The Red Saint

by

Warwick Deeping

The Red Saint
by Warwick Deeping

ISBN: 978-93-67145-45-6

Published by

DOUBLE 9 BOOKS

2/13-B, Ansari Road
Daryaganj, New Delhi – 110002
info@double9books.com
www.double9books.com
Tel. 011-40042856

ABOUT THE AUTHOR

George Warwick Deeping, an English novelist and short story writer, was best known for his work Sorrell and Son (1925). Warwick Deeping was born in Southend-on-Sea, Essex, to a family of physicians and attended Merchant Taylors' School. He went to Trinity College, Cambridge, to study medicine and science, then to Middlesex Hospital to complete his medical education. During World War I, he served in the Royal Army Medical Corps. Deeping later left his position as a physician to become a full-time writer. He married Phyllis Maude Merrill and spent the rest of his life at "Eastlands" on Brooklands Road, Weybridge, Surrey. He was a best-selling author in the 1920s and 1930s, with seven of his novels reaching the bestseller list. Deeping was a prolific short story writer whose work published in British journals such as Cassell's, The Storyteller, and The Strand. He also wrote fiction for various US periodicals, including The Saturday Evening Post and Adventure. All of the short stories and serialized novels in American publications were reprints of works originally published in Britain. More than 200 of his original short tales and essays, which appeared in various British fiction journals, were never published in book form during his lifetime.

CONTENTS

CHAPTER I

When Denise of the Hermitage went down to draw water at the spring at the edge of the beech wood, she saw the light of a fire flashing out through the blue gloom of the April dusk. It was far away—that fire, almost on the horizon, a knot of tawny colour seen between the dark slopes of two high hills. Yet though it was so far away Denise could see the long flames moving, sometimes shooting upwards, or bending and sweeping towards the ground.

Denise stood and watched these flames that waved and flickered yonder through the dusk where the smoke spread out between the hills into a kind of pearly haze. It was so still under the boughs of the great beeches that the distant fire seemed strange and ghostly, burning without a sound. The little pool where Denise had filled her pitcher was not more silent, the pool fed by an invisible spring, and believed to be miraculous and holy.

Yet though those far flames were so silent, Denise could set a sound to them, a crackling roar that would be very real to those who looked on the thing as on a sacrifice. There would be many watchers on the hills that night, sullen and silent folk to whom that blaze would speak like a war cresset teased by the wind on some great lord's tower. Peter of Savoy's riders, those hired "spears" from over the sea, Gascons, Flemings, Bretons, were out to keep the King's peace in the Rapes of Pevensey and of Hastings. Denise knew that private war had been let loose, for had she not heard from the priest of Goldspur, and from Aymery the manor lord, that many of the lesser gentry and the Cinque Port towns were calling for Earl Simon? The pot that had long been simmering, had boiled over of a sudden. And those who had scalded toes had only their own perversity to thank.

In such a fashion began the Barons' war in many a quiet corner of the land. Lawyers might orate and scribble, but when men quarrelled over a great issue, and the heart of a people was full of bitterness and discontent, the rush was towards the primitive ordeal of the sword. "God—and the King!"—"Earl Simon and the Charter!" These two rallying cries cut off brother from brother, and father from son. There had been years of verbiage, oath breaking, famine, peculation, and cynical corruption in high places. The law was no law, the King's oath a byword in brothels and in taverns. The great Father—even the Pope—had had both fists in the English money pots. Poitevins, Provençals, and Italians had scrambled together. The country was sick of it. Men who were in grim earnest hastened to get to blows.

As Denise, half hermitess, half saint, went back through the beech wood, the fire, like a great red brazier, still shone out on her, latticed by the black boughs, or hidden for a moment behind a tree bole. And though the wood was as still and solemn as a temple, it seemed full of a hushed and listening dread, waiting for the wind that should come roaring through the tops of the trees. Unrest was upon the hills, and in the deeps of the valleys. Denise felt it as she might have felt the nearness of thunder on a sultry night in June.

But if no wind stirred in the wood that night, there were other sounds more human and more passionate than the voice of the wind. Denise had said her prayers in her cell when the dead leaves under the beech trees whispered with the moving of many feet. Indistinct figures went in and out among the tree boles, the muttering of voices mingling with the rustle of the leaves. A full moon had risen, and begun to throw long slants of light into the darkness of the wood, outlining the black branches, and splashing the trunks of the trees with silver. In and out, through the still moonlight and the shadows, came the moving figures whose feet filled the whole wood with the shiver of dead leaves.

They straggled along by twos and threes, some silent and morose, others talking with the quick muttering intensity of men who have given and taken blows. A darker core moved along the woodland path in the midst of this scattered company. Men were carrying a litter of boughs piled upon the trunks of two young ash trees. The moonlight played intermittently upon the men about the litter, showing so many white faces, intent and silent, and a body that lay upon the bed of boughs with a shield covering its face.

A breadth of clear sky in the thick of the wood showed them that they were close on the glade where Denise of the Forest had her cell. The place was sacred and full of mystery to the woodlanders of those parts, and the scattered figures drew together under a tree where the path came out of the wood into the glade. Only the litter of boughs and the men with it went forward into the moonlight; the rest held aloof like dogs left by their master at the door of a church.

The men who carried the litter set it down outside the gate in the wattle fence that shut in Denise's garden. There was some whispering, but the men's voices were no longer harsh and angry. Grimbald, the parish priest, sent them back into the wood to wait. Two men remained beside the litter, one standing a little apart with a cloak wrapped round him, and a hood drawn forward over his face.

Grimbald, the priest from Goldspur village, opened the gate, and went up the path paved with rough, flat stones that led to the cell. Denise had heard the sound of voices, and the rustling of the dead leaves in the wood. Grimbald's voice warned her that they were friends.

"Sancta Denise," he said, crossing himself, "*ora pro nobis.*"

The door opened, under the broad black eaves of the hermitage. Denise stood there on the threshold, wearing a grey cloak that shone white in the light of the moon. Her hair clouded past her shoulders to her knees. It was miraculous hair, red as rust in the shade, but burning in the sunlight with a sheen of gold. Denise herself was miraculous, and this beech wood of hers was said to be full of many marvels. People who came for holy water from her pool, or to be treated by her for sickness, swore that they had seen a moving radiance, like a marsh fire, in the wood, and heard the voices of angels and the murmur of their wings. Denise was famed for her powers of healing. She knew all the precious herbs, and the touch of her hands could bring a blessing.

Grimbald told her the news.

"It is Waleran de Monceaux's lad," he said. "Come and see, Sanctissima, whether God will be merciful."

She bent forward and looked into Grimbald's face.

"There is war with us—then?"

Grimbald spread his arms.

"Peter of Savoy sent out his free-lances from Pevensey. They were too strong for us. The lad was shot through the body when they drove us into the woods."

"I saw a fire—about dusk."

"Waleran's hall—and outhouses! That was the end of it!"

He stood aside, and Denise went down the path, her bare feet making no sound upon the stones. Aymery, lord of the manor of Goldspur, knelt in the grass beside the litter holding the lad's cold hands. Waleran still stood aloof, his face hidden under his hood. No one spoke to him. They left him alone, knowing his mood, and the manner of man that he was.

Denise went on her knees beside the litter, her two hands putting back the masses of her hair. Aymery lifted the shield from the lad's face. The sleeve of his hauberk brushed against Denise's cloak. She glanced round at him, and their eyes smiled faintly at one another.

"We brought the boy to you. The arrow drove right through him. You can feel the point under his tunic."

Denise laid a hand over the lad's heart. There was not a flicker of movement there, but she could feel the arrow's head standing out a hand's breadth beyond the ribs. The lad must have died very quickly.

"He is dead," she said to the man at her side.

Aymery was staring at the boy's face. He turned, and glanced meaningly at the figure that stood apart in silent isolation.

"It is Waleran," he said in a whisper, "he would not believe the worst."

Denise gave a little shudder of pity. Aymery turned, and met her eyes.

"Pray for the boy, Denise. What is death, but a miracle! And an hour ago——"

She spread her hands helplessly.

"Lord, death is beyond me; I am not blessed with so much power. Someone must tell him."

"The pity of it!"

And she echoed him.

"The pity of it!"

A compassionate humility made her bow her head over the rough litter, for there was no place for the smaller remembrance of self in the conscious awe of her own helplessness. Denise had healed sick people, but she who could play the lady of healing, knew herself human in the presence of death.

"Tell him," she said, "it is almost shame to me that you should have brought the boy here."

Aymery covered the lad's face again with the shield.

"Pray for Waleran," he said.

"For the living rather than the dead."

Aymery rose and joined Grimbald the priest, who was standing by the gate. Denise still knelt beside the litter, holding the dead boy's hands. And if compassion could have given him life, compassion for that silent man who stood aloof, life might have flowed miraculously from Denise's body, and spread like fire into the limbs of the dead.

Grimbald left Aymery, and crossed the grass to where Waleran stood, Waleran that sturdy man with the fierce red shock of hair. Waleran had been the first mesne lord in those parts to bristle his mane against Count Peter of Savoy. This hardihood had lost him his only child, and made a bonfire of his home, though he would not believe at first that the boy was dead.

Aymery of Goldspur turned again to Denise. He could see that she was praying, and his eyes, that were frosty with the cold anger of a strong man helpless in the face of death, flashed suddenly as he saw the moonlight touching Denise's hair.

Grimbald had Waleran by the shoulders. They heard a short, sharp oath scatter the priest's whisperings as a puff of wind scatters a handful of feathers.

"Dead!"

There was the sound of heavy breathing.

"Let me alone! Am I a fool of a girl?"

"Patience, brother."

"Patience be cursed! What is the use of an idiot saint if an arrow between the ribs is too much for her?"

Denise let the boy's hands fall; Aymery saw her bow her head, and heard her whisper words that he could not catch. Then Waleran came forward, swinging his arms as though to keep off Grimbald who towered beside him like a great ship. Waleran stopped at the foot of the litter, and stood staring at the shield that covered the dead boy's face. Some impulse drove him to his knees, and he began to feel for the arrow, breathing heavily through set teeth.

Denise's nearness seemed to come between him and the savage tenderness of a dog for its dead whelp. Her humility and her compassion were not tuned to the cry of nature.

"Get up," he said. "This is my affair."

He leant forward, and pushed her back with a rough thrust of the open hand. Aymery caught Denise, and drew her aside.

"Forgive— —"

His arms lingered about her like the arms of a lover.

"Lord, I understand."

"That arrow has stricken two hearts."

Her eyes looked into Aymery's as he let her go.

"God have pity," she said.

Waleran had broken off the head of the arrow. He held it up in the moonlight, and his hood fell back from his face. The three who watched him saw his face contorted with laughter, though no sound came from the open mouth.

He ran the arrow's head through his cloak, as a woman pins her tunic with a splinter of bone.

"Here is a keepsake," he said. "Lord, but I shall cherish it! They have lit a candle for the boy, yonder. Some day I shall hang a bell on a rope, and ring him a passing."

He scrambled up, swaggering, and shaking his shoulders. It was his way of carrying the burden that the night had laid on him. He shouted to the men, roughly, and they came out from the shadows of the trees.

When they had lifted the litter, Waleran jerked himself on to it, and putting the shield aside, sat fingering his boy's face.

"A puff of wind, and the candle is out," he said.

The litter swayed under his weight.

"Spill me, you fools, and I shall have something to say to you. Off with you. To-morrow we must put this poor pigeon under the grass."

The men moved away, and Grimbald would have followed them, but Waleran ordered him back.

"Have I nothing better to do than to cut my own throat!" he said. "Shifts and cassocks are no good for me. The puppy is mine, by God! Let no one meddle between him and me."

Grimbald followed them no farther, and heard the swish of their feet die away through the dead leaves into the darkness.

In an hour from their first coming the beech wood was silent and empty, and Denise's cell lay with its dark thatch like an islet in the midst of a quiet mere. Not a ripple of sound played over the surface of the night. Aymery and Grimbald had gone to warn their own people that death was abroad on the White Horse. And Denise, sitting on her bed, wakeful, and filled with a great pity for Waleran and the lad, felt that the stealthy glamour of the moonlight was cold and unreal. If her compassion followed Waleran, a feeling more deep and more mysterious followed Aymery under the boughs of the beeches. Yet this feeling of Denise's was as miraculous as the moonlight which she thought so cold and mute.

The two men made their way through the wood by a broad green ride, and stood listening where the heathland began for any sound that might steal out of the vast silence of the night. Grimbald's great head, with its gaunt, eagle face, the colour of smoked oak, had the full moon behind it for a halo. Aymery of Goldspur stood a little below him on the hillside, leaning on his sword. His thoughts were back among the trees about Denise's glade, those towering trees whose boughs seemed hung with the stars.

Below them stretched wastes of whin and heather, hills black with forests, valleys full of moonlit mist. They could see the sea shining in the distance, a whole land beneath them, ghostly, strange, and still.

"It is all quiet yonder."

Grimbald's head was like the head of a hawk, alert and very watchful.

"They have done enough for one night," he said.

"To make us keep troth with the King!"

Both were silent for a moment. Grimbald spoke the thought that was uppermost in Aymery's mind.

"It is no longer safe for the girl alone, yonder," he said.

Aymery, that man with the iron mouth and the square chin, and eyes the colour of the winter sea, spread his shoulders as an archer spreads them before drawing a six-foot bow.

"I will see to it," he said quietly. "Nothing must happen to Denise."

CHAPTER II

The little red spider of a man who pattered along beside Gaillard's horse, looked up from time to time into the Gascon's face, and thought what a great pageant life must be to a soldier who had such a body and so much pay. For the little red spider was a cripple, and nothing more glorious than a spy, a thing that crawled like a harvest bug, and might have been squashed without ceremony under the Gascon's fist. As for Gaillard he was a very great man, cock and captain of Count Peter's chickens, those most meek birds who scratched up obstinate worms, and kept their lord's land clean of grubs.

They were marching back to Pevensey, bows and spears, along the flat road over the marshes, with the downs in the west a dull green against the April sky. Waleran de Monceaux had been chastened in proper fashion, a chastening that might calm the turbulent tempers of his neighbours. Of what use were such castles as Pevensey, Lewes, Arundel, and Bramber, to the King at such a crisis, if the great lords did not put pettifogging law aside and coerce as much of the country as they could cover with their swords? Men were tired of words and of charters. "Let us come to grips," said they, "and not quarrel over parchment and seals." And the great lords were wise in their necessity, kept—each in his castle—a dragon at his service, a dragon that could be sent out to scorch up those who had the temerity to threaten the King.

The little red spider thought Messire Gaillard a fine fellow. He had such limbs on him, such a voice, such a cheerful way of bullying everyone. The Gascon might have been made of brown wire, he was so restless, so sinewy, so alert; a rust-coloured man with red and uneasy eyes, a harsh skin blotched with freckles, hair that curled like a negro's, and a big mouth insolent under the aggressive tusks of its moustache. A vain man, too, as his dress and his harness showed, a man who put oil on his hair, wore many rings, and had a quick eye for a woman. He was just the lusty, headstrong animal, a born fighter, and a bully by instinct, inflammable, self-sufficient, a babbler, and a singer of love songs.

The waters of the bay were covered with purple shadows, and the marshlands brilliant as green samite when Gaillard's men came to the western gate of the castle, and rode two by two with drooped spears into the great outer bailey closed in by the old Roman walls. Gaillard came last, with the spy pattering beside his horse. The men went to their quarters, rough pent houses that had been built for them along the northern wall, for there was not room enough in Peter of Savoy's new castle within a castle for all those hired men from over the sea.

Pevensey would have astonished any rough Northumbrian baron, or the fiery Marcher Lords who fought the Welsh. For Peter of Savoy was a southerner, a compeer of the King's in his love of colour and of music. To dig a moat and build white towers was not enough for him, and the spirit of Provence had emptied itself within the Roman wall. A great part of the space had become a garden, shut in with thickets of cypresses and bays. The roses of Provence bloomed there in June. Winding alley ways went in and out, short swarded, and overhung by rose trees. There were vines on trellises, and banks of fragrant herbs. In the thick of a knoll of cypresses Count Peter kept two leopards in a cage, yellow-eyed beasts which glided silently to and fro.

Gaillard, skirting the cypresses of the pleasaunce, had his eyes on the window of the great tower where Peter of Savoy loved to sit playing chess with Dan Barnabo his chaplain, or listening to a woman singing to the lute. The lutanist sang to others as well as to Count Peter. Gaillard the Gascon knew the twitter of her strings, better perhaps, than Peter of Savoy himself.

"Give me a red rose, my desire,
And a kiss on the mouth for an *Ave*."

The words were those of Etoile of the Lute, and Gaillard hummed them under the shade of the cypresses as he rode towards the inner gate. But some hand threw a clod of turf at him that morning, and threw it so cleverly that the thing hit Gaillard on the ear, and spattered his blue surcoat over with soil.

The Gascon turned sharply in the saddle, and saw a white hand showing between two cypress trees, and a wrist that betrayed the golden threads embroidering a woman's sleeve.

A voice laughed at him.

"Throw me a clod of turf, my desire,
Give me a blow on the ear for a greeting!"

The arm put the boughs aside, and a face appeared, wreathed by the cypress sprays, a woman's face, white, mischievous, and alluring. Her black hair was bound up in a golden net. She showed her teeth at Gaillard, and put out the tip of a red tongue.

"Can I throw straight, dear lord?"

He turned his horse, glanced at the window in the tower, and then laughed back at her, opening his mouth wide like the beak of a hungry bird.

"Better at a man's heart, than at his head, dear lady."

"A Gascon has more head than heart, my friend."

"And a long sword, and a longer tongue!"

She tilted her chin, two black eyes laughing above a short, impudent nose, and a hard, red mouth.

"Go and have your gossip with good Peter. Barnabo has beaten him twice at chess, and he was ready to throw the board at me. The leopards are better tempered."

Gaillard snapped his fingers.

"I will be a leopard," he said. "Wait till I have washed the dust off. Peter always plays until he wins."

The white face disappeared behind the cypress boughs, and Gaillard rode on to his quarters, ready to wash the dust of the road away with wine and water, and thinking of Etoile, Count Peter's lutanist and lady. She was a Gascon also from the land of the Garonne. Etoile and Gaillard were excellent friends, especially when the Savoyard was playing chess.

There were peacocks strutting in the garden, sunning their gorgeous tails, when Gaillard fresh from the bath and the hands of his man, went out to Etoile among the cypresses. At the window above Peter of Savoy had his head over the chess-board. The game was such a passion with him, that his people left him in the throes of it, not even Etoile being allowed to touch her lute. The Savoyard, chin on the palm of his left hand, with Barnabo opposite him, had not so much as noticed Gaillard's return. The men had ridden to their quarters, but Peter's long fingers loitered over the board, and his ears might have been stuffed with wool. Barnabo, who had won two games, had enough worldly wisdom behind his smooth, Italian face to know that the time had come to put his lord in a happier temper. Barnabo always rose from the board a loser. It was part of his policy to pique the great man by defeating him at first, that he might delight him the more with the inevitable revenge.

"You are too subtle for me, sire," he would confess. "I can begin by winning, that is easy. When I have beaten you, you laugh, and turn to show me what a child I am."

The chess-players were so intent above, that Gaillard and the lute girl Etoile, had the half hour safely to themselves. They were blood cousins— these two Gascons, and yet nearer of kin in the intimate ambition that had sent them hunting in a strange land. How the Lady of the Peacocks had persuaded Peter of Savoy into loving her would be a tale fit for a French song. She could do very much as she pleased with him so long as he was not hanging his dyed beard over the chess-board. As for her and Gaillard, they understood one another. The man was driven at times to be rash and impetuous. Etoile was strange and fierce enough at a crisis to keep Gaillard's galloping passion from breaking its own neck.

These two Gascons had a common enemy, Barnabo the Italian, who was as clever as Etoile, and far more clever than Gaillard. The chaplain was a smooth man, a man who smiled when he was snubbed, and put the insult carefully into the counting-house of his memory. There was sometimes a glitter in his eyes, like the gleam of a knife hidden in a sleeve. He hated Etoile, and Etoile the woman, knew why he hated her. Barnabo would have had her for an accomplice, the Queen on the chess-board to play against Count Peter. Etoile had struck Barnabo across the face, and the chess-board and the lute had been at feud with one another. Peter of Savoy knew nothing of all this. Both Barnabo and Etoile were too wise to throw soot at one another, unless the chance should come when one could be safely blackened without so much as a pinch of slander falling upon the other.

It was of Barnabo they talked that morning, hidden by the cypresses, Etoile standing by the leopards' cage, the great beasts fawning against the bars, and letting her stroke their heads. There seemed some sympathy between her and the two sleek, sinuous cats. The voice and the eyes of Etoile cast a spell upon them. They would purr and rub against the bars when she came near.

The Lady of the Peacocks told Gaillard a piece of news that made the man's eyes grow more hard and restless.

"He had better not meddle," he said; "or I will twist his neck."

Etoile snapped her fingers.

"You are a great fool, my Gaillard, Barnabo is not so rough and clumsy. I know the man."

"But the rat is nibbling at our cheese!"

"What else can he do, the Savoyard cannot go to bed with him. A man is at a disadvantage. He can only call names."

"Behind our backs, my desire!"

"Over the chess-board, perhaps."

Gaillard put a hand through the bars, and scratched a leopard's head.

"It is a pity," he said, "that we cannot shut Barnabo up with these two innocents when they are hungry. They would play a pretty game with him, a game of knucklebones, with nothing left afterwards but some rags, two sandals, and a brain box."

Etoile laughed, and then looked shrewd.

"There are other people who would eat up Dan Barnabo, people in the woods—yonder. Every man has a foolish corner in his heart. If Barnabo asks you how the country seems, tell him the folk are as frightened as mice."

"Very lusty mice, my desire! Call them pole-cats."

"Pole-cats may serve as well as leopards. Be careful of that window in the tower; Barnabo has quick eyes. Go up now and see how the game goes."

Peter of Savoy and the chaplain still had the chess-board between them when Gaillard went up to the room in the tower. The window, widely splayed, had painted medallions in its frames. A song book and a lute lay on a red cushion, with a gaze-hound curled on the seat.

The third game was nearly at an end, and Peter of Savoy was rubbing his pointed beard, and chuckling inwardly as he hung over the board. Barnabo brooded, his puzzled, hesitating hands flattering the strategy of his lord and opponent. Gaillard sat down on the window seat to wait. Peter of Savoy was to triumph. Therefore the world went well.

A resigned sigh from Barnabo, the tap of a piece on the board, a shuffling of Count Peter's feet, and the end came.

The great man sat back, laughed in his chaplain's face, and turned a sharp and self-satisfied profile to Gaillard.

"So you are back, my Gascon. All our games have gone well, have they? See—I am about to steal his lady."

Gaillard leant forward to watch.

"Since he is a priest, sire, you are saving him from great temptation."

Peter of Savoy laughed, but for some reason Barnabo looked up at the Gascon sharply.

The game was lost and won, and Gaillard had told his news. Peter of Savoy had picked up the lute, and was twanging the strings complacently. Barnabo still pored over the chess-board as though to discover how and where he had been beaten. He was a clever artist in the conception of flattery, yet he was on the alert while Peter of Savoy and Gaillard talked.

"Quiet as lambs, to be sure. That will be good news for our friend here. You smoked Waleran out like a fox out of a hole. Excellent Gascon! Fire purifies, so thought the Greeks. There are the folk at Goldspur to be seized—unless they come in with halters round their necks."

The great man hummed a passage from a favourite song.

"Barnabo would not be persuaded," he said, half-closing his eyes slyly. "You must know, my Gaillard, that Barnabo is a man with a hot conscience. He has learnt six words of English—what does that matter? So many benefices to be served—in Latin; so many women to be shrived! Even when the wolves are out—Barnabo will not neglect his duties!"

The Italian was imperturbable and debonair.

"I have a charm against all wolves," he said, looking at Gaillard out of the corner of his eyes.

"Your sanctity, Father, to be sure. Most excellent St. Francis, the hawks even perch on your shoulders. Barnabo will mount his mule and ride out to comfort the sick, whatever I, his lord, may say."

Gaillard took the gaze-hound up into his lap.

"He will have nothing to fear there, now. I will answer for that."

Barnabo's eyes were studying Gaillard's face. He smiled, and began to gather up the chess-men.

"After the sword come the Cross and the mass book," he said. "You will not quarrel with my conscience, sire, if I ride out to-morrow."

"Who—in Christendom—is worth the labour of a quarrel? Command your friends, and tread upon your enemies. Go out, and heal the sick, when the husbands are not at home."

Etoile, who had been listening at the door, pulled Gaillard into a dark corner on the stairs when he came out to see to the guards.

"So Barnabo is going a-love-making," she said. "Good. Perhaps he will not come back again."

And she sang to Peter of Savoy that night, a desirable woman whose face betrayed no care.

CHAPTER III

Denise was so much the saint and the Lady of the Goldspur woods that the country folk had almost ceased to wonder whence she had come, and what her past had been. She was Sancta Denise to them, a woman to whom they went when they were sick or in trouble, who came and prayed for them, and smiled on their children with her miraculous eyes. All the woodland folk in the hundreds round looked on Denise as a saint, a child of mystery who dwelt up yonder amid the great beech trees under the clouds. Offerings were left before her gate, milk, bread, eggs, and herbs, the offerings of the poor. If there was digging to be done, or the grass to be scythed in the glade, some of Aymery's villeins would be there at dawn, working like brown gnomes in the dusk of the breaking day. Four times a year a pedlar brought her the gold thread for her orfrays work, for Denise had wonderful hands, and her embroidery had been worn by queens. The money that she earned Denise spent among the poor, and she might have walked from Rye to Shoreham, and no Sussex man would have laid hands upon her, save to touch her gown for a blessing.

Olivia, Aymery's mother, alone had known Denise's history, and Olivia was dead. Some had said that she was the "love child" of a great lady, others a "ward" who had fled from the King's court rather than be married to some creature who had offered the King money. But Denise was Denise, and her past was of no account, though any hind could have sworn that she was no peasant's child. The cell in the beech wood had been built for her by Dame Olivia, and the ground about it turned into a garden. Denise had become part of the woodland life, a tender and mysterious figure that threw a glamour over the hearts of all.

Her coming had been soon after the great famine, when the crops had failed after a wet summer. Death had passed over the land like a plague, and in the towns the dead had lain for days unburied. The famine had left sickness behind it, sick women, and sick babes at the breast, as though the whole countryside had grown feeble for lack of bread. Denise had come down from her cell in the beech wood, a veritable Lady of Compassion. It was not the bread that she had given, but the pity and the tenderness that had enshrined her in the hearts of all the people. It was as though she had magic power, a glory given of God and the Virgin. Men soon spoke of miracles. Sick children were brought to her, and water taken from her holy spring. The abbots and priors of the south heard of her, and more than one "house" considered the value that might be set upon a saint.

Perhaps Denise's power lay largely in her youth, for she was no ulcerous and lean recluse, but a woman in the morning of her beauty, a beauty that was strange and elfin-like, rich as an autumn in red leaf. She had but to look at men, and they felt an awe of her; at children, and they came to her like birds to a witch. The hair under the grey hood had the colour of copper, with tinges of red and of gold. Her eyes were between amber and the brown of a woodland pool, her skin so clear and white, despite the sun and the wind, that men believed her heart could be seen shining like a red gem beneath. Denise was tall, and broad across the bosom. Her fingers were so long, and slim, and white, that the superstitious believed that pearls might drop from them, and that not even the brown soil of her garden could cling to those miraculous hands.

Denise carried her pitcher to the spring the morning after they had brought Waleran's boy to her with an arrow through his heart. She stripped herself at the pool, and washed her body, scooping up the water in her palms, her hair knotted over her neck. Denise's naked figure might have stood as the symbol of her womanhood, clean, comely, unshadowed by self-consciousness. It was part of the infinite mystery of things, a mystery that dwelt in Denise's heart, and gave her power over women and over men.

Her brown eyes were sad that morning as she slipped on her white shift and her grey gown, and went back under the beech trees to her cell. With the fragrance of the wild flowers and the dew came the consciousness of the rougher world within that world of hers. She remembered the flames of the night before, Waleran's dead boy, the savage anguish of the man breaking out into bitterness and laughter. What more might not happen in the deeps of the woods? Denise was no ignorant child, she had lived in another world before Olivia had built her the cell under the Goldspur beeches.

Denise said her prayers, worked awhile in her garden, and then brought out her orfrays of gold, and sat in the doorway under the deep shade of the thatch. But though her fingers were busy with the threads, her mind was full of a spirit of watchfulness and of unrest. She felt as it were the stir and movement of another world beyond the towering domes of the trees. She had a premonition that someone would come through the wood that morning. It would be a man, and yet not Grimbald. Denise's hands were idle awhile, and her brown eyes looked thoughtfully into the deeps of the wood.

Nor was it very wonderful that Aymery's thoughts should turn towards Denise as a man struggles through the thick of a crowd when he sees a beloved head in danger. He and Grimbald had been at the burying of Waleran's boy, but Aymery had left Grimbald and the rest, and ridden back to Goldspur to see Denise.

The trampling of his horse's hoofs through the dead beech leaves came as no surprise to the woman who sat with the orfrays work of gold in her lap. She had watched her own mind, till, like a crystal, it had been full of the man's coming. Often in her life Denise had been able to foresee the faces of those dear to her, and to feel friends near while they were still far distant. She had the gift of inward vision, though the power became lost to her later when she had suffered many humiliations.

Aymery rode out into the sunlight of the glade, and Denise could see that he was armed. A surcoat of apple green covered the ringed hauberk, though the hood of mail was turned back between his shoulders. Aymery rode his big black destrier that day, and not the rough nag he used for hawking and cantering over his lands. He looped the bridle over the post at the gate, and came up the path with the air of a man who has more in his heart than his lips might utter.

Denise let her work lie idle in her lap. She had had no fear of Aymery from the first, his face had become so familiar that it seemed part of the life round her, like the trees, or the hills, or the distant sea. Yet from the instant that he opened the wattle gate that morning, a sense of strangeness took hold of both of them. Each felt the change and wondered at it, so simple in its significance, and yet so strange. The shadow of a cloud lay over them for the first time. The more intimate hour had come when the man looked into the woman's eyes and thought that thought which opens the eyes of the soul—"if any harm should befall her! If that dear head should suffer shame!"

"We have buried the boy," he said. "That will be the beginning of a long tale."

There was something satisfying about Aymery, a man who carried his head high, and looked fearlessly at the horizon. He had a quick yet quiet way with him had Aymery of Goldspur. Shirkers and cowards were afraid of those grey eyes of his, for they were not the eyes of a man to be trifled with or fooled.

He spoke to Denise, resting his hands on his sword, and looking at the golden orfrays work in her lap. She was leaning against the door-post, her face in the shadow, thought and feeling as intimately one as the rose and the scent of the rose.

"The woods are no longer safe. Peter of Savoy's riders will be with us again. Waleran will see to that."

Denise's brown eyes had a tremor of light in them.

"Have you proved me a coward?"

"We are cowards, Denise, where others are concerned. What do the days promise us? Waleran could not hold his house against those hired swarthies, nor can I mine; I am not fool enough to doubt it. A few arrows bearded with burning tow, the thatch alight, and the smoke and the flames would make us run like rats. It will be war in the woods where our bows can serve us, and where their men-at-arms cannot ride our peasants down."

Denise did not answer him for a moment. Her hands were turning over the embroidery in her lap.

"I have lived with you all in the sunshine," she said. "And now that trouble comes you would have me run away!"

"What man would not wish it?"

"But you— —"

"I—I am the worst of all."

She dropped her head suddenly as though hiding the light and colour that had rushed into her eyes and face.

"I am not afraid," she said.

"I am"—and he shut his lips on the words—"it is human to be afraid. If you knew this scum of Gascons, Flemings, and what not, you would wish them well beyond the sea. Would to God that we could whip them out of the land. But what would you! We cannot pull down such a rock as Pevensey with our hands. These castles that the King's men hold for him are too strong for us to meddle with. It is they who will do the meddling, and what do these hired men care for what we honour? You will be on the edge of a pit here. Women are best away when swords are out."

He bent towards her, looking down into her face, his manhood shining out on her, strong and honest, denying itself the right of a romantic beast.

"Come with me, and I will guard you against all Christendom." A weaker and vainer man might have spoken in such heroics. Aymery knew what he knew. Denise would be safer away from him when such men as Waleran were to be his brethren-in-arms.

"I tell you the truth, Denise, because— —"

She looked up at him suddenly, and their eyes met. Denise saw the deeper truth, that great mystery of life that cannot hide itself from the eyes of a woman.

"Lord, what shall I say to you?"

He spread his arms.

"Say nothing. Do what I, Grimbald, all, desire. I have good friends at Winchelsea. You will be safe there. The King wishes to win the Cinque Ports over. He will not be rough with them, as yet. They are too precious to be ravaged."

Denise looked at the sky beyond the boughs of the beech trees, letting her hands hang over her knees.

"Lord," she said, "I am still obstinate. I have lived among you all."

"Denise, I also am obstinate."

"I would not have you otherwise. And yet, how can I shirk the truth that I shall be deserting you all the moment trouble comes?"

He smiled at her, and shook his head.

"Should we be the happier if you fell into the hands of Peter of Savoy? No. That is unthinkable! I would rather see you—dead like Waleran's boy—before they carried you into Pevensey! Good God, you, to be touched by such hands!"

Denise understood all that was in his heart. She crossed herself as though against the evil things of the world.

"Lord," she said, "let there be this promise between us. If Goldspur is threatened, then—I will do what you desire. When the people take to the woods, I shall feel less of a coward. They shall not say that I fled from a shadow."

And thus it was agreed between them, Aymery riding back through the woods towards Goldspur, the face of Denise more wonderful to him than it had ever seemed before. Aymery had come by the truth that morning, and the world had a mystery—the mystery of the tenderness of spring.

Close by Goldspur village, on the edge of the manor ploughlands, he met Grimbald, who had come in search of him. The priest's face had the look of a stormy and ominous sky. He took Aymery's bridle, and turned back with him towards the village.

"Waleran has gone towards Pevensey," he said. "We must be ready for a whirlwind when such storm-cocks are on the wing."

CHAPTER IV

A poor rag of a man, with the pinched face of a sick girl, came limping on sore heels to the western gate of Pevensey. The man had a broken arrow through the flesh of his neck; his mouth was all awry, and his breath came in great heaves, for he had run ten miles that morning. When someone caught him round the middle as he tottered at the gate, he doubled up like a wet clout over a line, and emptied his very soul over the stones. The guards put him on his back awhile, rubbed his legs, and gave him a horn of mead to drink. One of them forced the back of the arrow through the skin, and whipped it out as a woman whips a broken bodkin out of a friend's finger.

The beer, and the blunt heroism of this barber surgeon brought Barnabo's man briskly upon his haunches. He clapped his hand to his neck, saw that there was blood on it, and promptly began to whimper.

"You've pulled the spiggot out," he wailed. "Lord, did ever a hogshead gush faster! Linen—oil, and linen, for the love of the Saints."

The men laughed at him. One of them took a smock that hung on a nail outside the porter's lodge, tore a strip from it, spat on the wound, and bandaged Barnabo's man till he had a gorget and whimple fit for a nun.

"Take a little more beer, comrade," he said. "Never a rabbit ran more bravely."

The fugitive sulked under their attentive and jeering faces.

"Go to perdition," he retorted. "It was fifty to one, there, in the woods. Messire Gaillard must hear of it. You will all be very brave, sirs, when these devils begin to shoot at you from behind a hundred trees."

Gaillard heard of it soon enough, as did Etoile, and Peter of Savoy. Barnabo had been waylaid in the woods that morning, and the pole-cats had clawed him off his mule. For no man was more hated than Dan Barnabo in those parts, a hard, shrewd man who held many benefices, and saw that his steward ground out the dues. The Italian could not speak ten words in the vulgar tongue. His ministrations would have been ridiculous had he ever troubled his soul about the people. It was told that a woman had once waylaid Barnabo, and demanded to be shriven. The Italian had understood nothing of what she said to him, but since she was pretty and importunate, he had created a scandal by misunderstanding her whole desire, and by seeking to comfort her in a fashion that was not fatherly. The woman had scratched Barnabo's face. There were many people who had lusted to scarify him more viciously. Barnabo baptised no children, sought out none of the sick, buried none of the dead. Twice a year perhaps he had said mass in the churches that belonged to him. Few of the people had come to hear Barnabo's Roman voice. He was a better lute player and lap-dog than priest, and the people knew it.

Gaillard had his orders from Peter of Savoy. Etoile laughed in his face when she met him upon the stairs.

"Let the pole-cats play a little with Barnabo," she said. "Do not ride furiously, dear lord! I can learn to serve at chess better than Barnabo."

Gaillard caught at her, but she slipped past him up the stairs.

"There are two sorts of fools in the world, my Gaillard," she said. "One is killed for the sake of a woman, the other through greed for a woman. Keep out of Barnabo's path."

Both Peter of Savoy and the Gascon knew whither Barnabo had ridden that April day. It was notorious that the Italian had kept a *focaria* or hearth-ward at a priest's house of his in a valley beyond the hill called Bright Ling because of the glory of its heathlands in the summer. The woman—a Norman—was more comely than was well for Dan Barnabo's name, and she had kept the house for him, and rendered it to him sweet and garnished whenever he chose to ride that way.

Gaillard and his men marched past Dallington, where Guillaume Sancto de Leodegario was lord of the manor, and on over Bright Ling with the furze in full bloom. The little red spy jogged along beside the Gascon's horse. He led them into a deep valley, a valley full of the grey-green trunks of oak trees, and the brown wreckage of last year's bracken. A stream dived and winked in the bottoms, and at the end of a piece of grassland the thatch of the priest's house shelved under the very boughs of the oaks. No smoke rose from the place. It seemed silent and deserted as Gaillard and his men came trampling through the dead bracken.

Gaillard's eyes swept hillside and valley, for he was shrewd enough to guess that many an alert shadow had dogged them on the march that day. He dismounted, sent his archers into the woods as scouts, and taking the pick of his men-at-arms, marched up to the silent house, holding his shield ready to catch any treacherous arrow that might be shot from the dark squints. A wooden perch shadowed the main entry, and Gaillard saw that the door stood ajar, and that the flagstones paving the porch were littered with rushes, and caked with mud as though many feet had passed to and fro over the stones.

Gaillard pushed the door open with the point of his sword. It gave to him innocently enough, and he crossed the threshold, and stood staring at something that the men behind him could not see.

The place had the dimness of twilight, lit as it was by the narrow lancets cut in the thickness of the wall. Not three paces from Gaillard, their feet nearly touching the floor, two bodies dangled on ropes from the black beams of the roof. The face of the one was grey; of the other, black and turgid; for one had died by the sword, the other by the rope.

The body with the black face was still twisting to and fro as a joint twists on a spit before the fire. The arms had been pinioned, and the man's tongue been drawn out, and the head of an arrow thrust through it. The face could scarcely be recognised, but by the clothes Gaillard knew him for Dan Barnabo, the Italian, lutanist, lover, spoiler of the poor.

Gaillard touched the body. It was still warm. His men were crowding in, peering over each other's shoulders so that the doorway was full of faces, shields, and swords.

Gaillard waved them back. He swung his sword, struck at the rope that held Barnabo, and cut it so cleanly that the body came down upon its feet. For a moment it stood, poised there, before falling forward to hide its black face in the rushes.

Gaillard looked at it a little contemptuously, thinking of Etoile, and the rivalry between her and this thing that had been a man.

"Only fools come by such a death," he said. "A dog's death. This man had a woman's hands."

Dusk was falling, and Gaillard and his men settled themselves to pass the night in dead Barnabo's house under the oak trees. Gaillard, who did not trouble himself about such a thing as a "crowner's quest," had the two bodies buried in the garden at the foot of a holly tree. Waleran de Monceaux had hanged Barnabo, and the priest was not pretty to look at with his black face and his swollen tongue. Nor was Gaillard going to quarrel with so convenient a coincidence. He called his archers back out of the woods, posted two sentinels, had the horses brought in and stabled in the hall. A fire was lit on the hearth, and the men gathered round it, and opened their wallets for supper.

Gaillard kept the red-headed hunchback at his elbow, and questioned him narrowly as to the woodways, and the manor houses, and the gentry with whom he would have to deal. These Sussex rebels had hanged Barnabo, and in the hanging, thrown down the blood gauge to Peter of Savoy. War was Gaillard's business. He had learnt the trade in Gascony, where neighbour went out against neighbour as for a day's hunting. Nor was it Gaillard's concern to trouble about the law of the land, and how far feudal faith bound this man or that. The King was the great over-lord, and Peter of Savoy stood as his champion in those parts. Hence if rebels popped their heads up, it was only necessary to strike with the sword.

Night fell, and the men lay down to sleep in the long hall, crowding about the fire, for the horses were ranged along the walls. The air of the place was close and heavy with the smoke from the fire, the animal heat of the crowded bodies, and the pungent scent of horses' dung. Faint flickers of light lost themselves in the black zenith of the timbered roof. Gaillard, sitting propped in a corner with his sword across his knees, could hear the wet murmur of the stream that ran close to the house. He could also hear the two sentinels answering each other, and since they seemed so whole-heartedly alert, Gaillard dozed off like a dog.

About midnight Gaillard opened his eyes, and sat staring at the dying fire, and though he remained motionless, his face sharpened like the face of one who listens. His eyes moved slowly from figure to figure, to rest at last on the shutter closing a window. And Gaillard saw that the shutter was shaking ever so little, and he knew that there was no wind.

Gaillard did not move. He could hear a vague scuffling as of many men moving about the house. But there were other sounds that made the Gascon's lips tighten and retract so that the teeth showed, a faint crackling as of dry brushwood being piled against the door of Barnabo's house.

The Gascon saw the shutter open. A white face peered in with eyes that moved like the eyes of a wonder-working image. Then the face disappeared, and the shutter closed again, but Gaillard was on his feet, and going to and fro, silently rousing his men. Hardly a word was spoken. The men caught up their arms, and stood like listening dogs, while the archers marked the windows.

Gaillard was at the door trying to lift the bar, but some weight from without had jammed it in the sockets. He stood listening, sniffing the air, and watching grey puffs of smoke come curling in through the crevices. Then he shouted an order through the hall, an order that brought his men crowding forward for a sally. Some of the strongest of them put their shoulders to the bar. It flew up, letting the door swing in with a gush of smoke and a crash of falling faggots.

"Out—out!"

Gaillard and his men broke through, hurling the brushwood aside, dragging it into the hall, cursing as they realised the devil's trick that had been played them. Only the outer faggots were alight. There was a gush of flame under the hooded entry, but Gaillard and his men sprang through it with a weird glitter of gold upon their harness, and an uprush of smoke and sparks. Dark figures flitted about the priest's garden. Arrows whistled and struck the walls as the Savoyard's men came tumbling out over the burning faggots.

There was a sharp tussle in the garden; blows were given and taken in the dark; arrows shot at a venture; torches thrust into hairy faces. Gaillard's men-at-arms in their heavy mail, for they had lain down armed to sleep, were more than a match for the woodlanders in their leather jerkins. Soon— scampering shadows went away into the moonlight. Gaillard and his men were left to put out the fire about the porch.

And savage men they were, men with the hot flare of that death trap in their nostrils. The two sentinels had been stalked and killed, and the brushwood piled against the door. The windows were so narrow that men could have been shot while struggling through them. The flames and smoke would have leapt in, making the place a hell of plunging, terrified beasts, and mad and half-dazed men.

Gaillard watched his fellows trampling on the brushwood. Now and again an arrow came whistling out of the moonlight.

"We will pay them for this," he said grimly. "God, but they meant to burn us like blind mice in a stack!"

The fire was soon out, and there was nothing left but to wait for the daylight, and to keep the house in darkness so that no lurking woodlander should have the outline of a window for a mark. Gaillard's men were very sullen and bitter over the night's adventure. They had brought in the two dead sentinels, and crowded about them, letting their fury break out in growls for to-morrow's reckoning. There was no more sleep for Gaillard's men that night; they squatted round the walls, telling each other what they would do to these people who murdered priests and set fire to houses where the King's men slept.

The dawn came with a thick mist hanging over the woods, even covering the crowns of the uplands of Bright Ling. Gaillard had made his plans, and in the garden the little spy was drawing a map on the soil with the point of a charred stake. The archers had gone out to scout, but had found nothing but fog and rotting bracken. Gaillard ordered his men to horse, and they were soon on the move through the mist, the drippings from the trees falling on them, and on grass that was grey with dew.

The hunchback, marching beside Gaillard's horse, led them towards Goldspur, following the high ground where there was less chance of an ambuscade. Gaillard had ordered silence. Not a man spoke. The grey shapes moved through the greyer mist with no sounds but the dull shuffle of hoofs, the occasional snort of a horse, the creaking of saddles, and the faint jingle of steel.

It was still very early when they came to the hill above Goldspur, and skirted the great beech wood whose topmost boughs were beginning to glitter in the sunlight. The mist lifted quite suddenly like a white diaphanous curtain drawn up into the sky. A broad beam of sunlight clove like a sword into the deeps of the beech wood. And to these rough riders of Peter of Savoy was revealed a vision, a vision such as a crystal-gazer might watch growing from nothingness in the heart of a crystal.

In the full sunlight at the opening of a glade a woman stood washing herself at a forest pool. The woman's figure gleamed like snow against the sombre trunks of the trees. Her hair blazed about her naked body like flames licking a white tower. As yet she had not seen that line of armed men winding along the hillside not a hundred paces from where she stood.

Gaillard reined in, and held up a hand for his men to halt. He looked from the woman to the hunchback who held his stirrup strap.

"Hallo, what have we here?"

The cripple crossed himself, cur that he was.

"It is Denise of the Forest, lording," he said. "They call her their Lady of Healing in these parts. She has a cell yonder, in the wood. She can work miracles, so they say."

The rough faces behind Gaillard were all agog. A short, yapping laugh came from some man in the rear. Gaillard turned in the saddle, and looked for the man who had made the noise.

"Enough of that, sirs," he said. "Shall we laugh because a saint happens not to cherish vermin."

Perhaps curiosity pricked Gaillard, perhaps something still more human. At all events he pushed his horse forward and rode alone up the stretch of green turf that sloped towards the beech wood. The men grinned like apes so soon as his back was turned. Messire Gaillard might be a great captain, but assuredly he was no saint.

Gaillard was laughing to himself with a coarse spirit of mischief, being inquisitive as to what this woman would do when she discovered that she was no longer alone. He carried his chin high in the air, his hard eyes gleaming like the eyes of a man who has drunk strong wine. But Denise made her womanhood a thing of pride and splendour that spring morning. Her tunic was still open at the bosom when the Gascon's horse threw a shadow on the grass close to the pool.

Denise looked Gaillard straight in the eyes, and yet not at him, but past him, as though he were so much vapour. Gaillard, Gascon that he was, had not a word to say for himself, though he boasted himself so debonair with women. Denise took her hair with her hands, put it behind her shoulders, and picking up the clean cloth that she had brought, turned and walked away into the wood.

For once in his life Gaillard felt a fool, and his arrant sheepishness did not please him. He comforted himself with that infallible sneer that is the refuge of a vain man who has done something mean and cowardly.

"Red-headed Pharisee, go your way," he said. "A woman's sanctity is as thick as her skin. Fool! I am not the first sheep that has bleated in these parts."

CHAPTER V

Grimbald the priest stood on guard under the ash tree where the road left Goldspur for the open fields. He had a buckler on his arm, and an axe over his shoulder. His short, frayed cassock showed the beginnings of a brown and mighty pair of calves, and the feet in the leather sandals looked like the feet of an Atlas whose shoulders wedged up the heavens.

There had been a panic at Goldspur that morning, when a lad had run in with the news that he had seen armed men riding through the mist, and that they were marching towards Goldspur. And Grimbald, stalking down into the village, had met some of the younger men skulking off as though there were no women and children to be remembered. Grimbald had twisted a stake out of the hedge, dusted some decent shame into these cowards, and driven them back into Goldspur much as a drover drives his cattle.

Grimbald had found the village in an uproar, for Aymery was away with Waleran, and the folk had tumbled over each other for the lack of a leader. Men and boys had herded in sheep and cattle, and the beasts were bolting all ways, and taking every road but the right one. Women, weeping, scolding, chattering, were carrying out their chattels from the cottages. One had a baby at the breast; another clutched a young pig; a third sat at her door, and screamed like a silly girl. Men were arguing, shouting, quarrelling, eager to do the same thing, but obstinate in trying to do it each in his several way.

Then Grimbald had come and shepherded the people, knocked together the heads of the men who quarrelled, and turned disorder into order. The sheep, cattle, and pigs were driven off towards the woods. Men, women, and children followed, carrying all that they could put upon their backs. In a quarter of an hour from Grimbald's coming Goldspur village was a row of empty hovels, with nothing alive there but a few chickens, and the sparrows, who trusted in God, and continued to build in the thatch.

Grimbald had set himself at the lower end of the village, and stood there like the giant figure of some protecting saint. He was about to follow his flock when he saw a man on horseback round a spur of woodland in the valley. He came on at a canter for the village, and Grimbald knew him for Aymery by the colours of his surcoat and his horse.

Aymery reined in, hot with galloping, his eyes keen and full of flashes of light. He had been with Waleran, and had ridden to warn his people of what they might expect that day.

Grimbald pointed with his axe to the open doors of the hovels.

"They are safe in the woods by now. Have you had view of Peter's gentry?"

Aymery turned his horse, and shaded his eyes with his hand.

"They left the priest's house under Bright Ling—at dawn. Waleran tried a trick there, but the dogs smelt the smoke. I saw their spears coming down the hill as I crossed the valley."

Aymery looked towards the beech wood on the hill, his eyes flashing back the morning sunlight. The muscles of his jaw were hard and tense.

"We must bide our time, and watch them," he said; "they are coming to make a bonfire here. They can burn every stick of the place so long as they have not meddled with Denise."

Grimbald shifted his axe from one shoulder to the other. If ever a man had cause to be jealous of a woman, that man was Grimbald. But his heart was too warm and too well tilled to harbour such a weed. He thanked God for the good he found in the world, and did not quarrel with it because it was not part of his own halo.

"She cannot be left yonder," he said.

Aymery still looked at the beech wood, head thrown back, grey eyes a-glitter.

"We must take cover and watch. They will be here soon, and we shall see. To-night, I will take her away."

A gleam of spears showed in the valley, and Aymery rode off to the nearest wood with Grimbald holding to his stirrups. They saw Gaillard and his men come over the fields to Goldspur village, and Denise was not with them. Aymery's eyes made sure of that. The Gascon found nothing but the empty hovels, the untroubled sparrows, and a black cock crowing and scratching on a dunghill. One of Gaillard's men fitted an arrow to the string, shot the black cock through the body, and laughed at the way the bird tumbled and flapped in the death agony.

"Brother Barnabo may find use for him," said someone, and there was a laugh.

"He will wake him before daylight," quoth another. "Such birds are useful to gallant clerks."

Goldspur village did not go up in smoke that morning, for Gaillard, cunning as a fox, did not always run straight for the game in view.

"We will take our dinner elsewhere, sirs," he said. "When we are over the hill, the fools may think that they will see us no more. When does a cat catch mice? We shall do better in the dark."

And Aymery and Grimbald saw him and his men ride on towards the west as though an empty village were too miserable a thing even to be burnt. Nor did they turn aside to where the gable end of the manor house showed amid the oak trees. It seemed that Gaillard had another quest in view. Goldspur was left to the sparrows and the dead cock on the dunghill.

Aymery and Grimbald watched the raiders till they had disappeared.

"We are free of them for one day, brother. What about our people?"

"We had better look to the fools," said Grimbald. "They are as frightened as rabbits."

And they went off together into the woods.

Aymery and the priest found the Goldspur folk penning their cattle in a wild part of the forest. The men had cut boughs and furze bushes, and the women were building rude huts for shelter at night. Aymery sent some of the boys to scout through the forest, and bring back any news of Gaillard that they could gather. About noon one of Waleran's men came in, with a word to Aymery that Waleran and the woodlanders were gathering to ambush the Savoyard's men. Grimbald and Aymery went off to join in the tussle, but saw nothing of Waleran though they sought him most of the day. A woodman who was felling oak trees to bark for the tanner, told them that young St. Leger had ridden by, and that Gaillard and his company had marched back beyond Bright Ling. Aymery and the priest turned homewards towards Goldspur. The long shadows of evening were purple upon the grass, and Aymery's heart remembered Denise.

They came to Goldspur manor as the dusk was falling, and the song of the birds went up towards the sunset, and everything was very still. The bridge was down over the narrow moat, and the gate open; no man had been there all that day, for Aymery's servants had fled with the village folk, and two men who could handle their bows had been sent two days ago with Waleran into the woods.

Grimbald drew the bridge, while Aymery went to the stable to feed and water his horse. They had no fear of Peter of Savoy's riders that night, and took their augury from the fact that Gaillard had left the place untouched that morning. Grimbald carried tinder and steel in his wallet, and he lit a torch in the hall, and went to the pantry and kitchen to get bread, beer, and meat for supper. He and Aymery sat down in the empty hall, and ate for a while in silence, like men who were weary, or were sunk in thought.

They were nearly through with their hunger, and were talking of Denise and the hermitage, when Grimbald, who was about to finish his mead, paused with the horn between the table and his mouth. The men's eyes met across the board. They were both listening, motionless as images carved in stone.

The night seemed dark and silent without, the woodlands asleep, the night empty of all unrest. Yet there had come to Grimbald a sense of something moving in the darkness. And as they listened there was a faint splash from the moat, and a sound like the creaking of wet leather.

Grimbald's eyes were fixed on Aymery's face.

"Listen!"

"A rat in the moat?"

Grimbald put his horn down on the table, rose up swiftly and silently, and taking his axe, went out into the courtyard. Aymery's sword and shield hung from a peg in the wall. He took them down, and had gained the door of the hall when he heard a sudden scuffling of feet, an oath in the darkness, the harsh breathing of men at grips, the splash of something into the water of the moat.

A scattering of arrows whirred and pecked at the walls, one slanting in and smiting the flagstones close to Aymery's feet. He heard the dull jingle of armed men on the move. Grimbald towered back suddenly out of the night, a red splash of blood on his forehead, his eyes shining in the torchlight.

He flung the door to, and ran the oak bar through the staples.

"Brother, we are trapped! I took the first of them and pitched him into the moat."

He shook his shaggy head, and looked round the hall. Aymery was buckling on his sword.

"There is the garden bridge," he said. "We can make a dash for it."

"Away, then; they are wading the moat, and climbing the palisade."

Aymery pushed in front of Grimbald as they hurried down a narrow passage-way that led from the hall and the kitchen quarters into the garden.

"I go first, brother," he said. "I have my steel coat; a stab in the dark might find your heart."

Grimbald passed a huge arm about Aymery as they went.

"Lad, what is that to me!"

They came out into the garden, and stood for a moment listening. They could hear Gaillard's men beating in the door of the hall, but towards the garden everything seemed quiet.

Aymery laid a hand on Grimbald's arm.

"If one of us is taken, brother, let not the other tarry. Remember Denise."

Grimbald understood him.

"Come," he said in an undertone, and they crossed the garden side by side.

Now there was a trestle-bridge from the garden over the moat, a footbridge made of a single plank that could be thrust across and withdrawn at pleasure. A wicket in the palisade led to the bridge. Aymery unbarred the gate, and ran the plank forward on to the trestles.

"We shall trick them," he said grimly, "quick, they have broken in."

He ran across the bridge, Grimbald following, the plank creaking and sagging under the priest's weight. Aymery had stooped to drag the plank away again, when he heard Grimbald give a short, deep cry, and saw him spring forward and smite at something with his axe.

"Guard, brother, guard."

Steel crashed upon steel, a glitter of sparks flying from axe and helmet. An arrow stopped quivering in Aymery's shield as he sprang forward to Grimbald's aid. Men rose at him out of the darkness. Dimly in the midst of the waving swords, he had a glimpse of two men clinging to Grimbald. He saw the priest shake them off, and beat them down before him as a boy snaps thistles with a stick. There was a rush of armed men in the darkness, the dash of steel against steel as they blundered one against another. The red splutter of a torch came tossing out of the night, with the hoarse shouting of men trying to tell friend from foe. Grimbald and Aymery lost each other, and fought each for his own hand.

CHAPTER VI

Through the darkness of the night went Denise, her grey cloak passing amid the beech trees like some dim ghost shape that drifts with the night breeze. She had been restless and distraught all day, her splendour of peace ruffled, her heart filling with a distrust of the near future. To begin with, out of the grey fog of the morning had come the man on the black horse, the man with the red eyes and the insolent scoffing mouth. Gaillard had made her shudder despite her pride, for she had learnt to hate the look of such a man before the woods had hidden her from the world. Feeling a shadow of evil near her, Denise had gone down to Goldspur after the Gascon and his men had ridden on, and had found the place deserted, so many silent hovels in a silent landscape. She had wandered up to the manor house, and found the same silence there, the same foreshadowings of tragedy.

The rest of the day had dragged slowly for her in the great beech wood, and she had found her thoughts wandering like children into a forbidden place. And Denise's pride would start up after these same thoughts, seize on them in that little pleasaunce of dreams, drag them forth, and bar the door. But there was a restless refrain in the mood of the day. The future seemed to fly open before her eyes like the magic gate of an enchanted garden, and she had a glimpse of paradise bathed in a mist of gold. Her thoughts were lured thither, though her pride arose and drove them back.

With the dusk the spirit of unrest in her had deepened, and she had seemed to hear voices calling through the twilight of the woods. A thrush had perched on the topmost bough of a beech tree, and had uttered his desire, till the plaint had rung and rung into Denise's heart. She had tossed her cloak at the bird, but none of the wild things feared her. And though the dusk fell, the song of the thrush seemed to thrill through the brown gloom.

Then night had come, and her cell had seemed small and stifling, a vault for a live soul. She had thrown her grey cloak over her shoulders, and gone out into the beech wood, following the path that led towards Goldspur manor. Her brown eyes had more than human vision in the darkness, and she knew the wood ways even at night. It was as though she went out to watch over the place, and to dispel the shadow of dread that had settled over her own heart.

Denise had come to the end of the wood where the grassland swept down into the valley, when she stopped to listen, putting her hood back so that she might hear more clearly. Her face was towards Goldspur, and she merged her body into shadow of the trunk of a great tree. Abruptly out of the night came the sudden sound of men shouting, a vague clamour that rose and fell like the noise of a wind through trees. Dots of light shone out in the darkness, jerking to and fro like sparks blown hither and thither by the wind.

Denise stood there watching these dots of fire, afraid yet not afraid, striving to understand what was happening down there in the darkness. The shouting died down suddenly, to change into the scattered cries of men running to and fro. The torches tossed this way and that as though Gaillard's fellows were hunting for fugitives, calling to one another as they doubled upon their tracks. One of the torches came some little distance up the hill towards the beech wood and then halted, and remained motionless, flaming like the eye of a cyclops.

Denise had drawn back behind the tree, when she heard the sound of something moving in the darkness. A black shape passed momentarily between her and the torch burning below upon the hillside. Footsteps came near to her, the stumbling, irregular, running steps of a man hard put for breath, and perhaps—for blood. He passed close to her in the darkness, labouring for breath, and staggering from side to side. She could still see the moving shadow in the gloom, when it plunged like a man falling forward over a cliff, and she heard the sound of a body striking the crisp, dead leaves. Fear was beneath Denise's feet for the moment. The man had fallen over the straggling root of a tree, and he was struggling to rise as Denise came up with him.

He had gained his feet, and stood rocking like a drunken man, trying to steady himself, and to win forward into the wood. But his legs would not carry him, and he went swaying as though struck on the chest, to stagger against Denise before she could avoid him. She felt the hard rings of his hauberk against her bosom, and to save herself she held the man, throwing an arm about his body.

Caught thus from behind, he turned his head and looked at her, not questioning the strangeness of it, being dazed and almost dead with what had passed. His face was so close to hers that Denise could not but know him, even in the darkness.

"Aymery!"

Her voice set his dull brain thrilling.

"Denise!"

She kept her arm about him, for there was nothing else for her to do, and he would have fallen had she not held him. Aymery's face was as white as linen, and she could feel him quivering as he stood.

"Peter of Savoy's men, we were caught yonder, Grimbald and I."

He spoke in jerks, and tried to stand apart from her, as though one purpose had carried him so far, and as though the same purpose dominated him still.

"I want breath, that is all; they pressed us hard, there, at Goldspur; we broke through, and I ran for the hills. You must go, Denise, to-night; make for one of the coast towns. I can look to myself."

He was at the end of his strength, however, for all his hardihood, with a sword cut through the shoulder, an arrow broken in his thigh. Denise could see nothing of all this, but she knew that he could hardly stand. Moreover, he had struggled up into the wood to warn her, and her heart was the heart of a woman though the people called her a saint.

Looking back over her shoulder she saw tongues of yellow flame rising from Goldspur in the valley. Gaillard's men had set fire to the place. The glow from it caught Aymery's eyes as he stood, swaying at the knees, great sickness upon him, even his wrath feeble in him because of his wounds and his weariness.

"They have lit me a torch to travel by," he said bitterly.

Denise was shading her eyes with her hand. She turned swiftly upon Aymery, for she had seen mounted men moving on the hillside between her, and the burning house.

"Lord," she said simply, "yesterday, you were afraid for my sake; to-night, it is I who fear."

Her eyes met his, and held them. The secret thoughts of the day no longer had their half treacherous significance. Denise had no thought of self in her that moment; the succouring hands hid the dull radiance of the heart beneath.

"To-night you must rest and sleep."

He looked at her, as though trying to understand. The darkness began to deepen about him, and he felt cold, and numb to the core.

"I can crawl to cover. If you could bring me wine and food, and a little linen— —"

She went close to him suddenly, and passed her hands over his hauberk. Touch told her the whole truth. She had no false shame to make her weak and careful.

"Wounds, and you would have hidden them!"

"A little blood, nothing more. Let me lie here, Denise."

"To die," and her voice had a deep, quiet passion in it; "lord, would you choose death for a piece of pride! Come, I know the ways."

She put an arm about him, as though she was stronger than Aymery that night, and had the will and courage to do for him what he, in his full strength, would have done for her. Suffering and sickness sweep the small prides of life aside. The heart of a woman is as elemental, then, as the wind or the sea.

"Lean on me."

He looked at her half rebelliously, and then hung his head, and obeyed.

How great his need was became apparent before they had reached the clearing amid the beech trees. The man stumbled and faltered at every step, his head fell forward, he muttered incoherently, like one in the heat of a fever. Denise felt his weight bearing more heavily upon her arm. His head drooped, and rested upon her shoulder. Before they reached the wattle gate of the garden the conscious life was out of him, and Denise, borne down like a vine-ladened sapling bent by the wind, let the man slip from her gently to the ground.

She stood irresolute a moment, then stooping and putting her two hands under his shoulders, she found that she could drag him slowly up the stone path into her cell. Once within she closed the door, and slipping off her cloak, she covered the slit of a window with it. There was a little earthen lamp in the cell, and Denise sought and found it in the darkness, also tinder, flint, and steel. Yet her hands shook so with her labour of bearing up under Aymery's weight, that it was a minute or more before she had the lamp burning.

Setting it upon a stone sconce in the wall, she bent over Aymery, the light of the lamp making his face seem white as the face of the dead. Her brown eyes grew frightened at the sight of his wounds, and at the way he lay so quiet, and so still. But there was something greater than fear in Denise's heart that night. In a corner of the cell were some rough boards covered with dry bracken, a coarse white sheet, and a coverlet of wool. Denise, putting her arms once more under the man's body, half dragged and half lifted him to her own rough bed.

CHAPTER VII

The night was far spent, and the oil in the earthen lamp had failed some hours ago. Denise, sitting in the darkness, with her chin resting on her hands, listened to Aymery's breathing, and waited for the dawn. Nerving herself, she had twisted the arrow's head from the flesh, unlaced his hauberk and bound up the wounded shoulder, and poured some wine between his lips. For a long time she had watched him for signs of returning consciousness. Then the lamp had died out and left them in the darkness, and Denise had sat wondering whether the man's quietude meant sleep or death.

Denise did not close her eyes that night. She was wakeful, strangely wakeful, almost conscious of the beating of her heart. More than once she had bent forward and touched Aymery's hand, and its coldness chilled her, so that she longed for the day. Often too in the strained suspense of the night's silence she would fancy that he had ceased to breathe, and she would fall a-praying with a passion that startled even her own heart.

A faint greyness beneath the door, a sudden tentative cry from some awakened bird. For a while silence, then sudden and strange, a thrilling up of note on note, a sense as of golden light mounting in sweeping spirals towards the sky. Wizard's magic in the grey of the great wood, a thousand throats throbbing in unison till the whole world seemed full of a glory of sound. The very air quivered within the cell. It was as though invisible wings were beating everywhere, while the trees of the forest were tongued with prophetic fire.

Denise rose, opened wide the door, and let the song of the birds come to her with the cold fragrance of the breaking day. As yet greyness everywhere, grey grass, grey trees. A gradual gathering of light, then, of a sudden, as though some god had hurled fire into the sky, a blur of gold, a cry of crimson from the mouths of the pale clouds. Soon, an arch of amber in the east, the forest black against the splendour thereof, the grass a-gleam, the sky in the zenith still dim like a woman's eyes dim with tears. A beautiful tenderness transfigured the face of the world; no wicked thing seemed thinkable while those birds were singing.

So the dawn came, and flung his torch into the cell at Denise's feet.

Now that the daylight absolved her from suspense, she turned, a little fearfully, and knelt down beside the bed. The man's face was in the shadow, so that it looked very sharp and grey to her, yet he was breathing quietly with his lips closed. Only a little blood had soaked through the bandages. Yet Denise knelt watching him, unable to shake off the haunting dread that he might not wake to see another dawn.

Whether it was the daylight playing on his face, or the long gaze of Denise's eyes, Aymery awoke without so much as the stirring of a hand, and looked up straight into the woman's face. And for some moments those two stared silently into each other's eyes.

Aymery half rose upon his elbow, but Denise's hand went to his unwounded shoulder.

"Lie still," she said to him, with a pressure of the hand.

He obeyed her, and sank back upon the bed. Denise saw his lips move, but no words came from them. His eyes wandered from her face about the cell, as though the slow consciousness of it all were flowing into his brain. And as the daylight broadened, his mind's awakening seemed to keep pace with it. He was lying in Denise's cell, and upon Denise's bed.

"How long have I been here?"

She bent towards him, her hair shining about her face. Aymery's eyes caught the sheen thereof, and seemed dazzled by its glory.

"Only lie still," she said. "In the night I thought that you would die. You are safe here. None but friends know the ways."

He seemed to feel the first burning of his wounds, for his hand went to his right shoulder, but Denise caught it, and laid it upon the coverlet.

"I have looked to your wounds."

"How did I come here?"

His eyes searched her face.

"You are safe, is not that enough; yet, you were very heavy," and she smiled at him.

"Have you seen Grimbald?"

"No, no one."

Aymery was silent for a moment, looking at Denise with a kind of quiet wonder. Her face was turned from him. And suddenly he caught her hand, and lifted it, and for a moment its whiteness lay across Aymery's mouth.

"God guard you, Denise."

Her eyes flashed down at him.

"You must live. I ask that."

"Assuredly, I cannot die."

Denise rose up and went out into the sunlight, for her face had blazed suddenly with blood that rushed from the heart.

The first thing that Denise did that morning was to take a pitcher that stood beside the door, and to go down to the spring to draw water. There were drops of the man's blood upon the stones of the path, and Denise, bringing back her pitcher, washed the stains away so that they should offer no betrayal. The beech wood seemed still and empty in the morning sunlight. Yet the peril of the night haunted her heart continually with an innocence that had no thought of self.

She went to refill the pitcher at the spring, looking watchfully down every dwindling woodway, and listening even for the rustle of dead leaves. Aymery was lying awake when she returned. His eyes watched her a little restlessly, and there was something in those eyes of his that made the blood come more quickly to her face.

Turning to a cupboard she took out bread, honey, and a little jar of wine.

"Is that water, there?"

He was looking at the pitcher.

"Yes."

Denise understood him instantly, for she found a clean napkin in the cupboard, moistened it, and bent over the bed.

"Your lips are dry."

She put a hand under his head, raised it, and washed his mouth and face. He held out his hands to her, and she washed those also, yet her eyes avoided Aymery's, and their deeps were hidden from him by the shadows of their lashes.

"Are you hungry?"

"No, not even a little."

"But you must eat for your strength's sake."

"I will do all that you desire."

She would not suffer him to manage for himself, but spread the honey on the bread, and held the wine flask for him to drink.

"It is all that I can give," she said simply.

He looked at her, but found no answer for the moment. Both of them had grown suddenly shy of one another and when their hands touched, the touch thrilled them from hand to heart.

Denise left him at last, and going to the doorway of the cell, stood to break bread for her own need. Yet though her face was turned from him, she could not put the man's nearness from her, and the bread as she crumbled it, fell in waste on the stones at her feet.

"Denise."

Aymery's voice startled her. He had not spoken loudly, but there was a return of strength in the tone thereof.

"Yes?"

"You shall be rid of me before nightfall. I only ask for a day's grace."

She had turned and was looking down at him with solemn eyes.

"It will be days before you must stir," she said. "Remember that I saw your wounds."

"They are nothing."

"Lord, I know otherwise. You will bide there on that bed."

She spoke quietly enough, but Aymery looked up at her restlessly, watching the sunlight shining through her hair.

"I cannot lie here, Denise."

"You are safe."

"Too safe, perhaps; it is not of my own safety— —"

He paused, but not before she had caught his meaning. The truth was difficult for Aymery to utter, and yet she honoured him for thinking of her honour.

"None but our friends come this way," she answered.

He half rose in bed with the strong and generous passion that made his pale face shine on her out of the darkness of the cell.

"Mother of God, child, am I so selfish, and so blind! Do I not remember what you are, to all of us in these parts. If these dogs found me here! I would rather crawl on my hands and knees than tempt that chance."

Her face flushed deeply, but not because of the mere words that he had spoken. A sudden impulse seized her, an impulse that came she knew not whither. Aymery had sunk back again, and the sight of this strong man's weakness went to her heart. In the taking of a breath she was bending over him, and holding the wooden cross that hung at her girdle. Kissing it she held it before Aymery's eyes.

"Lord, let this be as a sign between us, for I have no fear."

He looked at the cross, then at Denise, and his eyes seemed to catch the glimmer of her hair.

"Denise, but one day," he said. "To-morrow — —"

"Leave God the morrow."

"Yet, who knows what even the morrow may bring."

Denise turned from him, and going out, closed the door. She stood leaning against it, looking above the trees into the blue of a spring sky. Infinitely strange, infinitely wonderful seemed this mysterious fire that had been kindled suddenly within her heart. Quench it she could not, though she strove to smother and hide it even from herself. As for Aymery, the cell seemed very dark to him, for lack of the radiance that had streamed from her hair.

Denise went down through the beech wood towards Goldspur that morning, meaning to see whether Gaillard and his men had gone. The valley was full of sunlight, but over the village hung a thin dun-coloured mist, with pale smoke curling upwards into the blue. No live thing moved in the valley, and even her hope of the glimpse of a friend failed her. Still, her heart was glad that there were no riders there, and that the violence of the night seemed farther from her world.

Gaillard had gone. He and his men had passed the night, drinking and warming themselves before the burning house, none too pleased with the evening's handiwork. Soon after dawn a rider had come galloping in, beaconed through the darkness by the glare of the burning manor, and Gaillard, when he had spoken with the fellow, had ordered his men to horse, after they had buried two comrades who had fallen beneath Grimbald's axe. They had ridden away towards the sea, since my Lord of Savoy had called Gaillard back to Pevensey.

The night before, some thirty "spears" and a company of archers had marched in from Lewes, sent thence by John de Warenne, the Earl.

"Since the iron is hot in your parts, sire," ran the Earl's message, "I send you a hammer for your anvil. God keep the King."

Peter of Savoy had laughed at the message, and thrown a jewel into Etoile's lap.

"The book tells us that we should go a-hunting," he had said. "We will send for the Gascon back again. There are lusty rebels to be pulled down when the King's need is paramount."

Etoile had laughed in turn, with a gleam of black eyes and of white teeth.

"Let our horns blow, sire, I too will ride with you."

"A bolt in time saves twine," quoth her man.

When Gaillard returned that morning, and Peter of Savoy heard the news of Dan Barnabo's death, and the way the mesne lords had called out their men, he smiled at Gaillard very grimly, and twitted him with the little that he had done.

"You are clever at lighting bonfires, my Gascon," he said. "But singeing the bear makes him only madder. We have no need of our clerks and lawyers, for when such work is afoot we can shut justiciar, coroner, and sheriff up in the same box. Will any man tell me that I have no right of private war in my own manors. The King is defied! Go to now, we have our warrant."

Gaillard showed his teeth, and shot a stealthy, swaggering look towards Etoile.

"To catch the fox, sire, we must have hounds enough."

"Take them, my boaster, and sweep the countryside. We will ride with you to see the chase."

"And madame, also? We will show her how these pigs of Englishmen can run."

That same evening as the sun sank low, Denise went down to draw water at the spring. The woods were full of a glory of gold, and the chequered shadows of the trees fell upon the brown leaves, and the vivid grass. The gorse seemed lit as for the evening of All Souls. Perfumes rose out of the pregnant earth. A hundred thrushes seemed chanting a vesper song.

The heart of Denise also was full of strange, elfin music. There was a smile upon her mouth, and her eyes caught the enchanted distance of dreams. As she drew water at the spring and the ripples of the pool were inset with gold, she sang to herself softly, a song that she had learnt as a young girl, a song of the tower, and not of the cell.

Aymery heard her singing as she came across the glade to the gate of the garden. The door of the cell stood open, but Denise had hung her cloak so as to hide the bed.

When she came in to him, Aymery watched her with the eyes of a man whose heart is troubled. For he felt the guilt of his presence in that place, and the fairness of Denise had made him afraid. True, she had taken no formal vows, but to the world she was a creature whose very feet made the brown earth holy.

"No news of Grimbald?"

"None."

Her deep voice thrilled him, but he stirred uneasily upon the bed.

"I have gained strength to-day."

"Do not waste it, then, lord," she answered him.

His eyes pleaded with her like the eyes of a dog.

"Give me a hand, Denise; I will try if I can stand."

"No; why, you will but open your wounds again."

"My thoughts are more to me than my wounds, Denise."

He struggled up suddenly before she could hinder him, only to turn faint and dizzy, for the blood fell from his brain. He swayed, and went grey as Denise's gown.

"Are you mad, lord; you will die of your wilfulness!"

She put her arm about his shoulders, and her hair brushed against his cheek.

"Denise, if I could so much as crawl——"

His wistfulness woke a rush of tenderness in her.

"No, no, rest here."

"Rest! I cannot rest, cannot you understand?"

Denise's arm was still about his shoulders. They looked into each other's eyes, one long look full of mystery, of sadness, and unrest.

"My heart understands you," she said very softly. "Yet, is there shame in my wishing you to live."

She let him lie back on the bed, and taking the wine, she made him drink, and her hand brushed the hair from off his forehead.

"You must sleep," she said. "No harm can come while I am watching."

And Aymery's eyes were full of a silent awe.

CHAPTER VIII

There was a sound of horns in the woodlands as the morning of the second day drew towards noon, and Denise, who had gone down towards Goldspur to discover whether Grimbald or any of the villagers had returned, heard the distant winding of the horns, and stood still to listen.

The day was sunny, with a light breeze blowing, and Denise could see no live thing stirring in the whole valley where the ashes of Goldspur still threw out silver smoke. Yet those distant horns beyond the hills seemed to carry a cry of strangeness and unrest. Denise would have given much to know all that was passing yonder, but no man came that way and she dared not leave the beech wood, and the wounded man in the cell. The very silence and emptiness of the landscape filled her with vague dread. No one had dared to return to the fields or the burnt village. The hawk was still hovering, and the small birds kept their cover.

Aymery was asleep when Denise returned to the cell, but he woke at her coming, and looked up at her for news.

"I have seen nothing but the smoke from Goldspur," she said calmly enough. "Grimbald and the people still keep to the woods. They may be with us any hour."

Aymery lay quiet for a while as though sunk in thought. His consciousness reflected clearly the meaning of the past and the promise of the future.

"So they have burnt Goldspur," he said, as though speaking the words of a prayer.

Denise had set the door wide, and drawn a stool into the sunlight.

"Surely there is some law left in the land?"

"We have surfeited ourselves with law," he said bitterly; "only to learn that the law bows itself to the man with the sword and the title."

Denise leant back against the rough oak door-post.

"You will build the house again?" she asked.

He did not answer her for a moment.

"No, not yet," he said at last. "The sword is the first tool that we Englishmen must handle. These Frenchmen laugh at us, calling us English swine, but the day is near when the tusks of the English boar shall be red with their blood."

He spoke with the fierceness of the man of the sword, but Denise's heart was with him, though her hands were held to be hands of mercy.

"Such men as Hubert of Kent, they are our need," she said.

"Hubert! The land shall give us a hundred Huberts," and his face blazed up at her. "It will be the bills of England against the spears of this hired scum from France and Flanders, these dogs in the service of dogs who have plundered our lands and shamed our women. They have laughed at us, robbed us, made a puppet of our king. 'Get you to England,' has been the cry, 'It is a land of fools, of heavy men stupid with mead and swine's flesh. Take what you will. The savages will only gape and grumble.' But I tell you, Denise, the heart of England has grown hot with a slow, sure wrath. We are Normans no longer, nor Saxons, nor Danes. Men are gripping hands from sea to sea. God see to it, but the years will prove that England is England, the land of the English, and woe to those who shall trifle with our strength."

Like a mocking voice came the cry of a horn, echoing tauntingly amid the hills. Another took up the blast, and yet another, cheerily braying through the young green of the woods. The two in the cell were mute for the moment, looking questioningly into each other's eyes.

Aymery raised himself upon his elbow.

"The Savoyard's men!"

Denise's eyes were full of a startled brightness.

"Why not Waleran?" she asked him as she stood listening at the door.

"I know the sound of our Sussex horns."

She stepped out into the sunlight, and went swiftly down the path towards the gate.

"Lie still," she called to him. "I will go and see what may be learnt."

Denise knew every alley in the wood, and her grey gown glided westwards amid the dark boles of the trees. Ever and again the horns sang lustily to one another, coming nearer and ever nearer, swelled by the faint but ominous tonguing of dogs. Denise went forward more slowly, pausing often to listen, her brown eyes growing more watchful as the sounds came nearer to her through the maze of the woods. She could feel even her own heart beating; and her face sharpened with the keenness of her vigilance.

Denise drew back abruptly behind the trunk of a great tree. She had heard a crackling of dry leaves, a sound of men moving, voices calling in harsh undertones, one to the other. She crouched down amid the gnarled tree roots, her lips apart, her eyes at gaze. The heavy breathing of tired beasts came to her, with the rustle of leaves, and the quick plodding of many feet. As she crouched there she saw figures go scurrying away through the mysterious shadowland of the woods. Some were mounted on forest ponies, others fleeing on foot. One man passed within ten yards of Denise, his mouth open, his hands clawing the air beside him as he ran. None of them saw her, none of them looked back. They disappeared like so many flitting shadows, and a second silence covered their tracks as water closes behind the keel of a ship.

Denise tarried no longer, but rose and ran back towards the cell. Those flying shadows amid the beech trees had told her all that she could need to know. As for Aymery, she must hide him and take her chance. Her gown gleamed in and out through shadow and sunshine, while the tonguing of the dogs and the scream of the horns haunted her like the discords of a dream.

Denise had half crossed the clearing when she saw a sight that made her catch her breath. Close by the gate lay Aymery, propping himself upon one arm, his head drooping like the head of a man who has been smitten through with a sword.

She ran to him, her eyes a-fire.

"Lord, what have you done?"

He lifted his face to her, a face that was grey and moist in the sunlight. She saw that the linen swathings over his shoulder were red with vivid stains.

"I have time—yet."

Denise bent over him.

"You are mad, you are bleeding anew."

"Give me wine, Denise; I can crawl, if I cannot walk."

She put her arms about him and tried to lift him to his feet.

"No, no, come back to the cell. They are beating the woods. I saw men flying for their lives."

Aymery clung to her, and gained his feet.

"Denise, I must take my chance, help me into the woods."

But his eyes went dim and blind in the sunlight, and Denise, as she looked at him, uttered a sharp, passionate cry.

"Lord, you have tempted death enough. Come. There is no time to lose."

Denise was strong beyond her strength as she put an arm about him, and half led, half carried him into the cell. She let Aymery sink upon the bed, and covered him with the coverlet that he had thrown aside.

"For God's love, lie still," she said. "Should they come this way I will put them off with lies."

Denise went out from him and closed the door. For a moment a great faintness seized her, for she had taxed her very soul in carrying Aymery within. The sunlight flashed and flickered before her eyes, so that she put her hands up before her face, and leant, trembling, against the door. But the sound of the horns and the dogs grew louder in the beech wood, and Denise's strength came back to her with that fine courage that women show when life and death hang in the balance.

With one quick glance at the woods she went down on her knees on the stone-paved path, and began to pull up the few weeds that she could find in the borders. Her hair had become loosened in her flight through the wood, and hung in waves about her neck and shoulders. Denise kept her eyes on the ground before her, though her ears were straining to catch the slightest sound. She prayed as she knelt there, as she had never prayed for a boon before, that these men might pass by without seeing the dark thatch of her cell.

The trampling of many horses swelled the shrill whimpering and tonguing of the dogs. A horn blared close by. The wood seemed full of voices, of swift movement, of hurrying sounds. Denise heard the laughter of a woman peal out suddenly, strange and unfamiliar in the midst of such a chorus. A man's voice shouted a fierce command. The whole wood about the place seemed to become alive with colour, and the gleam and clangour of steel.

Denise bent her head over the brown soil and gave no sign. Her fingers plucked at a tuft of grass, but could not close on it because of their great trembling. Her heart told her that these people would not pass by. Swiftly, half fearfully, she raised her head, and looked up over the wattle fence.

Before her the shadowy wood seemed to swim with the faces and figures of armed men. Horses crowded in with tossing manes, shields flickered, surcoats with many colours. Brown-faced archers walked between the horses, their steel caps shining, bows ready with arrows on the strings.

Rangers and servants held the dogs in leash, sweating, panting men who cursed the beasts that strained, and yelped, and rose upon their haunches.

In the forefront of the whole rout, like a great gem set in the centre of a crown, Denise saw a woman seated on a milk-white horse. Her green gown was diapered over with golden lilies, and in her hand she carried a bow. The woman's face was flushed with riding, and her hair disordered in its golden caul. On her right hand rode a lord in a surcoat of purple, and the trappings of his horse were of white and blue. On her left, with a drawn sword over his shoulder, Denise saw the man who had surprised her at the spring.

Since there was no help for it, Denise sat back upon her heels, her face flushed with stooping over the soil. All those hundred eyes seemed fastened upon her. Yet there was a sudden silence save for the whimpering and the chafing of the dogs.

Over the wattle fence, and across the narrow stretch of grass, the eyes of the woman on the white horse met the eyes of Denise. And some instant instinct of enmity seemed to flash between the two, as though—being women—they could read each other's hearts.

Denise saw her turn to Gaillard, and point with her bow in the direction of the cell. The Gascon laughed, and pretended to pray to the cross of his sword. Then he flapped the bridle upon the neck of his horse, and rode forward to speak with Denise.

CHAPTER IX

Gaillard rode up to the wicket and saw Denise kneeling on the path with weeds and grass tufts scattered along the stones. Paltry, misplaced labour, this, for a woman with such a body and such eyes and hair! Gaillard had his grudge against Denise, and though his impulse was to humble her, he could not forget how the morning sunlight had struck upon her that morning at the pool.

"The best of matins to you, Sanctissima," he said. "I trust that you are rid of your sins as easily as you are rid of those weeds."

Denise rose to her feet, his scoffing voice bringing the colour to her face. The look in Gaillard's eyes made her hate him, a jeering, masterful, boastful look that showed that he was insolently sure of himself, and knew how to play the bully on occasions.

"What would you, messire?" and she felt her face hot under the man's eyes.

Gaillard stared her over, as though he had no high opinion of women, and especially of those who were comely and yet pretended to be righteous.

"Holy Sister," and his eyes looked beyond her towards the cell, "why do you shut your door so close of a May morning?"

His red eyes flashed down at her again, and Denise, with a fierce burning of the cheeks, felt that he was watching her, and that her secret might hang upon the tremor of a word.

"You are curious over trifles," she said curtly. "I live alone here after my own fashion. What would you with all your dogs and men?"

Gaillard heeled his horse close to the gate. Count Peter, Etoile, and all their company watched and waited.

"Come nearer, Sanctissima," said the Gascon, keeping his eyes fixed upon her face.

Denise did not stir.

"Come now, saint of the beech woods, put your pride aside, and let us talk together. And keep those eyes of yours from anger. It may be that I can give service for service."

He spoke softly to her, almost suggestively, but Denise hated his smoothness more than his insolence.

"I do not understand you, messire," she said.

Gaillard's eyes grew keen and greedy.

"Such a woman as you, my lady, should not be rash in refusing courtesies. Now, if I ask you to open yonder door?"

She tried to outstare him, but his eyes seemed to look her innocence through and through.

"Say what you please," she said. "Men fled through the wood here before you came. But I have not meddled in your affairs."

He tossed his head back suddenly and laughed, so that Denise saw the red roof of his mouth above his smooth, strong, shining chin.

"Sister, do they write of such things in heaven? Clerks tell us a tale that whenever a cock crowed, St. Peter was seized with a spasm of coughing. Who is it that you are hiding, yonder?"

Denise stood dumb before him. The man's face mocked her like the face of a mocking Faun.

"I have no answer for you, messire," she said. "Go back to those who sent you, and to your horns and your dogs."

She turned slowly, meaning to reach the cell and bar the door, hoping the last hope that these people would ride on and leave her in peace. But Gaillard was too shrewd to be cheated thus. He struck his horse with the spurs, set him at the low fence, cleared it, and trampling the garden under foot, put himself between Denise and the cell.

"A capture, a capture!"

He laughed down in Denise's face, as he waved his sword to those who were waiting on the fringes of the beech wood.

The flash of the Gascon's sword brought the whole rout swarming down upon the place, dogs, men, and horses, fur, steel and colour. The wattle fence went down before them; the herbs and the spring flowers were trampled into the soil. A horse plunged and reared close beside Denise, so that she had a glimpse of a black muzzle with the teeth showing, and soaring hoofs ready to crush her to the earth. Some unknown hand thrust her roughly aside, when a hound sprang at her, and was dragged back snarling on the end of a leash. Suddenly in the whirl of it she found Gaillard beside her on his horse, pushing the beast forward so as to shelter her from the rout that had stormed in as though half Waleran's rebels held the hermitage.

"Back, fools," and he struck at some of them with the flat of his sword. "Out, out! Who called for a charge?"

He turned his horse this way and that, driving the men back, and clearing a space about the cell.

"Roland, on guard there, man, by the door. Stand to your arms, sirs; am I captain of a drove of swine?"

There was something fine in the way he wheeled his great horse to and fro, driving men and dogs like so many sheep. Denise, her hair falling upon her shoulders, drew back towards the cell, her senses dazed for the moment by all this violence and roughness.

The crowd of armed men parted suddenly, and through the gap between their swords and lances came riding the woman on the milk-white horse, haughty, yet smiling, her bow across her knees. Peter of Savoy rode close beside her, a quiet, noiseless man, whose cold eyes were more dangerous than a dozen swords. Gaillard wheeled towards them, touching his horse with the spur so that the beast caracoled and showed off his lord's masterfulness in the saddle.

Peter of Savoy smoothed his beard with a gloved hand that showed a great ruby upon the leather.

"What have we here, my friend? The lady in the grey gown looks as though she would kill you an she could."

Gaillard laughed, and glanced at Etoile.

"That is our Lady of the Woods, sire, a saint whom the boors worship. Yet I might swear that she has more than her scourge, her stone bed, and her cross in that cell."

Etoile's black eyes covered Denise.

"Does a saint carry such a fleece of hair," she sneered. "This man-chase pleases me better and better, sire. See how Madame Dorcas is standing on live coals!"

She laughed, and looked at Denise, tilting her chin, her eyes inquisitively insolent.

"Have the door opened, sire, and let us see what her man is like."

Peter of Savoy glanced shrewdly at Etoile.

"How fair women love one another! Rosamond's cup is always ready to the hand."

Denise had drawn back close to the door of the cell, and stood leaning against the wall under the shadow of the overhanging thatch. Her hair seemed to burn under that band of shade like stormy sunlight under a ragged cloud. Her hands were folded over her bosom, her brown eyes fixed on the white forehead of Etoile's horse. There was no furtiveness about her face, no flickering of a half confessed shame. The open space between her and Gaillard's men seemed to symbolise something, perhaps an awe of her that made these rough men of the sword hold back.

Etoile pointed with her bow towards the door, and her eyes challenged Denise.

"Perhaps our Holy Sister will satisfy us with an oath," she said. "For the lips of a saint cannot utter a lie."

Denise answered her nothing, and Etoile's face darkened maliciously under her golden caul.

"Will you lay me a wager, sire?" and she tapped Peter of Savoy on the knee with her bow.

His eyes gleamed at her.

"A star is made wise by the stars; I keep an open mind."

"Then have the door opened, and let us see whether this good woman cannot hide a lover."

Peter of Savoy nodded towards the cell, and Gaillard wheeled his horse, catching a glimpse of Denise's white and waiting face.

"Roland, Jean, Guillaume!"

His strident voice rang out. The three men stood forward with their eyes fixed on him. Gaillard pointed with his sword to the door of the cell.

"Open it."

They turned to obey him, one of the fellows forcing the door back with the point of his sword, all three of them upon the alert with their shields forward as though expecting the rush of armed men.

The door had swung back showing nothing but a shadowy interior, a dark and deep recess in the midst of the day's sunlight. The three men craned their heads over their shields. Gaillard heeled his horse forward, and ordered the men aside. Stooping low in the saddle he looked into the cell, his face lean and intent, his eyes like the eyes of a suspicious dog. At first he could distinguish nothing. Then he laughed very softly, straightened in the saddle, and looked down at Denise.

"Perhaps, Sister, your bed works miracles!" he said.

He laughed a little more loudly, his mouth mocking her, his eyes sparkling over the humbling of her pride. The three men began to laugh also. The pother seemed as infectious as the cackling in a farmyard; the dogs opened their mouths, and bayed; the wood became full of stupid, Bacchic mirth.

Etoile laughed as loudly as any of the men, yet with a metallic hardness that was not beautiful.

"Here is a quaint tale," she said. "Who is it, the lord of Goldspur, did someone say? She has prayed over him like a saint!"

The woman's shrill laughter stung Denise like the lash of a whip. Her lips moved, but she said nothing.

They were all laughing, and looking upon Denise when a man appeared in the doorway of the cell. He was unarmed, with reddened bandages about one shoulder, and his white face blazed out from the shadows as though all the wrath in the world burnt like a torch behind his eyes. There was something so grim and scornful about that face that the men nearest him fell back, silenced, repulsed, crowding upon one another.

Aymery came out into the sunlight. He looked right and left, his eyes sweeping the circle of rough faces, and leaving on each the mark of his sharp contempt. Gaillard alone had a smile upon his face. He sat in the saddle with his sword over his shoulder, and pouted out his lips as though to whistle. Denise had not turned her head. Yet it was as though she were trying to look at Aymery without betraying the quest of her brown eyes, for Etoile was watching her with a sneer lifting the corners of her mouth.

Aymery glanced up at the Gascon, and then beyond him towards Lord Peter and the lady.

Gaillard laughed aloud.

"It is our friend who ran away from us two nights ago," he said. "I hope you were happy, sir, hiding under a lady's bed."

Aymery's knees shook under him, and his eyes had turned to grey steel.

"If your heart and mouth are foul," he said, "make no boast thereof, my hireling. God give me the chance some day, and I will choke you with those words."

He held his head high, and looked Gaillard in the eyes. But the strength was ebbing from him; he had lost more blood. Two of the Gascon's men caught him by the arms as he began to totter.

Etoile touched Count Peter with her bow.

"The man has courage in him. We have bated him enough."

The lord of the castles smiled like a cynic.

"We men are so deserving of pity, we are such fine fellows! Lend him your horse, my desire!"

Peter of Savoy laid a hand over his heart, looking at Etoile under half-closed lids as though she were a child to be humoured. He gave Gaillard his orders. A spare horse was led forward, and Aymery lifted into the saddle. He held to the pommel with both hands, trying to steady himself, a confusion of faces before his eyes.

"Wine, and I shall not hinder you."

A horn set with silver and closed with an ivory lid, passed from hand to hand. It had come from the wallet that hung from Etoile's saddle. A soldier held it to Aymery's mouth, steadying him with one arm. Aymery drank, his hand shaking, so that the red wine stained his chin.

"Thanks, friend, for that."

He gave the horn back again, raised his head, and looked round him for Denise. She was still leaning against the wall of the cell. Their eyes met for a moment in one quick look that left sadness and joy and pain in the hearts of both.

Gaillard's voice rang out. A horn screamed. Dogs, men, and horses moved suddenly like a crowd that has been held behind a barrier. Etoile remained motionless upon her horse, watching the men pass by her with Aymery in their midst. Already Gaillard's red surcoat beaconed towards the gloom of the beech wood, the sun shining upon it so that it looked the colour of blood.

Peter of Savoy loitered beyond the trampled garden, waiting for Etoile, and wondering what whim kept her near the cell. The men had streamed away before she turned her horse and walked the beast slowly past Denise. And she stared at Denise boldly as she passed, her black eyes mocking her from the vantage of her horse.

"Sweet dreams to you, Holy Sister!" she said.

And she rode on laughing, and leapt her horse over the wattle fence.

Denise stood there motionless, her face bleak and cold, her eyes looking into the distance as though they saw and understood nothing. Suddenly her face blazed with a rush of blood. She hung her head, and seemed to be praying.

CHAPTER X

So briskly did the Lord of Pevensey sweep the woods that Maytide, hunting his enemies with horn and hound, that he drove such mesne lords as had drawn the sword beyond his borders into other parts. The mere gentleman and the yeoman could make no fight of it as yet against a great lord who held the castles. The peasants were cowed by the lances of the troopers; a few still lurked in the deeps of the woods, chased hither and thither like wild things that fly from the cry of the hound. The finer and fiercer spirits fled with savage thoughts in their hearts, counting on the day when their chance should come again. Waleran de Monceaux took refuge in Winchelsea, and joined himself to the men of that town. Others galloped away to seek Earl Simon, and to ease their wrath under De Montfort's banner. As for Grimbald the priest, he lay near to death, hidden near a swineherd's hovel, stricken with the wounds that he had gotten him at Goldspur manor.

When Waleran de Monceaux, that man of the fierce face and the bristling beard, fled to Winchelsea town, he rode by the Abbey of Battle as the dawn was breaking and halted there and called for food. He and his men had touched neither meat nor bread for a day and a night. Some were wounded, all of them ragged, famished, and caked with the mire of the woodland ways. The hosteler looked sulkily at these savage and beaten men. Love them he could not because of their importunity, and their great hunger. And while they cursed him because of his slowness, he sent word to the Abbot, desiring his commands.

Abbot Reginald's message came to him with curt good sense.

"Feed them, and be rid of them."

So Waleran and his men had their paunches filled, because Reginald of Battle was a man of discretion and desired to keep his lands untainted. There were sundry inconveniences that clung even to the right of sanctuary and such high prerogatives. Reginald of Brecon was a smooth and astute man, a fine farmer, and keen as any Lombard. He would have no neighbour's sparks from over the hedge setting fire to his own hayrick. If fools quarrelled, he could pray for both parties, and hold up the Cross benignantly, provided no one came trampling his crops.

In those days Dom Silvius was almoner at the Abbey, a quiet, sharp-faced, gliding mortal, very devout yet very shrewd. Men said that Dom Silvius loved his "house" better than he loved his soul. Never was a mouse more quick to scent out peas. He knew the ploughlands in every manor, every hog in every wood, how much salt each pan should yield, the value of the timber and the underwood, the measure of the corn ground at the mills, the honey each hive yielded, the number of fish that might be taken from the stews. The Abbey's charter, and each and every several bequest might have been written on Dom Silvius's brain. He was ever on the alert, ever contriving, and such a man was to be encouraged. His brethren loved him, for he was not miserly towards the "girdle," and their pittances were bettered by Dom Silvius's briskness. What did it matter if a monk meddled with more than concerned him, provided the buildings were in good repair, and his brethren had red wine to warm their bellies.

Dom Silvius's ears were always open. He was a quiet man who did not frighten folk, but he learnt their secrets, and he often touched their money. Few lawyers could have snatched a grant from under the almoner's cold, white fingers. He was a man of foresight, and of some imagination. Property to him was not merely a matter of so many plough teams and so many hides, pannage for hogs, and grindings at the mill. The Church held all charters in the land of the Spirit; she could take toll from the lay folk, and make them pay for using her road to heaven.

The very day that Waleran rode through Battle, Dom Silvius walked with folded arms and bowed head into the Abbot's parlour. He stood meekly within the door, his face full of a smooth humility, his eyes fixed upon the rushes.

Abbot Reginald trusted greatly in this monk. The man was ever courteous and debonair, never turbulent or facetious, always inspired for the "glory" of his "house."

"The blessing of the day, Brother. What business lies between us?"

Dom Silvius lifted his eyes for the first time to his superior's face.

"If I repeat myself, Father, my importunity is an earnest failing. It concerns the Red Saint for whom Olivia of Goldspur built a cell."

Reginald of Brecon leant back in his chair, and closed the book that he had been reading.

"The woman whom they call Denise?"

Silvius looked demure, as though his sanctity were especially sensitive where a woman was concerned.

"Her fame has become very great these months," he said quietly.

"You covet it, Silvius."

The almoner bowed his head.

"I grudge no soul its good works, Father. But in these days of burnings, and of spilling of blood — —"

"The woods have grown perilous, Silvius, with Lord Peter's men abroad."

"That is the very truth, sir. There is no place safe outside the sanctuaries. I have heard it said that the Prior of Mickleham has offered protection to the woman."

Abbot Reginald smiled, the smile of a philosopher.

"Speak your thoughts, brother."

Silvius spread his hands.

"The woman is certainly a saint," he said. "It is common report that she has worked many and strange cures. And, lord, with the foresight of faith I look towards the future. From simple beginnings great things have arisen. We do not draw pilgrims here—to our Abbey. How much glory, sir, has the altar of Canterbury won by the swords of those violent men."

Reginald of Brecon saw Dom Silvius's vision.

"A hundred years hence, brother, we shall be blessed through the relics of St. Denise!"

Silvius had no mistrust of his inspiration.

"The maid is certainly miraculous," he said. "We could grant her a cell within our bounds."

He of the mitre put the tips of his fingers in opposition.

"Our brethren of Mickleham or of Robertsbridge would forestall us, if they could?"

"They love their 'houses,' Father, and for that I praise them."

"Worthy men! Where would you lodge her, Silvius?"

"There is that stone cot near Mountjoye, sir, with the croft below it. We could set up a cross there that would be seen from the road. If the maid can but work miracles here, people will flock to her; then gifts can be laid upon our altar."

A sudden clangour of bells from the tower brought the almoner's audience to an end. Reginald of Brecon rose, and laid aside his book.

"What does the woman say?" he asked, touching the core of Silvius's conception.

"That, lord, must be discovered. If I have your grace in this— —?"

"Go, Brother, and prosper."

And Silvius went out noiselessly from the parlour, his hands hidden in the sleeves of his habit.

Though the may was whitening in the woods, and the blue bells spread an azure mist above the green, May was a harsh and rugged month that year, with north winds blowing, and the sky hard and grey. And Dom Silvius when he mounted a quiet saddle horse and trotted away followed by two servants, drew his thick cloak about him, and was glad of his gloves and his lamb's-wool stockings.

Up in the beech wood above Goldspur the wind made a restless moan through the branches of the trees. Sometimes the sun struck through the racing clouds, and a wavering chequer of light and shadow fell on the thin forest grass. There was a shimmer of young green everywhere, yet the year seemed sad and plaintive as though chilled to heart by the north winds.

Denise, wrapped in her grey cloak, wandered that morning along the grass paths of her trampled garden, brooding over the wreck thereof. Here were her thyme and lavender bushes trodden under foot, or snapped and shredded by the browsing teeth of a horse. Crushed plants peered at her pathetically from the pits where hoofs had sunk into the soft soil; a bed of pansies seemed to scowl at her with their quaint and many-coloured faces, as though reviling her for having brought such barbarians to trample them. Almost the whole of the wattle fence had fallen, dragging down into the dirt the roses that had been trained to it.

Yet never had Denise's garden been a more intimate part of herself than that May morning with the wind tossing the beech boughs against a heavy sky. What a change from yesterday, what a breaking in of violent life, what revelations, what regret! The quiet days seemed behind her, far in the distance, for the vivid present had made even the near past seem unreal. As for her own heart, Denise was almost afraid to look therein. It was like her garden, with the barriers broken, and the life of yesterday trodden into the soil.

She had tried to put these passionate things from her, and to turn again to the life that she had known. There were a hundred things for her hands to do, but do them she could not, for the will in her seemed dead. Even the familiar trifles of her woodland hermitage were full of treachery and of suggestive guile. Her bed, Aymery had lain there. Her earthen pitcher, she had brought him water therein. The very stones of the path still seemed to show to her the stains of the man's blood. Memories were everywhere, memories that would not vanish, and would not pale.

Denise's face still burnt when she remembered Etoile's laughter, that hard, metallic laughter like the clash of cymbals. The woman's insolence showed her the mocking face of the world, yet for the life of her, Denise could not tear her thoughts from the happenings of those two days. Had the whole country risen to jeer at her, she could have suffered it because of the mystery that made of the ordeal a sacrifice. She had not saved the man, and yet she did not grudge all that she had borne, all that she still might bear. The violence of yesterday had opened the woman's eyes in Denise. The world had a new strangeness, and the chant of the wind a more plaintive meaning.

She had been unable to sleep with thinking of Aymery, and of what had befallen him, for she still seemed to see his white, furious face, throwing its scorn into the scoffing mouths of the Gascon's men. Nor could she forget the last look that had passed between them, the appeal in the man's eyes as though he would have said to her: "God forgive me, for all this." Where were they taking him, would they be rough with him, would he die of his wounds upon the road? What offence had he committed that his house should be burnt, and his life hazarded, and who was this Peter of Savoy, this Provençal that he should lord it over the men of the land, claiming to act for his over-lord the King? It was the right of the strong over the weak, the pride of the men who held the castles crushing those who refused to be exploited. The curse of a weak King was over the country. These hawks of his whom he had let loose in England obeyed no one, not even their own lord.

But Denise's conscience took scourge in hand at last, and drove her from her broodings and her visions. Work, something to fill the mind, something tangible to fasten the hands upon! What did it avail her to loiter, to dream, and to conjecture? There was no salvation in mere feeling. Her heart was turning to wax in her, she who had worked for others, and who had been knelt to as a saint. A rush of shame smote her upon the bosom. The peasant women, these men of the fields, what would they think of her if they could read her thoughts? She had held up the Cross before their eyes, and was forgetting to look at it herself.

So Denise drove herself to work that morning, lifting the fallen fence and propping it with stakes, gathering the wreckage, binding up the broken life of the place. It eased her a little this labour under the grey sky, with the wind in the woods, and the smell of the soil. For in simple things the heart finds comfort, and idleness is no salve to the soul.

It was about noon when Dom Silvius came to the clearing in the beech wood, and Denise, who was binding up her trailing roses, saw figures moving amid the trees. Her brown eyes were alert instantly as the eyes of a deer. But there was nothing fierce about Dom Silvius's figure, and nothing martial or masterful about the paces of his horse.

The almoner left the two servants under the woodshaw and rode forward slowly over the grass. Silvius's eyes had a habit of seeing everything, even when they happened to express a vacant yet inspired preoccupation. He saw the scarred turf, the hoof marks everywhere, the broken fence about the garden, the woman in the grey cloak at work upon her roses.

Silvius kept a staid and thoughtful face till he had come close to the hermitage. Then his eyes beamed out suddenly as though he had only just discovered Denise behind the spring foliage of her roses. And Dom Silvius could put much sweetness into his smile so that his face shone like the face of a saint out of an Italian picture.

"Peace to you, Sister; we were nearer than I prophesied."

Denise lifted her head and looked at him. A rose tendril had hooked a thorn in the cloth of her cloak. And to Silvius as he gazed down into the questioning brown of her eyes, that thorn seemed to point a moral.

"I come as a friend," he said, hiding his curiosity behind smooth kindness. "Silvius the almoner of the Abbey of Battle."

"I have heard of you, Father," she answered him.

Silvius smiled, as though there were no such thing as spite and gossip in the world.

"May my grace fly as far as yours, Sister," he said. "You are wondering why I have ridden hither? Well, I will tell you. It is because of the rumours of violence and of bloodshed that have come to us. Even here, I see that you have not been spared."

He looked about him gravely, yet with no inquisitive, insinuating briskness. His eyes travelled slowly round the circle of the broken fence, and came to point at last upon Denise.

"I have come with brotherly greetings to you, Sister, from Lord Reginald our Abbot. All men know what a light has burnt here these many months upon the hills. It is a holy fire to be cherished by us, and all men would grieve to see it dimmed or quenched."

After some such preamble he began to speak softly to Denise, for he was a good soul despite his shrewdness, and the woman's face was like a face out of heaven. He put the simple truth before her, speaking with a devout fatherliness that betrayed no subtler motive. Peace should be hers, and a sure sanctuary, roof, clothes, bed, and garden, and a daily corrody from the Abbey. The times were full of violence, lust, and oppression, and Silvius feared for those far from the protecting shadow of some great lord or priest. At Battle she should enjoy all the sweetness of sanctity; she should have even her flowers there, and he waved a hand towards the ruinous garden.

Denise listened to him with a pale and unpersuaded face. Perhaps a flicker of distrust had leapt up at first into her eyes. But the monk's simplicity seemed so sincere a thing that she put distrust out of her heart.

When he had ended, she looked towards the woods in silence for a while, and Silvius made no sound, as though he reverenced her silence, and understood its earnestness.

"For all this I thank you, Father," she said at last. "But come to you I cannot. It is not in my heart to leave this place."

Silvius smiled down at her very patiently.

"Who shall deny that the Spirit must guide you. Yet even St. Innocence may remember what God has given."

Denise reddened momentarily, and Silvius looked away from her towards the sky.

"I am not a child, Father," she said simply. "The people in these parts love me, and I, them. They will return home in time, and will come and seek for me. I should seem to them the worst of cowards, if they found that I had fled."

Silvius was too sensitive and too shrewd to press his importunity upon her, seeing that she was prejudiced in her heart. He could leave her to think over what he had said to her. Her pride might refuse to waver at the first skirmish.

"You are living your life for others, Sister," he said. "Nor do we live in the midst of a wilderness at Battle. Trust the Spirit in you; do not be misled. Yet I would beseech you to remember what manner of world this is. Had not St. Paul fled from the city of Damascus, the Faith would have lacked a flame of fire."

Denise looked up at him with miraculous eyes.

"And yet, I would stay here," she said.

"So be it, Sister; some day I will ride this way again."

So Denise sent Dom Silvius away, clinging with all this strange new tenderness of hers to a place that seemed sacred by reason of its memories. Yet if she had known what others knew, or guessed what was passing beyond her ken, she might have fled with Silvius that day, and left her cell to the wild winds, the sun, and the rain.

CHAPTER XI

It was possible for such a man as Gaillard to be in love with two women at one and the same moment, if indeed what Gaillard felt for a woman could be called love. Peter of Savoy was at Lewes, and the Gascon had the command at Pevensey, and had taken to oiling his hair, and having musk sewn up in a corner of his surcoat. He and Etoile saw much of one another, but the lute girl knew how to keep Gaillard at arm's length. He might play the troubadour, and make himself ridiculous by singing under her window at night. Etoile wished to try the man further before she trusted such a cousin as Gaillard with her power over Count Peter of Savoy.

One thing Etoile did not know, that Gaillard had ridden more than once to the beech wood above Goldspur, and that he had seen Denise, and come away feeling baulked and foolish. The Red Saint had shut herself obstinately in her cell, and as for singing her love songs, even Gaillard had not the gross conceit to treat Denise as he would have treated Etoile. Yet Gaillard had no sense of the comic in life, and accepted himself with such enthusiasm that anything was possible to so blatant a creature. Display was a passion with him, and any clouding of his conceit, an injury that made him scowl like a spoilt child. Life had to be full of noise and bustle, the blowing of trumpets, and the applause of women. Gaillard was so much in love with himself that he ran about like a fanatic waving a torch, and expecting all the world to listen to what he said.

The Gascon might be a fool, but he was a pernicious fool in those rough days, when there was a woman to be pleased. Denise had shut her door on him, but Gaillard did not doubt but that she would open it in due season. Her pride was a thing on the surface, so Gaillard told himself, and she had more to surrender than had most women. Etoile also was unapproachable, but in very different fashion to Denise. The one was a white glare that blinded and repulsed, the other a glittering point that lured and kept its distance. And Gaillard, like a great gross red moth, blundered to and fro, making a great flutter.

Etoile had much of the spirit of those Byzantine women who had the devil's poison under their tongues. Gaillard amused her. It pleased her to discover how far she could drive him into making a fool or a cur of himself, even as she might tease Count Peter's leopards, playing on their jealousy, or tantalising them by holding out food and snatching it away between the bars. And Etoile's ingenuity searched out an adventure that should show her how far Gaillard could be trusted. She was shrewd enough to realise that the man might be of use to her. Peter of Savoy was but a child with a play-thing. It was worth Etoile's discretion to have a man upon whom she could rely.

Gaillard grew more importunate, and was for ever offering her his homage. "Well," said Etoile to herself, "let him prove himself, but not in the matter of brute courage." She knew that it is always more dangerous for a man to be tempted than to be dared. And Etoile gave Gaillard a tryst at dusk among the cypresses of Count Peter's garden, and turning on him like a cat challenged Gaillard to prove his faith.

No man was ever more astonished than the Gascon when she told him what she would have him do. At first he hailed the devil of mischief in her, but Etoile was in earnest, and flamed up when he laughed at her. Gaillard shrugged his shoulders, and saw destiny stirring the live coals of his desire.

"It would be simpler to bring you her head," he said, wondering whether Etoile knew more than she had betrayed. "Cut off the woman's hair, indeed! The folk yonder would crucify me, if they caught me harming their saint."

Etoile looked him in the eyes.

"You are for ever shouting at me to prove you my Gaillard. Here is your chance. There is often some wisdom in a whim. You are to bring me her wooden cross, too, remember, as well as a piece of her hair."

Gaillard, uneasy under Etoile's eyes, hid his more intimate thoughts behind an incredulous obstinacy. He could have scoffed at the absurdity of the thing. And yet, when he looked at it squarely, the adventure was not so physically absurd. What did it mean but the robbing of one woman to win another, the plundering of one treasure house to use the spoil to bribe the keeper of other treasures! The fine rascality of the thing delighted him. He threw back his head and laughed, though Etoile mistook the meaning of his laughter.

"You have not the courage, Gaillard, eh? The man who sings under my window must be something better than a troubadour fool."

Gaillard bit his nails as though in the grip of a dilemma. The devil in him applauded. He could have clapped himself on the back over the broad humour of his cleverness.

"What a road to set a man on, my desire," he said, looking rather sullen over it. "There is a sin that they call sacrilege— —"

Etoile clapped her hands.

"Cousin Gaillard with a conscience! Oh, you fool, am I worth a piece of hair, and the wood of a cross?"

Gaillard spread his arms.

"Fool! Do you think that I want a man with weak knees to serve me, a boy who empties half the cup and then turns sick?"

Gaillard made a show of faltering, rocking to and fro on his heels, and looking at her under half closed lids.

"Assuredly," said he, "you are a devil. And to win a devil I will rob a saint."

Denise's inward vision helped her so little those days that she had no foreshadowings of Gaillard's treachery. He had shown none of his rougher nature to her when he had ridden through the beech wood to her cell. And Denise had let him talk to her once or twice, intent on discovering all that had befallen Aymery since he had fallen into the hands of Peter of Savoy. Only when Gaillard had tried to come too near had she closed the door on him, frightened by the look in the man's eyes, and yet feeling herself very helpless in that solitary wood. For some days she had seen nothing of the Goldspur folk, nor did she know whether Grimbald was dead or alive. Gaillard had gone off sulking from the frost that she had thrown out on him. Denise believed herself rid of the man. And yet in her unrest, and loneliness, she thought of what Dom Silvius had said to her, and was half persuaded to put herself within sanctuary at Battle.

Gaillard had told her nothing about Aymery, save that he was alive, and waiting the King's pleasure. And of all these happenings Aymery knew nothing as he lay on the straw in a tower room at Pevensey. His wounds were mending, for Peter of Savoy had some of the instincts of a Christian, and had sent his own barber surgeon to minister to Aymery's needs. Yet the lord of Goldspur manor thought little of his own wounds those days.

Though Aymery's flesh was free from fever, the spirit chafed in him, tossing and turning with an unceasing flux of thought. Those happenings at the hermitage haunted him, and in the spirit he drank wine that was both bitter and sweet, cursing himself for the helplessness that had brought such things to pass, and laying to his own charge all the shame that had fallen upon Denise.

Yet Aymery had other thoughts to trouble him, for those hours at the hermitage came back more clearly and vividly, as though they had happened in the twilight, and been remembered in the day. He felt again the touch of Denise's hands, saw the gleam of her hair, and caught the mystery of tenderness that had flashed and faded in the deeps of her eyes. Aymery would be very still in the narrow room, still as one who lies dead with a smile on his lips, and in blind eyes a vision of things splendid.

Sometimes Aymery would take to preaching to himself, growing sensible and almost prosy, like a merchant looking methodically into his ledgers. Without doubt Grimbald would be at Goldspur, the people would come back to the village, they would think no shame of Denise, even if they heard of the thing that she had attempted. The quiet life would begin again, for there was no cause now for my Lord Peter to harry the countryside. No harm might come of all these adventures, and to insure that end, Aymery preached to himself still further.

"Heart of mine," said he. "Denise is for no such worldly desires. True, she has taken no sworn vows, but for all that, my friend, she is as good as a nun. Take heed how you tempt sacrilege. For to the people Denise is a lady of many marvels. She is not of mere clay, there is mystery yonder—and her love is the love of the angels and the saints."

In some such simple and sturdy fashion Aymery spoke often to his own heart. Yet there was always an enchanted distance shining beyond these vows of his like a sunset seen through trees. Flashes of passion lingered that should not linger. A look of the eyes, a touch of the hand, such things are not forgotten.

As for his own fortune, Aymery had no grip thereon; he could only eat his food and shake up the straw of his bed for comfort. He was mewed there, "waiting the King's pleasure," a useful phrase in the mouth of a lord who shared with others in persuading the King. Aymery might have stood at his window and shouted "Charter" till the barber surgeon decreed that he was turgid and feverish, and should be bled. There was no such thing as a rescue to be thought of. Presently he might scheme at breaking out in other and grimmer fashion if they did not release him. For there was still much talk in the land of "Stephen's days," and it was said that when the saints saved a soul, the devil erected a castle.

CHAPTER XII

Denise had some sign at last from the Goldspur folk, for she found that offerings had been left at her gate, and since her store of food had fallen to half a very dry loaf and a pot of honey, she was carnally glad of such a godsend.

The evening of the same day while she was at work in her garden, two of Aymery's villeins came out of the wood, each carrying a bundle of ash stakes and an axe, for they had heard that the saint's fence was as flat in places as the walls of Jericho. The two men, Oswald and Peter, were a little shy of Denise, as though the Goldspur conscience had accused the community of neglecting the Red Saint. They told her that the cattle had broken out from the pen, and strayed far and wide through the woods. It had taken them days to recover the beasts, and they had been hampered by the knowledge that the men of Pevensey were still sweeping the hundreds of the rape.

Both of the men knew that Aymery was a prisoner at Pevensey, but they did not know that he had been taken at the very doorway of the Red Saint's cell. Nor did Denise betray to them all that had passed; she had too much pride and a sacred sense of secrecy for that. Oswald and Peter set to work, their axes catching the sunlight that sifted through the trees, white chips flying, their brown faces intent and stolid. Denise stood and watched them for a time, and Oswald, the elder of the two, told her what had befallen Father Grimbald. A swineherd had found him half dead in the woods, and had hidden him in a saw-pit for fear of Gaillard and his men. It had been a sharp escape, and a sharp sickness for Grimbald. He was still in hiding, and being healed of his wounds, and there was not a woman in the whole hundred who would not have had her tongue cut out rather than betray Grimbald to Peter of Savoy.

Dusk was falling before the men had finished mending the fence, and a wind had risen like a restless and plaintive voice, making the twilight seem more grey and melancholy. The whole beech wood had begun to shiver with a sense of loneliness that made the earth itself seem cold. Oswald and Peter knelt down before Denise, and asked her to bless them before they shouldered their axes and marched off into the wood.

The two men followed the winding path that struck the main "ride" running through the heart of the wood, and they walked fast because of the twilight, and because it was believed that the wood was haunted. For the wilds were the haunts of the evil things of the night, and when a saint lived a holy life in such a place she was sure of being tempted and vexed by devils. The tale of St. Guthlac of Crowland was a tale that was told of many a saint. When the lamp of sanctity was lit in some such wilderness the spirits of evil would fly at it in fury, and seek to beat it out with the rush of their black wings.

Oswald and Peter were no more superstitious than their neighbours, but they were as timid as children in the thick of that dark wood. And to frighten their credulity a strange sound seemed on the gallop with the gusts of the wind, a sound that was like the trampling of a horse under the sad gloom of the trees. The sound came so uncomfortably near to them, that Oswald and Peter bolted into the underwood like a couple of brown rabbits. And looking back half furtively, as they scrambled through brambles and under hazels, they had a glimpse of a great black shape rushing through the darkness on the wings of the wind.

The two men did not wait to see more of it, but got out of the wood as fast as their legs could carry them.

"It was a ghost or a devil," they said to one another. "God defend us, but surely it is a terrible thing to be a saint."

They pushed on, heartily glad to be free of the far-reaching hands of the spectral trees.

"It was good for us that we had the saint's blessing."

"God and St. Martin hearten her. The devil vexes those who live for good works."

"Father Grimbald must know of it. He is man enough to come and take a devil by the beard."

So Oswald and Peter went back to their womenfolk and their cattle, glad to be near warm bodies, snug under their woodland huts. The night passed, and the dawn came, a slow, stealthy dawn muffled in silver mist. Rabbits scampered in the glades, brushing the dew from the wet grass. Birds hunted for worms, and fluttered away to feed their young. And the devil whom Oswald and Peter had seen, sent the rabbits bolting for their burrows as he rode away through the beech wood towards the sea.

Before noon Etoile the lute girl had a wreath of hair curled like a snake about the little wooden cross in her lap. Gaillard had brought them to her, hiding a guilty memory in the eyes behind a laughing swagger. The Gascon's voluble tongue was driven to deal very fancifully with the adventure, since Etoile was very curious, and intent on hearing everything. The Red Saint was very ready to be worshipped, such was Gaillard's explanation. She was a little vainer than the majority of women, and Gaillard shrugged his shoulders and laughed.

"A red apple is always a red apple," he said. "Mother Eve taught us that."

The mischievous devil in Etoile was not yet satisfied.

"Never trust a saint, Gaillard," she said. "I have not forgotten that the man in the tower might be glad of this piece of hair. It will give him something to think about while he sits and nibbles straws. Take it up and push it under his door, and tell him it comes from his lady."

The joke caught Gaillard's fancy. He climbed the tower, and pushed the trophy under Aymery's door with the point of his poniard.

"A woman gave it me, my man," he said. "But since I have something better for a keepsake, you can have the hair."

He went away, laughing, a thorough Gascon in his gross self-satisfaction. And Aymery picked up what Gaillard had left him. He knew it for Denise's hair, for there was none like it in all those parts.

CHAPTER XIII

The may was budding into bloom, and Dom Silvius came riding Goldspur way again, thinking of the many things that may occupy the mind of a man who keeps both eyes fixed upon the affairs of the "house." Silvius's soul felt very comfortable within him that morning. The bloom was setting well upon the orchard trees, such a sea of foam that the autumn should be red with fruit. Word had come from the shepherds in the pasture lands that hardly a lamb had been lost that spring. There was little sickness anywhere, but few poor to need alms, and no shortage of dues from the tenants. Dom Silvius made it his business to know of all these things, even though they might not concern his authority. He was like a child and a miser in his joy and carefulness in working for the wealth and honour of his Abbey.

So Dom Silvius came to the beech wood above Goldspur, and followed the main ride, talking to himself like a happy starling, for he rode alone that morning. And he would lean forward and fondle his nag's ears, for the beast was provided by one of the tenants, and Dom Silvius loved the horse because he had not to feed him.

"A little more roundly, my good Dobbin," he prattled. "But beware of worldliness, for the sake of my dignity; we must not bump like a butcher to market. What will Sancta Denise say to us this morning? The child should not set herself alone here like a white dove for any hawk to swoop at. *Mea culpa*, but the girl has hair like dead beech leaves touched by the sun, saving, Dobbin, that the leaves have no glitter of gold. And what eyes! God bless us, but we may hope for miracles. And if the folk flock to be healed, they shall lodge in the Abbey, and surely their gratitude will make us rich."

The almoner sobered himself however when he turned aside by the white stone that marked the path leading to the hermitage. The woodlands might have eyes and ears, and it would not be seemly for a man of Silvius's age and estate to be overheard babbling like a lover who must talk even though it be only to his horse. So he rode very demurely into Denise's glade, with his chin on his chest, and his lips moving as though he said a prayer for every furlong.

The door of Denise's cell was shut, nor could Dom Silvius see her stirring in her garden. "Perhaps she is abroad," thought he, "or maybe she is at her prayers," so he rode up quietly, dismounted, and looped his bridle over the post of the wicket gate. Then he went in and up the path, and was about to knock softly, when the door opened under his very hand, and Silvius saw a figure in grey standing upon the threshold.

Dom Silvius dropped his eyes suddenly as though he blamed himself for being surprised into staring at a woman's face.

"The grace of Our Lady to you, Sister," he said. "I was in doubt whether I should find you at home or no."

Now Silvius was not a shred embarrassed, though he pretended to a kind of saintly coyness. He had his eyes on the sandalled feet that showed under the hem of the grey gown. They were very comely feet, with the brown straps of the sandals contrasting with the nut brown of the skin, and Dom Silvius was thinking how different these feet were with their arched insteps and straight toes from the gouty and behumped members that shuffled and progressed in the Abbey cloisters. Yet in looking at Denise's feet the almoner missed the first shadows of a tragedy.

Denise stood very still, her hood drawn forward, one hand holding the edge of the door. The face under the hood expressed nothing, if despair be nothing more than a pale, mute mask. Yet the eyes that looked at the monk were the eyes of one whose blood was full of a spiritual fever.

"It is Dom Silvius?" she asked at last, and her voice sounded steady and even tame.

Silvius folded his hands together, and raised his eyes to the level of Denise's knees.

"You may remember, my Sister, how I said that I might ride this way again."

She was silent, as though absorbed by some memory that pervaded all her consciousness. Silvius's eyes climbed a little higher and rested upon her bosom.

"We did not agree then, Sancta Denise. It may be that you still love the life in the wilderness. The winter is past with us, for which God be thanked; you will have summer here, and the woods are pleasant in summer. Perhaps you have your birds to feed. The fruit promises well. I am never one for importunities."

He spoke like a man who had rushed too quickly towards the point aimed at, and who covered up his retreat with irrelevancies. For Dom Silvius felt that his wisdom had slipped for the once, and that he should have begun with a digression. Women like love tokens hidden in a posy of flowers, and passion pledged in a song. But Denise's directness saved Silvius from tracking her whims through a maze.

"Your words have been with me," she said.

Her voice surprised him, so much so that he looked up sharply into her face. The hood was drawn, but an immovable mute pallor, a kind of deadness, struck on Silvius's eyes like the whiteness of a whitened wall.

"I am not unthankful for that, Sister."

"And you are of the same mind?"

"What God and the Church offer is ever an offer," he said, dropping his eyes again, and finding his intuition in touch with something that was invisible, and yet to be felt.

He heard Denise draw her breath in deeply.

"Sometimes we seem wise, sometimes foolish," she said. "Life teaches the heart many things. You offer me some such place as this to lodge in? And that I shall be alone?"

Silvius threw aside vague conjectures, to seize the prize he had long coveted.

"It is a sweet place," said he. "With a garden, and fruit trees, and a croft below it. The garden has a good quick hedge all about it. As to the flesh, your soul shall be as Solomon's lily, Sanctissima. We have no ritual for those whose eyes see into Paradise."

So as the great purple cloud shadows drifted over the young green of the beech wood, and the sun shone forth with moments of gold, Dom Silvius warmed with his own words, and in his kindling never so much as saw that Denise listened like one who struggled against some inward anguish. What light and shade were there over her own soul as Silvius put his visions into his voice? The monk thought her calm and sensible, a little cold perhaps, but then the snow of her chastity would make her that. Silvius was no coarse colourist, no noisy twanger of strings. There should be mysticism, aloofness, a play of pearly light about such a part. His exultation burnt delicate flattery. For Silvius knew that many sacred souls loved their sanctity as a gay quean loves her clothes. How many Magdalenes were there who dreamt of being seen while they washed the feet of God and the Saints! And Silvius wished to lead this child of the Miraculous Heart so that she should walk in a path of his own conceiving, a sweet saint who should draw the country, aye far countrysides, as the moon draws the sea. The coming of Denise to the bounds of Battle should be as the coming of the Bride to the Church of God.

It should be a pageant, and a poem. For in those days pageantry preached to the people, and through the eyes the heart was persuaded.

Denise heard him, like one very weary, one who listens because there is no escape. And in good season Silvius had the wit to see that he had pressed wine enough for the day. Denise had given him her promise, and he took his leave of her with sweetness, and all reverence, putting himself beneath her, and speaking of her wishes as commands.

"Would their most blessed Sister take up her new cell soon?"

Denise leant her weight against the door, feeling that if she were not rid of Silvius she would drop at his feet and weep.

"Before the moon is full," she answered.

And the monk mounted his horse, and rode away like one who has received a pallium, dreaming miraculous dreams, and beholding innumerable pilgrims, peasant and prince, knight and lady, riding and journeying towards Senlac over hill and dale.

As for Denise she stood at the door of her cell long after Silvius had left her, as though she lacked even the power to move. What help was there, what other means should she devise? This cell of stone had become a den of evil dreams for her; the tenderness and mystery had fled. She had no heart to live there any longer, no heart to meet those who had knelt to her before this thing had happened.

CHAPTER XIV

Since the fight at Goldspur Father Grimbald had lain hidden in a saw-pit on one of the forest manors, the swineherd who had hidden him being also woodman and sawyer when his hogs were rooting amid the beech mast and the acorns. Saw-dust with heather spread over it made none so miserable a bed, and the swineherd had fortified Grimbald against wind, rain, and the inquisitiveness of enemies by covering the mouth of the pit with faggots. For a month Grimbald had lain there, his shirt and cassock clotted to great wounds that no man dared to touch. At first a fever had taken him, and he had roared and stormed at night like some sturdy saint at grips with Apollyon in a corner of hell. The swineherd had banked up the faggots to deaden the sound, praying God to abate Father Grimbald's fever, for a dozen of Gaillard's men were camped that very night not two furlongs from the saw-pit. Yet Grimbald's shouts had come rumbling out of the earth, "Strike, strike, St. George!" "Shine, brown bills, and beat the Frenchmen into the sea!" And so strenuous and bellicose had the fever grown in him, that the swineherd, staking purgatory or peace on a pail of water, had lifted the faggots and doused Grimbald to cool him. Nor had any harm come of it, but rather good, for Grimbald had grown less fiery, and fallen into a deep sleep.

About the time that Dom Silvius made his second pilgrimage to the beech wood above Goldspur, Grimbald was so well recovered of his wounds that he could sit up on his bed, and take his food with great relish. Being also an industrious soul he made the swineherd throw him down billets of seasoned oak, a knife, and a hatchet, and set himself to carve heads of the saints for decorating the corbels of his little church. But either St. Paul and St. Simon were in an ill humour, or Grimbald knew little of his craft, for the saints emerged pulling most villainous faces, sour, evil, and grotesque, with flat noses, and slits for eyes. So Grimbald gave up his struggle with them, and heaved them up out of the pit to be burnt, and took to pointing and feathering arrows, for your woodlander was often his own fletcher.

The flesh prospering so well with him, and the end of his sojourn in the saw-pit seeming near, Grimbald sent the swineherd for some of the Goldspur folk. The very same evening the swineherd brought in the two men Oswald and Peter, both of them full to the brim with gossip, and ready to empty themselves at their spiritual father's feet. Grimbald sat on his bed in the pit, whittling a yew bough with his knife; Oswald and Peter squatted side by side on a faggot like a couple of solemn brown owls on a bough.

"Father," quoth Oswald, "we have seen the devil in St. Denise's wood."

Peter chimed in to add to the impression.

"A black devil with a black horse that breathed fire and smoke."

"And he came and went like the wind, Father!"

Even such honest men as these had imaginations wherewith to decorate an experience. Grimbald's face looked the colour of brown earth in the darkness of the pit, and to Oswald and Peter his eyeballs seemed to glare like two white pebbles at the bottom of a well.

"And you ran away from this devil?" he said. "Yes, you ran, my sons, as fast as your legs could carry you. When shall I come by a Christian who is not afraid to stand on his own feet, and to astonish us by making the devil run?"

Though Grimbald scoffed at them, the two men knew his methods. No one had anything to fear from Grimbald so long as he looked him straight in the face and spoke the simple truth. But a liar or a fawner were likely to be thrashed, since Grimbald's chastening of souls was not wholly a matter of the tongue. He used his hands like a Christian, and for the love of their flesh he did not spare them.

"Assuredly, Father, it was the devil we saw in the beech wood. Night was just falling——"

"So! And he was very black was he? Just as black as charcoal, and had two live coals for eyes?"

The good man's grim irony drove neither Oswald nor Peter from his breastwork of conviction.

"We would take oath it was the devil, Father."

"Oswald, Oswald, you seem too familiar with the face of Satan! You are too fond of the mead-horn, my man."

The accused one accepted the charge meekly, knowing that it was true in the abstract, and that Father Grimbald knew it, for there had been an occasion of second baptism in a somewhat dirty ditch. But Oswald was stolidly sure of his innocence on the night in question, nor had he as yet finished his confessions.

"I had no mead froth on my beard that day, Father," said he. "Whether it was the devil or no we saw, we saw him with these eyes of ours. And he rode like a black north wind. But what is worse, Father, we have never had sight of our saint since then."

This was news that struck the irony out of Grimbald's mouth. He laid the yew bough aside on the heather, and became at once the demi-god, and the seer.

"What is that you are saying, man Oswald? Why are you troubled for Denise?"

Oswald looked like a wise dog that has come by kicks undeservedly, and is now to be commended.

"The door of the cell is always shut," he said, "and never a word or a sound have we now from our lady. What is more, Father, the stuff we took there two days ago was still by the wicket when one of the lads went up this morning."

Grimbald looked thoughtful.

"Have you tried the door?" he asked.

"We durst not, thinking she might be in a vision or in prayer."

"Did you call to her?"

"Not above asking her blessing, Father, and telling of the food, and news of you. And it was four days ago that her voice answered us, but since then we have heard no sound."

Grimbald stood up slowly on the bed, propping himself with his arms against the walls of the pit.

"God helping me, I could sit a horse," he said. "This must be looked to. Oswald, my son, you had a fat pony. Bring the beast here to-morrow, at dawn."

"It shall be done, Father."

And they departed with his blessing, but Grimbald was awake all that night, troubled lest any harm should have befallen Denise.

"Devil!" thought he. "Oswald's devil was one of good human kidney, or I have no sense of smell. Satan need not heat himself with galloping in these parts. We have enough of him in the flesh."

Meanwhile at Pevensey, Aymery of Goldspur had thrown the preaching part of himself aside, for that which Gaillard had thrust under his door had stung the manhood in him, and left the poison of a great fear in his blood.

The hair was Denise's hair; he could have sworn to that on the relics of the Cross. How had they come by it, here in Pevensey? Was Denise also a caged bird, and if not, what had happened in that beech wood, where the great trees built dark winding ways with the sweep of their mighty branches? Aymery's thoughts plunged in amid those trees, grimly and passionately, yet with the sheen of a woman's hair luring him on like the mystic light from the Holy Grael. Had evil befallen her because of him? What devil's mockery might there be in the way the truth had been thrust into his ken! Had Gaillard any hand in it? And at the thought of Gaillard, Aymery twisted Denise's hair about his wrists, and yearned to feel those hands of his leaping at the Gascon's throat. God! What did it avail him to pretend that he feared for Denise as he would have feared for a sister? She was the ripe earth to him, the dawn of dawns, the freshness of June woods after rain. He could cover his eyes no longer as to what was in his heart.

To break out into the world, to gallop a horse, to feel his muscles in their strength, that was the fever in him, the restless fever of a chained hawk beating his wings upon a perch. To be out of this hole in a stone tower, but how? He had no weapons, not so much as a piece of wood, or the rag of a linen sheet. They had taken his leather belt, but left him his shirt, tunic and shoes, and he laughed despite his grimness, for they might as well have left him naked. The man who brought him bread and water, filled a cracked flask for him, and took the water-pot away. And what a weapon that great earthen jar would have made, swung with the verve and sinew of a young man's arm.

Impatient with his own impotence, he stood at the narrow window looking seawards, drawing Denise's hair to and fro between his fingers as he would have drawn a swath of silk. A thought came to him, but at first he revolted from it as from a piece of sacrilege. His sturdy sense saved him, however, from being fooled by a shred of sentiment, and he twisted the strands of hair till he had wound them into a fine and silken cord. Wrapping the ends about his wrists he looped the cord over his bent knee, tried the strength thereof, and smiled as though satisfied.

That evening there was the sound of a scuffle when the bread bringer drew back the bolts and pushed the heavy door open with his foot. The fellow had made light of his duty of late, for Aymery had seemed quiet and tame, and still feeble after his wounds. He had marched in perfunctorily while Aymery waited for him behind the door. There was the crash of the pitcher on the stones. The jailer's knees gave under him; he sank sideways driving the door to with his weight.

Aymery had no wish to end the poor devil's life, so he left him there to get back breath and consciousness, after robbing him of his rough cloak and the knife he carried at his girdle. Pushing the body aside, he swung the door to cautiously, and shot the bolts. Almost instinctively he had wound Denise's hair about his wrist, and as he descended the winding stair he tossed the man's cloak over his shoulders, turned up the hood, and kept the knife hidden but ready for any hazard. Going down boldly he came out into the inner court, crossed it and reached the gate without being challenged by any of the men who loitered there.

Aymery's heels were itching for a gallop, but he held himself in hand, and walked on coolly, whistling through his teeth. He was under the gateway, through it, and crossing the bridge. Someone called to him, but he laughed, crowed like a cock, and gave a wave of the hand.

The outer court with its great garden still lay before him, and he followed the paved track, praying God to keep all officious fools at a distance. Fifty paces, twenty paces, ten paces, and he was at the outer gate, with the cypresses black behind him, and no betrayal as yet. The gate still stood open, though it was closed at sunset, and to Aymery it was an arch of gold, a dark tunnel way with a tympanum cut from the evening sky.

He was half through it, when a lounger at the guard-room door lurched forward and caught him roughly by the cloak. It may have been a mere challenge to horse-play or the grip of a swift suspicion. Aymery did not wait to decide the matter, but struck the man across the face with the knife, broke loose, and ran.

CHAPTER XV

They brought the Red Saint to Battle when the meadows were a sheet of gold, and the thorn trees white above the lush green grass. Dom Silvius and two of the Abbey servants came for her in the morning, bringing a white palfrey to carry her on the way.

Denise had kept vigil all that night, praying, and striving to quiet a heart that would not be quieted. And when the dawn had come she had gone out into the garden and stood there silently, looking at the familiar things that had mingled with her life. Yet very strange had garden, hermitage, and woodland seemed to Denise that morning; the strangeness of leave-taking was over them, and the sadness of farewell. Even the rose trees that had been given her, and which she had cherished, had seemed to catch her memory, with their thorns. Memories, memories! Some infinitely dear; others, brutal and full of shame. The thatch would rot, the walls crumble, the garden beckon back the wilderness. And a great bitterness had fallen upon her, because of what she was losing, and of what she had suffered, and yet might suffer. She had felt glad in measure when she had heard the tinkling bells on Dom Silvius's bridle as he had come riding through the beech wood. Her love of the place had hurt her. The very stones had cried out, and the pansies had scowled at her as she went down the path.

At Battle there was joy that day, and a ringing of bells, for Abbot Reginald had ordered it. And the song of the bells went over the woodlands that gleamed or grew gloomy as the clouds drifted. The cuckoo called; green herbs rose to the knees; the meadows rippled with gold; the oaks were in leaf. Over the blue hills, and through slumbrous valleys filled with haze, Silvius and Denise came to the Abbey lands.

Before her there, beside a wayside cross, Denise saw many people gathered to welcome her, but her heart wished them away. She would have come quietly to this new refuge, nor had she foreshadowed Dom Silvius's pageantry. Here were gathered the Abbey singing boys in white stoles, the precentor with them; also a number of the Brethren, two and two, solemn figures with hoods and hanging sleeves that seemed to catch the shadows. All the townsfolk had streamed out from their boroughs, old and young.

Some carried green boughs, the girls had their bosoms full of flowers, even toddling children had their posies.

Denise's blood became as water in her when she saw all these people gathered there, ready with their gaping awe, and their inquisitive reverence. The bright colours of their clothes, the greens, blues, and russets became a blur before eyes that felt hot with bitter tears. It was all so much mockery to Denise. The precentor's arms waved; the singing boys moved off two and two to lead her, singing some quaint chant. The people were down on their knees beside the road, all save the girls who strewed their flowers before her. And Denise rode by on her white palfrey, her eyes blind, her cheeks burning, a strangle of humiliation in her throat, knowing what these people could not know, and shamed to the heart because of it. She saw neither the silent faces under the row of cowls, nor the green boughs that waved, nor the hands that were stretched out to her by children and by women. Nor did she see Dom Silvius's subtle and happy face as he rode beside her, carrying a wooden cross upon his shoulder.

So the white-stoled boys chanted, the bells rang and the slow and sombre Brethren threaded their way between the green boughs and the colours. The people followed on, and began to buzz and to chatter. "The Lady of Miracles has come to dwell with us," they said. Their mouths were full of all manner of marvels, and each began to think of the advantage that might be dreamed of.

"She shall keep the sheep rot from us," quoth one.

"And cure the bone ache and the rheumatics," said another.

A fat, pork butcher with a face the colour of swine's flesh remembered that his dame was to take to her bed in a month, and that he would have her blessed by Denise. A charm against "the staggers" was the desire of a carrier. Wuluric, a wax chandler, wondered whether his trade would be increased. One old woman was eaten up with a sore that would not heal. "I shall beg me a little of her spittle," said she, "a holy virgin's spittle on a dock leaf is a wondrous cure."

So they brought Denise to her cell near Mountjoye Hill, and from that hour they began to call the little field below it "Virgin's Croft."

All this had happened the day before Oswald and Peter had told the Lord of the Saw-pit the tale of the devil in the Goldspur beech wood. According to Grimbald's bidding they brought the pony to him at dawn, helped him from his hiding-place, and set him upon the beast which bore up bravely though Grimbald's heels nearly ploughed the ground. They started off through the woods, thinking to make Goldspur within two hours, but their reckonings were without the sanction of heaven, for Grimbald's pony stumbled over a red ant's mound, and threw the priest heavily, for he was weak after his many days abed. And Grimbald lay on his back with his arms spread out like the arms of a man crucified, and Oswald and Peter stood and stared at him, and wondered whether he was dead.

They knelt down and chafed his feet and hands until Grimbald came to his senses again, and cheered them with the uttering of a few godly curses. The men lifted him up, and for their clumsiness he cursed them further, and bade them put him with his back against a tree. Grimbald, being a heavy man, had broken his right collar-bone in the fall, and he was still weak for such rough byplay.

"Give me a mouthful of water," he said.

But neither Oswald nor Peter had water with them, nor was there a pool near, nor a running brook. Grimbald looked at them with mighty disdain, and Oswald, sneaking off, mounted his pony to get what he could. Five miles rode Oswald that morning before he came to Burghersh village, and begged a hornful of mead there, and a bottle of water. He bumped back again at a rollicking canter, till his pony's coat was as wet as if he had swum a stream. Grimbald had been sick as a dog with the twist of the fall, but the mead heartened him, and he bade Oswald splash the water on his face. Then they bound his right arm to his body with their girdles, and when he had rested awhile, he made them put him again upon the pony.

Nor was this mounting an easy matter, though approached in subtle and backward fashion over the pony's tail. Happily the beast had no kick in him, being tired and subdued. So they had Grimbald astride, and started off once more, the men walking one on either side, and steadying him as they went.

What with the time wasted, and the slow travelling that they made, evening was making the beech wood brilliant as they climbed up out of the valley. The great sentinel trees that stood forward from the main host cast purple shadows upon the grass. A small herd of red deer went trotting into the green-wood, and there was a great silence save for the sucking patter of their hoofs.

One corner of Denise's glade was still steeped in sunlight when Grimbald and his men came from under the beech trees. They could see that both the wicket gate and the cell door stood open. Grimbald dismounted at the wicket, and leaning on Oswald's shoulder, went up the path towards the cell. They were close to the threshold when a brownish thing flew forth into their faces, screamed, and sped away on noiseless wings. It was only a great owl, but Oswald had covered his face with his arm like one who fears a blow.

"Assuredly it was the devil, Father!" said he, uncovering a pair of round and credulous eyes.

Grimbald pushed on alone and entered the cell. One glance showed him that it was empty. He saw the rough bed with the coverlet spread awry, the wooden settle, the hutch where Denise had kept her clothes, the great water-jar in the corner. In the cupboard he found nothing but a dry loaf, a drinking horn, and the lamp that she had used. There seemed no sign of violence, nor even of a hurried flight.

Grimbald stood there awhile considering, and then went out into the gathering dusk. It seemed probable to him that Denise had not been in the cell for some days, for was not the bread dry and the water-jar empty? He walked about the garden, turning his beak of a nose this way and that like an eagle, his weakness and his broken bone forgotten in the unravelling of this coil. The little lodge built of faggots where Denise had kept her tools and wood, enlightened him no further, and he was ruffling his brows over it when he heard Oswald calling. The man had caught all Grimbald's spirit of unrest, just as a dog catches the moods of his master, and searching the ground he had found hoof marks on the grass.

Grimbald found him kneeling outside the wattle fence, pointing at something that lay across a grass tussock, something that glistened like a few shreds from a woman's hair. Oswald went on his hands and knees with his face close to the turf. He beat to and fro awhile, crawled forward across the glade, lay almost flat a moment, and then started up with an eager cry. He had found the fresh print of a horse's hoofs in the grass under the fringe of a tree whose boughs nearly touched the ground.

Grimbald went to see what Oswald had to show him. Dusk was falling fast, and they both stooped low over the marks in the grass. But Oswald started up on his haunches and sniffed the air like a dog.

"Hist!"

His eyes dilated as he turned his head to and fro, staring into the deepening gloom under the trees. Something was moving out yonder. They heard one bough strike another, a dead branch crack, the faint brushing of feet through leaves and grass. Oswald laid a hand on the knife at his belt; his teeth showed between snarling lips.

But Grimbald caught him by the shoulder, and they turned back towards the cell where Peter loitered at the wicket in the dusk, and the pony stood with tired and drooping head. They were half across the glade when a man came running after them, and they could see that he was armed.

Grimbald swung round instantly, and stood with head thrown back, shoulders squared. A sword flashed not three paces from him before his lion's roar made the dusk quiver. The man's sword dropped, and he came to a dead pause.

"Grimbald!"

They caught each other as men do who love greatly, and for a moment neither spoke. Then Aymery stood back, and picked up his sword.

"Denise? Is she here?"

Grimbald's forehead became seamed with lines. His short silence betrayed perhaps more than he could tell.

"We came to find her, brother," he said.

"And she is gone?"

"The cell is empty."

Aymery's voice sounded harsh as the rasp of a saw. He swung his sword up and let it rest upon his shoulder. Even in the dusk Grimbald saw that glitter in the eyes, that fierce closure of the lips, that spreading of the nostrils.

"The cell has been empty some days, I judge. I was troubled for the sake of Denise, for I had heard a strange tale from Oswald here. We came, and found nothing."

Aymery swung to and fro with swift, sharp strides. Then his sword shot out and pointed Oswald away.

"Go. Out of earshot."

The man went. Aymery brought his sword back to his shoulder, stretched out an arm, and showed Grimbald something coiled about his wrist.

"Look, a coil of her hair!"

Grimbald bent his head, and then straightened with a deep-drawn breath.

"This— —?"

"They put it under my door at Pevensey, the dogs! Yesterday I broke out and hid in the marshes. They gave chase, and I killed one of those who followed, and took his horse and arms. That was to-day. Then I galloped here."

He tossed his head, shaking back his hair, his eyes hard as a frost. Then he pointed towards the hermitage with his sword.

"What is there in yonder?"

He seemed to stiffen himself against the truth, challenging Grimbald to tell him all.

"There is nothing, brother, but her bed, hutch and cupboard and the like."

"No more than that?"

"Nothing."

Aymery bent forward slightly, and looked into Grimbald's face. For a moment they stared each other in the eyes as though asking and answering silent questions. Then Aymery seemed to understand.

"There has been some devil's work here," he said, and Grimbald told him Oswald's tale, and showed where the hoof prints might be seen by daylight.

"God knows the rest!" he said, smoothing his beard.

But Aymery was kneeling, and praying to the cross of his sword.

CHAPTER XVI

Twilight had fallen, a twilight of blue mists and vague, mysterious distances. A young moon was in the sky, and in a thicket near Denise's cell nightingales were singing. She was to offer herself at the high altar that night, to strip her body before God, St. Martin, and Our Lady, for Dom Silvius had so persuaded her, arguing that her chaste holiness would be the more miraculous when offered publicly to God. Denise had had no heart to determine for herself, and to withstand Dom Silvius's arguments. Her womanhood stood mute and humbled, feeling that some subtle virtue had fled out of her, and left her without purpose. She had lost faith in her own genius; in the magic crystal of her heart she could no longer see visions. And like one very weary she was leaving her destiny in the hands of others, letting them think for her, and guide her as they pleased.

When the twilight had fallen Denise went out into the little grass close before the cell, a close that was shut in by a high thorn hedge. She carried with her a jar of water that Abbot Reginald had blessed, a napkin, a vial of perfumed oil, and a pure white shift and tunic, given by the devout. No one could see her there, and Denise stripped off her old clothes, washed her body from head to foot, dried it, and anointed it with oil.

Now the warmth of her bosom made the perfume of the oil rise up into her nostrils, and the perfume seemed to steal straight into Denise's heart. The night was very still, save for the song of the nightingales. Dew had fallen on the grass, yet a sweet warmth rose out of the earth, a warmth that is rare in the month of May. There was the moon yonder, and far hills faint under a mysterious sky. And Denise who a moment ago had felt miserable and weary of soul, in one breath was blushing as red as a rose, her whole body quivering in the moonlight, her eyes full of some inward fire.

A call from the unknown had come to her, and her heart had answered it, and for the moment she stood transfigured. The night seemed magical, a-whisper with mystery. She felt that she must steal away into the sweet green gloom of the woods, taking all hazards, dreaming a great love. She stretched her arms above her head, so their white and anointed sheen caught the faint light of the moon. Then as a white flame leaps and falls again into the darkness, so Denise's arms fell suddenly across her bosom. The warmth and the perfume had gone again, and she felt cold in body and in heart.

What could it avail her that she was a woman and could dream dreams? The torch was quenched, the wine spilt from the jar. There was no other path than this even though it was strewn with thorns. She must follow it to the end, forgetting that other life, and yet remembering it, hating the world, yet thinking of one heart that might have stood for the whole world. If she escaped bitterness and shame, surely she should be grateful, and contented with such mercies. There was no other life for her but this one of self-renunciation.

Slowly, and very sadly she put on the white shift and tunic, emblems of what the world believed in. She bound up her hair and the touch of it brought back the memory of that night, a memory that stung like an asp at the breast. When she had dressed herself, she knelt on the threshold to pray until the midnight offering. But her misery fled forth into other ways, and she thought of man before she thought of God.

Hours had passed, and there was a sense of stir somewhere over yonder where the abbey lay. A bell began to toll, slowly and sonorously, the first clang of its clapper sounding a note of dismal sanctity. Torches were being lit, for a faint glare began to rise above the orchards and the thickets, and Denise, kneeling on the bare stones, knew that the hour of her renunciation was near.

The sound of their coming was still a sound in the distance when Denise heard the trampling of a horse along the road that ran not very far from her cell. It ceased suddenly, and a murmur of voices came up to her in the darkness. Then all was still again save for the tolling of the bell, and the solemn chanting which told her that Dom Silvius and the Brethren who had charge of her were coming with torches over the hill.

Now Denise had risen and gone out into the green close when the trampling of hoofs came along the thorn hedge with the creaking of harness, and the snorting of a horse. Denise stood still, holding her breath as she listened. The moon had gone, and the only light was the glare of the torches that were topping the hill.

Denise heard a voice calling.

"Denise," it said; "Sancta Denise."

The trampling of hoofs had ceased, and there was silence save for the chanting of the monks upon the hill top. Something moved beyond the hedge, and Denise heard the latch of the gate lifted. The heart stood still in her a moment. Someone was near her in the close, for she heard the sound of breathing, and the rustling of feet in the grass.

A man's whisper came to her out of the dark.

"Denise!"

In a moment, she knew not how, the warm silence of the night grew full of love and life. He was close to her with a white, passionate face looking into hers, questioning her very soul. Perhaps their hands touched. It was like the tumult and yearning of waters in a dark and narrow place.

Denise was trembling from head to foot. Aymery had touched her hand, no more than that, yet nothing but a thin film of darkness seemed to hold the two apart. Denise heard the outpouring of his words, a man's words, poignant and tender, striking her very heart. What could she say to him, with this renunciation of hers so near.

"Denise, why have you left us?"

She covered her face with her arms.

"Lord, lord, was it not you who told me to seek a surer refuge?"

His hands were straining back, and straining forward, as though to touch her, and not to touch.

"Yes, but that was a while ago. Things happen in this world, when a man is tied to his bed. If all has been well with you— —"

She let her arms fall from before her face, and there, above them, the dark hillside was seamed with a stream of light. And in the flare of the torches she could see many shadowy figures moving, and the outline of a great cross carried in the van.

Aymery had seemed blind to all save the white figure before him. But the torch flare struck across his face, and he seemed suddenly to understand.

Then Denise spoke, as though compelling herself.

"They are coming for me," she said. "To-night, I offer myself at the high altar. They must not find you here."

He did not answer her for the moment, but stood looking at the torches, almost stupidly, like a man stunned. Then he bowed his head before her, spoke her name, and went out into the night.

Aymery remembered all that followed as a man remembers few things in the course of his life. He hid his horse in a thicket, and followed on foot when the cross and the torches turned back towards the abbey. The abbey town seemed full of strange curious faces, of shadowy figures that jostled him, of the light of torches, of folk whispering together. There were many people moving under the gate, and on towards the abbey church. Aymery moved with them, silently, dully, like one carried along in the midst of a stream. They flowed in at the doors, these people, and on between pillars that towered up into darkness, and along aisles that were shadowy and dim. The high altar alone was lit with many waxen candles. The Brethren were in their stalls, the sound of chanting came from somewhere out of the dusk.

Then began in that great church the last episode of Dom Silvius's pageant. Aymery, leaning against a pillar in the darkness, saw Denise kneeling before the altar, Reginald of Brecon near her, and two of the most aged of the monks. A bell rang; a strong and strident voice spoke some prayer; then the chanting soared and rolled into the far vaultings of the roof. Heads were bowed everywhere; the monks in the choir had their faces hidden. But Aymery's eyes were turned towards the altar where the candles flickered and the smoke of incense seemed to curl and ascend.

He saw Denise rise, drop her white tunic and shift, and kneel naked upon the altar steps. An old monk bent over her, and clipped away her hair so that it fell like light about her body. She bent before the altar with outstretched arms, and holy water was sprinkled upon her body and her clothes. A voice sounded. She rose slowly and re-arrayed herself. One long murmur seemed to pass like a wind through the darkened church.

The year of a novitiate had begun, a season of probation that should pass before more solemn and final vows should be put upon her. Silvius, shrewd man, had advised Denise guardedly for the sake of the honour of his "house." There should be a ceremony, a kneeling before the altar. That would please the people, and bring her more solemnly before their eyes. Then let Denise prove herself as a child of miracles, and they could talk of the greater and more lasting vows.

Then the aisles seemed alive with swirling water. The people were moving forth with lowered heads, while Denise knelt again before the high altar with its candles. Aymery went with the people, looking back but once when he had reached the western door. The night struck warm after the cold air of the great church. He found himself in the abbey town, walking aimlessly in the midst of many moving, whispering figures.

Then a great hunger to be alone seized him. He almost ran through the straggling town, up past Mountjoye to where he had hidden his horse. And when the first grey of the dawn came he was galloping northwards along the forest roads as though trying to distance the memories of the past night.

CHAPTER XVII

At Pevensey that June-tide Peter of Savoy discovered something that concerned him, thanks to Gaillard's foolhardiness, and the Gascon's boastful, passionate nature. There were bitter words between the Lady of the Lute, and Peter of Savoy, though much of the bitterness was in Etoile's mouth, for the Count could be cold as a frost, when cheated.

"Madame," said he, looking her coolly in the face, "it is every man's privilege to see that he is not fooled. Let us be merciful to one another. You will find a horse at the gate."

Now Etoile might have persuaded most men with her beauty, but in my Lord Peter's eyes there was a look that told her that he would use steel if she made a mocking of his pride. She smothered her words, and dissembled her wrath before him, for he was too cold and clever a man to be treated as she would have treated Gaillard. "Go," his eyes said to her, "and be thankful in the going." And Etoile hid her rage, and went, half wondering the while whether some man had orders to stab her in the back.

Then Peter of Savoy sent for Messire Gaillard, but the Gascon had become suddenly discreet, and betaken himself early to the stable.

His master snapped his fingers.

"Let the fool go," he said. "Madame will need company on the road to the devil."

One of his gentlemen, a very young man, showed some concern for the Lady of the Peacocks.

"Will you turn her out next to naked, sire?"

Peter of Savoy laughed in his face.

"Are you a fool, also, Raymond? Go with her if it pleases you, you will have to fight the Gascon. God knows, I would prevent no man drinking green wine."

So they turned Etoile out of Pevensey, suffering her to take nothing with her but the horse, the clothes she rode in, a little money, and such jewels as were hers.

Peter of Savoy had not judged the case amiss, for if Raymond of the Easy Heart had followed Dame Etoile some miles that morning, he would have found Gaillard waiting for her under the shade of a beech wood near the road. But at first Etoile would not look at the man, for her anger was still hot in her because of all that had passed. She reviled Gaillard without mercy, letting the whip of her tongue flay him as he rode along beside her horse, half loving her and half hating her for her taunts and for her fury.

Whether Gaillard spoke up well for himself, or whether Etoile began to consider her necessity, it came about that she gave up mocking him, and let him ride more peaceably beside her. Probably it was not what Gaillard said, but what Etoile thought that brought them to softer speaking. The woman looked at once to the future, and the future to her was a forecasting of the importunities of self. Here was she, worse off in pride than any beggar woman, she whom Peter of Savoy had brought with pomp and homage out of the South. Gaillard had brought all this upon her, and Gaillard seemed her necessity since she was set adrift in a strange land. Perhaps she loved him a very little, with the treacherous, transient love of a leopardess. For the present he must serve her. The husk of to-day might be the gold shoe of the morrow.

Matters were so well mended between them that they halted to rest under the shade of a tree. And there Gaillard knelt in his foolish, passionate way, and swore many oaths on the cross of his sword. Etoile curled her lip at him, and bade him save his breath. She was in no mood for such philanderings, and had other thoughts in her head.

"Come, Messire Gaillard," said she, "you and I must understand each other if we are to travel the road together. Those who are turned out of doors must learn to face rough weather."

Gaillard showed his temper by pulling out a purse, and pouring the gold in it at her feet.

"Such stuff is to be won. I will fight to win pay for you, my desire, as never man fought before."

Etoile touched the money contemptuously with her foot.

"Put it back again, you may need it."

Gaillard shrugged, and humoured her. He spun one of the coins, caught it, and balanced it on his thumb.

"A woman is made a wife for less," he said.

"And kept, for less. Listen, fool, we are not a girl and a boy."

She spoke to Gaillard a long while, looking in his eyes as she spoke. At first Gaillard carried his head sulkily, but little pleased with what she said.

Presently his eyes began to glitter, he protruded his chin, and once more his shoulders seemed ready to swagger. Before Etoile had ended she had made him her man, ready to skip to the tune she piped.

"Splendour of God!" and he began to laugh. "That is a game after my own heart. In a year the King shall give us the best of his castles. What Fulk de Brauté did, I can do even better."

He sprang up, happy, vain, and audacious, not thinking to read into the deeps of Etoile's eyes.

"You are a great man, my Gaillard," she said. "You and I shall make our fortunes without waiting for Peter's pence."

Hardly three leagues away from these two worldlings the Church took cognizance of holier things, and sought to boast of a miracle at the hands of Denise. More than a month had passed since the Lady of Healing, as the folk called her, had knelt at midnight before the altar, and offered her body to the glory of God. Dom Silvius, dreaming his dreams, and chaffering over his ambitions, thought the time ripe for Denise to prove her sanctity. For a month she had been left in solitude to commune with the saints, save that an Abbey servant had daily brought her food and drink. The thoughts of all the people turned to the thorn hedge and the brown thatched cell that stood on the northern slope of Mountjoye Hill; and human nature being self-seeking, especially in its prayers, each soul had some hope of profiting by the miraculous hands of Denise.

While Etoile and Gaillard rode together in the course of adventure, Dom Silvius came to Virgin's Croft, and a servant with him bearing a young child in his arms. Several women followed devoutly at the almoner's heels, keeping their distance because of Dom Silvius's carefulness towards the sex. The child was said to be possessed by a devil, and when a fit took him he would fall down foaming, struggle awhile, and then lie like one dead. The devil had brought him to such a pass, that he seemed frailer and feebler after each seizure. The boy was the only son of his mother, the brawny wife of a still more brawny smith, and they had great hopes for the child now that Denise had come.

Silvius had the child laid before her door.

"A devil teareth him, Sister," said he. "Your purity shall drive the devil out."

And they left the child with her, and went their way.

Now Denise was very miserable that day because of something in herself that she had begun to fear, and she needed her own heart healing before she might dream of healing others. The world remained with her, though she was shut up as a saint, and the solitude and the loneliness had preyed the more upon her mind. At Goldspur the wild woodland life and the life of the people had been hers. Here she had only her own haunting thoughts, and a voice that whispered that the virtue had gone out of her, and that she no longer had the power to help and to heal.

It was with a kind of anguish that she watched over the child, taking him to her bed, and praying that the devil of epilepsy might go forth. All that day she watched and prayed, the boy lying in a stupor with wide eyes and open mouth. So the night came, and Denise lit her taper, and knelt down again beside the child. All that night she pleaded and strove with God, beseeching Him to show His grace to her for her own sake and the child's.

Just before dawn the boy was taken with a strong seizure, crying out at first, and then lying stiff and straight and silent as a stone image. Denise took him into her lap, put her mouth to his mouth, and held him against her bosom. As the dawn came, so the truth dawned also that the boy was dead, dead in her lap despite her prayers. And a great horror came upon her, as though God had deserted her, nor had the saints listened to her prayers. A new shame chilled her heart. The virtue had gone out of her, she felt alone with her own thoughts, and the dead.

When Dom Silvius and the women came some two hours after dawn they found Denise seated upon the bed with the dead child in her lap. A kind of stupor seemed upon her. She did not so much as move, but sat there with vacant face.

"He is dead. Take him."

That was all she said to Dom Silvius. The almoner took the boy, not able to hide the mortification on his face as he carried the dead child to his mother. Denise heard the woman's cry, though the cry seemed far away like a voice in a dream. Dom Silvius sought to comfort her, but comfort her he could not, because she had hoped so much from Denise's prayers. And as is the way so often with the human heart, the woman went home in bitterness and anger, holding the dead child to her breast, and murmuring against Denise.

If Denise felt herself deserted of God, there was one Sussex man who did not lack for inspiration, and whose heart was possessed by both God and the devil. Aymery of Goldspur had ridden from the Thames to the Severn, to join Earl Simon's army that was on the march from the Welsh borders. The great Earl was like a rock in a troubled sea, or a beacon that drew all those who loved their land, and who strove for better things. The King might call him a "turbulent schemer"; sneers never killed a man like De Montfort. For the heart of England was full of turbulence, and it seemed that England's heart beat in Earl Simon's breast.

Aymery, wild as a hawk, borne along by the storm-wind of his restless manhood, grieving, exulting, torn by a great tenderness that could have no hope, came within the ken of the People's Earl. For it was Aymery's need that month to throw himself at the gallop into some cause, to live in the midst of tumult, to let his face burn wherever the banners blew. Perhaps fortune set her seal on him because he was ready to hazard his life with the fierce carelessness of a man who had no traffic with the future. Be that as it may, Simon's host marched down from the West, taking Hereford and Gloucester on its way, and Aymery had caught the great Earl's eye before they came to Reading Town.

Moreover, on the march from Reading to Guildford, over the heathlands and wild wastes, there were skirmishes with the King's men who had pushed out from Windsor. Sharp tussles these, horsemen galloping each other down, spear breaking on the hillsides, men slain on the purple heather. Here the fiercer, bolder spirits were to be found, the young eagles who would redden their talons. In one such skirmish Aymery charged in, and rescued young John de Montfort who had been taken prisoner through too much zeal and daring. At Reigate again there was more fighting, though the place soon fell, yet Fortune pushed Aymery into a lucky chance. Certain of the King's men, hired ruffians most of them, had barricaded themselves in a church, nor would they budge, though an assault was given under the eyes of the Earl himself. Fortune helped Aymery as she so often helps the man who is careless as to his own end. He found the window of a side chapel unguarded, broke in, and held his ground desperately till others followed, and the place was won.

Earl Simon himself came into the church, and knelt there before the altar, close to where two of the King's men lay dead in their blood. When he had finished his prayer, he stood on the altar steps and called for the man who had leaped down first into the church. And they put Aymery forward, finding him standing behind a pillar, and so gave him the glory.

Simon made ready to knight him there in the church, but Aymery begged seven days to chasten himself, keep vigils, and be blessed with his sword and shield. Simon looked at him steadily, for he was a man after his own heart, grim, resourceful, dangerously quiet, and no boaster. He granted Aymery the seven days, telling him to come to Tonbridge whither the host went towards the siege of Dover.

"God first, man afterwards," he said. "You have chosen as I would have you choose."

So Aymery slept that night at Guildford before the altar of the church. When the dawn came he mounted his horse, and rode southwards, alone.

CHAPTER XVIII

A man's chivalry must have a queen to crown it with the crown of a high purpose, and Aymery had no will to forget Denise, nor the mystical beauty of her womanhood. The thought of her drew him as the Holy City drew those who had taken the cross. Since he was to be made a knight, she should bless his arms for him, and serve as a Lady who looked at him out of Heaven. Thus Aymery went riding southwards in the July heat, saying his prayers devoutly at dawn and at sunset, bathing his body when he found clear water; and filling his soul with the thought of Denise. He had broken himself to the belief that she was lost to the world, though he was still troubled as to the happenings that had driven her from Goldspur. Denise's silence seemed sacred to him, and her unapproachableness made his love the greater. Now, like a man who has found a good excuse, he returned again to win a glimpse of her face.

Late on the afternoon of the first day Aymery turned aside from the road under the shade of an oak tree to rest his horse. Below him stretched a deep valley with the road running through it like a white thread; the place seemed very desolate, while on the farther side of the valley the woods came down close to the road. The day was full of a shimmer of gold, and no mowers had come to mow the summer grass.

As Aymery sat there under the shade of the tree, he saw a man in a blue surcoat riding a grey horse along the road below. Aymery had hardly set eyes on him when he saw the man halt, and remain motionless under the July sun that glittered on him and showed that he was armed. A woman had come out from the woods close to the road, a woman with black hair and a scarlet tunic that shone up against the green. What was passing between them Aymery could not tell, but he saw the woman disappear into the woods and the man on the grey horse follow her.

Some time had passed, and Aymery's thoughts had flown elsewhere, when a cry rose out of the summer silence, held a moment, and then died down. Presently he saw a grey horse and a rider in blue reappear out of the woods with another horse and rider beside him. The second man wore green, and carried a plain, black shield.

Aymery saw them ride away westwards into the golden light that covered the woods and the valley. The way they rode seemed strange to him, for the horses went shoulder to shoulder, and one arm of the man in green lay about the body of the rider in blue. He was puzzled moreover by the thought of the woman in the red tunic, and the cry that he had heard, and it crossed his mind that there had been foul play yonder.

When he had mounted and come down to the place where the blue knight had turned aside, Aymery turned aside also into the woods. A little way in, under the trees where a bank rose covered with bracken, he found a track that had been trampled leading to a place where someone seemed to have lain. But he saw nothing else beyond the tree boles, the cool green foliage, and the bracken splashed here and there with sunlight. When he called, no voice answered him, so he rode out of the wood and went his way. Yet there was more in the wood than he had seen, nor did he guess that he would meet again with the rider on the grey horse.

On the evening of the second day Aymery came to the hills by Montifeld, and saw the Senlac uplands smitten by the evening light. Beyond Watlingtun he found a man mowing grass beside the road, and stopped to question him concerning Denise. The man pointed towards Mountjoye Hill, for they could see from where they stood the thatched roof of the cell above the thorn hedge.

"The Virgin's cell is yonder, lording," he said, thinking perhaps that Aymery rode thither to be cured of some wound, and that he would be disappointed, for the Lady of Healing had worked no cures since they had brought her to the Abbey lands.

Denise was at her prayers, kneeling on the threshold with the door of the cell wide open, when she heard the trampling of Aymery's horse, a sound from the outer world that made her heart stand still and listen. There was a minute's silence before she heard the latch of the gate lifted, and someone moving through the unmown grass.

"Aymery! Lord!"

He saw the wave of colour go over her face, for he had come upon her suddenly as she knelt there upon the threshold. The rush of blood from the heart died down again. She looked at him, and prayed that he should not see that she was trembling.

Denise rose up from her knees as though the sound of her own voice had broken some spell. A kind of dumb discomfiture possessed them both. Aymery, with the sunlight shining on his battle harness, felt challenged by his own silence. The words he had meant to utter stuck in his throat, for that wave of redness over the woman's face had somehow made him feel ungenerous and a coward. What right had he to come galloping into her life again, when they had put a day of dreams behind them?

And like a man who would be honest, he stumbled to the blunt perfunctoriness of a boy going down on his knees in a church. There was something to be gone through with, and the sooner the better, since he had begun so clumsily. Many women would have misunderstood the mood in him. Denise understood it, perhaps more clearly than Aymery himself.

"Yes?"

Her eyes questioned him, more than her voice. Aymery put his shield before him as he knelt.

"I have been with Earl Simon," he said, looking at his shield. "It is to be the sword on the shoulder, and a pair of spurs."

He spoke, with a slight shrug of the shoulders, a man ill at ease under his own eyes, even though self-consciousness was not part of his normal nature. Denise's heart had dropped to a steadier rhythm. The quicker wit of the woman has always the advantage of the man.

"Earl Simon gave me some days, to keep vigils, wash, and be cleansed. I would have my arms blessed also, they will serve in a good cause."

He drew out his sword, set it point downwards in the grass, and looked at it, and not at Denise.

She had her two hands over her bosom, and seemed to draw several breaths before she could speak.

"There is the Abbot Reginald."

"Should I ride forty miles to be blessed by Reginald of Brecon? Here are my sword and shield. Bless them, or they shall go unblessed."

She looked at him, recoiling upon the consciousness of all that had happened to her since the days at Goldspur.

"I?"

"You can bless them, Denise. Who better?"

The fog in the air between them thinned and vanished. But neither Aymery nor Denise noticed its passing. Life, and the infinite earnestness thereof had both their hearts in thrall.

"Is it so great a thing to ask, Denise?"

He was looking at her steadily now, the self-consciousness had slipped from him.

"Lord, if my blessing were but worthy."

"Need you ask that!"

"It is I who ask it of my own heart," she answered.

He flung out his arms suddenly, and his face blazed up at her.

"For England, for the land, not for me alone, Denise. Mother of God—I will have no other. Am I not wise as to my own desire?"

His ardour caught her spirit and sent it soaring above the earth as a wind blows a half-dead beacon into flame. The miserable self-fear, the consciousness of coming shame fell away from her like a ragged garment. She was the Denise of the woods again, with miraculous eyes and hands.

"Give them to me."

She stretched out her arms, took his shield, held it to her bosom, and spoke words over it that Aymery could not hear. Yet how much love and how much supplication there were in those words of hers, the heart of a woman alone could tell. She took his sword also, kissed the cross thereof, and held it on high.

"Break not, fail not. Keep troth, rust never."

She gave him the sword again, and Aymery kissed it, and knelt awhile with bowed head, as though in prayer. Then he rose up out of the grass, holding the cross of the sword before his eyes.

"I would keep my vigil here," he said. "Yonder where there is a thicket of young oaks. Before dawn, I shall be gone."

Denise's face was still transfigured. The realisation of her earthliness had not returned as yet.

"God guard you in the wars," she said to him.

Aymery lifted his head, and for a moment they looked into each other's eyes. Then he turned from her as though his own heart bade him go. And it seemed to each that they had snatched a moment of joy from that half-closed hand of life that holds more pain than gladness.

There were some children standing staring at his horse when Aymery came out from the wicket in the hedge of thorns. He paid no heed to them however, and taking his horse by the bridle, led him to the oak thicket on the hillside below Virgin's Croft. The children ran away into the town, and told their mothers that they had seen a knight come out of St. Denise's gate with a naked sword over his shoulder. The children's tale-bearing caused some tattle in the Abbey town, and the Abbey servants heard it.

Thus these two, soldier and saint, passed the night within call of one another; Aymery kneeling bareheaded under the stars, with sword and shield before him; Denise pitiably wakeful in her cell, conscious of the darkness, and of that shadow of darkness that grew each day more heavy about her heart. She prayed for Aymery that night, prayed for herself, and against the future that she dreaded. They were so near to each other, and yet so utterly apart. It seemed to Denise that night that she had fled to this place of refuge, only to meet the greater bitterness and shame.

At last the dawn came, and with it the sound of a horse moving over the grass. She heard Aymery come riding up to the hedge of thorns. She saw his sword flash out against the dawn as he stood in the stirrups and called her name.

"Denise, Denise!"

"God keep you," she answered him in her heart.

He went away into the world at a gallop, as though it was easier to leave her thus in the gold and green of a summer morning.

Aymery had been gone but half an hour when a monk and two lay brethren came hurrying over Mountjoye Hill. Their figures looked dark, intent, outlined against the virginal clearness of the dawn. The monk was Dom Silvius, and his eyes were sharp and watchful.

He came alone to Denise's cell, leaving the two lay brothers at the gate in the hedge. Denise was washing her neck and bosom; she had closed the door, and suffered Silvius to speak to her from without. She soon learnt that he had heard of Aymery's coming, and that he desired to discover the reason thereof.

"It was one who rode here, Father, to have his arms blessed. He is on the eve of knighthood, and kept his vigil in the wood, yonder."

Silvius's face was very astute, he stroked his chin and considered. There was nothing of the dreamer about him that morning.

"And the offering, Sister, the offering?"

Denise did not choose to understand.

"What offering, Father?"

"That which the man left, for the blessing."

"He left no offering with me," she said.

"No gift, Sister, nothing out of gratitude for the blessing?"

"No."

"Not even a ring or a piece of money?"

"Nothing."

Silvius's face condemned such vagrant meanness. He hid his vexation, and spoke softly, remembering that he was dealing with a certain sensitive thing called woman.

"Sister," said he. "Perhaps the man was poor. We grudge nothing to those who are blessed with poverty. But an offering should always be made, even though it be but the half of an apple. God loves not niggardliness, my sister, and I would not have our good Lord, St. Martin, offended."

Denise could not see Silvius because of the closed door, but there was something in his voice that made her see him as a sharp-faced, shrewd, insinuating figure hiding covetousness under the cloak of humility.

"I asked for nothing, Father," she said.

Silvius's face was very cunning.

"True, my Sister, we do not barter with our own souls. But there are the poor to be remembered, the fabric of the church, the glory of St. Martin. There is no shame in holding out the hand for these."

Denise's hands were fastening her tunic. And in the darkness of the cell she seemed to understand suddenly, as one comes by the understanding of the deeper things of life in the midst of some great sorrow, the reason of their eagerness to win her to the Abbey. The realisation of it was like the discovery of simony and self-seeking in the character of one beloved. She stood motionless, staring at the door beyond which Silvius listened. And the day seemed bitter and sordid to her after the night of Aymery's vigil.

"Such things as I receive," she said, "shall be laid before the altar," and from that moment she felt that she hated Silvius because she had seen the motives that moved his soul.

"That is well, Sister," he answered her. "St. Martin is generous to all who give."

The almoner went away grumbling to himself, disgusted as any Jew that a man who had benefited should have left nothing in return.

"The woman needs more shrewdness," he thought. "Nor have we had any marvel from her yet to open the people's hearts, and purses. God grant that we have not made an indifferent bargain. We are losing rental, and giving food and gear," and he returned in a temper, and thought mercenary thoughts all through Matins in the Abbey Church. For to Silvius his "house" was a great treasure-chest to be guarded, and enriched.

Denise was glad when Silvius had gone, and though she strove to put the sneering suspicions from her, they remained like dead trees, white and ugly in the green of a living wood. To count the money in the alms-box, to clutch at the offering, with the prayer hardly gone from the mouth! It was not in her soul to suffer such a traffic.

The day seemed very grey to her, though the sun was shining, because of that other thing that haunted her more than the thought of Dom Silvius's keenness. She felt more and more that the virtue had gone out of her, and that the Lord of the Abbey would have no miracles to bring him treasure. If this thing were to mature, what then would follow? She shut the eyes of her soul to it, and tried to think of that night in May as but the memory of an evil dream.

CHAPTER XIX

From the gold of the wheat harvest to the picking of red apples no great time passes, yet in those few weeks the people began to scoff openly at the healing powers of Denise. She had been brought in with such quaint pomp and ceremony, with such singing, and such a show of blossom on the boughs, that folk had looked for a wonderful fruiting, and for an especial blessedness that should show itself in each man's house.

Denise, poor wench, had come into the wilds of life, to find primitive things dragging her beautiful altruism into ruins. She had lost her wings and could no longer soar, because of the earthliness that grew more apparent to her day by day. Everything that she attempted failed with her, and faith in her own power dwindled out of her heart. Long ago she had noticed the prophetic change in Dom Silvius's attitude. He was suspicious, grieved, hesitatory, always hoping for some lucky miracle, some splendid coincidence that might fire the beacon of his imaginings. He had boasted a little of this Virgin Saint out of the woods, and the eyes of some of the Brethren were beginning to twinkle.

One sunny day early in October Dom Silvius went down to the stews to fish. There happened to be some of the younger monks there, and Guimar the hosteler, a long, lean quiz of a man whom Silvius hated.

"Brother," said he to the almoner. "Have you come to fish?"

Dom Silvius answered the question by settling his stool with great deliberation at the edge of the pond. Guimar glanced at the rest.

"My Brothers," he said. "See, here is Silvius come a-fishing. Let us kneel and pray for him, and perchance his saint may catch a miracle!"

They all laughed at the joke, all save Silvius, who bit his lips. And from that moment his pride began to work like a slow poison in him, filling him with a hatred of Denise.

Once only, and that in August, Father Grimbald had come stalking up the hill to Virgin's Croft, when the people were busy with the harvest, and there were none to see his coming. What he said to Denise, and she to him, no man knew, for Grimbald held his peace concerning it. But Denise wept when he had gone, bitter, impassioned tears that welled up out of her heart. Grimbald's brow was heavy with a thunder cloud of thought as he trudged home to Goldspur over the hills. He opened and closed his great fists as he went, as though yearning to smite something, or to take an enemy by the throat. He had been unable to learn much from Denise, save that she seemed unhappy, and that she had left Goldspur because of the violence of the times. Grimbald had his own suspicions, but speak them he could not, though he was troubled within himself for Denise's sake. He knew that it had not been a matter of vainglory with her, a desire to be flattered by the worship of a wider world. Oswald's tale of the Devil on the Black Horse loomed largely in the background of Grimbald's mind. Denise had hidden something from him. Of that Grimbald felt assured.

The burgher folk of Battle and the people on the Abbey lands began to have their grievances against Denise, grumbling with superstitious pettiness because their hopes had profited so little. There was a multitude of small things remembered against her, for of what use was a holy woman if her sanctity brought no blessings. Grubs had attacked the apples; why had not Denise prevented that? The sheep had been worried with the "fly"; again Denise had been besought to pray against the pest. Many of the wells had run dry with the hot summer; what was the use of a saint who could not bring back water?

There were many more things quoted against her.

Mulgar the carrier had brought a horse cursed with "wind sucking" and the staggers. A holy woman should be able to conjure such trifles, and Mulgar had brought three pennies as an offering. The horse had died on the road next day.

Gilbert the miller was plagued with rats. And the rats prospered, even though he had brought a dead buck rat to Denise, and besought her to curse the vermin.

Olivia, the goldsmith's wife, brought a girl with a purple birth-mark on her cheek. She desired Denise to touch the stain that it might disappear. The birth-mark remained for all to see.

A woman in child-bed sent for Denise's blessing. The child was still-born the very same night.

Well might Denise feel that the virtue had gone out of her, that the people were beginning to mock, and that her prayers were as so much chaff. The bitterness and the humiliation were not of her own seeking. They had set her upon a pinnacle, crowded about her open-mouthed, ready for the blessings she should bestow. Her white garments, and her burning aureole of hair had dazzled them, and the power of her beauty remained with her still. But the mystery was passing; she had profited none of the people; her prayers had burst like bubbles in the air. And since the human heart is ever a fickle thing, ready to scoff and sneer, and think itself cheated when its own fancies fall to the ground, the very children began to catch the spirit of their elders, and to throw surreptitious stones at Denise's door. They invented a game, too, that they called the Silly Saint, in which one of the girls wore a halo of straw and attempted to work wonders which were never wonderful, till the audience rose and rolled her in the grass. No one chided them for such indecent blasphemy. Even Dom Silvius was ready to wash his hands of Denise.

There were more sinister whisperings in the air as the autumn drew on and merged into the winter. Bridget, the smith's wife, whose boy had died on Denise's knees, had set her tongue and her spite against the saint. The woman had been very bitter against Denise all through the summer, laughing maliciously over her failures, and nodding her head with the air of "I could have told you so." When neighbours had still seemed credulous, she had put her tongue in her cheek, and mocked.

Bridget and some other women were spreading their linen on the grass one windy October day, and their talk turned upon Denise. As women will, they spoke of the things that had been noised abroad of late. There were some that said that Denise was no saint, that she was no better than they themselves were, far worse in fact because of her vows. It had been told that a strange knight had kept a vigil near her cell, and the women laughed, as only women of a kind can.

Bridget, the smith's wife, was the bitterest of them all, because of her dead child, and the spite that she had nurtured against Denise. And as they spread their linen on the grass she began to tease the women, and to tantalise them with all manner of cryptic nods, and sneers, and insinuations. The end of it all was that much of the linen blew hither and thither because the women were so eager to listen to Bridget, and forgot to weigh the sheets and body gear down with stones.

Bridget was the fat hen with the worm in her beak, and they all crowded about her as though to thieve it. But all she did was to laugh and to smooth her frock with her two hands.

The women set up a great cackling, and then ran to and fro to catch the linen that was blowing in the wind.

"Blessed Martin," said one, "when the Abbot hears of it!"

"A mighty poor miracle for Dom Silvius to boast of! I could do as well myself."

CHAPTER XX

The early days of December found Earl Simon lodged at Southwark, while the King and his men prowled to and fro in Kent, coveting England's sea gate, Dover, that the barons had taken in the summer. Earl Simon had no great gathering with him in Southwark, for he had London at his back, an ant's nest into which the King would not venture to thrust his spear. There had been much bloodshed and violence in the land, and it was De Montfort's hope that Henry would show some wisdom now that he had seen many of his great lords in arms against him. A truce had been mooted, with Louis of France to judge between the two parties. Yet no man trusted Henry, because of his fickleness and his foolish cunning, and because of the favourites who had his ear.

Henry had hated the Londoners with exceeding bitterness since they had pelted his Queen from London Bridge when she had sought to escape to Windsor in the summer. They had thrown stones and offal at her barge, and the King, and Edward his son, talked of the blood of the city as though it were the blood of swine. It was even said that they had sworn upon relics to make a slaughter there that should be remembered for many years. Yet a number of the wealthier merchants were for the King, partly because they hated the lesser men and the mob, and partly because they had taken bribes. There was treachery afoot of which Earl Simon knew nothing, nor had he any foreshadowings of the peril that was near.

Early in December Henry had attempted to win his way into Dover. The attempt had failed miserably; and the news was that he and his men were still lingering on the coast. No one thought of him as within ten leagues of London; the traitors in the city were alone wise as to his plans. Earl Simon remained in Southwark, debating the future with the barons who were with him, and with the Londoners who would hear of nothing but that the King should swallow the Great Charter, and that the Provisions of Oxford should hold. They had not forgotten Richard of Cornwall's corn ships, and the way Henry had attempted to play the Jew at the expense of the starving poor.

It so happened that Aymery was in the saddle one December evening as the darkness came down over the land like a rolling fog. Rain had begun to fall, a fine drizzle that made the fading horizon in the west a dim grey streak. Infinite mournfulness breathed in the gust of a wet winter wind. Tired horses plodded past Aymery as he sat motionless by the roadside, the hood of his cloak turned over his helmet. A party had been out to bring in forage, and Aymery had had the handling of the escort, a few archers and men-at-arms.

The last tired horse had gone splashing by, and the creaking of the saddles and the breathing of the beasts were dropping into the darkness before Aymery turned to follow his men. He was about to push his horse to a trot when he heard the sound of a man running along the wet, wind-swept road. Aymery drew up across the road, and saw a figure come out of the darkness, head down, hands paddling the air.

The man seemed to see neither horse nor rider till he was almost into them. He stumbled, recovered himself, and drew back out of the possible reach of a possible sword.

"Montfort—Montfort?"

Aymery reassured him, and he staggered forward and leant against Aymery's horse, panting out his news, for he had run two miles or more.

"Lording, there is an army on the march down yonder. I was carrying faggots from a wood, when I saw them riding out of the dusk. Their vanguard halted under the wood, and I hid myself, and listened, and then crept away and ran like a rabbit."

He panted, pressing his ribs with his two hands, as though his heart was gorged with blood. Aymery bent down, and looked into the hind's mud-stained face.

"Quick, good lad——"

"It was the van of the King's host, lording, they are riding on Southwark out of the night."

"How near are they?"

"The wood is a mile beyond the cross where the roads branch. They were resting their horses, the beasts had been hard ridden, and their bellies were all mud."

Aymery straightened in the saddle, and sat motionless. The night gave no sound for the moment save the soughing of the wind through some poplars that grew near. Half a furlong away the darkness thickened into a black curtain, hiding the world, tantalising those who watched with the wraiths of a thousand chances.

Yet, as they waited there on the wet road, a confused sense of movement came to them from somewhere out of the darkness, like the sound of the sea galloping in the distance over a mile of midnight sand. Aymery swept round, pulled off his glove with his teeth, and threw it at the man's feet.

"Look to yourself, my friend," he said. "They are coming through the night yonder. Bring that glove to the Earl, and you shall have your due."

Aymery clapped in the spurs, and went away at a gallop. He did not doubt that it was the King's arms behind him, pouring upon Southwark to surprise De Montfort's weak force there, and take him or slay him before the Londoners could gather to his aid.

As Aymery galloped through the night, the lights of Southwark and of the city beyond the river came to him in a blur through the mist of rain. He did not slacken even when he came to the outskirts of the place, but rode straight for the Earl's lodging, shouting to those whom he passed in the street.

"Arm, arm," was his cry as he galloped through. "The King's men are on us."

And so he brought the news to Simon the Earl.

De Montfort and his knights and gentlemen were at supper, but they left the wine cups unemptied, and made haste to arm. The Earl sent his son Simon to ride across the bridge and rouse the train-bands in the city. The narrow streets and alleys of Southwark were soon in a great uproar with the running to and fro of men, the tossing of torches, and all the tumult of a hurried call to arms. A bell began to clash somewhere up in the darkness. The narrow ways were full of movement, of an infinite confusion that struggled and chafed like waters meeting and beating against one another. Trumpets blared. Leaders sought their men, men their leaders. From beyond the river also bells began to peal, the city was bestirring itself, and humming like a hive of bees.

Aymery, rushing out from the Earl's presence, ran against a man with a fiery tangle of bright-red hair. It was Waleran de Monceaux, that rebel of rebels, driven by Gaillard out of Sussex. He caught Aymery by the shoulder, and blessed God fiercely because the Sussex men were the first to show their shields.

"Brother," he shouted, "I have thirty spears for a charge home. I heard you were here. Come. We shall have the van."

They went out together into the street where some of the Earl's men were already under arms. None the less there was a dire tangle everywhere, the place choked with disorder that promised well for the King's men if they lost no time. Aymery and Waleran found their bunch of Sussex spears standing steady and stiff for the night's need. They were soon joined by other knights and their men who gathered out of the wet gloom. De Montfort himself came out, and ordered his archers forward into the outskirts of the suburb, to scout and discover what was happening in the darkness yonder.

A shout rose suddenly, and went from mouth to mouth. Young Simon came out of the darkness with torches, riding his white horse, and a mob of half-armed men with him.

"Sire, treachery, the gates at the bridge are locked."

Such in truth was the case, for the King had planned the trick, and those of the wealthier citizens who were in his pay had locked the gates and thrown the keys into the river.

Simon saw his imminent hazard, but his sword was out to hearten his men.

"Break down the gates."

And then, standing in his stirrups:

"Sirs," said he, "let the King's men come to us. They will find it hot here, despite the rain."

A number of archers came running back out of the night, shouting that masses of men were pouring along the dark streets at their heels. A blare of trumpets tore the darkness. The narrow main street began to roar with the rush of mounted men. The Earl's trumpets gave tongue in answer. In an instant a black torrent poured forward as though a dam had broken, and fell with fury upon the flood that lapped from wall to wall.

A man has no time to remember what happens in such a fight when he is caught by a whirlwind of human fury, and driven this way and that. Horses reared, fell, and crushed their riders. The narrow street rang like a hundred smithies. Blows were given and taken in the darkness, men grappled together in the saddle, for there was no room often for the swing of a sword. Aymery found himself and his horse driven against the wall, and pinned there by the mass that filled the street. He struck out, with cries of "Montfort, Montfort," and was struck at in turn by those who bawled for the King.

Aymery found himself being forced along the wall his horse, scared and maddened, backing along the street. The tide had turned in the King's favour. The Earl's men were being driven by sheer weight of numbers. The night had a black look for Earl Simon and his party.

Of what followed Aymery could have given no clear account, all that he knew was that he went on striking at those who struck at him, and that he remembered wondering that he had not been wounded or beaten out of the saddle. His brain seemed to become dulled by the din and clangour, and by the tumult in the darkness and the rain. A roar of voices rose suddenly, flowing from somewhere out of the night. "Montfort, Montfort!" A great rallying cry came up like the sound of the sea, for the Londoners had broken the gates, and were pouring over the bridge into Southwark to rescue the Earl.

For a while the fight stood still, and then slowly, and with a sense of infinite effort it began to roll towards the fields. New men seemed to come from nowhere, streaming up alleys and side streets to break in on the flanks of the King's party. Aymery found himself with space to breathe; his sword arm ached as though he had been swinging a hatchet for an hour. Comrades came up on either side of him, they gathered and pushed on, shouting for Earl Simon, and fighting shoulder to shoulder, Aymery found the street opening suddenly upon a small square before a church. In one corner a torch had been thrust into an iron bracket on the wall of a house, and still burning brightly, despite the rain, it seemed to serve as a rallying point for those whose stomachs were not sick of the fight.

It was becoming a hole and corner business now, a question of group fighting against group, man against man. Each party had been tossed into so many angry embers, like a fire scattered by a kick of the foot. The Londoners were still streaming over the bridge. Their shouts of "Montfort, Montfort," held the night. The surprise had failed, thanks to the hind who had run two miles in the mud.

Aymery was pushing his horse across the square, battered shield forward, right hand balancing his sword, when his eyes were drawn towards a skirmish that was going on where the torch burnt in the bracket on the wall. A big man in green surcoat, and mounted on a black horse was keeping some of the Londoners at bay. And behind the green knight, just under the torch, Aymery saw a knight in a blue surcoat on a grey horse, a contrast in colours that struck him as familiar. The blue knight was taking no part in the tussle. His comrade seemed to be defending him, backed up by a few men-at-arms whose harness gleamed in the light of the torch.

Aymery spurred forward, and came to blows with the man in green. Nor had he had much to boast of when a mob of Londoners came up at a run and broke into the thick of the scrimmage. Aymery found himself driven close to the knight in blue. He struck at him, but the other seemed to have lost his sword, for he did nothing but cover his head with his shield. Aymery caught the blue knight's bridle, and urged both the horses out of the press. He had a glimpse of the man on the black horse trying to plunge through the Londoners towards him. But he was beaten back, and disappeared, still fighting, into the night.

Aymery got a grip of the blue knight's belt. The man appeared to have little heart left in him, for he dropped his shield, and surrendered at discretion.

"Quarter, messire, quarter."

The voice that came through the grid of the great battle helmet seemed more the voice of a boy.

Aymery kept a firm hold of the gentleman, and rode back with him into the main street. The grey horse went quietly as though thoroughly tired of the night's adventure. Aymery had no trouble with either beast or man.

A great crowd had gathered at the bridge head. Earl Simon was there, guarded by an exultant and shouting mob of Londoners who were carrying him across the bridge into the city. The crowd was so great that Aymery had to halt with his prisoner, and bide his time. Torches had been lit and their glare and smoke filled the street where a thousand grotesque faces were shouting "Montfort, Montfort."

Aymery felt a hand touch his arm, for he still had hold of the blue knight's sword belt.

"Ah, messire, see what manner of prisoner you have taken."

The blue knight had lifted the great helmet and let it fall with a clash upon the stones. Aymery saw masses of dark hair flowing, and a white face looking into his.

"Mother of God," said he, "what have we here?"

"A woman, lording," and she laughed a little, and then said again, more softly: "A woman."

Aymery scanned her by the light of the torches, and it seemed to him that he had seen her face before. Her hair was dark as night, her skin the colour of a white rose, and she looked at him with eyes that seemed full of an amused yet watchful glitter.

For the moment Aymery thought of letting her go free, but the lady herself appeared to have no such ambition.

"I am in your hands, messire," she said. "Keep me from the mud and the mob, and I will thank you."

Aymery asked her name, being puzzled to know what to do with such a prisoner.

"My name?" and she laughed, and gave him a look that was meant to challenge a possible homage. "I dropped my name with my shield. Nor would you know it if I told it you."

Aymery was asking himself what had best be done with this lady in man's guise. To many men the answer would have been gallant and none too difficult. But Aymery coveted neither the responsibility nor the possible romance. Nor was he sorry when a happy chance intervened between him and the dilemma.

A number of knights came riding out of Southwark with Simon the Younger on his white horse at their head. And Simon who was an adventurous and hot headed gentleman with the eyes of a hawk when a woman was concerned, caught sight of Aymery and his prisoner, and swooped down instantly towards the lure.

"Hallo, my friend, who are you, and what have you here?"

Aymery showed his shield, but the Earl's son recognised his face.

"Sir Aymery, out of Sussex! And what is this treasure, messire, that we have taken?"

At the sound of Aymery's name the woman's eyes had darted a look at him, like the momentary gleam of a knife hidden under a cloak. Then she moved nearer to young De Montfort, and was soon speaking on her own behalf.

He bowed gallantly to her when she had done.

"Since you offer us no name, madam," he said. "Let us call you Isoult of the Black Hair. I am Simon, the earl's son. Also, I am your servant, unless our friend here stands between us."

Aymery renounced all prestige, not having Simon's capacity for instant infatuations.

"It is no concern of mine, sire," he said, with a bluntness that was hardly courteous to the lady.

A laugh hailed this frankness. De Montfort's son was looking at Etoile.

"Will it please you to command my courtesy?" he asked.

Etoile smiled at him. He took her bridle, and they went riding together over London Bridge into London City. Nor did Simon guess that this was the first ride along a tortuous road that would lead him to bring death upon the great earl, his father.

CHAPTER XXI

Winter had come, and since Denise's cell stood on the northern slope of Mountjoye Hill, it was bitter cold there, nor would the north wind be stopped by such things as a thorn hedge or a closed door. To Denise the cold was but part of the misery that was closing upon her, for people were hardier in those days, and less softened by the luxury of glass and carpets. But it was not the cold that kept her wakeful through the night, but the blank and unpitying face of the future that never departed from before her eyes. Denise knew the truth now, and soon the world might know it also.

The Abbey folk had sent her no winter gear, but that was Dom Silvius's affair, perhaps due to his meanness, or his discontent with her, or to the feeling that a recluse whose prayers went unanswered needed to be chastened by wind and frost. It seemed very far from that day in May when the meadows were sheeted in gold, and the singing boys sang her into the Abbey *leuga*. Denise would have had no winter clothes, had not a good woman who distrusted Dom Silvius, sent her a lamb's-wool tunic, and a cloak lined with rabbit's skin.

So the winter deepened, and Denise saw always that shame that was coming nearer day by day. She knew now how utterly she had failed, and the reason thereof seemed in herself. Life had thrust hypocrisy upon her insidiously and by stealth. She would have fled from it, but the wide world seemed cold and empty, nor was she free to follow her own will. Reginald the Abbot was her lord now, both in the law and in the spirit, he could have her taken if she fled, condemned, whipped, and turned forth with contumely in the eyes of all. Denise had her woman's pride, a pride that shrank from the thought of a public scourging and of open shame.

Two weeks or more after Christmas, on a clear frosty morning, three women came to Denise's cell, and one of these women was the smith's wife, Bridget. They had loitered on the road awhile, talking volubly, priming one another for some enterprise. No one had come near Denise for a month or more, save the Abbey servant who left food at the cell, but never saw her face.

So the three women came to Denise's cell, and stood before the closed door, smirking and making a mystery of the event. They had christened each other "Warts," "Sterility," and "Thorn-in-the-Thumb," and their business was to win a glimpse of Denise.

Dame Bridget, or "Thorn-in-the-Thumb," made a devout beginning. She was a big woman with a high colour, and a mouth that was generally noisy, a woman of coarse texture, and of gross outlines that showed Nature as a craftswoman at her worst.

Bridget had picked up some Latin words, and she began with these, as though such a prelude would impress Denise with their seriousness in coming.

"Sister," she said with a snuffle, when she had come to the end of her Latinity. "Here are three poor women in need of a blessing. We pray you to come out to us, Holy Sister, and to touch us with your hands."

Denise had no thought of treachery that morning, and she opened her door, and stood there on the threshold. The three women were kneeling humbly enough in the wet grass, their hoods drawn forward, their hands together as in prayer.

Bridget showed a thumb red and swollen about the pulp.

"There was a thorn twig in a faggot, Sister," she said. "I laid my hand to the sticks, and the thorn went into my thumb. It has kept me awake o' nights with the pain of it."

Then Sterility had a hearing, and while Denise bent over her, for the woman chose to whisper, Thorn-in-the-Thumb nudged Warts with her elbow, and stared Denise over from head to foot.

Lastly, Warts displayed her imperfections, looking most meekly into Denise's shadowy eyes. And when Denise had touched them all and given them her blessing, the three women departed, walking very circumspectly till they gained the road. Then Thorn-in-the-Thumb flung her arms about the necks of her neighbours, crumpled them to her, and laughed gross laughter that was not pleasant to hear. And they went up the hill together, gaggling like geese, blatantly exultant over the thing that they had discovered.

Very soon hardly a man or woman in the five boroughs of Battle had not heard what Bridget and her neighbours had to tell. Rumours had been rife of late, but this last cup was spiced with the palatable truth. The women spoke more loudly than the men, were more strenuous and vindictive, more self-righteous, more eager to have the hypocrite proclaimed. Mightily sore were some of the worthy folk who had gone on their knees for nothing before Denise's cell. They were quick to cry out that they had been cheated, more especially those who had left an offering to bribe the Blessed Ones in

Heaven. The insolence of this jade, setting herself up as a virgin and a saint! "Out with her," was the common cry. As for Dom Silvius he was little better than a fool.

With all these hornets humming even in the midst of winter, some of the older burghers and the head men of the boroughs went secretly to speak with Dom Silvius, and to show him discreetly how matters stood. Such an open sore needed healing; it was an offence and an insult to St. Martin, and the saints. Old Oliver de Dengemare was their spokesman, a man with a wise eye and a sagacious nose. Dom Silvius kept an imperturbable countenance, and heard them out to the bitter end, though inwardly he was aflame with wrath and infinite vexation. "The jade, the impudent jade." His brain beat out such imprecations while the old men talked.

No sooner had they gone than he crept off to whisper it all to Reginald the Abbot. Now Reginald was a man of easy nature, bland, kindly, one who chose a suave word rather than a sour one. Silvius came to him, cringing yet venomous, slaver dropping from his mouth as he stuttered and spat his wrath. He took the thing as infamous towards himself; the greed, the self-love, and the ambition in him were tugging at the leashes.

"Let them hound her out and spit upon her," he said, driving the nails into the palms of his hands, the muscles straining in his pendulous throat. "Let them spit upon her."

Abbot Reginald placed the sponge of his placidity over Dom Silvius's mouth.

"Brother," he cautioned him; "such things should not be spoken till the anger is out of one. A hot head at night calls for penitence in the morning."

He saw very clearly how matters were with Silvius, that the monk's zeal had turned sour, and sickened him; and that he was mad that all his astuteness should have taken, in the eyes of his little world, the motley of the fool.

"You are too hasty, my brother," he said. "Does a man whose wife has lost her virtue, shout it from the house-tops? Come, my friend, let us consider."

But Silvius would not be appeased. The fanatical cat had spread its claws, a beast more cruel than any creature out of the woods. Reginald of Brecon watched him, as a fat man who had dined well might watch the petulant tantrums of a child. He took to turning the ring upon his finger, a trick habitual with him when he was deep in thought.

"It is growing dark," he said at last, glancing at the window.

Then he rose and stood awhile before the fire. Silvius had ceased to spit and to declaim.

"My cloak and hood, Brother Silvius. You will find them there in the recess."

The monk obeyed his lord. When he returned with the cloak, Reginald held up two fingers, and spoke one word:—

"Peace."

There was not the glimmer of a star in the sky when two dim figures climbed Mountjoye Hill. A north wind was blowing and whistled coldly into Reginald's sleeves. Dom Silvius jerked from side to side, looking restlessly into the darkness as though his blood were still hot and bitter in him despite the cold. Reginald understood the savage impatience that possessed his monk, for he bade him wait at the gate in the hedge, and went on alone to the cell.

Silvius kept watch there, striding to and fro, blowing on his nails, and beating his arms against his body like a great black bird. He envied his Abbot the rights of an unbridled tongue, for Silvius would have been a libertine that night in the matter of godly invective and abuse. He could hear voices, the dull, half-suppressed voices of people who spoke earnestly, and yet with passion. Once he thought that something stirred in the hedge near him, for he was startled, and stood still to listen. A prowling fox might have taken fright, or a bird fluttered from its roosting place.

Meanwhile on the threshold of that dark cell stood Reginald the Abbot, shocked, unable to retain much store of anger. A shadowy something knelt there close to him. The very heart of Denise seemed under his feet.

"Lord, let me go," was all that she could ask.

And again—

"Lord, let me go, away yonder, into the dark."

Reginald looked down at her from the serene height of his abbacy.

"Daughter," he said at last, with no sententiousness, "go, and God pity you. It is better that this should end. Yet, wait till the day comes. You would lose your way on a night such as this."

"I will wait, lord," she answered, utterly humble because of his kindness, and her own poignant shame.

When Abbot Reginald returned through the gate in the thorn hedge, Dom Silvius's voice hissed at him out of the darkness, for the cold had sharpened a venomous tongue.

"The jade, has she confessed?"

Reginald was possessed by a sudden unchristian lust to smite Dom Silvius across the mouth.

"My son," he said very quietly, "take care how you cast stones."

And he was more cold to Silvius on the homeward way than the breath of the winter wind.

But Silvius, that dreamer of dreams, that most mundane monk, who thought more of the jewels crusting a reliquary than the Cross of Christ, did a vile and a mean thing that night. Denise, poor child, was to slip away, so Reginald said, at dawn; but Reginald did not tell Dom Silvius that he had left money on the stones whereon she knelt. And Silvius, still venomous because he deemed himself befooled, took pains to betray Denise's secret going. And the method of the betrayal was the meanest trick of all.

When he had seen Abbot Reginald safe within the Abbey, he called two servants and went out with a basket of victuals to visit certain of the sick poor. That the hour was a strange one for such charity counted for nothing with Silvius whose head was full of the ferment of his spite. Many of the folk had gone to their beds, but some few he found still lingering about the covered embers on the hearth.

It was counted for holiness to Silvius that he should come on God's errand at such an hour.

"Feed my sheep," the Lord had said.

And Silvius fed certain of them that night with hypocritical humilities, shaking his head sadly, and dropping a few treacherous words like crumbs into mouths that hungered.

CHAPTER XXII

A red, wintry dawn was in the east when Denise stood ready for her flight from the Abbey lands, her rabbit-skin cloak about her, and the hood drawn over her head. She had knotted the money that Reginald had given her into a corner of her under tunic, and the food that she had saved from yesterday she carried wrapped in a clean cloth. Denise had thought of seeking Grimbald, but her heart had failed her at the thought of meeting the familiar faces of the people who had looked upon her as something superhumanly pure and wonderful. The passion that obsessed her for the moment was the passion to escape from the inquisitive eyes of those who knew her, and to slip away into the world where she would be nothing more than a mere woman.

A robin twittered on the thorn hedge as she left the cell and, crossing the grass, went out by the wicket gate. The land was white with hoar frost, each twig and blade beautiful to behold, and the arch of the east red with an angry dawn. The hills looked big and blue, and very sombre, and in the north the sky had an opaqueness as of coming snow.

The brittle silence of a frosty morning seemed unbroken as yet, and Denise, after looking half fearfully about her, came out from the shadow of the thorn hedge, and walked quickly in the direction of the road. She would be away and over the Abbey bounds before anyone knew in the town that she had gone. Reaching the road, she climbed down the path into it, for the road ran in a hollow there. A bramble had caught the latchet of her shoe and pulled it loose, and Denise bent down to refasten it, putting the cloth with the food on the bank beside her.

Now Dom Silvius's treachery had betrayed her to the people, and Denise, as she fastened her shoe-latchet, was startled by a shrill, gaggling laugh that seemed to rise out of the ground close to her. The banks on either side of the road were covered with furze bushes, and a number of these bushes were suddenly endowed with the miraculous power of movement. They rose up from where they had grown, and came jigging down the steep banks into the road.

Moreover these same furze bushes burst into loud laughter, and began to crow with exultation.

"A miracle, a miracle!"

"St. Denise has worked a wonder, at last!"

"Holy virgin, see how the bushes dance!"

Denise stood still at the foot of the bank, and the furze bushes came jigging round her like mummers in a mask. Flapping skirts and shuffling feet gave a human undercurrent to the green swirl of the furze. Now and again she saw a red, triumphant face, or a pair of brown arms holding a bough, while the frolic went on with giggles and little screams of laughter. Then, at a given shout from one of them, these women of the winter dawn flung their furze boughs upon Denise, as the Sabines threw their shields upon Tarpeia.

The thorns were as nothing compared with that circle of coarse and jeering faces that stood revealed. Old hags with white hair, skinny arms, and flat bosoms; women in their prime, rough and buxom, with hard features and loud mouths; young girls, whose tongues were pert and insolent. Bridget, the smith's wife, led this wolf pack, like a hungry and red-eyed dam.

Denise's face was bleeding, but she did not flinch now that her pride had been driven against the pricks. She looked round at the women, holding her head high, although they had beaten her across the face. And for the moment the women hung back from her as she pushed the furze boughs aside, and made as though to pass on without answering a word.

Bridget, the smith's wife, stood in her path. She flung up her head and laughed like a great raw-boned mare, and an echo came down from Mountjoye Hill like the answering neigh of a horse. On the ridge above, where the dawn light shone, were crowded the men who had come out to see their women bait Denise.

Bridget began the savage game with a word that brought the blood to Denise's face. The women shrieked with delight. Taunts struck her on every side as they crowded close on her, gloating, screaming, their mouths full of cursing and derision. They began to shake their fists, and to stretch their claws towards her, and the smell of their bodies was in her nostrils.

Bridget swung forward, and spat in her face.

"She would work miracles, this jade, this wanton! Where is my boy, you minion? Answer me that, I say!"

"Where is your man, eh?"

"We know him, we know him! Let him show his face here!"

"Look at her, the pretty jade!"

"Spoil her beauty. Strip her naked."

"Out with the harlot. Let her freeze."

Warts, Sterility, and fifty more were howling about her, drunk with the very noise they made. For a moment Denise stood white-faced in the midst of them. Then she disappeared in a swirl of coarse and violent movement, like a deer that is dragged down and smothered beneath the brown bodies of the wolves.

The road that morning was a martyr's way as the redness of the dawn waned and the sky became cold and grey. Mouths spat upon her, hands smote her, and clutched at her clothes. Buffeted at every step, jostled, and torn, she was brought to the boundary of the Abbey *leuga*, and driven out thence into the world. The women even caught up stones and pelted her when they had let her go, screaming foul words, and laughing in loud derision.

Denise was as dazed and as exhausted as though she had been wrecked, and washed ashore half dead by some lucky wave. Her face was bruised and bleeding, her clothes in tatters, her tunic torn open so that her bosom showed. She drew her ragged clothes about her, and went unsteadily down the road, with the cries of the women still following her as she went. Denise's pride made a last brave spreading of its wings. It carried her beyond the sound of those voices, though her feet dragged, and her knees gave under her, and a kind of blindness filled her brain.

Perhaps she struggled on for a mile or more before she turned aside, and lay down under some hazels beside the road. And as she lay there, dull-eyed, grey-faced, and still half dazed, the power to think came back like the sense of reviving pain. Horror of herself and of the world took hold of her by the throat. It was as though those women had spat upon her soul, and made her revolt from herself as from something unclean. Those mocking faces symbolised the mercies of her sister women. All those who knew the truth would scoff, and draw away their skirts. She was an outcast, a thing whose name might broider a lewd tale.

Denise was no ignorant child, but a grown woman, yet she was weak and in pain, and her very weakness made her anguish the more poignant. She lay there a long while under the hazels, not noticing the cold, nor the sodden soil, for her heart seemed colder than the frost. Life held its helpless, upturned palms to the unknown. What use was there in living? God had deserted her, and had suffered her innocence to be put to shame. She was too weary, too miserable even for bitterness or for rebellion. Inert despair had her, body and soul.

Presently a boy came along the road towards Battle, driving an ass laden with paniers full of bread. Close to the spot where Denise lay under the hazels, the ass was taken with the sulks, and stood obstinately still. The boy tugged at the bridle, shouted, thwacked the beast with his stick, but make her budge he could not. Denise sat up and watched him, this piece of byplay thrusting a wedge between her and the apathy of despair.

The boy was a sturdy youngster, with brown face, brown smock, and brown legs splashed with mud. He rubbed his nose with a brown hand, and catching sight of Denise, took her to be a beggar, and perhaps a bit of a witch.

"Hi, there," he shouted, "give over frightening the beast."

"It is none of my doing," she said, surprised somehow at the sound of her own voice.

"She stopped here, none of your tricks, old lady," said the boy.

Denise put back her hood, and the youngster stared.

"Lord," said he, "you have been fighting, and you are not old, neither!"

His curiosity was curtailed by the curiosity of the ass, who took to kicking, sending sundry loaves rolling on the road.

"Hi, there, come and help."

Denise rose up, and went towards the struggling pair. She took the bridle from the boy, and began to pull the donkey's ears, to rub her poll, and talk to her as though she were a refractory child. The beast grew suddenly docile, and the bread was saved.

Denise helped the boy to pick up the loaves. He looked hard at her when they had refilled the paniers, and then offered one of the loaves to Denise.

"Take it," he said almost roughly, yet with the brusqueness of a boy's good-will.

"It will be missed."

The boy gave a determined shake of the head.

"Father's bread. The jade served him the same trick last week, kicked the loaves on to a dung heap. He can't blame me."

He thrust the loaf into Denise's hand, gave her a friendly grin, and cut the ass viciously across the hind-quarters with his stick. The response on the beast's part was a wild and hypocritical amble.

This simple adventure on the road heartened Denise in very wonderful fashion, even as the voice of a child may interpose between a man and murder. It was like a mouthful of wine in the mouth of one ready to faint upon a journey. Denise watched the boy disappear, hardly thinking that she had been saved from despair by the obstinacy of an ass. She had the loaf in her hand and the boy's smile in remembrance, and the mocking voices of the morning seemed less shamefully persistent.

Denise broke and ate some of the bread, and finding a ditch near with a film of ice covering it, she broke the ice with her shoe, and soaking one corner of her tunic in the water, she washed the blood from her mouth and face. It was then that she found the money that Abbot Reginald had given her still knotted up in her clothes. And these two things, the bread and the money, comforted her with the thought that she was not utterly forgotten of God. Both blessings had come to her by chance, but when a soul is in the deeps it catches the straws that float to it, and believes them Heaven-sent.

Despite her wounds and her bruisings Denise walked five miles before noon. The passion to escape from familiar faces and to sink into the outer world, had revived in her. She skirted Robertsbridge and its Abbey, crossing the Rother stream by a footbridge that she found. On the hill beyond she met a pedlar travelling with his pack, and taking out a piece of money bought a rough brown smock from him, a needle and some thread. About noon she found some dry litter under the shelter of a bank of furze. She put on her brown smock, and mended her cloak, and then despite the January cold, such an utter weariness came upon her that she fell asleep.

When Denise awoke it was with a rush of misery into the mind, a misery so utter that she wished herself asleep again, even sleeping the sleep of death. She was so stiff with the cold and her rough handling that it hurt her to move, and the infinite forlornness of her waking made her shudder. Something soft touched her face, like the drifting petal of apple blossom out of the blue. A wind had risen and was whistling through the furze bushes, and buffeting them to and fro. The sky had grown very sullen. Snow was beginning to fall.

Denise dragged herself up and drew her cloak closer about her. She must find shelter for the night somewhere, unless she wished to tempt death in the snow. Yet she had gone but a short way along the road when a sudden spasm of pain seized her, pain such as she had never felt before.

Denise stood still, clenching her hands, her eyes full of a questioning dread. The spasm passed, and she went on again slowly, the flakes of snow drifting about her, the sky and the landscape a mournful blur. She had walked no more than a furlong when the same pain seized her, making her catch her breath and stand quivering till the spasm had passed. Nor was it the pain alone that filled her with a sense of infinite helplessness and dread. The birth of a new and terrible consciousness seemed to grip and paralyse her heart. She knew by instinct that which was upon her, a state that called up a new world of shame and tenderness and fear.

Denise went on again, a woman laden with the simple and primitive destiny of a woman. It so happened that she came to a wood beside the road, and at the edge of the wood under the bare branches of the trees she saw a lodge built of faggots, and roofed with furze and heather. The place seemed God-sent in her necessity, and her anguish of soul and body. Denise found it empty, save for a mass of dry bracken piled behind some faggots in one corner of the lodge. The place had a rough door built of boughs. Denise closed it, and hid herself in the far corner of the lodge, sinking deep into the bed of bracken. The pangs were upon her, and all the dolour and the foreboding that take hold of a woman's heart.

It was bitter cold that night, and the snow came driving from the north, a ghost mist that wrapped the world in a garment of mystery. The wind roared in the trees whose bare boughs clapped together, creaking and chafing amid the roaring of the storm. It was a night when sheep would die of the cold, or be smothered in the snow drifts banked against the hedges.

The sky began to clear about dawn, patches of blue showing between ragged masses of grey cloud. The sun shone out fitfully at first, flashing upon a white world, upon a world of brilliant snow schemes and glittering arabesques, with the wood's sweeps of black shadow across a waste of white.

The wind had dropped, and there was the silence of snow everywhere, not a voice, not a sound, save the occasional creaking of a rotten bough and the swish of its falling snow. The sun climbed higher, and the whiteness of the world became a pale and blinding glare.

Now, the silence of the wilderness was broken that morning by a slow and steady sound that grew on the still air. It was the muffled beat of hoofs upon the snow of the road that ran southwards along the ridge of the hill. Presently the snorting of the horse, jingle of metal and the creaking of leather were added to the plodding of the hoofs. A man's voice rang out suddenly into a burst of song. The white world was glorious in the sunshine, marble and lapis lazuli, with flashes here and there of gold.

The muffled beat of hoofs ceased by the wood where stood the lodge built of faggots. The snow was virgin about it, and the man turned his horse towards the wood, swung out of the saddle, and began kicking the snow aside as though to give the beast a chance of cropping the grass. Taking wine and meat from a saddlebag, he brushed the snow from a log that lay outside the lodge, and sat down to make a meal.

And as he sat there in the sun he talked to his horse, and gave the beast some of the bread from his own breakfast. The horse nosed against him like a dog, its breath steaming up into the frosty air, its eyes the colour of sapphires seen against the snow. And there were no sounds save the man's voice, the breathing of his horse, and the dripping from the boughs as the snow thawed in the sun.

In due course the man remounted, and rode off down the road with the morning sunlight upon his face. Cowering on the bracken in the lodge Denise lay dazed, and weary, hands and feet numb with the cold. She had prayed to God that the man might not enter the place, and find her there on her bed of bracken. He had been so near to her that she had been able to hear the sound of his breathing, and even the breaking of the crust of the bread.

Beside her on the bracken lay a white thing that neither moved nor uttered a cry. Denise lay and stared at it, half with dread and mute wonder, half with a passion of primeval tenderness that was too deep for tears. And as Aymery rode away from her into the morning, she kept her vigil beside that innocent thing that did not whimper and did not move. The snow and the secret silence thereof seemed part of her life that morning, and the eyes of the world were full of a questioning mist of tears.

CHAPTER XXIII

Aymery went riding southwards over the snow, a cloak of furs over his harness, and the leather flaps of his steel cap turned down to cover cheeks and ears. He rode alone, for though the gilt spurs were at his heels, his purse saw little of the colour of gold, and his horse and his arms were all that he had.

There was peace in the land that January, for men had put up their swords, and delivered their quarrel into the hands of the King of France. It was the month of the Mise of Amiens, when Louis, Saint and King, sat to judge between Henry of England and his people. Men trusted in that Holy Heart, that Flame of Sacred Chivalry, that had brought peace to France, and given God martyrs on Egyptian sands. But Louis was a King judging between a King and turbulent towns and still more turbulent barons. Nor was it strange, therefore, that a saint, from whose mouth should have sprouted an olive branch, hurled back over the sea a two-edged sword.

A truce had been called, and with the sheathing of his sword, Aymery had seized the chance and the time to ride southwards into Sussex. Goldspur manor house was a black ruin, but the manor folk were there, with Grimbald to see that an absent lord was not forgotten. No forfeiture had been proclaimed, and Aymery had saddled his horse Necessity, and ridden to see whether his villeins and cottars were honest men. Aymery had left no steward over them, but Grimbald was more to be trusted than any steward; no one would play him any tricks.

Aymery's road ran a devious way that January morning, the road of a man who galloped ten miles out of his path for the glimpse of a woman's face. And Aymery rode wilfully towards Battle, though Goldspur lay over and away beyond the white hills in the west.

About noon Aymery let his horse take his own pace up the hill from Watlingtun. The slope of Mountjoye seemed one sweep of virgin snow, and Aymery, looking for Denise's cell, marked it out above the thicket of oaks where he had kept his vigil that summer night. When he came to the place where the path should turn aside from the road, he saw a muddy and much trampled track leading over the snow towards the cell with its hedge of thorns. It looked to Aymery as though the whole countryside had made a pilgrimage to Denise of the Hill. He followed the path in turn, giving Denise her glory with the sadness of a man who cherishes an impossible desire.

The ground about the gate in the thorn hedge had been trampled into a quagg of mud as though many people had passed to and fro that morning. Aymery dismounted, and threw his bridle over the gate post, numbering himself among those who had come for Denise's blessing. But the sight he saw startled him not a little, for there was no benediction to be won there that morning.

The door of the cell stood open, and before it, in the middle of a space of trampled snow, two of the Abbey servants were heaping up straw and faggots as though for a fire. The trampling of Aymery's horse had been deadened by the snow, the men had not heard it, and he stood at the gate, watching them and wondering what this meant. The two men went to and fro into Denise's cell, carrying out the wooden bed, the straw, and the sheets thereof, her prayer stool, and cross, and other lesser things, for Silvius in his first ardour had seen her better housed than a mere recluse. The men piled everything upon the faggots, and then stood aside in silence as though waiting for someone's coming.

Aymery tarried no longer, but marched out from the shadow of the thorn hedge, a voice crying in him: "Can it be that she is dead?" The two servants saw him, and for some strange reason began to handle their staves, while one of them went to the door of the cell, and spoke to someone within.

Dom Silvius and Aymery came face to face outside Denise's cell that morning, for the monk had been within, watching the unclean things carried out for the burning. He came out with a lighted torch in his hand, ready with canonical curses, hot and hungry for the chance of scolding the whole world. But when Silvius saw Aymery, he seemed to grow cold of a sudden, and thin with a malicious carefulness.

For Silvius saw the hauberk and the gilt spurs, the long sword at the girdle, the shield slung across the back, the shoulder plates painted with a knight's device, the golden claw of a hawk. And Silvius sprang to sinister conclusions with the intuition of a woman. Here, no doubt, was the woman's paramour, some hot-headed gentleman who had ridden in to discover how things fared with Denise.

Silvius took no notice of the Knight of the Hawk's Claw, but plunged his torch into the straw, and watched the flames spring up and seize the wood. The smoke rose straight up into the still air, turning to a pearly haze as the sunlight touched it. The monk stood there, with bowed head and folded arms, as though too busy with his own prayers to be troubled by any stranger. But prayer was very far from Silvius's soul. His eyes were wide awake under their lowered lids.

Aymery came two steps nearer. Silvius raised his head and looked at him, and saw at a glance the face of a man who was not to be repulsed or fooled.

"Whom may you be seeking, my son?" he asked, watching Aymery out of the corners of his eyes.

The Knight of the Hawk's Claw turned his head towards the cell. Silvius seemed to enjoy an inaudible chuckle.

"Perhaps you have come for a blessing, messire?"

As yet Aymery had not spoken a word, but Silvius read his thoughts by the puzzled frown and the alert eyes.

"Ah, my son," he went on, beginning to sneer, "you are wondering what has become of our saint."

Aymery looked from Silvius to the flames that were leaping through the wood.

"Has death been here?"

Silvius's eyes were netted round with cynical wrinkles.

"Assuredly your saint is both dead and alive," he said. "Some of you gentlemen have slain the saint in her. I will not ask you, my son, whether the guilt of the sacrilege is yours."

His sly, sneering face made Aymery's manhood grow hot in him. He was in no temper for sardonic subtleties. Silvius saw a look in his eyes that betrayed a lust to take someone by the throat. And Silvius kept the fire between him and the man of the sword, nodding to the two servants, and hinting without deceit that they should be ready with their staves.

"My son," he said, licking his lips; "we are burning the unclean relics of an unclean woman. If you ask me for reasons, I send you to my lord, Reginald, at the Abbey. His word is law here. I am but a humble servant in God's house."

Aymery looked Silvius in the eyes, and then turned on his heel, with a face like ice. He mounted his horse, and went up Mountjoye Hill at a canter, choosing to gallop at the core of the truth rather than suffer Dom Silvius to lick his lips and sneer. Nor had horse and rider disappeared below the sky line before Silvius called the two servants to him, gave them their orders, and sent them away into the town. He himself tarried there awhile, warming his hands at the fire that consumed those relics of an unsaintly saint.

When Aymery came out from the presence of Reginald of Brecon that day his face had the frozen bleakness of a winter land. He walked stiffly, almost rigidly, with nostrils that twitched, and hungered for air. The Abbey servants fell back before him as he mounted his horse at the gate. Here was a man who was not to be meddled with. His face sobered them more than the face of a leper.

Aymery struck his horse with the spurs, and the beast leapt his own length, stood quivering a moment, and then went away at a sharp gallop as though he had the devil on his back. Aymery's eyes looked straight before him, eyes that caught the white glare of an inward fury, and were blind to the outer world. The snow lay white upon the roofs of the little town. Smoke ascended tranquilly into a shimmer of sunlight.

Aymery was not to ride out of Battle town at his own pace; Dom Silvius had seen to that. At the sound of a horn a crowd of figures seemed to start from nowhere; men, women, and children came running together; the whole wasps' nest was on the wing.

Aymery drew up sharply, for the crowd in front of him filled the street. He did not grasp the meaning of it at first, but stared round at the people as though he were but a chance actor in some chance scene. A stone thrown from the crowd carried a rude hint, striking him upon the shield that hung at his back. And with the throwing of the first stone the whole mob sent up a sudden roar of anger.

"Out, out, seducer!"

"Pelt the sacrilegious dog!"

"Here is Dame Denise's man, neighbours."

"Drag him off."

"Roll him in the mud."

The uproar and the fury of the fools might have dazed any man for the moment. The crowd came tossing about Aymery's horse, keeping a coward's distance, content as yet with stones, and filth, and curses. Thorn-in-the-Thumb and her women were there, obscene and violent, howling like cats, and urging the men on. Some of them cut coarse capers, leering up into the knight's face.

Aymery sat still in the saddle for a moment, looking neither to right nor left. His lips were white and pressed hard together, his eyes full of that shallow glare that fills the eyes of an angry dog. The yelling and distorted faces began to close upon him. A stone thrown by a man near struck Aymery upon the mouth.

Blood showed, but with it a blaze of wrath so terrible and yet so silent, that hands which were uplifted did not fling their stones. Aymery's sword was out. He struck his beast with the spurs, and rode straight into the thick of the crowd. And though he smote only with the flat of the blade, they tumbled over each other in their hurry to give him room, while those who were safe stood open-mouthed, staring like stupid sheep.

Aymery rode through them as he would have ridden through a cornfield, swinging his sword, and laughing, the terrible laughter of a man who has no pity. No sooner did the rabble see his back, than their courage came again, the courage of dogs that yap at a horse's heels. They scampered after him, shouting, screaming, pelting him as they ran. Thorn-in-the-Thumb, with a bloody poll from the flat of Aymery's sword, panted along with the very first, her apron full of filth that she had brought with her from her kitchen, and kept gloatingly until too late. But Aymery never turned his head, and leaving the slobbering pack behind, rode at a canter out of Battle town.

CHAPTER XXIV

One day early in March when dust and dead leaves were whirling everywhere, old Fulcon the baker, the meanest man—so it was said—in Reigate town, went to and fro along the passage beside his house, carrying in faggots that had been unloaded from a tumbril in the street. The carter had thrown the wood against the wall, knowing that Fulcon would not give him so much as a mug of water for helping to carry the faggots into the shed behind the bakehouse.

Fulcon went to and fro along the passage like a brown crab, a man whose back seemed built for burdens, and whose bowed legs and hairy chest gave promise of great strength. He carried the faggots two at a time, and neighbours who loitered to watch him at work saw nothing but the sheaves of wood crawling along upon a knotty pair of legs. The boys of Reigate, who hated the baker because he had good apple trees and used a stick vigorously in defending the fruit, called him "tortoise," and "snail in the shell." Sometimes a boy would make a dash and pretend to try the snatching of a loaf from the stone counter of the little shop. But Fulcon had a dog who was as surly and as wide awake as his master. Nor was it to be wondered at that dog Ban had a sour temper, since the number of stones that were surreptitiously thrown at him would have paved the path in old Fulcon's garden.

The baker had come near the end of the load, and had disappeared up the passage, leaving the last two faggots lying on the footway. He came back, picking up the odd bits of stick that littered the stones. A bent body seemed such a habit with Fulcon that his eyes often saw nothing more than the two yards of mother earth before his feet. Hence he had already laid a hand to one of the remaining faggots before he saw the grey folds of a cloak spread out under his very nose.

Fulcon straightened up, and showed his natural attitude towards the world by closing a big brown fist. He saw a woman sitting upon one of the faggots, a woman in a grey cloak with the hood drawn over her head. The woman's back was turned to him, and by the stoop of her shoulders she seemed very tired.

Fulcon took her for a beggar, and Fulcon hated beggars even more than boys.

"Get up," said he.

And since she did not stir he repeated the command.

"Get up, there," and he reached out to take her by the cloak.

The woman rose, and overtopped Fulcon by some five inches. She turned and looked at him with great brown eyes that seemed tired with the dust and the wind. The baker stared hard at her, catching the gleam of splendid hair drawn back under the grey hood. The woman's face had a silence such as one sees on the face of a statue.

"The wood's mine," he said, grumbling into his beard, and pointing a very obvious finger.

The woman looked at him, and then at the shop.

"I want bread," she answered.

Fulcon's eyes retorted "pay for it."

The woman had a leather bag in her hand. She felt in it, and brought out money. Fulcon's frown relaxed instantly. He stooped under the wooden shutter propped up by its bar, picked up a loaf, and handed it to her.

To his astonishment she sat down again on the faggot, as though she had a right there now that she had bought the loaf. Fulcon opened his shrewd but rather sleepy eyes wider, and stared. The words "get up" were again on the tip of his tongue. But he smothered them, picked up the other faggot, and giving a warning whistle to the dog Ban who was lying in the shop, went away up the narrow passage.

When Fulcon returned, he stared still harder, for the dog Ban was sitting with his muzzle resting on the woman's knee, and looking up steadily into her face. She was breaking the bread slowly, and giving the dog a crust from time to time. Fulcon might have reasoned with her over such extravagance, had he not been the creature of a strong affection with regard to the big brown dog, one of the two living things in the world to whom he grudged nothing.

The baker stood by, scratching his beard, something very much like a smile glimmering in his eyes. Then he gave a half audible chuckle as though the scene seemed peculiarly quaint.

The woman turned her head, but Fulcon's face was as blank as a piece of brown sandstone. He looked indeed as though he had never uttered a sound in his life. Dog Ban lifted his head and stared at his master as though it was unusual for Fulcon to chuckle.

The woman asked a question.

"How far is it to Guildford?"

Fulcon jerked his head like a wooden doll worked by string.

"Guildford? It may be eighteen miles," and he reconsidered the number carefully as though he were handing out loaves.

The woman laid a hand on the dog's head.

"I am tired," she said suddenly. "I want a lodging."

"A lodging."

Fulcon always echoed a neighbour's sentences, a trick that suggested caution, and a desire to gain time for reflection.

"There are hostels in the town," he said.

"No."

"There are hostels in the town."

"No," and yet again she repeated the blunt monosyllable "no."

Fulcon echoed the "no," and stared hard at the opposite wall.

Ban opened his mouth suddenly, and laughed as a dog can laugh on occasions. It was as though the matter was so absurdly simple that he was tickled by the way these humans bungled it.

Fulcon caught the dog's eye. Ban's laughter had been silent, his master's came with a human gurgle.

"You want a lodging?" and he approached the question as something wholly new and astonishing, a matter that had never been previously mentioned.

"I can pay."

"You can pay."

The woman put back her hood, and gave Fulcon a full view of her face. Perhaps he felt what Ban had felt, for there was something in the woman's eyes that made both these surly dogs quite debonair.

"I should give you no trouble," she said simply. "I have had trouble enough to teach me to be contented."

Fulcon nodded.

"Trouble," he agreed. "There are many things that bring trouble, more especially such a thing as a King."

"My trouble began with the King," she said.

"Ah, to be sure; his men took all my bread one day last year, and I had not so much as a farthing."

His voice grumbled down in the bass notes, and Ban sympathised with a growl.

The woman felt in her bag.

"I can pay you," she said, "a little. I can work, too, if you wish it."

Fulcon narrowed his eyes suspiciously, and looked at Ban as though for advice. The dog wagged his tail. That wag of the tail decided it.

"Come up and see," he said. "I have a little room under the roof."

And all three went in together, Fulcon, the dog, and Denise.

Whether it was Ban's friendship, or Fulcon's complacency in turning a good penny by letting his attic, Denise tarried there in the baker's house, glad to find a corner in the world where she could rest awhile in peace. Fulcon lived quite alone, though an old woman came in now and again to cook, clean, and sew. The house was of stone, and roofed also with flags of stone, because of sparks from the bakehouse furnace. The upper room where Denise lodged was reached by an outside stairway from the yard. There was a small garden and orchard shut in by the walls and gable ends of other houses. As for Fulcon he lived in his bakery behind the shop, he and Ban sleeping together in one corner like two brown dogs curled up in a heap. Often there was baking to be done at night, and then Fulcon dozed in the shop by day, the dog keeping an eye open for customers, boys, and thieves.

It is one of the facts of life that gruff and surly people are more to be trusted than those with burnished faces and ready tongues, and so it turned out with old Fulcon. For Denise found him steady and honest. The neighbours declared that Fulcon was a miser. True, he worked like a brown gnome, round-backed, laborious, and silent. No man baked bread better than Fulcon; nor had he ever sold short weight.

So Denise found herself tarrying day after day in the town under the chalk hills, where the beech woods clambered against the sky, and life seemed still and quiet. Though Earl Simon had taken Reigate the year before, no memory of violence and of bloodshed seemed to linger there, and the valley amid the hills waited peacefully for the spring.

Denise had come very near to death that year, and the heart in her still carried a deep and open wound. She had changed, too, in those few weeks. Her glorious hair was growing long again, and her eyes had a more miraculous sadness. She was thinner in face, yet plumper at the bosom. Some people might have discovered an indefinable air about her, a subtle, human something that was not to be seen on the face of a nun.

A great gulf had opened for Denise between the present and the past, and what her thoughts and emotions were, only a woman could understand. She had lost something of herself, and there was a void of tenderness and yearning in her that hungered to be filled. A chance touch of kindness could melt her almost to tears. She was very silent, and very gentle. Even the dog Ban was something to be loved and fondled, and in winning Ban she won old Fulcon, that brown gnome who toiled and hoarded, hoarded and toiled.

One day he called Denise from her upper room, and showed her the door that led into the garden. Within were herb beds, brown soil turned for planting vegetables, and a stretch of grass where the apple and pear trees grew.

"Grass turns white under a stone," he said in his grumbling way. "You will see more of the sun here."

And Denise was grateful to the old man, and she went down into the orchard of an evening, and heard the blackbirds sing.

Old Fulcon had taken a fancy to Denise. He began to look upon her as a house chattel that was familiar, and even as a possession to be treasured. She was silent and gentle, and Fulcon was silent and gentle under that gruff, ugly, and laborious surface. Denise paid him her money, and though Fulcon took it, he kept it apart from the hoard he had in a secret hole in the wall.

"Times are hard, dog Ban," he would say sulkily. "Only a priest takes a child's last pence."

Ban would approve, knowing that his master was less mean than he seemed.

"Be sure, it is no common wench, dog Ban. Noble folk fall into the ditch, as well as beggars. She may be a great lady, who knows? No kitchen girl ever had such hands."

So Denise tarried there, and old Fulcon seemed quite content that she should tarry, and even began to show less reticence and caution. Old men are often like children; they turn to some people, and run from others. Nor was it long before Denise discovered why the baker toiled and hoarded as he did.

Fulcon had an idol, an idol that fed upon the father's gold, and that idol was a son. Denise heard of him as a big, black-eyed, tan-faced sworder who had run away to the wars before the down was on his chin. Fulcon's boy had swaggered, fought, and shouldered his way up hill. He rode a great horse now, wore mail, and carried a long spear. He earned good pay in the service of those who hired such gentlemen, even had men under him, and was a great captain in his father's eyes.

"God of me, child," he would say, "the boy was a giant from the day his mother bore him! I can stand under his arm, so," and he would show Denise how his head did not reach to his son's shoulder.

"The handsome dog, he must have money," and Fulcon chuckled and rubbed his hands, "there is not a finer man at his arms in the whole kingdom than Hervé. He has fought as champion often, and no man can stand up to him. Lord, child, and the way some of the ladies have shown him kindness, but that is not a matter for your ears. Hervé must have money, the handsome dog! A lad of such promise must live like the gentleman he may be."

Then Fulcon waxed mysterious, and looked at Denise with cunning pride.

"I have not given him all my money, oh no, I am wiser than that, I bide my time. For though I have never dreamt it, my dear, I know that some day Hervé will win the spurs. Lesser men have fought their way to it. And then, child, the old baker of Reigate will come out with a store of gold. Arms, and rings, and rich clothes shall the lad have. He shall not be put to shame for lack of the proper gear."

Denise was touched by the old man's love for his son, and also by the trust he showed her in telling her such a thing. For to one who had been driven out into the world with shame and ignominy, such human faith is very dear. Denise might be touched by old Fulcon's pride, but whether she believed Messire Hervé worthy of it was quite another matter. The fellow was probably a gallant rogue, with wit enough to possess himself of the old man's gold. It seemed strange to her that Fulcon, who was so shrewd and grim, should be dazzled by gaudy trappings, a loud presence, and a handsome face.

Denise had at least found peace in the little town, a time of tranquillity that stood between her and despair. She had space there for quiet breathing, and no fear for the moment but the fear of a chance betrayal. She needed sleep and strength before the march into the future, that future that seemed as dim and formless as a strange and distant land. Her heart seemed doomed to lose the very memory of a most dear dream. If she thought of Aymery she thought of him as a man who had made her soul thrill in past years, and was dead. Her vows were broken, but what did that avail? The past was dead also, after what had happened.

One evening late in March, Fulcon came to her in the garden, and she could tell that he was troubled.

"The bloody sword is out again," he said. "Bah, I thought they would let us have peace awhile. The accursed Frenchman has thrown poison into the pot."

Denise was ignorant of much that had passed in the world around. She knew nothing of the Mise, and of the blight that had fallen on the Barons' cause. Pope Urban, good man, upheld King Henry in the breaking of oaths and the casual selfishness of misrule. Time-servers and waverers were going over to the King, because of the award St. Louis had made. Yet Simon had carried his head high, and acted in all honour, he and the chief lords who were with him. They had surrendered Dover, and prepared to treat loyally with Henry about the Mise.

Now news had come into the town that the firebrands on either side were flaming in arms. Roger Mortimer had ravaged De Montfort's estates on the Welsh marches. There had been skirmishes in the west country. The Earl of Derby had hoisted his banner against the King. Henry himself had issued writs calling his followers to arms on the last day of March. The peacemaking of Louis of France seemed likely to bring on a yet bitterer war.

Fulcon shook his head over it, and grumbled.

"The King pipes the tune, and poor John pays. There will be bloody work again. God give Earl Simon a heavy hand."

And then, as is always the case, he discovered compensations.

"Hervé will have his chance," he said; "how can a soldier show himself without a battle!"

Two days passed, and news came suddenly that Simon the Younger was near at hand, and likely to pass through Reigate on the way. The news set Fulcon all agog, for Hervé followed the Earl of Gloucester's banner, and some said the earl was with young Simon, and Fulcon was as eager as any woman to see his lad. He went out into the town, leaving Denise and Ban to look to the loaves in the shop. And while Fulcon was away De Montfort's son marched into Reigate with a following of knights and men-at-arms.

Denise saw the people running to and fro like ants in a nest that have been stirred up with a stick. A crowd began to gather, an anxious, whispering, restless crowd, uneasy as a wood under the first puffs of a threatening storm. For armed men in a town were too often the devil's retainers, were they friends or foes.

The sound of shouting came from one of the gates, with the blare of trumpets.

"Simon is here!"

The news spread, and men who had wives and daughters, pushed them within doors, bidding them look through cracks in the shutters if they must look at all. A knight came riding by, carrying a black banner with a white cross thereon. A few stray dogs ran hither and thither, to be hooted, and pelted by the boys in the crowd. Then suddenly, with the thunder of hoofs along the street, came the clangour of young Simon's company, their spears set close together like black masts in a haven.

Denise stood at the door of Fulcon's shop, with Ban bristling and snarling beside her. A splendid knight on a white horse rode in the van. His helmet was off, and he laughed, and looked about him as he rode with a certain good-humoured vanity. Beside him, mounted on a black mare, Denise saw a woman in silks of blue and green, and a cloak of sables over her shoulders.

The way was narrow, and the crowd greatest just by the baker's shop. Simon the Younger reined in his horse, holding his spear at arms length as a sign to those behind him to halt.

"Room, good people," he said, gracious and debonair. "We are not here to trample on honest men's toes."

Denise's eyes met the eyes of the woman who rode at young De Montfort's side. And in that look the shame of the near past leapt up into Denise's face, for the lady in the cloak of sables was the woman who had ridden with Gaillard and Peter of Savoy the day they dragged Aymery from her cell.

Etoile's black eyes had flashed as they stared at Denise's face. She also had not forgotten. And once again she looked down upon Denise, and mocked her with lifted chin, and laughing mouth.

The street had cleared, and Simon and Etoile went riding on together, with spear and shield following along the narrow street. Denise had drawn back into the shadow of the shop, her face still hot with Etoile's sneer. Her shame seemed to have been flung at her like a torch out of the darkness. Denise felt as though it had scorched her flesh. And while she hid herself there, Aymery rode by among young Simon's gentlemen, but Denise neither saw him, nor he her.

Soon Fulcon came back panting, having pushed his way through the crowd in the street. He blessed God and Denise when he saw his bread untouched.

"Five score loaves for Simon's men," he said gloating. "I had the order yonder up at the Cross. Simon is a lord who pays."

Fulcon was very happy, but Denise went to her room above, sorrowful and sad at heart. The peace seemed to have gone suddenly from the place.

Aymery, who had passed so near to her for whom he would have pledged his spurs, served as knight of the guard that evening at De Montfort's lodging. Young Simon and Dame Etoile were very merry together, drinking and laughing into each other's eyes. Aymery distrusted the woman, and feared her power over the earl's son. It always seemed to him that he had seen her face before that night in Southwark, but where, for the life of him, he could not remember.

And as he kept guard in Reigate town that night, he thought of Denise, and of that dolorous thing that had befallen her. The shame of it had not driven her out of Aymery's heart. Little did he guess that he had been so near to her that day.

CHAPTER XXV

Simon the Younger went on his way, and Aymery with him, Aymery whose face had lost some of its youthfulness and caught in its stead the intensity of the life that stirred the passions of those about him. All who had kept troth with Earl Simon after the Mise were men whose hearts were in their cause, and who set their teeth the harder when the odds grew greater against them day by day. Earl Simon's spirit seemed like light reflected from the faces of the stern, strong men who rallied to him. De Montfort had no use for time-servers, or the half-hearted.

"Let them go," he would say; "we want no rotten timber in our house."

When Prince Henry, Richard of Cornwall's son, sought the earl's leave not to bear arms against his father and his uncle, Simon bade him go, and return in arms.

"For," said he with scorn, "I would rather have a bold enemy, than a cock that will crow on neither dunghill."

Then Hugh de Bigot, and Henry de Percy left him, but Simon would not be daunted.

"I, and my sons will stand for England, and the Charter," he said. "I will not go back from my purpose, though I sacrifice my blood, and the blood of my children."

Such was Simon the Earl when fate seemed against him, and such were the men who gathered about him with grim and silent faces, and the determination to go through to the end. Ardour and high purpose were theirs those months. The Mise had purged the cause of slackness and mere self-seeking. The people of England were to read the King a lesson that was never to be forgotten by his masterful and more kingly son.

Some days after Simon the Younger had passed through Reigate, a party of the King's men came riding into the town. They were very insolent and high-handed gentlemen who swore that Reigate was a nest of rebels because the townsmen had lodged Young Simon and his following, and given them food. None other than Gaillard commanded this company, Gaillard who was furious over the news that a spy had brought him, the news that Etoile had won young Simon as a lover. Gaillard spared neither tongue nor fist in Reigate. These fat pigs of English should be bled in return for the way De Montfort had trampled on Gascony.

Gaillard was never so happy as when he could tease and bully. He and his men, who were mostly mercenaries from over the sea, took possession of Reigate, and established themselves strongly there. They terrorised the place, doing much as their passions pleased, taking all they needed, and robbing even the churches. So many of them were drunk at night that had the townsmen showed some enterprise, they could have risen and rid themselves of the whole pack.

Old Fulcon had shut up his shop, and baked only such bread as he could serve out secretly to his neighbours. But Gaillard soon heard of Fulcon's frowardness, and came riding down one morning to see such impudence properly chastened. His men beat in the shutterflap of the shop with their spear staves, and found Fulcon waiting sulkily within.

The baker had shut Ban up in an outhouse, knowing that the dog would show fight, and have a sword thrust through him for his pains. Gaillard's men dragged Fulcon out into the street, and brought him beside the Gascon's horse.

"Hullo, you rogue, how is it that you bake no bread?"

"Because I have no sticks," said Fulcon surlily.

"We will give you the stick, dog, unless you send us thirty loaves daily."

Fulcon shrugged his shoulders.

"I have no flour left," he said, "and no fool will send flour into the town," and he grinned from ear to ear.

Gaillard cursed him.

"What, you goat, you horned scullion, are we to be starved! I will see to it that you have flour and faggots. You shall bake us bread, you dog, or we will bake you in your own oven."

Denise was in her room when Gaillard's men broke into Fulcon's shop. There was no window looking upon the street, and since Denise was no coward and wished to see what was happening to Fulcon, she opened the door and came out upon the stairway. As she stood there, two of Gaillard's men caught sight of her, and began to call to her from the street.

"See there, the old dog has a pretty daughter."

"Hallo, my dear, come down and be kissed."

Gaillard himself turned his horse, and looked up at Denise. And Gaillard knew her, and she, him.

Denise would have fled in and closed the door, but she seemed unable to move, held there by Gaillard's eyes. The man's face had flushed at first, but he covered a moment's sheepishness with a smile like the glitter of sunlight upon brass. Perhaps he saw how Denise shrank from him, and for a woman to shrink from him made Gaillard the more insolent.

"Sweet saint," said he, laughing and looking up at her, "what do we here? Have we grown tired of the beech wood, and Gaffer Aymery, and the Sussex pigs?"

Denise closed her eyes, and stood holding the hand-rail of the stair. She heard Gaillard laugh, and the sound of his horse trampling the flints of the street. When she opened her eyes, he was still there below her. And the sight of the man filled her with such sickness and loathing that she turned her head away as she would have turned her head from some brutal deed.

"Courage, Sanctissima," said he, "only ugly women have no friends. Master Flour and Faggots shall be treated gently for your sake. Speak for me in your prayers."

And he called his men about him, and rode away up the street.

Denise went into her room, and barred the door, and sitting down on the bed, looked with blank eyes at the walls of the room. A sense of utter helplessness possessed her, so that she could neither pray nor think.

So great was her loathing of the man, so poignant her repulsion, that she fell into a fever of unrest that night, and could not sleep because of Gaillard. Denise knew how much pity to expect from a man of Gaillard's nature; bolts and bars would not avail in the town if the Gascon's whim sought her out. She felt driven out again into the world, to hide herself, to escape from the very thought of the touch of Gaillard's hands.

By dawn Denise had made up her mind. She would slip out of the town, and throw herself once more into the unknown. Life had so little promise for her, nor was it in her heart to turn nun after what had passed. She was ready to work as a servant for the sake of a home.

Denise was not destined to leave Reigate town that day, for Fulcon came climbing up the stairs soon after dawn, and knocked softly at her door. He had been at work that night, perforce, baking bread for Gaillard's men, but Fulcon had heard news, news that made him grunt exultingly as he laboured.

"Child," he said, "come down into the garden. I have a word for you."

Denise unbarred her door, and followed Fulcon down the stair. He saw that she was fully dressed, but he said nothing, for Fulcon made a habit of sleeping in his clothes.

When they had gained the garden the baker shook his fist at some invisible figure, but looked very sly and cheerful.

"The Gascon dog, the bully, the thief! They are coming with whips to whip him out of the town."

He went close to Denise, and touched her on the bosom with a thick forefinger.

"Sweeting, I was afraid last night because of that hot-eyed wolf. But last night we had news, we English pigs. Tell me now, can you hear a bell ringing?"

Denise could not.

"No, child, it is Paul's Bell in London City. They are up, the men of London, and have flung the Frenchman's judgment back into his face. 'King stands by King, and cobbler by cobbler. No Mise for us, but the sword of Earl Simon.' Bold lads, let them shout that! London City has risen. Hear the wasps humming. They are on the wing everywhere, stinging fire into Richard the Roman's manors."

Denise had never seen the little brown man so excited before. His taciturnity had become voluble. Dog Ban, sympathetic cur, set up a militant barking.

"This pig of a Gascon knows nothing. We were sick of his wallowings, and we sent out our messengers. To-night the men of London will be here. The Gascon and his fools will be full of mead and wine. We shall open a gate. Then let these foreign dogs die in the gutter."

So Denise said nothing to Fulcon of her intended flight, but chose to bide her time on the chance that Gaillard would be driven out of Reigate. She had found a refuge in the town, and she loved dog Ban, and trusted Fulcon. Where else could she find a surer shelter?

CHAPTER XXVI

Denise kept watch in her room that night, sitting at her window that overlooked the garden. She could hear old Fulcon moving restlessly to and fro below, opening the door of the shop from time to time, and going out into the street to listen. There was a full moon that night, and though the town gleamed white under the chalk hills, the narrow passage-ways and streets were in deep shadow.

About midnight a suggestion of secret stir and movement rose in the town. Denise heard footsteps go stealthily by, as of people creeping along under the shadow of the houses. Men stopped to whisper to one another, and once she heard the sound of a sword dropped on the cobbles. Fulcon had opened his shop door again, for she heard the creak of the hinges. Then silence once more smothered the town, save for an occasional flutter of sound, like the flicker of leaves on a still night in summer.

Half an hour had passed, and Denise had begun to think that nothing was to be done that night, when a burst of shouting rose in the very centre of the town. So loud and sudden was it, that all the dead might have risen with one great and exultant cry, a cry that set the moonlit night vibrating with the thrill of a coming storm.

Then a bell began to ring, quickly, volubly, with an angry clashing to and fro. Denise heard men go rushing by with a clatter of arms, laughter and loud oaths. Soon, the whole town was in an uproar, and old Fulcon, standing in the doorway of his shop, shouted and clapped his hands together.

"Tear them, good lads, tear them."

The wave of war had broken over the town, and went splashing and plunging into every court and corner. Denise opened the door at the top of the outside stair, and stood listening to the roar of the fight, the wall of the next house throwing a black shadow across her and the stair. She could hear shouts and rallying cries, and a sullen under-chant that seemed made up of blows, curses, and the trampling of many feet. Confused and shadowy figures went tearing hither and thither, appearing and disappearing in the moonlight. A wounded and riderless horse galloped by, screaming with terror. Presently the glow of a fire coloured the sky with a blur of yellow light.

Denise was leaning against the jamb of the doorway when she saw a man come running down the street, a naked sword in his hand, his shield held up as though to hide his face. He stopped outside Fulcon's shop, dropping his shield arm, and looking about him cautiously, yet thanks to the deep shadow he did not see Denise. She took him for Gaillard, and was about to shut and bar the door, when she heard Fulcon's voice shrill and thin with an old man's joy.

"Hervé, Hervé!"

The man had disappeared round the angle of the house, and Fulcon dropped his voice to a cautious whisper. The door creaked and closed. Fulcon and the soldier were together in the shop. Denise did not doubt that it was Hervé his son who had come with the Londoners, and such of De Montfort's men who were with them that night.

Denise heard them talking together, the younger man's voice loud and rather aggressive, Fulcon's a mere gentle and deprecating grumble. The son seemed to be asking the father something, Fulcon to be putting Hervé off with reasons and excuses. Before long the younger man's voice changed its tone. It began to plead and to persuade with an insinuating light-heartedness that Denise did not trust. Old Fulcon's grumble became more persuadable. Denise heard a door opened, and then the sound of a man's voice singing.

The singing ceased. For some moments silence held, to be broken by a sudden scuffling noise, and a voice, thick and choking, crying "Hervé, Hervé!" A dog's growl joined in, fierce and threatening, to end in a piteous and wailing whimper. Something seemed to struggle to and fro with inarticulate anguish and horror. Then silence fell. Nothing moved in the room below.

Denise was caught by an impulse that took no account of self and of fear. She went down the stairway and into the street, only to find the door of the shop barred. Her hand was still on the latch when the door opened. The man Hervé came out, huddling something under his surcoat, his sword in the moonlight showing a shadowy smear. He stopped dead on the threshold, staring at Denise, and then pushed past her roughly, and fled up the street.

There was a light burning somewhere behind the shop, probably in the bakehouse where Fulcon and dog Ban lived and slept. Denise went in, wondering what she would find there, nor was she long in discovering Messire Hervé's handiwork. A candle was burning in a sconce on the wall, and close to the great brick oven lay Fulcon, stretched upon his back, one arm covering his face as though to shut out the sight of something, or to break the force of a blow. Ban, in his death agony, had dragged himself to his master, and crouched there with his forepaws on the baker's chest. They were dead, both of them, Fulcon and the dog. A black hole in the wall showed above the place where Fulcon had fallen, and the stone that had closed the hole lay close to the old man's head. Fulcon had hidden his hoard there, the money that he had scraped together with infinite labour for the sake of Hervé his son. Denise could guess what had happened. Fulcon had not been willing to part with the whole sum, because of his dream that Hervé would need it when he came by knighthood. And the son had watched the father go to the hiding-place in the wall, and then had beaten him down, and taken all that he could find.

A great horror of the place seized on Denise, with the two dead things lying there, and the brutal violence of the deed making old Fulcon's end seem pitiful and ugly. The horror of it drew her out into the night, as though to escape the sickly odour of freshly shed blood. Shuddering, she went up to her room, put on her cloak, and tied such money as she had left into a corner of her tunic. The grossness of the deed had shocked her, so that she fled away like a child from a haunted wood, forgetting such a thing as justice, and the fact that her tongue might drop a noose over Master Hervé's head.

Whither she was going, or what her plans were, Denise did not consider for the moment. Blind panic carried her away from a thing that had filled her with pity, and yet with disgust. She seemed hardly conscious of the fact that fighting was still raging in the town. Houses were on fire not fifty yards away, but the scattering sparks and the glare above the house-tops seemed hardly to strike her senses. The burning houses threw up a flare to match the horror that possessed her; such surroundings seemed natural and to be expected after Hervé's slaying and robbing of his father.

Denise found herself at last in an open space where many people were gathered, and torches threw up tawny light under the white face of the moon. Here was much shouting, much running to and fro, much uproar and exultation. Now and again a sword or axe flashed above the black mass of humanity. As Denise came out of the darkness a party of men went charging through, carrying ladders, hatchets, and iron bars. "Room, room," they shouted, for they were bent on stopping the spread of the fire by pulling down some of the flimsy houses.

In the middle of the square sat a knight on horseback, a knot of torches about him, and a pennon fluttering faintly above the smoke. The motion of the crowd seemed towards the knight, as though he were Lord and King of the Play. Denise was caught in the crowd and carried slowly towards the knight on the horse.

He sat there bareheaded, calm and a little grim, the torchlight flickering on his face, and on the harness that glittered under his tawny surcoat. Men went to and fro carrying his commands, figures in red, blue, and green, going and coming through the crowd. He spoke so quietly that at a little distance no one heard his voice, but saw only the lips move in his stern and watchful face.

It was Aymery, lord of Goldspur, Knight of the Hawk's Claw, who had the command of the Londoners who had rushed on Reigate. The crowd carried Denise close to him, within an arm's length of the circle of torches. And with her nearness she seemed suddenly to awake with a great cry of the heart that did not reach her lips.

"Aymery, Aymery!"

Her utter loneliness in the midst of that crowd seemed to her symbolical of the past and of the future. She was just a child that moment, with the passionate and pathetic longing of a child, touched with the deeper instinct of the woman. And by chance Aymery looked straight at Denise, so that it seemed to her that he was looking at her, and at her alone. She did not realise that Aymery could see nothing but a moving mist of faces because of the torch flare and the smoke. His face was so grim and intense, and his eyes so hard, that Denise shrank back, believing that he had recognised her, and that he looked at her as a thing of shame. She hid her face from him with bitterness and humiliation, and crept away into the thick of the crowd.

Of all that happened afterwards that night in Reigate town Denise had but a confused memory. She remembered being hurried along by the crowd, with shouting and tumult in the dark alleyways and streets. She had a memory of being crushed against a group of panting and fiercely exultant men who had blood upon their hot hands and faces. One of them had thrown an arm round her and kissed her, laughing when she shuddered and broke away. Once a couple of heads went dancing by on the points of spears, heads that seemed to mock with dead, open mouths at the jeering crowd below. Men were still fighting in one corner of the town, for Gaillard had got the remnant of his followers together, and was struggling to break through. Denise, still carried onwards, saw a black mass like the mass of a town gate rising before her. She was pressed against a wall as the crowd opened to let a file of mounted men ride through. She saw Aymery in his surcoat of tawny gold go riding under the arch of the gate, shield forward, sword swinging, his men crowding after him like sheep through a gap. Then the rush of the people carried her through the town gate into the space outside the barriers. And when the dawn came she found herself a mile from Reigate town, sitting under a tree, with a cold wind driving grey clouds across an April sky.

CHAPTER XXVII

Said Marpasse to Isoult:

"If the Lord had loved us he would have kept the King at Oxford until we came there to drink wine."

And Isoult, a little woman, the colour of ivory, lithe and strong as a snake, threw a handful of sand at Dame Marpasse, and laughed.

"Since they have taken Young Simon prisoner," she said, "there will be no chance for the like of us under the banner of the Old Earl. God grant that Simon be soon put under the sods. He would freeze all the young men in the country. God prosper the King."

Marpasse had taken off one of her stockings, and was darning a hole in the heel, and darning it very clumsily.

"They have slaughtered the Jews in London, and the King should come south again to see after the remnant of his flock. They say his host is moving nearer the river. We must look to our manners, my dear; I will be nothing under a great lady."

Isoult shot out a red tongue.

"Supposing I look no lower than Prince Edward himself! We must fill our purses soon. These cursed marchings to and fro have left us out in the cold. Once in the King's camp, I will sleep in a lord's tent, and no other. And I will have siclatouns and silks, for there will be London and half the country to plunder."

Marpasse looked solemn.

"They must beat Earl Simon out of the country first," said she; "the old watchdog keeps the meat from being stolen. Phew, I would give something for a loaf of bread. We shall have to bide the night here, and chew grass. What a curse it is sometimes to wear gay clothes, and to have no gentleman near to take one up on his horse."

Great contrasts were these two; Isoult, black as midnight as to eyes and hair, sharp, peevish, slim of body, red of mouth and white of skin; Marpasse, with large handsome face brown as a berry, hard blue eyes shining under a mop of tawny hair, and a mouth ready to break into giggles. They were resting on the road, these excellent gentlewomen, in the shelter of a sand-pit on the hills beyond Guildford, their baggage, such as it was, spread about them in happy confusion. Isoult had a great slit in her poppy-red tunic, a slit that showed the white shift beneath. She was waiting till Marpasse, that tawny woman who loved bright colours, should finish with the needle. But Marpasse's darning was slow and clumsy, and Isoult plucked grass and gnawed it, watching the sandy track that went winding down into the valley.

Marpasse finished her botching at last, and wiping the sand from between her toes, pulled on her stocking. She stuck the needle into a wisp of thread, and tossed it into Isoult's lap. But Isoult was still gnawing grass, and staring down the road with a brooding alertness in her eyes.

"Here comes a grey goat," she said suddenly, spitting out a blade of grass, and wiping her chin, "maybe she is worth being gentle to. Who knows! At all events, we are hungry."

Marpasse wriggled forward so that she had a view of the road. One stout leg protruded from under the skirt of cornflower blue, and the Juno's limb betrayed a further need of the needle.

"Hey, grey gull, but you are tired, my dear."

"Tired! Bah!" and Isoult bit her lips, "only married women walk so, as though they had a stick laid across their shoulders each morning."

Marpasse held her ground.

"You should know enough of the road, little cat, to tell when a padder is footsore, and far spent. God a' me, but she is good to look at, though she be lame. And a bag, too. If she has bread in it, I will call her dear sister."

The woman in grey whom Isoult had sighted, came to the mouth of the sand-pit, and saw these two wenches in their bright clothes watching her; and when one of them smiled and beckoned, Denise stood hesitating, and then smiled in return. But the smile was so weary and so sad, that Marpasse, that big woman with the head of a sunflower, jumped up, and went out into the road.

Marpasse looked Denise over from head to foot, yet behind the rude and bold-eyed stare there was the instinctive good nature of a coarse, generous, vagrant spirit. Marpasse's self-introduction was like a friendly slap of the hand. She spoke straight out, and did not stop to parley.

"The roads might be strawed with peppercorns in this dry weather. It is hot in the sun too, on these hills."

She glanced at Denise's feet. The shoes were dusty and worn, with the pink toes showing. Marpasse laughed. She was a hardy soul, and her brown feet were like leather.

"If you are going to Guildford, you will not make the town to-night."

"I know the road, I travelled it only a week ago."

"God o' me, mistress, so do I. Come in, and rest, we are two quiet women. And we have wine and no bread. If you have bread, I will strike a bargain."

Denise looked from Marpasse to Isoult, that slip of ivory swathed in flaming red. The two women puzzled her. She had neither character nor calling to give them, but Marpasse looked buxom, and good-tempered, and Denise had no cause to trust people who pretended to great godliness. Moreover she was very weary and very footsore, and very thirsty, as Marpasse had hinted.

The first thing she did was to give Marpasse the bag she carried.

"There is bread there," she said, "and some apples."

Marpasse stared, but took the bag. Isoult had crept up, and her eyes were bright and greedy. She snatched at the bag, but Marpasse caught her wrist, and gave her a slap across the cheek.

"Play fair, little cat," said she, "I cheat no one who does not try to cheat."

Then she turned to Denise with a laugh, her hard eyes growing suddenly soft and bright.

"Take your share, sister, and welcome," she said, "two mouthfuls of wine for a crust of your bread. Come in. I will keep Dame Red Rose's fingers quiet. There are worse places to sleep in than a sand-pit."

Peaceable folk might have fought shy of these boldly coloured, and bold-eyed women, but Denise had suffered so many things at the hands of the world that she did not stand upon dignity or caution. Marpasse and Isoult puzzled her, being so gaudy and yet so ragged, so broad and merry in their talk. When they had drunk wine and broken bread together, Marpasse came and sat herself at Denise's feet. She unlaced the worn shoes, and finding blood and chafed skin beneath, made a noise like a clucking hen.

"You are not used to the road yet, my dear," said she, "it is time I played the barber."

In her blunt and practical way she pulled off Denise's stockings, doing it gently enough, for the feet were chafed and sore.

"Black cat, throw me the oil flask."

Isoult demurred, looking a little sullenly at Denise. For Isoult was fond of oiling and smoothing her black hair, and there would be no oil left for the toilet.

Marpasse took it by force.

"I understand these matters," she said, "you are a selfish brat, Isoult."

Marpasse's broad face was so brown and kind, and her hands so motherly, that a wet mist came into Denise's eyes. She was astonished that the woman should take so much trouble, and was touched by her great gentleness. Isoult, who was watching, saw two tears gather in Denise's eyes, and she started up with an angry toss of the head, and a snap of her white teeth. Marpasse, bending over Denise's feet, saw those two tears fall on to Denise's skirt. She looked up suddenly, and for some reason showed her roughness. Such women as Marpasse and Isoult had a ferocious contempt for tears.

"Bah, come now, no snivelling. I have not hurt you, don't pretend that."

"You have not hurt me at all. It was not that."

"Oh, not that! Then what are you blubbering for?"

"Not many people would have troubled about my feet," said Denise, almost humbly.

"Bah, many people are fools."

The two women looked at each other, and Marpasse seemed to understand. She went red under her brown skin, laughed at herself contemptuously, and began to drop in the oil.

"The Black Cat has prowled away," she said, "and the cat is a selfish beast. Now for some cool grass."

She scrambled aside, and tearing grass from some of the tussocks on the bank, moulded the stuff about Denise's feet, binding it in place with pieces of rag.

"You will walk easier to-morrow," she said, smiling, "and you had better buy new hose in Guildford town."

She was still smiling when Denise bent down and kissed the coarse, laughing, good-natured mouth.

"Bah, if you had a beard, it might please me," quoth Marpasse.

But from that moment she and Denise were friends.

The three of them slept that night in the sand-pit, Marpasse showing Denise how she could scoop a hole in the sand, and lie in comfort. And

Denise slept till after the dawn had broken. When she woke, the two were packing their belongings into a sack.

Denise felt that they had been talking about her while she slept, for they eyed her a little curiously, but with no cunning or distrust. Nor was Denise's instinct at fault. "She is not one of us," Marpasse had said, "not yet, at all events, poor baggage." And Marpasse had looked almost pityingly at Denise, for her face was beautiful yet very sad in sleep, bathed by its auburn hair. "She has had trouble," Marpasse had gone on to declare; "curses, I was more like that myself once." Whereat Isoult had jeered.

Marpasse came over, and unbound Denise's feet, and in the doing of it, asked a few blunt questions.

"Maybe you would not be seen with us on the road?" she asked.

Denise's brown eyes answered "why?" Marpasse looked at her and smiled.

"Where may you be going?"

This time Denise's eyes were troubled, they had no answer.

"Nowhere, and anywhere? God o' me. I learnt that road long ago, and a rough road it is. Come with us, if it pleases you. I am a wise crow."

Denise looked puzzled. She liked Marpasse, and human sympathy was something, but she could make nothing either of her or of Isoult, save that Isoult had a jealous temper. They were so very gay for beggars, nor had they the air of being upon a pilgrimage.

"Perhaps you are for Canterbury?" she asked.

Marpasse sat back on her heels, and opened her mouth wide to laugh.

"No, my dear, we are not for St. Thomas's shrine. We are in search of service, Isoult and I. Isoult is travelling to find service in the household of some lord."

Denise's eyes were innocent enough as she looked at Isoult, but the girl bit her lips, and turned away. Marpasse had mastered her laughter. On the contrary she was studying Denise with a questioning frown.

"Are you after St. Thomas's blessing, my dear?" she asked.

Denise did not know how to answer her, and Marpasse, who was wondrous quick for so big a woman, picked up Denise's shoes and began to lace them on.

"You can come with us as far as you please, my sister," she said, "and when that body there is asleep some time, you and I can talk together. I am called Marpasse, and I am a very wicked woman, and the good priests curse me, and the bad priests curse me also, but look after me along the road. I am so wicked that I shall certainly be claimed by the devil one day. That is what I am, my dear; but a speckled apple is sometimes sweet under the skin."

She laughed with a kind of fierce bravado, and Denise saw her eyes flash.

Isoult broke into a sharp and malicious giggle.

"What a good girl you were once, Marpasse!"

"I was that," said the elder woman, looking at Denise's feet; "men make, men break, and good women prevent the mending. That is what life has been to many."

They set out for Guildford that morning over the blue hills where the gorse blazed, and a few solitary firs rose black against the sky. It was a wild country, and Denise was in wild company had she known it, for little Isoult had had blood on the knife she carried at her girdle, and Marpasse could use a heavy hand. They trudged on over the heathlands, Isoult walking a little ahead, sometimes humming a song, sometimes glancing back sharply and impatiently at Denise. For Marpasse took her time, remembering that Denise was footsore, and she talked to Denise freely, telling her where she was born, and how she had lived, and how she had come to the road.

"For we are beggars, my dear," she said, "though Madame Isoult there has a red dress. We must live, and the good women turn up their noses. But good women often have sharp tongues and sour faces, and the poor men run to the mead butt and to us for comfort."

Marpasse was so frank that she could not but doubt that Denise knew what company she was in. But Denise had taken a liking to Marpasse, and perhaps for that reason she did not read very clearly the truth that the woman put honestly upon her own forehead. It was not surprising that Marpasse should draw her own conclusions, yet she was sorry in her heart for Denise.

The day passed, a day of blue haze, of blue distances, and of sunlight shimmering over purple hills. Bees were on the wing, humming here and there amid the gorse. At noon the women shared out the bread, wine, and apples, and Marpasse looked at Denise's feet. It was near evening when they came over the last hill towards Guildford town, with the west a pyre of peerless gold.

Isoult, who walked ahead of the other two, turned suddenly, and waved to them, and pointed towards the sky line. And against the deep blue of the northern sky they saw a line of spears moving, with here and there the black dot of a man's head. A banner was displayed at the head of the company, but neither Isoult nor Marpasse could decipher it at such a distance.

The line of spears went eastwards towards Guildford, and dropped slowly out of view. Denise saw that Black Isoult's nostrils had dilated and that her eyes had the glitter seen in the eyes of a beast of prey. She ran on ahead, light on her feet as a young lad, and they saw her stand outlined against the sky line, and then turn and wave her arm.

Below, towards the valley, dark masses of men were moving on Guildford town. The faint braying of the trumpets came up on the evening breeze. Isoult saw a part of the King's host on the march.

She tossed her head, laughed, and spread her arms.

"The good saints have blessed us," she said, and she looked at Denise curiously under her black brows as though searching her inmost heart.

Marpasse beamed.

"Our grey sister has brought us luck. We must keep our wits sharp to-night."

They went on down the hill, and Isoult, walking softly and lightly as a cat, pointed out where a great baggage train lumbered with a crowd of people like black ants about it. Already they were pitching tents and pavilions in the meadows outside the town. The evening sunlight seemed to strike upon water, for the glitter of the King's host was like the glitter of a river flowing in the valley. Everything looked so peaceful and minute, so orderly, and yet so human. It was like the green grass over a quagg, bright and rich at a distance, but covering rottenness beneath. Up on the hills one did not smell the sweat of the horses nor hear the men's foul talk, nor see the savagery that was loose in their eyes.

Isoult turned, and looked sharply at Marpasse.

"Shall we try the town?"

Marpasse shook her head. Her face was hard now, and her eyes watchful. Denise wondered at the change that had come over the two women.

"A quick bargain is a bad one," said Marpasse, "let us bide our time, and listen. We are good enough to take our choice. I shall keep my knife in my hand to-night."

And they went on down hill towards the camp that was being pitched about the town.

CHAPTER XXVIII

Night came while Marpasse and Isoult were building a fire under the lee of a grass bank in a meadow outside Guildford, for Marpasse, shrewd woman, had no sooner heard the din that the King's men were making in the town, than she had chosen to pass the night in the open rather than within the walls.

"They will all be drunk as swine," she said, "and a drunken man is no bargain. Out with your knife, Black Cat, and run and cut some of that furze yonder. Some lazy soul has left faggots in that ditch."

Marpasse made Denise sit down under the shelter of the bank, for the grey sister's feet had hurt her through the last two miles. So Denise sat there in the dusk, lost in a kind of vacant wonder at life, and at herself, and at the strange way that things happened. She felt tired, even to stupidity, and the sounds that came up out of the town were not more audible than the roar of a distant mill.

Marpasse and Isoult made the fire, Isoult using the flint, steel and tinder they carried with them, Marpasse playing the part of bellows. The fire proved sulky, perhaps because of Isoult's temper, and her muttering of curses. Marpasse knelt and blew till her brown cheeks were like bladders. The flames seemed pleased by her good-natured, strenuous face, for they shot up, and began to lick the wood.

Marpasse sat back suddenly on her heels, her face very red, and shading her eyes with her hand, she looked out into the darkness.

"Poof, is it the blood in my ears, or do I hear something?"

Isoult was also on the alert, her eyes bright under a frowning forehead.

"Horses," she said.

"What are they doing this time of the night?"

From somewhere came the dull thunder of many horses at the trot. Nothing was distinguishable but the fires that had been lit here and there about the town, fires that shone like golden nails on the sable escutcheon of the night. Isoult, who was very quick of hearing, swore that more than a thousand horses must be moving yonder in the darkness.

"Curses, but it must be the rear-guard," said Marpasse; "God send them clear of us, or we shall be over-crowded. The fire will save us from being trampled on."

The thunder of hoofs came nearer, a sound that sent a vague shudder through the darkness as though something infinitely strong and infinitely savage were rushing on out of the gloom. The earth shook. A sense of movement grew in the outer darkness, a sense of movement that approached like a phosphorescent wave swinging in from a midnight sea. Then a trumpet screamed. There was a rattling and chafing like the noise made by the tackle of a great ship when she puts about in a high wind. A shrill, faint voice from somewhere shouted an order. The belated rear-guard of the host, for such it was, halted within a furlong of the women's fire.

Marpasse shook her fist at the dark mass.

"Fools, you should have been drunk down yonder in the town by now! We can do very well without you. And as likely as not you will thieve our fire."

Isoult laughed.

"Some thieves might be welcome," she said.

And Denise, who had listened to it all with tired apathy, seemed to wake suddenly and to feel the cold, for she shivered and drew nearer to the fire.

Despite the newcomers, Isoult, Marpasse and Denise sat round the burning wood, breaking their bread, and listening to the shouts of the men, and the trampling and snorting of horses. It was pitch dark beyond the circle of light thrown by the fire, though torches began to go to and fro like great moths with flaming wings. Marpasse and Isoult both had their ears open. They were rough women in the midst of rough men, and their instincts were as fierce and keen as the instincts of wild things that hunt or are hunted at night.

Voices seemed to rise everywhere in the darkness. A waggon went creaking by, with the cracking of a whip, and the oaths of the driver. Mallets began to ring on the polls of stout, ash pegs and Isoult pricked up her ears at the sound.

"They are pitching a tent yonder!"

Marpasse nodded as she munched her bread.

"Some of the lords must be near," Isoult ran on, "we may be in good company. The saints bring us luck."

Her eyes met Denise's, and there was a startled something in Denise's glance that made Isoult flinch, and then burst into spiteful laughter. Isoult had the wine flask in her hand, and she lifted it, and drank deep.

"Blood of mine, have we an unshorn lamb here?"

She stared at Denise impudently as though challenging her. Denise looked away.

Isoult's face sharpened, the face of a little vixen ever ready to snap and bite.

"Lord, how proud we are! Coarse sluts, that is what we are, Marpasse."

The big woman held up a brown hand.

"Keep your claws in, cat," she said, "you were born quarrelling. Curse you, be quiet."

And Isoult obeyed, having felt the weight of Marpasse's fist.

It was not long before a couple of soldiers passed close to the fire, and seeing the three women, red, blue, and grey, they stopped, and began to talk banteringly to Marpasse and Isoult. The women returned the men better than they gave, and showed them plainly that they had no need of their company, for the fellows were rough boors, and sweeter at a distance. Denise sat and shuddered, huddling into herself with instinctive disgust, and understanding why Marpasse had a naked knife in her sleeve. The men slunk off, sending back jeers out of the darkness, for Marpasse had shown her knife.

"The sting of a wasp keeps such flies from buzzing too near," she said; "we are great ladies on occasions, Isoult and I. We cherish our dignity for the sake of the gold."

They went on with their meal, hearing movement everywhere about them in the darkness. Isoult's eyes were fixed upon a fire about a hundred yards away, whose light seemed to play upon the rose-coloured canvas of a tent. Men were going to and fro there, and Isoult guessed that it was some great lord's pavilion. As for Marpasse she ate, drank, and kept eyes and ears upon the alert.

Denise had nothing before her but the black half sphere of the night chequered with the yellow flutter of the fires. Isoult and Marpasse sat facing her and looking towards the town. Therefore they did not see what Denise saw, the tall figure of a man in war harness, unhelmeted, and wearing a blue surcoat blazoned over with golden suns. He came along the bank out of the darkness, and stood looking down at the three women round the fire.

Now Denise's hood was back, and the firelight shining on her hair and face. Gaillard stood on the bank above, and stared at her, intently, silently, and she at him. Denise felt stricken dumb, and the heart froze in her, for Gaillard was near enough for her to recognise his face. It seemed to Denise that he stood there and gloated over her, opening his mouth wide to laugh, but making no sound. She saw him raise his hand, touch his breast, and then make the sign of the cross in the air, watching her as a ghost might watch the confused and half-stupefied terror of one awakened out of sleep.

Marpasse happened to raise her eyes to Denise's face, and its bleak, fixed stare put her upon the alert.

"Heart alive, sister, is the devil at my back?"

She twisted round in time to see a man moving off into the darkness, and Marpasse caught a glimpse of the gold suns on the blue surcoat. She jumped up, looked hard at Denise, and then went a few steps after Gaillard into the darkness. But the man did not wait for her, and she was recalled by a sharp cry from Isoult.

Marpasse saw Denise climb the bank, and disappear into the darkness, and in a moment Marpasse was after her, knowing more than Denise knew of a camping ground at night. She still had view of the grey cloak, and Denise fled like a blind thing, and like a blind thing she was soon in trouble. She had run towards the place where the night seemed blackest, but the passion of her flight carried her into nothing more sympathetic than an old thorn hedge. It was here that Marpasse came up with her, while she was tearing her cloak free from the clinging thorns and brambles.

She caught Denise and held her.

"Fool, where are you running?"

"Let me go, Marpasse."

Denise's voice was fierce and eager, the eager fierceness of a grown woman, not the petulance of a child. She struggled with Marpasse, but the woman kept her hold.

"Let me go, take your hands away!"

Marpasse found Denise stronger than she had thought.

"Fool, I am holding you for your own good. Strike me on the mouth, I am used to it. I know what a camping ground is like at night. Some great, fat spider will have you in a twinkling."

Denise struggled for breath.

"I must go, Marpasse, take your hands away."

"Saints, don't shout so, they are as thick here as flies on a dead horse! Ssst, listen to that!"

She dragged Denise close to the hedge, for they heard men stumbling and calling in the darkness.

"Hallo there, hallo!"

"Come here, you squeakers, and keep us company."

"Find 'em, good dog, find 'em."

Marpasse laid a hand over Denise's mouth, and they crouched there while the men beat the hedge and shouted like boys bird hunting with clap nets at night. They were on the wrong side of the hedge, however, and soon grew tired of the game. The women heard them move off into the darkness.

Marpasse took her hand from Denise's mouth.

"There, you grey pigeon, the night hawks would have had you!"

"Help me, Marpasse. My God, I cannot stay here."

She was still in a fever for flight, but more reasonable towards Marpasse. The woman sat down under the hedge, and pulling Denise after her, held her in her arms.

"Let me play mother," quoth she gently, "keep to a whisper, my dear. I know something about trouble."

So with the camp fires about them, and with the sound of trumpets blown madly and at random in the town below, these two women opened their hearts to one another. Denise told Marpasse how Gaillard had served her, how she had seen him that night, how she loathed and feared the man, and Marpasse understood. She was wise, poor wench, in the ways of the world, and Denise's tale might have been her own in measure. But Marpasse had not been wholly hardened and brutalised by the life she had led. She had the instinct of generosity left in her, and she could be superlatively honest when she was not rebuffed by sneers.

Marpasse had an honest fit that night. She told Denise the truth about herself, and knew by Denise's silence and a certain stiffening of her body that the truth had roused a counter-shock of repulsion. Denise's instincts recoiled from Marpasse. The woman was sensitive to the change. She drew aside from Denise, and sat with her knees drawn up, and her arms clasped over them.

"You are like the rest of the world, sister," she said, with a laugh on edge with bitterness; "even when we try to be honest, good people spit on us, and draw aside their clothes."

Denise stretched out a hand and touched Marpasse's shoulder.

"It is not that," she said.

"Bah, I am used to it! We are never forgiven, and I want no forgiveness. Fawn and cringe on the godly? To hell with their smug faces! But after all, you and I, my dear——"

She stopped, and began to pull at the grass with her hands. Denise's eyes were shining.

"God forgive us both, Marpasse. Sometimes fate is stronger than we are. We are sisters, in that."

Marpasse did not move. It was Denise now who played the comforter. Marpasse did not repel her a second time.

"Bah," said she, "what is the use of talking? The good people will never let me be other than I am, and even a pig must live. But you, you can climb out of the quagmire, my dear. The Gascon devil, I would stick my knife in him for nothing. Listen to me now, we must go back to the fire, and wait till the morning. It will be easier to bolt then. You must not risk it in the dark."

Denise still clung to the darkness, as though it could keep Gaillard at arm's length. Marpasse scolded her.

"Why, you chicken, you have never learnt how to rule a man! Who is this Gaillard, indeed? I tell you I am not afraid of him, Marpasse is a match for any Gascon."

She held out her arms, and the Denise she held in them was white-faced, and very earnest.

"You have a knife, Marpasse," she said, "you can strike me if needs be."

Marpasse held her close.

"There, now, there, what mad things are you saying?"

But Denise clung to her passionately, looking straight into Marpasse's eyes.

"Promise to strike with the knife, Marpasse. Promise or I will run, and take my chance."

And Marpasse promised so far as the knife was concerned, knowing that she would strike Gaillard before she struck Denise.

CHAPTER XXIX

When they returned to the fire Isoult was no longer there, but she had left some sign behind her that Marpasse understood, for the elder woman showed no concern. She was discreetly curt with Denise when the latter began to wonder what had befallen Isoult.

"Lie down and sleep, my dear," she said, "and take care of your feet, for you will want them on the morrow. The black cat can see in the dark, she will come to no harm, will Isoult."

Marpasse might as well have told Denise to love Gaillard as to sleep. Her brain was full of a listening wakefulness that started uneasily when a stick cracked on the fire. So she and Marpasse kept vigil together, while a gradual silence spread over the valley with its armed host and its sombre town. Nor were Marpasse and Denise disturbed that night, for the men of the rear-guard had been marched and counter-marched that day owing to some mad rumour, and they were dead tired, and glad to snore under any hedge.

The dawn came listlessly, and without colour. The birds were awake and singing, and with their song, bizarre and discordant came the blowing of trumpets and the stupid curses of the stirring men. The dawn seemed heavy, and full of a dull discontent. Yet the birds sang, and the men cursed perfunctorily, sulkily, the creatures of a habit. So with the voices of the morning thrilling from the throats of the choir invisible, the camp of the King was one great oath.

Denise was ready, and shivering to be gone. The fire was out, her body stiff and cold, the dew heavy upon the grass. The dawn had shown Denise how hemmed in she and Marpasse were. Horses stood tethered everywhere, gaunt, clumsy waggons waited like patient mammoths, not a hundred yards away a red pavilion had been pitched, its coloured canvas swelling and falling lazily with the morning breeze. The babel of coarse, rough voices that rose out of the green earth made Denise shudder and yearn to be gone.

But Marpasse held her ground.

"Food and drink first," she said.

Denise's restless eyes betrayed her desire.

"Rest easy," Marpasse assured her, "men are meek in the morning, though they curse all heaven and earth. Eat and drink, and see that your shoes sit comfortably."

Denise ate with such hurry and such artificial greed that Marpasse could not help but laugh.

"My teeth are not so good as yours," she said; "if your legs are as sound we shall not do amiss."

Denise's eyes were on the red pavilion. The flap thereof was open, and in the black slit that clove like a wedge into the colour, Denise thought that she saw a man standing and looking towards where she and Marpasse sat. Marpasse was still at her meal, when two men-at-arms came out of the red pavilion, carrying their shields as servers carry dishes to a table. They came over the grass towards the women, while a man in a blue surcoat appeared at the door of the pavilion, and stood as though to watch.

Denise half rose, but Marpasse caught her, and pulled her back.

"Sit still. You are far too simple."

"It is Gaillard, yonder!"

"Yes, yes. Fool him first, my dear, and then run away when he is not looking. That is what we women have to do when men are the stronger."

The two soldiers came up, and stood before Denise. One carried food and a flask of wine in the hollow of his shield; the other, a red scarf and a silver girdle.

"Messire Gaillard, our lord, yonder, begs for the Lady Denise's good-will."

Marpasse beckoned with her arm.

"Give them here, sirs, my good will is worth homage."

The men grinned, and inclined their heads with quaint accord towards Denise.

"It is the grey, not the blue," said one.

Denise stared at the grass, and did not catch Marpasse's urgent nods and winks.

"I take no gifts from Messire Gaillard," she said.

Marpasse made an impatient clucking with her tongue. How prejudiced people did bungle matters, to be sure!

"Think twice, my dear," she said meaningly.

Denise repeated the same words. The men grinned, looked at one another, and did not stir.

"Messire Gaillard," said they, "has set us at your service. It is proper that you should be guarded when all men are not as honourable as our lord."

Denise saw herself trapped, and went red, and then white. She looked at Marpasse, but Marpasse stared obtusely into the distance, knowing that they were in the Gascon's hands, and that the men had been sent to see that they did not flit. Marpasse remembered the promise of the knife, but the morning was cold and grey, and Marpasse too practical and hopeful to indulge in such heroics. Therefore she put the best face she could upon it for Denise's sake, and Marpasse knew how to deal with men.

"Sit down, gentlemen," said she, "I am sorry the fire is out, but we shall be moving before long. You, there, with the beard, since my sister is in the sulks, I will take some of that baked meat and wine you have brought us. Now, good health to the King, and all soldiers."

Marpasse ate and drank with relish, a second breakfast not coming at all amiss to her, and she talked and laughed with the men, and soon had them at her service. Denise would touch nothing, though Marpasse smiled, nodded and whispered in her ear. "Courage, girl," she said, "leave it to me, a laugh and a flash of the eyes work marvels, even with pigs. We will spread our fingers at them before the day is old." But Denise sat like one stunned, and would not believe that Marpasse meant what she said. The red tent had a fascination for Denise, and she saw Gaillard and two other knights come out, sit down on cloaks their servants spread for them, and make a meal. Then they were washed, barbered, and armed in full view of the two women, while a boy stood near, and sang to the sound of a lute. The whole camp was full of stir and movement. Already, black columns were pouring out of Guildford town. In an hour the whole host would be on the march.

So it befell that Denise found herself walking beside Marpasse that morning at the tail of Gaillard's company of spears. The two men-at-arms who had been set to guard them, walked their horses one on either side. Marpasse trudged along, merry and insolent; Denise, with her thoughts humbled into the dust. Gaillard had ridden up and spoken to her, not mockingly, but with the arrogance of a man in power. "Sanctissima," he had said, "before long I will find you a palfrey, and you shall ride at my side. Hold up your head, my dear, and be sensible; I have something on my conscience, and by my sword, I am not unready to right a wrong." Denise had answered him nothing, for she was bitter with the humiliation of it, and that Gaillard of all men should look at her as on one whom he might graciously lift up out of the mire. Chance had joined her to these two women, and she guessed that Isoult's red gown had coloured Gaillard's vision.

When they had gone a mile or more Denise asked Marpasse in an undertone for her knife. But Marpasse shut her mouth firmly, and shook her head.

"Have patience, my dear," she said in a whisper, "I have my trick to play. Be ready when I give the word."

And Marpasse trudged on cheerfully, mocking at herself in her heart.

"Fool," she said to herself, "what is the girl to you? Why burn your fingers pulling cinders out of the fire? You may get kicks for it, and no money. And you may lose your chance, too, of getting a lover. Fool! You have had a heart of pap ever since you were born."

Yet though Marpasse talked to herself thus, her mind was set on cheating Gaillard of Denise.

The King's host went winding through the green valleys that spring morning, marching Kentwards, where Earl Simon had taken the town of Rochester by assault, and pressed hard upon John de Warenne who held out in the castle. Horse and foot, archers and camp-followers, baggage-waggons, sumpter mules, and loose women, made up the stream of steel and colour. It was a rough, careless, confident march, for had not the first triumphs fallen to the King? Northampton had been taken, and Simon the Younger made prisoner, with Madame Etoile, his lady. Leicester and Nottingham had fallen, and Gifford's seizure and destruction of Warwick was all that the Barons could claim on their side. The Mise had gilded Henry's cause. Even the King of the Scots had sent aid to his Brother of England; a Balliol, a Bruce, and a Comyn were among his captains. John de Warenne should keep Earl Simon under Rochester's walls, until the King should come and crush him, or drive him headlong over the sea.

Henry, weak, persuadable, false, yet brilliant gentleman, might count himself strong that spring, with his Poitevins and his adventurers, and the rougher lords who preferred the licence of a weak King to the justice of Earl Simon. But the old lion was not driven to bay yet, much less cowed or beaten. De Montfort and his men were not asleep, nor over confident like the King's party. Rochester might be many miles away, but Earl Simon had sent some of his most trusted men to watch the march of the King's army, to judge its strength, and keep him warned as to all that passed.

Waleran de Monceaux and Sir Aymery, woodlanders both of them, and wise in woodland law, lay that morning in a coppice close to the road and watched the King's host go by. These Sussex men were men whom De Montfort trusted to the death. And they lay on their bellies in the thick of the dead bracken and the brambles, two wise dogs that saw and were not seen.

Aymery was stretched at full length, his chin upon his two fists, his grey eyes at gaze, while Waleran, more restless and impetuous, carried on a mumbling monologue, and chewed grass with hungry jaws. They were counting the banners and the pennons, and marking as best they could the lords and knights who were with the King. Aymery lay still enough till Gaillard's company came up, the Gascon riding bareheaded, his blue surcoat ablaze with its golden suns. Gaillard had found favour with the King, despite the happenings at Pevensey, and the anger of Peter of Savoy. Aymery knew Gaillard at the first glance, and set his teeth hard so that the muscles stood out about his jaw.

Yet the tail of Gaillard's company brought a far fiercer inspiration, for Denise walked there beside Marpasse, Denise with her hair of red gold shining like a torch against the green. She walked as one going to the ordeal of fire, white-faced, mute, looking neither to the right hand nor left. Her grey cloak went like a cloud beside Marpasse's azure blue. The two men-at-arms rode stolidly behind, while the men in the rear rank of Gaillard's troop were laughing and joking with Marpasse.

Aymery stiffened as he lay, and his hand went to the sword in the dead bracken beside him. He scrambled suddenly to his knees, with a fierce, inarticulate cry deep down in his throat. Waleran seized him, and dragged him back to cover, for they were so near the road that the slightest movement might betray them.

"God, man, are you mad!"

Aymery lay there a moment with his face on his arms. He said nothing to Waleran, but when he raised his head again his face was grim and full of thought. He kept watch there in silence, but the road was empty now save for a few camp-followers, women and beggars. Aymery rose on one elbow, and looked towards the drifting dust that hung on the heels of the King's host.

He turned suddenly to Waleran.

"Brother, you and I must part company for a while. Go back to our men. I must follow the march farther."

Waleran looked at him curiously out of half-closed eyes.

"I know the man you are. Simon trusts us both."

They scrambled up out of their "forms," and went back through the wood till they came to a dell where they had left their horses. Aymery laid his hands on Waleran's shoulders.

"Brother-in-arms," he said, "trust me. I have a book to read, and a debt to pay. There is nothing of the traitor in my heart."

Waleran hugged him like a bear.

"Blood of my father, I know that! I can carry the news."

They parted there, two men who loved and trusted one another. Aymery took spear, shield, and helmet, and mounted his horse to follow the march of the King's host, that splendid stream that seemed to gather and to carry with it all the pomp and music, the violence and passion, and the suffering sinfulness that the land held.

CHAPTER XXX

A halt was called at noon, and Denise, who had walked for four long hours, felt that hopeless weariness that yearns only for some corner where the body may lie relaxed. Her feet were burning, and she and Marpasse had been trudging in the dust made by the horses, dust that had clogged the air, and made the eyes tingle. Denise was glad to throw herself on the grass beside Marpasse, who was much less weary, being tougher, and more used to the road.

Marpasse was very wide awake. She looked narrowly at Denise, and rolled to the side on one elbow so as to be nearer.

"We have our chance now, are you strong enough?"

Denise's dull eyes brightened, and she moistened her lips with her tongue.

"If we only had water! What can we do—here, Marpasse, with the men all round us?"

Marpasse gave her the stone bottle of wine that Gaillard had sent them that morning.

"Drink," she said in a loud voice, "nothing like wine on a dusty road. Heigh-ho, I shall soon be sleepy," and she rolled on her back so that she touched Denise, and stretched her arms and yawned.

"Listen," she said in a whisper, "there is that wood yonder, I have my plan," and she went on speaking softly to Denise, and still stretching and yawning as though there was nothing hazardous to be considered.

It was plodding along an endless road, with aching feet, and gloom in her heart, that had made Denise's courage droop for the moment. Above all it was the hopelessness that had tired her. Marpasse's words were as warm and as heartening as strong wine. The spark fell on the tinder and red life began to run again through Denise's being.

"I am strong enough, Marpasse."

Marpasse seized her hand, and pretended to bite it, like a dog at play.

"Don't look red and eager, my dear. Limp, as though you had worn your feet to the bone. Now, good St. George, bless all fools!"

Marpasse jumped up, and crossed the road to where the two men-at-arms who had charge of them were making a meal. She spoke to them jauntily, her hands on her hips, her brown face insolent and laughing, her eyes unabashed. The men laughed in turn, and nodded. Marpasse recrossed the road, held out a hand to Denise, and pulled her roughly to her feet. Marpasse put an arm about Denise, and Denise, prompted by her comrade, limped as she walked, and leant her weight upon Marpasse.

Fifty yards from the road was a patch of scrub that jutted out like a pointed beard from the broad chin of an oak wood. Marpasse and Denise went slowly towards the trees, thinking each moment that they would hear some voice calling them back roughly to the road. Marpasse felt Denise straining forward instinctively upon her arm. She was breathing rapidly like one in a fever.

They reached the scrub, and skirting it, came to the ditch that bounded the wood. Marpasse still kept her arm about Denise.

"Gently, sister, gently; it would be a shame to spoil everything by bolting like a hare. Be sure, our friends behind are watching us."

Marpasse turned her head to look.

"Curses!" and the strain of the moment showed in her impatience, "one of the fools is strolling after us. We cannot go far with only our shadows for company. Over! No muddy shoes this time."

They were across the ditch, and on the edge of the wood, Marpasse still holding Denise as they went in amid the trees. She kept looking back till the open land and the sky were shut out by the dense lattice work of the boughs. The men had not followed them across the ditch, and Marpasse blessed their luck when she saw that the underwood had been cut that winter so that it would be quicker running between the stubs. Only the dead leaves troubled Marpasse, rustling and crackling under their feet.

"Now for it, run, run!"

She let go of Denise, and they gathered up their skirts and started off, scudding between the tree boles, never stopping to look back. Denise did not feel her feet under her. The brown leaves, the coarse grass, and the wild flowers were like so much water over which she seemed to skim, yet not so swiftly as her fear fled. She was quicker than Marpasse, because her passion to escape burnt at a greater heat. Marpasse had torn her skirt on a stub and was panting when they came to the farther edge of the wood.

They paused a moment, and stood listening, and could hear the confused hum of the host like the humming of bees. A meadow lay before them, bounded by a second wood that towered up the steep slope of a hill. Against the blue a lark hung with quivering wings, and quivering song. As they stood listening a shout rose in the deeps of the wood behind them. Denise was off like a deer, her whole soul quivering like the wings of the lark overhead. Marpasse stayed a second to pull up a stocking that had slipped to her ankle, and then ran on after Denise across the meadow.

They were close to the outstanding trees of the second wood, when Denise looked back and saw that they were followed. The two men-at-arms who had had the guarding of them had been too shrewd to go beating through the trees on foot when they had begun to suspect Marpasse of playing a trick on them. They had mounted their horses, and ridden different ways so as to circle the wood and gain a view of the two vixens when they took to the open.

Marpasse cursed them for their pains.

"Another minute, and we should have been out of sight," she said; "we may yet trick them in the wood."

They kept together now, labouring uphill with faces that began to betray distress. Marpasse had a stitch in her side, her stockings were at her ankles, and her hair over her shoulders. They could hear the men shouting, but paid no heed to it, for if there were but thicker cover on the other side of the hill, they might take to it and escape.

As they topped the slope they heard the trampling of horses in the valley behind them. Marpasse looked eagerly to right and left, and an angry cry escaped her, for a wood of great forest trees dipped gently away from them, the trunks pillaring broad aisles that were carpeted with sleek and brilliant sward. A man could see through the wood as though looking along the aisles of a church, where children could do no more than play hide-and-seek round the piers and pillars.

"No luck for us! They can ride us down here almost as well as in a meadow."

Denise caught Marpasse's arm.

"The knife, Marpasse; give it me."

Marpasse was panting, one hand at her side.

"No, no, not that, my dear!"

"I will not be taken alive, Marpasse. Give me the knife, and run. They will not trouble you when they find me here."

Marpasse drew Denise behind the trunk of a great tree, for she had seen a helmet come up over the edge of the hill, to be followed by the tossing mane of a horse.

Marpasse took Denise in her arms.

"My sister," and she was greatly moved, "take it not to heart. In a week, or a month, it may seem different."

But Denise was in earnest as her white face showed.

"No, no, Marpasse, I cannot. Give me the knife."

Marpasse fumbled for it, great passionate tears rushing to her eyes. Had she not once passed through the same pain, and shirked the crisis, only to become a stroller and a courtesan! Denise had a more sensitive surface, a deeper courage. Yet Marpasse's heart cried out against the thing.

The two men were close upon them now, riding slowly and at some distance from one another so that the two women should not play hide and seek behind the trees. Marpasse turned her head away as she gave Denise the knife.

"My sister, am I wrong in this?"

Denise caught her, and kissed her on the mouth.

"Truest of friends, go, now. It will not be so hard to end it, for I am very tired."

Marpasse broke away with a spasm of the throat. The thought seized her suddenly that by running she might draw the men away from Denise. Yet she had not gone three steps before her wet eyes saw something that made her start, and then stand like a deer at gaze.

What Marpasse saw was a knight on a black horse riding up furiously through the wood. He was bending low in the saddle behind his shield, with spear feutered, and the steel mass of his great helmet flashing in the sunlight that sifted through the trees. His horse seemed to gallop almost silently over the soft turf. Yet he came on like the wind, and with no doubtful intent.

Marpasse whipped round, and ran back to Denise.

"Not death yet," she said, "nor the devil either, pray God."

There was the thud of hoofs on the soft turf of the woodland rides, and the two women saw the man on the black horse go by at the gallop, bending low behind his shield. Marpasse stood out to watch him, her mouth wide open as though howling a blessing. She saw one of Gaillard's men kicking his heels into his horse's flanks as though to gather speed against the shock of that feutered spear. The knight on the black horse was on him before the fellow could gain much ground. Marpasse saw a spear break in the middle, and a body go twisting over the grass like a bird with an arrow through it, while the dead man's horse went off at a canter.

Marpasse caught Denise by the hand, and drew her from behind the tree.

"Glory of God, my dear," and her eyes glistened, but not with tears, "Lord, how I love a lusty fighter. Here is a man who can strike a blow. And here are we like damoiselles in a French romance, my dear. Save us, Sir Launcelot, or Sir Tristan of Lyonnesse, whatever your name may be! La, I could kiss you for being so lusty!"

The second of Gaillard's men had ridden in to help his comrade. Swords were out, and sweeping in gyres of light under the boughs of the oak trees. But he of the black horse set about Gaillard's man as though he were thrashing corn. There was only one sword at work so far as the issue was concerned.

Denise looked on with dull eyes, and feverish face. It was like a violent dream to her, those struggling figures, and the body lying there thrust through with the broken spear. Marpasse was dancing from foot to foot, her brown face flushed, her eyes flashing.

She threw up her arms, and shouted in triumph.

"He has it, he has it, in the throat. Oh, brave blow! Would I were a man, and that I had an arm like that!"

The man on the black horse had beaten Gaillard's fellow out of the saddle. He slid down his horse's belly, a dishevelled figure with limp arms and fallen sword. One foot had caught in the stirrup, and the horse took fright, and cantered off through the wood, dragging the body after it.

The knight watched the body go sliding over the grass, tossing its arms as though in grotesque terror. He turned his horse, and rode back slowly towards the two women, and they saw that he carried a hawk's claw in gold upon a sable shield. His surcoat was a dull green, a colour that was not too crude and conspicuous for forest tracks. The great helmet, with its eye cleft in the shape of a cross, hid his face completely.

Marpasse, impetuous wench, ran forward and kissed the black muzzle of his horse.

"Lording, good luck to you," and her blue eyes laughed in her brown face, "never were distressed damsels in greater need. King Arthur's gentlemen were never more welcome."

The man did not look at Marpasse, but at Denise. She was leaning against the tree trunk, her hair hanging about her shoulders like red light, her face a dead white by contrast. Her brown eyes had a feverish look, and she still held Marpasse's knife in her right hand.

The man on the black horse waved Marpasse aside with his sword. And there was something about the silent, massive figure with its iron mask that made Marpasse move back.

"Go yonder, and watch," he said, pointing towards the outskirts of the wood.

"But, lording——?"

"Go. Is my blood the blood of that dead thing yonder!"

And Marpasse, who had obeyed very few people in her life, obeyed him without a word.

When she had gone the man put his sword up into its scabbard, dismounted, and stood holding the bridle of his horse. Denise's eyes were fixed upon the helmet with its shadowy cleft in the shape of a cross. The man saw her bosom rising and falling, and that her eyes were troubled. Marpasse's knife was half hidden by the grey folds of her gown.

The man put both hands to the helmet, lifted it, and let it fall upon the grass. And it was Aymery whom Denise saw.

She looked at him with wide, eloquent, and frightened eyes, a rush of colour crimsoning her face, for Denise remembered the Aymery of Reigate Town, the stern-faced captain hounding Gaillard into the night. And all the shame and ignominy that she had suffered seemed to fall and break upon her head. She stood speechless, her eyes looking at him like the eyes of one who expects a blow.

"Denise!"

He held out his hands to her, but she covered her face, and leant against the trunk of the tree. Yet she did not weep or make any sound. It was a dry, frozen anguish with her that could neither move nor speak. Aymery watched her as a man might watch one in bitter pain, knowing not what to do to help or comfort.

"Denise!"

Perhaps the pity in his voice stung her. God, that it should have come to this, for she had read the truth upon his face. Denise raised her head, and their eyes met. Her mouth was quivering, but she looked at Aymery as though challenging the whole world in that one man. Perhaps Denise could not have told what made her do the thing she did. The fever of fatalism was in her blood, and Marpasse's knife was in her hand. And Aymery, stupefied, watched the red stain start out against the grey cloth of her gown.

CHAPTER XXXI

Denise slipped slowly to her knees, still leaning the weight of her body against the trunk of the tree. The languor of death seemed upon her, but her eyes could still meet Aymery's, brown eyes swimming with the death mist, and growing blind to the sunlight. The man's shocked face, and his outstretched hands were the last things that she remembered.

"Lord, it is better so."

Her head drooped, her hair falling about her face. The long lashes flickered over the eyes like the flickering light of a taper before it dies in the darkness. Aymery dropped on his knees beside her. He was awed, shaken to the deeps, a man who looked upon the face of death, and knew that the great silence was falling upon the mouth of the woman whom he had kissed in dreams.

"Denise."

He took her into his arms, for there was no power to gainsay him, and death, dread lord, still watched and waited. They were heart to heart for the moment, though life was melting within the span of the man's arms. Denise opened her eyes once, and smiled, but it was the ghost of a smile that Aymery had.

"Denise!"

His mouth was close to hers.

"Lord, it is the end; do not judge me hardly."

"Denise, my desire, am I here to judge?"

"It was Gaillard's doing," she said, "and God deserted me. I am very tired, so tired. Now, I am falling asleep."

She gave a great sigh, and let her head lie upon his shoulder, her skin growing more white under the clouding of her hair. Aymery felt her hands grow cold as he knelt there looking at her in a stupor of awe, and wrath, and rebellious wonder. He believed that Denise would open her eyes no more, that the eternal silence was falling upon her mouth. This was death indeed, death that found him inarticulate and helpless.

He let her lie there upon the grass with her head resting upon a mossy root of the tree, and turned to call Marpasse back through the wood. And Marpasse came running, to stare at the deed her knife had done, and then to fall on her knees with a kind of blubbering fierceness, that was combative in its grief. She laid her hand on Denise's bosom, and bent over her till her mouth nearly touched the silent lips. But Denise still breathed, and Marpasse sat back on her heels and began to unlace Denise's tunic.

Aymery was standing by, looking down at them as though stunned. His helplessness maddened Marpasse, and she turned and stung him.

"Fool, will you let her bleed to death?"

She had laid bare the wound in Denise's bosom, a narrow mouth from which the red life was ebbing slowly.

"Fool! Have you such things as hands? For God's love, something to staunch the flow!"

Her words were like cold water dashed into his face. Aymery ripped his surcoat, tore a great piece away, folded it, and gave the pad to Marpasse. She pressed it to the wound with one hand, and with the other beckoned Aymery to take her place.

"Shall we give in without a fight?" she said, "you are better with a sword than with a sponge, lording. I have some linen on me, though it might have come white out of the wash."

She turned up her blue gown, and tore strips from the shift beneath.

"Blood stops blood, they say," and she ran back between the trees to where the dead man lay with the spear through him. The stuff and her hands were red when she returned.

"Lift the pad, lording."

He obeyed her, and she pressed some of the linen into the wound.

"A bandage, what shall we do for a bandage?"

Aymery tore his surcoat into strips, and knotting them together, he gave the end to Marpasse.

"Raise her, gently, gently, my man."

While Aymery held Denise limp and still warm, with her head and her hair upon his hauberk, Marpasse wound and rewound the bandage about her body, drawing the swathings as tightly as she could.

When she had ended it, she put her mouth to Denise's mouth, and felt the white throat with her fingers.

"Life yet," she said.

Then she and Aymery looked into each other's eyes.

"What next?"

That was what they asked each other.

Now Marpasse knew the country in those parts, having lived near at one time in the house of a lord's verderer, and gone a-hawking, and a-hunting in the woods. When she and Denise had started on their flight from Gaillard and the King's army, Marpasse had had a certain house of Sempringham nuns in her mind's eye. It was a little convent hid in a valley, aloof from the world, and very peaceful. Marpasse told Aymery of the place. They could carry Denise there, a forlorn venture, for both felt that she would die upon the road.

"The Prioress is named Ursula," said Marpasse, "and she is a good woman, though that may be worth little. They may know something of leech-craft."

Aymery mounted his horse, and Marpasse lifted Denise, and gave her into the man's arms.

"While the torch flickers there is light, lording," she said; "God grant that she may not die on the way."

They set off through the April woods, Aymery with Denise lying in his arms, Marpasse walking beside the horse, a Marpasse who was solemn and pensive, and unlike her ribald self. Aymery hardly glanced at the woman who walked beside the horse, for his whole soul was with Denise, Denise so white and silent, with the death shadows under her eyes. Her hair lay tossed in a shining mass over Aymery's neck and shoulder, and he held her very gently as though afraid of stifling those feebly drawn breaths. Sometimes he spoke to his horse, and the beast went very softly as though understanding Denise's need.

They came out of the wood and found themselves on the edge of a valley, a green trough threaded by a stream running between meadows. Marpasse stood looking about her for some familiar tree or field or the outline of a hill. They saw smoke rising in a blue column from a stone chimney behind a knoll of trees. Marpasse's eyes brightened. They had stumbled on the very place that she sought.

"The luck is with us, lording," she said, "I will come with you as far as the gate. But a devil's child may not set foot on so godly and proper a threshold."

She spoke a little scornfully, and Aymery looked down at Marpasse as though he had hardly noticed her before. She had been a mere something that had moved, and exclaimed, and acted. Of a sudden he seemed to touch the humanism and the woman in her.

He bent over Denise, and then looked again at Marpasse.

"She is yet alive. How did you two come together?"

Marpasse had not discovered yet why Denise had used the knife, though Aymery had saved her from Gaillard's men. But Marpasse had her suspicions.

"We met on the road, lording, where we wastrels drift. She was not one of us. No. She told me her whole story. That was last night outside Guildford Town."

Aymery's eyes were on the priory beneath them amid its meadows. He kept silence awhile, and when he spoke he did not look at Marpasse.

"Part of the tale I know," he said, "and God forgive me, I had an innocent share in it."

His eyes were on Denise's face again, and he smiled as a man smiles with bitter tenderness at death.

"Tell me what you know."

Marpasse plodded along, staring at the grass. And presently she had told Aymery all that Denise had told her, and told it with the blunt pathos of a rough woman telling the truth.

They were nearing the convent now with its grey walls and trees, its barns and outhouses with their dark hoods of thatch. Aymery's face was grim and thoughtful. He touched Denise's hair with his lips, and Marpasse saw the kiss and, being a woman, she understood.

"The devil snatched at her lording," she said, "but God knows that she was not the devil's, either in heart or in body."

Aymery rode on with bowed head. He was thinking of Gaillard, and how he would follow that man to the end of the world, and kill him for the death he had brought upon Denise.

They came to the convent, and Marpasse sat down on a rough bench outside the gate. The portress was waiting there, a very old woman with a dry, wrinkled face, a harsh voice, and grey hairs on her chin. She screwed up her eyes at the knight, and at the burden that he carried in his arms. Aymery was blunt and speedy with her, a man not to be gainsaid.

"Peace to you," he said, "soul and body are hurt here. Go and tell your Prioress that we are in need."

He rode into the court, though a most sensitive etiquette might have forbidden an armed man to ride into such a place. The portress went her way with a hobbling excitement that was very worldly. Presently Ursula the Prioress came out, and two nuns with her and since Aymery held out Denise to the women they could not let him drop her upon the stones.

CHAPTER XXXII

Ursula the Prioress was a prim woman, a woman with a long, thin face, and a small mouth. She had no knowledge of life, but being very devout and religious, her devotion and her religiosity made her conceive infallibility within herself.

Ursula had seen nothing more in Denise than a young woman with gorgeous hair, a deathly face, and blood upon her bosom, and Ursula's nostrils had caught a rank flavour of godlessness from the affair. The woman had stabbed herself or been stabbed. She was probably nothing more than a common courtesan, for Ursula had a vague knowledge that the sisterhood of Rahab still existed. And like many religious women, Ursula was very sure of her own cleanliness, and very suspicious of the cleanliness of others.

The woman could not be left to die, there was her "state of sin" to be remembered; yet Ursula was conscious of great graciousness in suffering Denise to be carried within her doors. Then there was the knight to be dealt with, and the Prioress who knew nothing of men, minced before Aymery with prim haughtiness, folding her hands over her lean body, giving him to understand that it was no concern of hers to please him. Aymery, in the deeps and on the heights in one and the same hour, and stricken to the inmost humanism of his soul, had no eyes for Ursula's prinnickings and prancings. He was in the throes of a tragedy, a strong and impassioned man whose thoughts and desires moved with the headlong naturalness of a stream in flood.

Ursula, half eager to be rid of the man, and yet equally curious, and prying, received him, under a hinted protest, in her Prioress' parlour. To be sure, she had a couple of nuns outside the door, but some of her prejudicial tartness vanished when she heard the name of Simon the Earl. Even the pinpoint of the Prioress' womanliness caught the gleam of Aymery's intensity that burnt at a white heat. She showed herself old-maidishly ready to hear the truth about Denise, since a knight trusted by Earl Simon could not be wholly a dissolute rogue.

Aymery made a mistake that day, a mistake that many a generous and impassioned man has made. Here was a devout woman, a mother of souls, and Aymery took her for what her religion should have made her. Denise, poor child, with the flicker of life still in her, was to be laid to rest in Ursula's lap. No woman could withhold pity in such a case, and Aymery told Ursula some part of Denise's tale, not seeing that he was throwing a rose into a pot of sour wine.

The Prioress' starched figure looked lean and stiff. She was interested, but, dear St. Agnes!—greatly shocked. Aymery's words fell on an ass's hide like blows on an empty drum. The drum resounded, made some godly stir, but held nothing more than air.

Aymery had money in his purse. It was not much, but Ursula was a woman whose skin had the colour of gold. She took the money, and his promises of a bequest should the people's cause prosper, thinking it easily earned by burying a lost woman and putting up prayers for her soul. Ursula would have prayed religiously. She was perfectly sincere in her own corner of the world.

"God give rest to all sinners," she said sententiously, "we will do what we can for the girl. It is a pity that she should not have been shrived."

Aymery's face would have made Marpasse weep. It had no meaning for Madame Ursula.

"I would see her, before I go," he said.

And his heart added:

"Perhaps for the last time."

Ursula's sympathy was purely perfunctory. They had carried Denise into the little infirmary, and laid her upon a bed. She still breathed, and two of the nuns who had some knowledge of leech-craft, had unwound the swathings, but feared to touch the pad that Marpasse had forced into the wound. They had poured oil and a decoction of astringent herbs thereon, wiped the blood-stains from the bosom, and swathed Denise in clean linen. Then they had given her into the hands of the saints, and sat down to watch, whispering to each other across the bed.

The slant of the late sunshine came into the room when Aymery entered at the trail of Ursula's gown. The sunlight struck upon the bed where Denise lay white as a lily with the glory of her hair shining like molten gold. And to Aymery it seemed that she smiled sadly like one dreaming the end of some sad dream.

Ursula's starched wimple creaked in the still room. She stood looking down from a pinnacle of righteousness; the two nuns rose and went to the window, taking care to see all that passed.

Their bodies shut off the sunlight from Denise's face, and threw it into shadow. Aymery was standing beside the bed. The two nuns glanced at one another, and were ready to titter when he knelt down in his battle harness as though praying, or taking some vow.

Before he rose he touched one of Denise's hands, and it was as cold as snow when he laid it against his lips. Ursula made a sharp sound in her throat. Such happenings were not discreet before women who were celibates.

Aymery rose and, looking at none of them, marched to the door.

"If she lives," he would have said, "be kind to her until I can return."

But death seemed to hover so close above Denise that he went out in silence, putting all human hope aside.

Ursula followed him, debonair by reason of her good birth, and superficially courteous after the habit of such a gentlewoman. Would Aymery take wine and meat? Aymery had the heart for neither, but he remembered Marpasse. Ursula had his wallet filled for him, and he took leave of her, finding little to say to show his gratitude. The old portress had watered his horse, and given the beast a few handfuls of corn.

It was growing dusk when Aymery rode out of the gate, and found Marpasse still sitting there on the bench. The figure looked lonely, with a dejected droop of the shoulders, and a hanging of the head. Marpasse's worldliness was down in the dust that evening.

She got up from the bench and made Aymery a reverence. A spirit of bitter mockery possessed her, for the day's tragedy had hurt Marpasse more than she would confess.

Aymery reined in. He said nothing concerning Denise, but held out the wallet that the nuns had filled for him.

"There is food there. You must be hungry."

Marpasse's eyes flashed up at him, and dropped into a hard and sidelong stare. She took the wallet, and stood biting her lower lip.

"How are things, yonder?" she blurted.

Aymery's fingers twisted themselves into his horse's mane.

"Still, a little breathing. They have put her to bed."

Marpasse nodded.

"I have no great hope ——"

"The devil will make sure of that," said Marpasse; "he loves a nunnery," and she grimaced.

Aymery walked his horse along the track, but Marpasse did not follow him. She stood there morosely, biting her lip, and holding Aymery's wallet in her hands. He glanced back, and finding that she had not moved, he reined in again and waited.

Marpasse came on slowly, one hand in the wallet, her eyes on the grass. When she had rejoined Aymery she stopped and stood unsolicitous and silent. The man appeared to be considering something. Yet he saw that the woman's face was hard and gloomy in the twilight.

"What are your plans?" he asked suddenly.

Marpasse stared.

"A ditch has often served me well enough, lording. We strollers count for little."

She laughed, fished a loaf out of the wallet, and broke off a crust.

"Do not trouble your head about me, lording," she said, "go your way. One pull at the bottle, and you shall have your wallet back."

She took out the flask, drank, and replaced it in the leather bag.

"Good-night to you, lording. We have our own ways to go. Mine is a common track, and I know the tread of my own shoes."

Aymery still held his horse in hand. He had something to say to Marpasse, and the words did not come to him easily. The woman was more human than Ursula, and his heart went out to her because of Denise. But before he had spoken twenty words, Marpasse broke in with a rough and bitter laugh.

"Lording," said she, "you cannot make silk out of sackcloth, however much you try. Go your way, I am safe enough on the road. I have a bit of bread here, and I shall sleep soundly under a bush. And to-morrow and the next day, I shall be, just what I have been these five years."

Aymery's eyes were still troubled on her behalf. Marpasse shook her hair, and shrugged her shoulders.

"The mule must carry its load, and be given the stick if it kicks, or turns aside. Bah, I know what I am! Denise, there, that was a piece of gold to be picked up out of the dust. Go your way, lording, and do not waste your words. I should only laugh in your face to-morrow, and call you a fool."

She sat down in the grass and began to eat her bread, ignoring the man on the horse, as though that were the surest way of answering him. There was nothing for Aymery to do but to go, and leave Marpasse to her own road.

"God's speed, lording," she said as he turned his horse.

"God's speed to you, sister."

"Ah, that would be too slow for me, sir!" and her laughter rang out with forced audacity.

So the night came, and these two solitary ones took up the strands of their several lives, strands that had been tangled by the martyrdom of Denise. Earl Simon's trumpets called Aymery into the east, whither the King's host went marching with dust and din. No sword could stay in the scabbard those days, and Aymery had pledged his to Earl Simon, who needed every sword.

Marpasse had watched Aymery ride away into the gathering darkness. She sat there in the grass, sullen, brooding, yet touched by what he had said.

"Bah!" said she, "what would be the use? Brave heart, go your way, and God bless you, for being brave, and honest. Wake up, fool! What, thick in the throat, and ready to blubber like a sot in his cups! Marpasse, my dear, you are a slut and a fool! This is what comes of letting your heart run away with your heels. You will be back to-morrow on the old devil-may-care road."

But for all her self-scorn—Marpasse could not conjure her own emotion. Her heart hurt her and was troubled, nor could she sleep that night, though she huddled close under the forlorn remnant of a haystack that she found in a meadow. Marpasse felt alone, utterly alone in the world, and conscious of the raw night and the darkness. Who would have cared, she thought, if she had used her knife as Denise had used it? Strangers would have kicked her into a hole, and covered her with sods; that would have been the end.

CHAPTER XXXIII

Rochester city had been stormed on the vigil of Good Friday, but De Warenne still held the castle, and two great Sussex lords, William de Braose of Bramber, and John Fitzallan of Arundel were with him. They knew that the King was on the march; nor was Earl Simon to remain much longer before the walls, for Henry forced him to raise the siege by threatening London with his host. It was Waleran de Monceaux who brought the news of the King's march, and Aymery, who rode into Rochester but a day behind his brother-in-arms, found De Montfort preparing for a retreat. Their spears were rolling on London when the next dawn came up behind the great tower of the castle, for London was the heart of England that year, and a sudden stab from the King's sword might have let the life-blood out of the cause.

Earl Simon and the Barons' men marched through Kent, and pushed in between the King's host and the city. The Londoners rang their bells, and came shouting over the bridge to bring the Great Earl in. The burghers had been busy since the rejection of King Louis' award. They had imprisoned some of the King's creatures on whom they had been able to lay their hands, and sacked and devastated the royalist lands in Surrey and Kent. The week before Palm Sunday the Jewry had been stormed, its inmates massacred, and great treasure taken. London had pledged itself in blood, and De Montfort tarried there, waiting for men to gather to him from the four quarters of the land.

While the roads smoked with these marchings and counter-marchings, and while spears shone on the hill-tops, and steel trickled through the green, Denise cheated death in that quiet valley amid the Surrey hills. Marpasse's knife had turned between the ribs, missed the heart by the breadth of a finger nail, and let Denise's blood flow, but not her life. Marpasse's rough sense had saved her, Marpasse who had saved the body, while Aymery had been busy with the soul. And yet to the nuns Denise's return out of the valley of the shadows had seemed nothing short of a miracle. Ursula, true to her belief, had seized the first glimmer of consciousness and sent for the priest who served the convent as confessor. But Denise had put the good man off, pleading that she would not die, and that she was too weak to tell him so long a tale.

The first few days Denise lay in her bed, very white and very silent, taking the wine and food they brought her, and speaking hardly a word. She was like one half awakened from sleep, able to feel and think, but with the languor of sleep still on her. She felt that it was good to lie there in peace, aloof from the world, with the quiet figures gliding in and out, and the sunlight moving in a golden beam with the floor of the little room for a dial. The ringing of the convent bells came to her, and the singing of the nuns in the chapel. Denise lay very still through the long hours in a haze of dreamy thought.

How much did she remember? Enough to inspire her with a new desire to live, enough to make her realise how mad had been the impulse that had set Marpasse's knife a-flashing. They seemed so far away, and yet so near and intimate, those happenings in the April woodland. In moments of deep passion the human heart seizes on what is vital and utterly true, even as those who are dying sometimes seem to see beyond the bounds of the material earth. So Denise remembered that which a woman's heart would choose to cherish. It had been no mere golden mist of pity glazing the cold truth. She had lain in Aymery's arms, arms that had held her with something stronger than compassion.

Thus as Denise lay there abed, a slow, sweet faith revived within her, a belief in things that had seemed dry and dead. Her woman's pride had been in the dust, and she had given up hope, save the hope of hiding in some far place. It might have been that Aymery's arms had closed an inward wound, and that the strength of his manhood had given her new life.

What had the "afterwards" been? What had happened after she had lost consciousness, and what had become of Aymery and Marpasse. She longed to ask the nuns these things, and yet a sensitive pride tied her tongue. The women were kind to her, and yet, as Denise's consciousness became more clear, she could not but feel that the eyes that looked at her were inquisitive and watchful. Now and again came a note of pitying tolerance that jarred the rhythm of her more sacred thoughts; and as the woman in her grew more wakeful she became aware of the shadows that stole across her mind.

On the third day the nuns unswathed her body, soaked the clotted pad away, and looked at the wound. It was healing miraculously with nothing but a blush of redness about its lips. There had been no fever, no inward bleeding. Denise could sit up while they reswathed her in clean linen.

"There is cause for thankfulness here," said the elder of the two nuns who had the nursing of her; "you will have many prayers to say, and many candles to burn to Our Lady and the Queen Helena, our Saint."

She spoke with brisk patronage, but Denise took it for the spirit of motherliness in the woman.

"I owe you also a debt," she said, looking up into the nun's face.

The sister licked her lips as she smoothed the linen about Denise's breast.

"The man and the horse are also to be remembered," she said, a little tartly, "you have much to be thankful for; even I can tell you that."

There was a sharpness in her voice, and a certain insinuating and inquisitive look on her face that made Denise colour. The woman was watching her out of the corners of her eyes, as though she were quite ready to listen if she could persuade Denise to talk. Minds that are cooped up in sexless isolation are often afflicted with morbid imaginings, and an unhealthy curiosity with regard to the more human world. The monastic folk were prone to a disease that they called "accidia." The life was very dull, very narrow, and led to introspection. What wonder that a woman should sometimes hanker to dip her spoon into the world's pot, and smell the stew, though she was not suffered to taste it.

Denise was thankful, and at peace, but she had no desire to open her heart like a French tale for these women to pore over. The nun won no confession from her, and therefore thought the worse of Denise's soul. People who were silent had much to conceal, and the religious sometimes prefer a vivid and garrulous sinner to one who cherishes a reserve of pride.

The two nuns were but mead and water when compared with their Prioress, who was sharp and biting wine. The miraculous swiftness with which Denise had been healed flattered St. Helena, and the piety of her convent. Ursula the Prioress was an earnest woman, cold, bigoted, well satisfied with her own spirit of inspiration. She began to see in Denise a brand to be snatched from the eternal fire, a soul to be humbled and chastened, and purified of its sin.

On the fifth day of Denise's sojourn there, one of the nuns bent over her, and told her in an impressive whisper that the Prioress was coming to sit beside her bed.

"Be very meek with her, my dear," said the nun, "and if she speaks sharply to you, remember that it is for the good of your soul."

So Ursula came, white wimple about yellow face, severe, admonitory, stooping very stiffly towards the level of this mere woman. She sat down on the stool beside Denise's bed, and began at once to catechise her as she would have catechised a forward child.

Denise went scarlet at the first question. It was flashed upon her without delicacy that Ursula knew her secret, and that either Aymery or Marpasse had told her something of what they knew. And Denise's pride was not so frail and weak that she could suffer Ursula to take her heart and handle it.

"Madame," she said, "I have much to thank you for. Yet I would ask you not to speak of what is past. Being wise in the matter, you will know what my thoughts must be."

Ursula was not to be repulsed in such easy fashion, for she knew a part of Denise's tale, and had decided in her own mind that Aymery had treated the subject with too much chivalry. Compassion had softened the harsher outlines, and Ursula had no doubt that Denise was less innocent than she may have pretended.

"My daughter," said she, "for the good of your soul, I cannot let such things pass unheeded."

Denise lay motionless, staring at the timbers of the roof. Ursula talked on.

"Our Mother in Heaven knows that we are frail creatures, and that sin is in the world, but it is the hiding of sin that brings us into perdition. It is meet for your penitence that I should speak to you of these infirmities. There is no shame so great that it may not be retrieved. But you must own your sin, my daughter, and humble yourself before Heaven."

Denise's hands moved restlessly over the coverlet.

"I have confessed it," she said, "though it was not of my own seeking. God himself cannot condemn that as a lie."

Ursula's face grew more austere and forbidding. She detected hardness and obstinacy in Denise, and overlooked that sensitive pride that may seem reticent and cold.

"You speak too boastfully," she said. "It may be that God wills it that I should bring you to humbleness and a sense of shame."

"It is the truth, that I have suffered," said Denise.

"Not yet perhaps, have you suffered sufficiently, for the proper chastening of the spirit. Think, girl, of God's great goodness, and the compassion of Our Mother, and St. Helena, in snatching you from death, and the flames, you—one who had fallen, a broken vessel by the roadside, the companion of low women——"

Again Denise's face flashed scarlet, but this time there was anger in the colour.

"Madame," she said, "hard words do not bring us into Heaven. I have never been what you would have me pretend to be. And the woman, Marpasse, stood by me, and was my friend. She has a good heart, and for me, that covers a multitude of sins."

Ursula, cold fool, was instantly affronted.

"What!" and she seemed to smack her lips with unction, "you, who have worn the scarlet, speak thus insolently to me! It is plain that you have no sense of shame. Hard words indeed are what you need, young woman, the bread of bitterness and the waters of affliction. Pity for your soul moves me to speak the truth."

The flush had faded from Denise's face. She lay there very pale and still, as though suffering Ursula's harsh words to pass over her like the wind.

"How is it, madame," she said at last, "that you believe so much that is bad of me?"

Ursula had her answer ready, the answer such a woman was destined to produce.

"Earl Simon's knight warned me, as was but right and honest."

"Aymery!"

"Sir Aymery, would be more fitting. It was he who besought me to take you in, knowing your misery, and the madness that sin must create in the mind. Pray to God that he may be blessed for snatching you from the devil, and for bringing you here, where, Heaven being willing, we will humble and chasten you."

Denise lay there as though Ursula had taken Marpasse's knife and stricken her, this time to the heart. She had nothing to say to the Prioress. The woman's hard morality had broken and bruised her re-born pride and hope.

Ursula rose, and stood beside the bed.

"Let the knowledge of sin and of humiliation sink into your heart," she said.

And never did woman speak truer or more brutal words.

When Ursula had gone, Denise lay in a kind of stupor, mute, wondering, like one who has been wounded and knows not why. All her dreams were in the dust. Ursula, the iconoclast, had broken the frail images of tenderness, mystery, and compassion. Aymery had said this of her? Denise had no strength for the moment to believe it otherwise.

And so she lay there, humiliated indeed, very lonely, and without hope. There was no bitterness in her at first, for the shock that had destroyed her vision of a new world, had left her weak and weary. She thought of Aymery with pitiful yearning and wounded wonder, and with the wish that he had suffered her to die. Marpasse alone might have comforted Denise in that hour of her defeat.

CHAPTER XXXIV

Denise soon found that the frost of Ursula's displeasure had fallen on her, and that she was to be humiliated and chilled into a proper state of penitence. The temper of the nuns changed to her; they came and went without speaking, their impassive faces making her feel like a child that is in disgrace. It was Ursula's wish that Denise should be mortified in soul and body. Her food and drink were water and bread, and lest the devil of comfort should remain to tempt her to be obstinate, they took the straw and sheets from the bed, and let her lie upon the boards.

Moral frost at such a season was like a severe night in the late spring. Denise's need was to lie in the sun, and to be smiled upon by kind eyes. It was the warm humanism of life that she needed, sympathy, and a clasp of the hand. The utter injustice of the humiliation that they thrust upon her began to awake in her a spirit of revolt. Had she not suffered because of her innocence, and borne what these women had never had to bear?

Why should she fall at Ursula's feet, and pretend to a penitence that she did not feel? And Aymery, too, was she to believe that he had spoken as Ursula had said? If that was the truth, and why should Ursula lie, she, Denise, would pray that she should never be driven to look upon his face again.

Yet her bodily strength increased despite her spiritual unhappiness. The wound in the breast had healed, and she had been able to leave her bed, and move slowly round the room, steadying herself against the wall. And as her strength increased the instinct of revolt grew in her till she began to understand the mocking spirit of Marpasse. To be reviled, humiliated, made to crawl in the dust, to regain a little grudging respect by cringing to her sister women, and by pretending to emotions that she did not feel! These good souls seemed set upon making the re-ascent to cleanliness hard and unlovely. And Denise, like Marpasse, felt a passionate impatience carrying her away.

Meanwhile Ursula, magnanimous lady, had taken pains to spread Denise's story through the convent, and the two nuns who had nursed her had been women enough to know that Denise had borne a child. Ursula had issued her commands; the contumacious devil was to be driven out of Denise; she was to be humbled, and taught to pray for penitence and grace. The nuns who served Denise now opened their mouths once more, and became oracles whose inspiration had been caught from Ursula's lips.

One would enter with the water-jar, set it under the window, and retreat without so much as glancing at Denise. She would pause at the door, and let fall some pious platitude that might act like yeast upon the perverse one's apathy.

"Flames of fire shall subdue those who are stubborn in sin."

"While the vile flesh lives, the soul is in peril. Mortify the body therefore, that the soul may be saved."

"A proud heart means death. Let your pride be trampled under your feet."

"Live, repent, and sin no more."

Such exhortations spaced out Denise's day, but her obstinacy and her bitterness of heart increased till she was nauseated by their piety, and filled with a gradual scorn. Twice Ursula visited her, to depart with the impatience of one whose words were wasted. Had Ursula suffered but once in life, it might have been so humanly simple for her to understand Denise. On the contrary, she found the victim less ductile than at first. Nearly three weeks had passed, and Ursula decided that the woman was well in body, but utterly diseased in heart. The Prioress began to bethink herself of sharper measures. Ursula believed that she had the devil in arms against her, and that the battle was for Denise's soul.

It was the night of May-day, the day of green boughs and garlands, and Denise had stood at her window and watched the sun go down, thinking of the May a year ago, and of her cell in the beech wood above Goldspur manor. The sun had set about an hour when Denise heard footsteps in the gallery, and saw the light of a lamp shining under the door. Ursula came in to the dusk of the room, shielding the lamp from the draught with the hollow of her hand. Her austere face was hard and white, and from one wrist hung a scourge set with burs of wire.

Ursula had brought two of her strongest nuns with her. She set the lamp on a sconce, and was as abrupt and practical as any pedagogue. She bade the women close the door, and commanded Denise to strip and stand naked for a scourging.

"Since words will not move the evil spirit in you," she said, "we must try sharper measures."

Denise put her back against the wall.

"Have a care how you touch me. I am not a dog to be whipped."

Ursula told the two nuns to take her by force, and to strip her of her clothes. But Denise was no longer the patient saint bowing her head before her destiny. She did what Marpasse would have done in such a storm, and taking the water-jar that stood by her, held Ursula and the nuns at bay.

"Off!" she said, "I have some pride left in me. I have eaten your bread, but I will not bear your blows."

She was so tall and fierce, and untamable, that Ursula was the more convinced that Denise had a devil in her, and a devil that was not to be treated with disrespect. She called the nuns off, not relishing an unseemly scuffle, and having some reverence for a stone water-pot that was not to be softened by formulæ. It would be easier to catch Denise asleep, tie her wrists, and scourge her till she showed some penitence.

"Woman," she said, "the evil spirit is very strong in you. But God and my Saint helping me, I will subdue it in due season."

But Ursula, whose piety was given to stumbling rather ridiculously over the hem of her own gown, had no second chance of scourging the devil out of Denise. For Denise had suffered St. Helena's hospitality sufficiently, and she made her escape that night after losing herself in dark passage-ways and listening at doors which she hardly dared to open. She made her way into the court at last, and found the old portress sleeping in her cell beside the gate. The key hung on a nail behind the door, and Denise, who had brought a lighted taper that she had found burning in the chapel, took the key and let herself out into the night.

Denise had made her escape not long before dawn, choosing the time when she knew that the nuns would be in their cells between the chapel services. She waited for the grey dusk of the coming day, sitting under an oak tree on the hill above the convent. And when the birds awoke and set the woodlands thrilling, Denise sat counting the last of the money Abbot Reginald had thrown down at her that winter night, and which Marpasse had sewn up for her in her tunic. Denise thought of Marpasse as she broke the threads and counted out the money into her lap, for Marpasse seemed the one human thing in the wide world that morning.

Life stirred everywhere when Denise started on her way with half a loaf, some beggarly coins, and her old clothes for worldly gear. Brown things darted and rustled in the underwood and grass. A herd of deer went by in the dimness of the dawn, and melted like magic shapes into the woodland as the great globe of fire came topping the eastern hills. The light fell on a dewy world, a world of well-woven tapestry dyed with diverse and rich colours. And Denise saw bluebells in the woods, and thought again of Marpasse and her blue gown. Marpasse would understand. She tried not to think of Aymery that morning.

Denise struck a track that came from nowhere, and led nowhere so far as she was concerned. She went on aimlessly till noon, meeting a few peasant folk who took her for a pilgrim or a beggar. And by noon her body that had lain so many days in bed, cried loudly for a truce under the May sun, and Denise, finding a pool by the roadside, knelt down there and drank water from her palms. The sun had dried the grass, and lying at full length she was soon asleep, with the brown bread held in one white hand.

The bank hid Denise from anyone who passed along the road, and a knight on a black horse came by as she slept. The sound of his horse's hoofs woke Denise. She raised herself upon one elbow, looked over the bank to see who passed, and then sank down again out of sight. The clatter of hoofs died in the distance, but Denise lay there and stared at the clouds in the sky. It was Aymery who had ridden past to hear from Ursula of Denise's life or death. But Denise let him go, hardening her heart against the thought of any man's pity. She would not be beholden to Aymery after the words that Ursula had spoken.

So the Knight of the Hawk's Claw came to the convent that day in May, hardening himself against all possible hope, and prepared to hear nothing but the tale of Denise's death. Ursula received him in her parlour, Ursula who had set her final condemnation upon Denise because of the perversity and ingratitude she had shown in escaping like a thief in the night. And Ursula cursed Denise before Aymery's face, pouring out her indignation against the woman, as though Aymery would sympathise with her over Denise's "contumacy and corruption."

Ursula had no eyes to see the change that had come over the face of the man before her. She was so busy with her denunciations that she did not mark the wrath rising like a cloud on the horizon. Aymery's silence may have deceived her, for he heard her to the end.

He looked hard at Ursula, and the gleam in his eyes would have made a less confident woman wince.

"So you thought that she needed scourging!"

Ursula was very dense that day, refusing to see what a tangle she was weaving.

"The scourge is an excellent weapon, messire," she babbled, "my own back has borne it often, and to the betterment of my soul. But this girl had no gratitude, and no sense of shame. She was obstinately blind, and would not see. I sought to move her by forcing your compassion upon her, and showing her that it was your desire that she should mend her life."

Aymery looked at Ursula as though tempted to strangle the consequential voice in that thin, austere throat.

"You told her that, madame!"

"I held her shame before her eyes, for the tale of her innocence was not to be believed. Her whole character contradicted it."

"And she has fled from you."

"With ingratitude, and cunning."

"Before God, I do not blame her."

He stood motionless a moment, looking down on Ursula with such fierce contempt, that, like many stupid people, she wondered how the offence had risen. Her eyes dilated when Aymery drew his sword. Her mouth opened to call the nuns who waited in the passage, but his laugh reassured her, the laugh that a man bestows on a thing beneath his strength.

"Madame," he said, "you have nothing to fear from me but the truth. You see this sword of mine"—and he held the hilt towards her, grasping it by the blade.

Ursula stared at him as a timid gentlewoman might stare at a rat.

"That hilt is in the form of a cross, madame; I would beg you to look at it. You may have heard that the Cross has some significance for Christians."

Ursula began to recover her dignity. It was borne in upon her suddenly that this man had stern eyes, and an ironical, mocking mouth. And Ursula began to dislike those eyes of his.

"Your words are beyond me, messire," and her normal frostiness struggled to pervade the atmosphere.

Aymery looked at her as a man might look at something that was very repulsive and very ugly.

"Madame," he said quietly, "if you have slain a soul, God forgive you; there are so many fools in the world, and so many of them are godly. There was no sin in Denise that called for the sponge full of vinegar, the scourge, and the spear."

Ursula opened her mouth, but no sound came. Aymery put up his sword, and turned towards the door.

"I would rather have left her," he said, "in the hands of the woman you have called an harlot. Nor need your zeal have put lies into my mouth. Suffer me, madame, to recommend you a saint. St. Magdalene might give you the religion that you lack."

And he went out from her, leaving Ursula speechless, and amazed at his insolence.

Yet Aymery's wrath was a greater and nobler wrath than Ursula's as he mounted his horse and rode out into the world, that world for which Christ had bled upon the cross. Bitterly plain to him was Denise's spirit of revolt, and her passionate discontent with Ursula's morality. What was more, this woman had put her taunts and her homilies into his mouth, and made him harangue and edify Denise! Aymery cursed Ursula for a meddlesome, cold, and self-righteous fool. He would rather have left Denise in Marpasse's hands, for Marpasse had a heart, and no belief in her own great godliness.

And Denise, what would befall her now that they had driven her like an outcast into the world? He was gloomy and troubled because of her, feeling that she had been wounded the more deeply than she had ever been wounded by Marpasse's knife. He remembered too how Denise had sought death in the woods that day. The impulse now might be more powerful, seeing that she had suffered more, and had no friend.

Ride after her into the blind chance of the unknown he could not yet, for Aymery was pledged to Earl Simon and his brethren-in-arms. The Barons' host had gathered at London; they were on the eve of marching southwards into Sussex, for the King was threatening the Cinque Port towns which were loyal to Earl Simon. Aymery had seized these two days to ride and discover the truth about Denise. His knighthood was pledged to the man who had knighted him, nor could he break the pledge to chase a wandering shadow.

CHAPTER XXXV

Marpasse of the blue gown had fallen in with old friends on the way to Tonbridge, where the King had taken the castle of Gilbert de Clare, and these same friends, ragamuffins all of them, were following the glittering chaos of the King's host on the road to the sea. There would be plunder to be had if St. Nicholas would only persuade King Henry to take and sack the Cinque Port towns; and all the beggars, cut-throats and strollers in the kingdom rolled in the wash of the King's host, terribly joyful over the happenings that might give them bones to pick.

The passing of fifty thousand armed men, to say nothing of the baggage rabble, was no blessing to the country folk whom it concerned. Lords, knights, men-at-arms, bowmen, scullions, horse-boys, and harlots went pouring southwards in the May sunshine, ready to thieve whatever came to hand. King Paunch ruled the multitude, for the host ate up the land, and called like a hungry rookery "more, more!" And since a hungry mob is an ill-tempered one when once its patience has leaked out of its tired toes, the King's followers began to grow very rough and cruel before they had marched five leagues. Hunger does not stand on ceremony, and such brutal things were done that the country folk took to the woods and swore death to any straggler. Bludgeon, and axe, and bow took toll of the King's host, and many a rowdy was caught and left grinning at the heavens, with his stiff toes in the air.

Now Marpasse and her friends were as hungry as the rest, and coming as they did, like fowls late for feeding time, their genius for theft was developed by necessity. Yet it is not so easy to steal when everything eatable has been stolen, and when a crossbow bolt may come burring from behind a wood-stack. None the less, Marpasse and her company were in luck not ten miles from Tonbridge Town. They saw a sow feeding on the edge of a beech wood close to the road. There was much pannage in the neighbourhood, and Marpasse and her comrades tucked up their skirts, and went a-hunting, and were blessed with the sight of the black backs of a whole drove of swine.

Great and grotesque was the joy that hounded and hunted through the beech wood, a mob of men-at-arms, beggars, boys, and women trampling the bluebells and the brown and crackling bracken. They shouted, laughed, and cursed as they rounded up the swine, and chased them hither and thither amid the trees. God Pan and his minions went tumbling over tree roots after the black beasts that bolted, and squealed, and flickered like grotesque shadows under the boughs of the beeches.

Marpasse, her skirts tucked up, and her knife flashing, shouted and ran with the lustiest till the sweat rolled into her eyes. As she stood to get her breath, a fat sow came labouring by with a young pig close to her haunches. Chasing them came a long, loose-limbed boy, his hair over his face, his mouth a-gape, his thin legs bounding, striding, and ripping through the bracken. He came up with the chase close to Marpasse, and threw himself on the young porker as a leopard might leap upon a deer. Brown boy and black hog rolled in a tangle into a clump of rotting bracken, and Marpasse, holding her sides, laughed at the tussle, and then ran on after the sow.

The sow, grunting and labouring, led Marpasse away from the rout, and back towards the road. Marpasse, intent on bringing the dame to book for supper, ran on till she came suddenly into a glade with a slant of sunshine pouring through it, and the open land and the road showing at one end thereof. Marpasse followed the sow no farther, for she had stumbled on another adventure that showed more importunity.

Marpasse saw a woman in grey leaning against the trunk of a tree. Not ten paces from her stood an old black boar, with the broken shaft of a spear protruding from one shoulder, and a broad trickle of blood running down his left fore-leg into the grass. The beast tottered as he stood, swinging his head from side to side, his little eyes malevolent, his wiry tail twisting with savage spite.

Marpasse gave a whistle, and looked like one who has run against a ghost. She saw the boar make a dash at Denise, Denise, who was playing hide-and-seek for her life with him round the tree. The beast missed her, and came to earth, only to struggle up, lurch round, and charge once more.

Marpasse clutched her knife, and made a dash for the tree. The boar had missed his blow again, and stood, resting, still dangerous despite the spear head in his side. Marpasse gained the tree with its roots clawing the soil. She gasped out a few words to Denise like a breathless swimmer joining a comrade on a rock in the thick of a boiling sea.

"May marvels never cease! You, child, you, as I shall live to kill pigs! Lord, now, keep an eye on this limb of a black satan!"

She peered round the tree trunk, and pushed Denise round it as the boar charged again, white tusks showing, snout bloody, his little eyes like two live coals. He swerved and missed Marpasse, but she was on him before he could recover and turn. The knife went home where six inches of steel might reach the heart, and Marpasse, springing aside to escape the mad side slash of the tusks, saw that the gentleman had the *coup de grâce*. He rolled over, struggled up again on his belly, scraped the earth with his fore trotters, and then wallowed amid the beech leaves. Marpasse sat down at the foot of the tree, panting and laughing, her brown face red and healthy. She threw the knife aside, caught Denise by the skirt, and pulled her down lovingly into her lap.

"God alive," she gasped, "what a girl it is! Am I always to be rescuing you from Gascons, and from pigs?"

Marpasse was quite joyous. She kissed Denise on the mouth, and then held her away from her, and looked at her with blue eyes that shone.

"Heart of mine, is it you in the flesh, my dear? Why, we left you for dead, Sir Aymery and I! And mightily gloomy he was too, poor lording. To think of it, that I should fall on you in the middle of a wood, while I was chasing an old sow!"

Though she was very voluble, Marpasse's eyes were scanning Denise as one looks at a friend after a long sickness. Marpasse's eyes were very quick. She could have told the number of wrinkles on Denise's face, had there been any. But Marpasse saw something there much more sinister than wrinkles.

"Well, sister," said she, "here is indeed a miracle. But I am not so strong as the lord on the black horse, so please to sit on the grass and let me get my breath. Now for the story. How did St. Helena and all the saints heal you, and how do you come to be here?"

Denise slipped aside from Marpasse, and sat down at the foot of the tree. It was a hard, brooding look about her eyes that had struck Marpasse. Things had not gone with pious facility. Marpasse could tell that by Denise's silence, and by the half-sullen expression of her face.

"Your knife turned between my ribs, Marpasse," she said, "I was a fool to bungle so easy a stroke; I had only to lie still, eat and sleep."

Marpasse clapped her hands.

"This is gratitude, and I swaddled you up like a baby! How is it that you are not still lying abed, and eating and sleeping? You look thin, eh, and what does Sir Black Horse know about it all? Lord, but what a lot of running away you have done in your life! So you fell out with the pious folk, was that it? I could never abide the smell of a nun."

She pinched Denise's cheek, watching her narrowly, for Marpasse had learnt to use her wits, and the philosophy that she had learnt upon the road.

"Well, my dear, what happened?"

"I ran away."

"What a soldier you would make! Madame Ursula was too good a woman. They are all too good for us, my dear; that is where the mischief comes, they tread on us, and expect us to be meek and grateful."

Marpasse grew serious and intent. She looked steadily at Denise, and then reached out and caught her hands.

"No more jesting," she said, "look in my face, sister. I have learnt to read a face."

She held both Denise's hands, and drew her a little towards her. For a moment they were silent. Then Marpasse pressed Denise's hands, sighed, and allowed herself a bluff round oath.

"Curse them," she said, "curse their godliness. So you told them the whole tale."

Denise hung her head.

"Messire Aymery told Ursula."

"The fool! Too much in love to be wise, I warrant. Come now, my dear, love is great of heart, but love is blind, and love talks when it should shut its mouth. Show me the way out of the wood."

She drew Denise close to her, so that her head was on her shoulder. Yet for the moment Denise seemed cold and mute. Marpasse kissed her on the mouth, and the one woman's lips unsealed the other's soul. Before long Marpasse had drawn the whole tale from her, and Marpasse looked fierce over it, and yet more fierce when Denise betrayed the bitterness that had poisoned her heart.

"God in Heaven, child," she broke in suddenly, "do you know what you are saying?"

"I know what you are, Marpasse. They were ready to whip me; I had no pity."

Marpasse set her teeth.

"This life, the devil pity you! For me, yes, but you! I have a brazen face, a conscience like leather, and talons that can tear. But you! Bah, you would kill yourself in a month."

She thrust Denise away from her, as though thrusting her from some influence that was dangerous and to be feared. Denise did not resist her, but sat hanging her head, mute and obstinate, her eyes sweeping up now and again to the face of the woman beside her.

"I am weary of it all," she said, "they made the soul sick and bitter in me."

Marpasse sat with her chin on her fists, her forehead one great frown.

"Ssh, and you thought of me, and the road! Am I such a damned witch as that!"

"You do not curse, and preach."

Marpasse turned on her with sudden, fierce sincerity.

"Yes, I do not preach, because I am down in the ditch, but I know what the mud is like, and I do not want you with me. Bah, let me think. What shall I tell you, that you had better be as dead as the black boar there, before you take to the road."

Marpasse hugged her knees with her arms, staring straight before her, and working her teeth against her lower lip. Denise kept silence, hanging her head, and flying in the face of her own bitterness like a bird that dashes itself against a window at night.

Marpasse awoke suddenly from her musings, and caught Denise by the hood of her cloak. She twisted her hand into the grey cloth, held Denise at arm's length, and threw one word straight into her face.

Denise's eyes flashed. She reddened from throat to forehead, while Marpasse watched her as a physician might watch the workings of some violent drug. Presently the brown eyes faltered, and grew clouded with the infinite consciousness of self. Marpasse burst into a loud, harsh laugh. The next moment she had her arms about Denise.

"Soft fool, the word stings, eh? You are innocent enough; it is all temper, and anger and discontent. Your conscience answered to the sting. I throw your own word in your face, and you redden like an Agnes. No, no, you are not made to be one of us, thank God!"

Denise felt this big woman's brown arms tightly about her. A great spasm of emotion had gathered in Marpasse's throat. She held Denise with a straining, inarticulate tenderness, as a mother might hold a child.

"Heart of mine," said she, "God forgive me for throwing that word in your face. It was the slap of a wet cloth on the cheek of one about to faint. Look up, sister, listen to me, by the Holy Blood, I have the truth to tell."

Marpasse was trembling with the passion in her.

"Take my knife again, Denise, before that! Do I not know, stroller and slut that I am! No, no, not that, not the dregs of other folks' cups, not the shame and the sneers, and the curses thrown back in defiance. Why should these good folk drive us down to hell, why should their fat faces make cowards of us? There, I have been the coward, take the truth from me, and be warned, heart of mine. Better death, I say, before the ditch, for it is death in a ditch that we wretches come to. Brave it out, sister, and for God's love keep your heart from bitterness, and from poisoning its own good blood."

She still held Denise close to her.

"What did the woman St. Aguecheek say? Bah, all lies, I tell you. Such cow-eyed women lie for the sake of piety. The man say that of you? I know better. Come, Denise, listen to me; I know a man when I have looked him in the eyes."

She turned Denise's face to hers and kissed her.

"That was a clean kiss," she said, "and by its cleanness I'll swear that beldam Ursula lied. What of Messire Aymery? A man, child, a rock man with an arm that can smite. Grace be with me, but he would have given you his own heart to mend your broken one. I spoke with him, and I know."

Denise lay at rest in Marpasse's lap.

"Why should Ursula have lied?" she asked.

"Why do dogs eat grass, and vomit? What! I know the woman, eyes that see the point of a pin and miss the moon, and a tongue like a clacker in a cherry tree. Love is lord of all, my dear, and what does that beldam know of love? Messire Aymery had his heart in his mouth that night. I judge that he let the old crow peck at it, and she took the pieces and poisoned them, and pushed them into your mouth. Go to now! Have a little faith."

She looked into Denise's eyes and saw a change in them. A more dewy and credulous April had followed a dry and stormy March. Marpasse's hand had stopped the former wound. She was healing the wound now in Denise's soul.

"God grant that you are right, Marpasse."

"Better, my dear, better. Lie in my arms and think them a man's, and that man as honest as ever loved a woman. May I die in a ditch if I am mistaken! And now, what's to do, as the sluggard says when all the rest have been three hours a-mowing."

Denise slipped out of Marpasse's lap, and sat down close to her, but not so close that their bodies touched. This act of hers seemed to betray that she had come by her stronger self again. Marpasse's scolding had set her upon her feet.

"I shall stay with you," she said simply.

Marpasse opened her mouth wide, a black circle of mute expostulation.

Denise looked in her eyes.

"Why not both of us?" she asked.

Marpasse's mouth still stood open as though to scoff at her own redemption. Denise closed it with her own.

"There is a clean kiss," she said, "let us keep it for each other."

And Marpasse caught her to her, and was a long while silent.

Whatever these two women may have said to one another, the fact was proven that Marpasse did not rejoin her band of vagabonds that night, for she and Denise sat on under the tree, and counted up the money that they could boast between them. They were like a couple of girls talking over some new dress, their heads close together, and their hearts lighter than they had been for many a day. But Marpasse had her whims. She would not mix her money with Denise's, but kept it apart with a sort of scorn, handling it gingerly as though the coins were hot.

Moreover Marpasse had a practical nature, and an attitude towards the ways and means of life that betokened that they were the accursed riddles that gods put to men each inevitable day. In truth Marpasse's life had been one long riddle, and she had grown sick of seeking to solve it, and had put the enigma out of her mind.

"Heart of mine," said she, "we are very much on a dust heap, so far as I can gather. My mouth was made to eat and drink! I cannot turn beast like the king did and eat grass. I have a little bread here in my bag," and she brought out the small sack that she carried slung to her girdle under her cloak.

Denise was drinking in new hope.

"We have the money," she said, "we can buy food, and I have enough for to-night."

"Innocent, there is not a loaf to be bought for miles round. The King's paunch would have made short work of the very trees, only they are too tough. And a word in your ear, treasure your money as though it were your blood. For when a woman is starving, and her pocket is empty, the devil comes in with a grin, and offers to pay for a meal."

"How can we get more money?"

Marpasse grimaced.

"We must go as mendicants," she said. "I will thieve an old cloak, and cover up my colour. At all events, here is our Lord the Pig. We will make some use of him. If you are dainty, go and sit on the far side of the tree."

Marpasse turned butcher that night, nor was it the first time that she had used a knife on a carcase, for people who live by their wits go poaching at times, even after the King's deer. Marpasse had no intimate knowledge of The Charter, or the Forest Laws, save that she had known men who had been caught, and mutilated. Being strong and skilful she had a good skinful of meat beside her before the dusk came down. Then she cut a hazel stake, slung the skin with the meat on it, and going down to a stream that crossed the road, washed the boar's blood from her hands and arms, and came back clean and smiling.

"Silver John will soon be up," she said, nodding towards the east; "if he would only drop us a few coins the colour of his face, I should feel the happiest beggar in the kingdom. Come along with you. We will tramp a little farther from my gossips. If you fell in with them you might not like their tongues."

Denise and Marpasse set out together, keeping a little distance from the road, and walking under the shadows of the trees. Soon the moon came up, and made the May woods magical, and full of a mystery that was clean and pure. Nightingales sang in the thickets, and the scent of the dew on the grass and dead leaves came with the perfume of wild flowers out of the dusk.

Marpasse was in a happy mood despite a day's tramp, and the adventure with the boar.

"I have a feeling in me," she said, "that Silver John looks at us kindly out of the sky. Throw us a penny, good Lord Moon, or some hair out of your silver beard. Hear how the birds are singing. They shall sing a merry jingle into our pockets."

Denise walked beside Marpasse with a smile of peace and of human nearness stealing upon her heart. And the Moon who looked down on the world must have been as wise as the breadth of his solemn face. "Strange," he may have thought, "here are a saint and a stroller hand in hand, comforting one another, and making the night mellow!" But they were both women who had suffered as only women suffer, and the wise Moon may have understood life, and sped them on with a glimmer of good luck.

Marpasse's sense of a blessing that was to be, saw its fulfilment as in the magic of an Eastern tale. They had walked a mile or more, and were looking about them for shelter for the night, when Marpasse stood still to listen, with one hand at her ear.

"Ssh," said she, "what's in the wind?"

It was the sound of a bell that she and Denise heard, a faint melancholy ripple like the sound of falling water in the stillness of the night. Sometimes it ceased and then broke out again, coming no nearer, nor dwindling into the distance.

"A chapel bell?"

Marpasse shook her head.

"No, nor a cow bell either. Poor soul, I know the sound of it. That bell has a voice if ever a bell had."

She listened awhile, and then touched Denise's arm.

"It comes from yonder, there, by that black clump of yews. A leper's bell, or I have never been a sinner."

They went towards the thicket of yews that stood there as though a black cloud covered the face of the moon. The sound of the bell grew more importunate and human. Marpasse whispered to Denise.

"It is the death toll," she said, "I have heard such a sound before at night. The poor souls do not like to die alone in the dark. And those who hear the bell sometimes take pity."

Stretched at the foot of the yew tree with the black plumes curving overhead, Marpasse and Denise found an old man whose face was as white as the cloak he wore. A hand was rocking to and fro ringing the leper bell, whose melancholy sound seemed to die away with the moonlight into the midnight of the yews.

Marpasse bent over him, she had seen too much of the rougher aspects of life to be greatly afraid of a leper.

"Hallo, father," she said, "here is company for you, you can stop your ringing."

The man's arm fell like a snapped bough, and the bell came to the earth with a dull, metallic rattle. The skull face, unmasked now that the end was near, betrayed that the bell carrier had been starved by the famine that the King's host had left behind them in those parts. He was blind and deaf with the death fog, nor did he know that Marpasse was near him till she spoke.

"Good soul, have pity."

He turned his blind face towards Marpasse.

"I am going yonder out of the world, and it is bad to be alone when the evil spirits are abroad, and to hear no prayer spoken. I rang my bell, good soul, for St. Chrysostom, he of the golden mouth, promised me that I should not die alone in the dark."

Marpasse sat down beside him, and beckoned Denise to her.

"Rest in peace, brother. What would comfort you?"

The man lay very still, with a face like ivory. He scarcely seemed to breathe.

"A Pater Noster," he said presently, "I cannot come by a prayer, for the words run to and fro in my head like rabbits in a warren."

Marpasse looked at Denise.

"Here is a Sister who knows all the prayers," she said.

"Ah, there is the smell of good meat a-cooking in a prayer. I saw the Host through a leper squint not a month ago. Pray, good souls, and I will ask the Lord Christ to shrive me."

Denise knelt in the grass, with Marpasse huddled close to her, and spoke prayers for the leper's lips, and found comfort and sweetness for her own soul in the praying. Presently the man held up a shaking hand, and made the sign of the Cross in the air.

"Good souls," he asked them, speaking as though he had a bone in his throat, "unfasten my girdle from about my body."

Marpasse's hands answered his desire. The girdle had a leather pouch fastened to it, and the pouch was heavy. Marpasse gave it into his hands, and he laid it against his mouth, and then held it towards Denise.

"I would rather you had it, Sister, than some begging friar. There is money in it, the alms of five years, and God bless the charitable. Take it, good souls. Dead men want no gold, though you will have candles burnt, and prayers put up for Peter the Leper."

He felt for his bell and they heard a great sigh come out of his body like the sound of a spirit soaring away on invisible wings. The bell gave a last spasmodic tinkle that was muffled and smothered by the grass. Then all was still, save for a light breeze that stirred the black boughs of the yews.

Denise knelt there awhile in prayer. Marpasse had gone aside and had cut down a yew bough with her knife, and was shaping the end thereof into the shape of a narrow spade. She began to turn the sods up clear of the roots of the trees, and Denise came and watched her, holding the dead man's girdle in her hands.

It took Marpasse till midnight to scratch a shallow grave. They laid the leper in it, with his bell in his hand, and his staff beside him, and covered him with sods and boughs.

Then Marpasse and Denise lay down under a tree and slept in each other's arms. They did not look into the pouch that night, for the nearness of death and the infinite pathos thereof possessed them.

And when Denise opened the pouch next morning, a rattle of silver came tumbling out, with here and there a piece of gold that shone like the yellow flower of the silverweed in the midst of its dusty foliage. Marpasse's blue eyes stared hard at the money. Both she and Denise were silent for a minute.

"Poor soul! We will put up prayers for him."

Marpasse hugged her bosom.

"God see to it," she said. "The tide turned when the old man's ship put out over the dark sea."

CHAPTER XXXVI

The King and his lords marched southwards through Sussex, boasting themselves lords of the land, and very much doubting whether Earl Simon would dare to follow them, and meet them in the open field. At Flimwell the King put to death certain of the country folk who had surprised and slain some of his people in the woods. Already many of the rough troops in Henry's service had begun to grumble at the emptiness of the land through which they marched, for they had had but little pillaging to keep them in a good humour, no great cellars to drain dry, no towns to trifle with. The King, being a generous man where other folks' coffers were concerned, as he had proved in the Sicilian farce, turned royal pimp and purveyor to his army. The Abbey of Robertsbridge lay in their path, and Henry let his men loose to plunder the place, and despoiled the monks still further by making them pay heavy ransom for their lives.

The news of the sacking of Robertsbridge came to Abbot Reginald five miles away at Battle, and though he may have rejoiced over the humbling of a rival, he was warned by his brother Abbot's flaying, and made haste to appear loyal. The Cistercians of Robertsbridge had been shrewd and greedy neighbours, and had snatched manors and land that might have fallen to the children of St. Benedict. Grants in Pett, Guestling, Icklesham, Playden, and Iden, and also lands in Snargate, Worth, Combden, Sedlescombe, and Ewhurst, showed that there had been cause for jealousy between the two. Reginald of Brecon may have had some thought of a possible transference of land from the Cistercians to his own "house." To show his loyalty he called out his tenants, and marched out in state as a war lord to meet the King, carrying presents with him, and wearing a mild and pliant manner. Riding back beside the King he spoke sadly of the poverty of St. Martin, and how the Pope's perquisitions and pilferings had emptied his treasure-chest. The King should have had it, had he not pledged much of the Abbey plate to the Jews, but his sweet lord was wholly welcome to such food and drink as could be got together.

Abbot Reginald's presents were perilously mean, and were not to be bulked out by pompous language. Even then, his discretion might not have miscarried but for the over anxious zeal of that cunning fox, Dom

Silvius. The almoner had bleated a "gaudeamus" over the humbling of the Cistercian upstarts at Robertsbridge. He had sought an audience of Abbot Reginald before the monks met in the chapter house, and had put forward the plan that his superior actually accepted. It might be possible to follow the middle path, pay little, and make some profits, and at least escape from being robbed. Silvius took upon himself the secret burying of the Abbey treasure, and Silvius's zeal for St. Martin was so notorious that none of the brethren quarrelled with his energy.

Battle that night was like a garden smothered in locusts, so thick was the swarm of armed men, servants, vagabonds, mules and horses. Henry, Prince Edward, the King of the Romans, and the great lords were lodged in the Abbey, and dined in state in the abbot's hall. Swarthy, swaggering men were everywhere, crowding and jostling, poking their noses into every corner of the five boroughs, kissing the women, and taking the food and drink that the monks and burghers surrendered to them for the blessing of peace and piety. Troops crowded the gardens, the orchards, and the Abbot's park. And though some measure of order reigned, the atmosphere was surcharged with thunder, Reginald and his people feeling themselves like Roman provincials at the mercy of a host of Huns.

In the thick of all this sultriness Dom Silvius must needs discover that some of the reliquaries had been left in the Abbey church. Silvius soon had the sacristan by the girdle, protesting fervently that the reliquaries must be saved from possible sacrilege, and buried with the rest of the Abbey treasure. Silvius played the part of a mad miser and busybody that night. He had spades brought, and sneaked out into the darkness with the sacristan and two of the younger brothers at his heels.

It so happened that Dom Silvius spoilt the whole plot by being over anxious for the property of St. Martin. Some of Comyn's Scotch soldiers, slinking about for anything to thieve, caught the monks burying the reliquaries in a piece of garden ground beyond the great *garde-robe*. The Scotchmen were quick to scent a trick, collared Silvius and his comrades, brought torches and tools, and set to work on their own authority. Not only did they discover two of the reliquaries that had been buried, but struck their spades on the whole of the Abbey treasure that had been hidden in a pit. Scotchmen, monks, treasure, torches, and all went in a whirl to the great hall where the King was dining. And Abbot Reginald hid his face in a flagon when he saw Silvius dragged in, spitting like a furious cat.

The King's eyes were not pleasant to behold. He had the "merry-thought" of a chicken in his hand, and was scraping the flesh from it with a silver knife. He looked attentively at the treasure that Comyn's men tumbled on the floor below the dais. Then he broke the "merry-thought" in two, and folding the pieces in his fist, bade Reginald choose his lot.

Reginald of Brecon pulled out the shorter of the two. The King laughed, a dry cackle that was ominous.

"The shorter the bone, the shorter the shrift, gentlemen," he said. "We will take care of this treasure for you, my lord Abbot. As for the cellars, storehouses, burgher tenements, and all such belongings, we make a night's gift of them to those who thirst and hunger."

There was loud laughter, and a babel of voices. The flushed gentry at the table shouted "God strengthen the King." One monk alone was mad enough to throw himself between St. Martin and the pleasantry of the royal spite, and that monk was Dom Silvius.

He broke loose, and rushed with furious and stuttering face to the high table, brandishing his cross, fanatical as any Egyptian hermit out of the desert.

"Spoiler of the houses of God!"

The bacon was following the fat into the fire. Abbot Reginald, good man, lost patience, and threw his platter in Silvius's face.

Silvius, with a gobbet of gravy on his nose, looked comic enough, but still burnt like a Telemachus.

"God shall revenge sacrilege! Let the curse of St. Martin——"

Someone from behind took him by the collar, and twisted a fist into the folds till Silvius was in danger of being choked.

The King lay back in his chair and laughed.

"Take the prophet away, and let him be washed," he said. "By the heart of King Richard, I have no use to-night for an Elijah!"

In this way it came about that Dom Silvius took a ride on the back of an ass, with his feet lashed under the beast's belly, and a dirty pot forced down over his ears. The mob pelted Silvius with stones and offal till he was a mere image covered with blood and dirt. Comyn's Scots had the privilege of bringing the martyrdom to an end. They took Silvius from the back of the ass, and carrying him into the place where the treasure had been buried, pitched him into the *garde-robe* drain, and so left him.

Silvius's blundering had, however, a grimmer significance, for it brought upon the Abbey and the town that straggled about it the same fate that had befallen the despised Cistercians. The King had given the place over to plunder, and it was at the mercy of the rough soldiery who were doubly insolent with the fumes of mead and wine. The folk of the borough of Battle might well have cursed Silvius and the Abbey treasure, for the devil was let loose among them that May night.

Nor did the darkness hide the violence and the horror, for the very furniture was thrown out into the street and piled up amid the faggots to help the bonfires that lit the sport of war. Women and children fled like frightened birds into the darkness, and were thrice blessed if they were not caught, and held. The gaudy queans who had followed the army played King of the Castle on the high altar of the church, pulling each other down by the skirts, shouting, and tumbling over one another on the steps. Drunken men burst in the door of the bell tower, and set all the bells clanging in huge discords. Others caught the monks, and made them race naked round the cloisters, whipping them with their girdles to make them nimble.

Gaillard and some of his fellows had come by a cask of wine, and Gaillard had Black Isoult, Marpasse's comrade, under his arm, and was well content with the lady. They needed a house for a night's revel, and chose one in the main street, a stone house that joined a forge. Gaillard's men broke down the door, while their captain held a torch, and Isoult sat on the wine cask, laughing.

When the door gave way they were met in the dark entry by a virago with a hatchet, none other than Bridget, the smith's wife, who had stormed against Denise. The men fell back from her, but Isoult showed herself more valiant, and quite a match for the lady.

"Make way, Gammer Goodbody," she said, "make way for the red gown."

Bridget answered her with an oath, and a word that was too familiar to Isoult's ears.

The little woman's black eyes sparkled with spite.

"Here is a respectable slut," she said, "who has not learnt to kiss the foot of a lady."

And she cut Bridget across the forearm with her knife, so that the smith's wife dropped her hatchet.

Gaillard sent his men in, and they overpowered the woman. But Isoult would not let them harm her. Her own spirit of wickedness was equal to taming the big shrew.

She made them cut off Bridget's hair, dress her in some of her man's clothes, tie a lamb's skin under her chin, and truss her with her hands fastened to her ankles. Then while she drank wine with Gaillard and made merry, seated on a bench, her red gown the colour of freshly shed blood, she had Bridget rolled across the floor and propped up near her like a sick duck. Isoult made a mock of the smith's wife that night because of the thing she had called her, asking her where her marriage lines were, and why her man had not come home. Sometimes she threw the dregs from her ale horn into Bridget's face, and called her a she-goat and a rabbit. Bridget still had the courage to curse back again, though her tongue was less clever than Isoult's. But when Isoult took a burning stick from the fire, and began to singe Dame Bridget's stockings, the woman took to screaming, and pleaded for pity.

So Dom Silvius let the devil loose in Battle, and the memory of that night lingered for many a long day.

As for Isoult's comrade Marpasse, she and Denise had come to Grinstead amid the woods, and were lodged in the house of a woman who fed swine and kept a wayside inn. At Grinstead they heard the news that Earl Simon and the Barons' host had left London with fifteen thousand burghers to swell their ranks, and were on the march to deal with the King. The army would pass not far from Grinstead, so said the woman of the inn, and Marpasse and Denise took counsel together and put their plans in order.

"Love carries the sword," said Marpasse, and laughed and kissed Denise.

"I can never look him in the face again."

"Bah, grey goose! There will be wounds to be healed. A woman's hands are useful when the trumpets are hoarse and tired."

CHAPTER XXXVII

On the evening of Tuesday, the 13th of May, the Barons lay amid the woods about Fletching, knowing that they were to march on the morrow to offer the King battle outside Lewes town. All hope of peace had gone, and both parties had thrown away the scabbard. Henry believed that he had Earl Simon at his mercy, for the royal host far outnumbered the Earl's, and where De Montfort could count in part only on burgher levies, the King and his favourites had the flower of the foreign mercenaries in their pay. Henry had refused to listen to the Bishops of London and Worcester, who had come from the Earl. God was delivering Simon and his turbulent following into the royal hands, and the King was not to be cheated of his opportunity by the tongues of meddlesome priests.

As the evening sun sank towards the west, the Barons' host gathered and stood to their arms with the fresh green of the May woods spreading a virgin canopy above their spears. It was no gorgeous pageant so far as pomp and circumstance were concerned. There were many banners and pennons brilliant in the evening sunshine, but the bulk of De Montfort's army was made up of the lesser gentry, and their retainers, and the burghers of the towns, plain men, but men who were in grim and sober earnest. Many of them had never fought in their lives before, and Gaillard, and such gallants in the King's service, laughed when they spoke of the herd of hogs they were to chase through the Sussex woodlands. But the stocky, brown-faced men of the English towns, and the English manors were not to be trampled on so easily. Men who could fell timber, and handle the scythe, the bill and the hammer, were tough in the arms, and sound and strong at heart.

The Barons' host went on its knees that evening, its lines of steel seaming the green woods. Lords, knights, gentlemen, yeomen, burghers, knelt with their shields before them, their swords naked in the grass, their heads uncovered. Between the ranks of these silent, steel-clad figures came the Bishop of Worcester, and many priests with him, chanting as they came. The whole host was confessed, absolved, and blessed under the oak trees of the Fletching woods. It was as though the heart of England was shrived that day, before the national ordeal of battle.

"Holy Cross, Holy Cross."

Men came running and shouting through the ranks, carrying bales of white cloth which they spread on the grass, and tore into hundreds of strips. Every fighting man was to carry the White Cross on his breast. And in the midst of it all Earl Simon and a great company of lords and gentlemen came riding through, wearing the White Cross on their surcoats. Swords and spears were tossed aloft, and the heart of the host went up in sound like the long roar of a stormy sea.

Under a great oak tree De Montfort knighted many of the younger lords and gentlemen, among them Robert de Vere, John de Burgh the son of the great justiciary, and young Gilbert, Earl of Gloucester. Then he and his sons and his captains went everywhere, heartening their men, bidding them rest and eat, and keep strong and lusty against the morrow.

As De Montfort was riding back with young Gloucester, and a few knights and gentlemen of his own household to the manor house where he had his quarters, he came upon several women standing under the shade of an old yew. It happened that Earl Simon had put abroad an order that no women should be suffered to follow the army on the march. If the King and his host had seven hundred courtesans in their camp, that was the King's affair; De Montfort would have none of it.

Earl Simon ordered his gentlemen to halt, and turned aside alone towards the yew tree. Two of the women had come forward, and were waiting as though to speak with the Earl. De Montfort had a frown on his face. Great soldier that he was, he had his rough and passionate moods; his strong sincerity sometimes ran away with his tongue.

The two women went on their knees before Earl Simon's horse.

"Sire," said the elder of the two, "put your anger away. We are here for love of the White Cross."

Straight speaking, and a straight look of the eyes were things that De Montfort loved. The armed men who watched and waited, wondered why Earl Simon tarried there talking, and did not send the women away.

De Montfort's face had begun to shine like the face of a saint. He looked very thoughtfully at the two women as they laid their lives in the hollow of his hand. The plan was Marpasse's, but Denise would not suffer her comrade to carry it out alone. Their plan was to go as spies to Lewes that night, and bring back any news that they could gather as to what the King purposed to do on the morrow.

Earl Simon would have none of it at first. Perhaps he doubted their honesty; yet the two women contrived to convince him, Marpasse sly and valiant, Denise with the quiet eyes of one who has chosen a certain part.

De Montfort appeared puzzled by Denise. Marpasse saw the look, and broke in in her blunt, bold way:—

"She is not of my clay, sire, but we were baked in the same oven. She has seized this trick of mine, and will not let it out of her hands."

"Is that so, child?"

Denise's eyes met his.

"I am not afraid, sire," she answered.

The Earl still shirked accepting a possible sacrifice. Marpasse put in a final word.

"Though it be to my shame, lord," she said, "I have learnt how to tread among thorns. There is only one thing that I would ask, and that is the right to choose the man who shall take us within two miles of Lewes town."

She flashed a look at Denise as though to silence her, and went close to De Montfort's horse. A smile came over his face as he listened to Marpasse, and there was sadness in the smile, and the quiet compassion of a man who had held children in his arms.

"God guard you both," he said, "it shall be as you desire."

Aymery had command of the guard that evening at the manor house where Simon, the Earl of Gloucester, and the great lords had their quarters. Word was brought him by an esquire of De Montfort's son Guy, that the Earl was calling for him, and that Simon was to be found in the great barn where the Bishop of Worcester was to preach to the lords and gentlemen before sundown. Aymery found the Earl sitting on a barrow that stood on the threshing floor, a knot of knights standing behind him, and the evening sunlight that poured in striking silver burs from their battle harness.

Simon looked straight into Aymery's eyes as he gave him his orders.

"Go down to the yew tree near the pond where we water our horses, messire. You will find two women waiting there. They have sworn to spy out the land for us. Take a guide and ten spears, and see the women as near to Lewes as you can without breaking cover."

Earl Simon always eyed his men as though he were looking into the brain behind the eyes. Aymery saluted, and turned to obey. His face betrayed no surprise, though it was a new thing for De Montfort to rely on the wits of two women.

Simon called him back.

"Wait, and keep watch in the woods," he said, "the women will try to bring back news. We shall be on the move before dawn."

He rose from the barrow, and crossing the threshing floor, laid a hand on Aymery's shoulder.

"It is in my heart to catch the King napping to-morrow," he said. "I trust England with you, in this, and some of us may have to suffer."

He stood considering something a moment, frowning a little, his hand still on Aymery's shoulder.

"The two women yonder, brave hearts, have talked me into suffering this. I would not put such work upon a woman, but then, my son, we all carry the Cross. Hasten, and God speed you."

And Aymery went out from before him, thinking of the two women as women, and nothing more.

Marpasse, who had spun her net very cleverly, and whose hope had been to catch and entangle a man and a woman therein, was bitterly disgusted at the way things happened. She had made up her mind that she herself would go to Lewes, but she had no intention of taking Denise into the hell of the royal camp. She certainly caught these two people in her net, but they broke the threads, and would not do as she desired. Yet Marpasse might have seen how it would be had she not been too eager to sweep away Denise's pride.

Denise was standing by her, with the sunlight on her hair and face, waiting in all innocence for the escort that Earl Simon was to send for them. A prophetic fore-gleam of self-sacrifice played in the deeps of her brown eyes. She had seized on Marpasse's plan and clasped it as something precious and something actively alive. The solemn shriving of that great host under the oaks of the Fletching woods had sent the blood to Denise's brain. She felt herself in the midst of strong men who held their swords aloft and prayed. She was as one who saw a sacred fire burning, and was driven to throw herself therein with the ardour of a soul that seeks martyrdom in some great cause.

Marpasse, who had a corner of each eye very wide awake for the coming of the man on the black horse, began to wonder how Denise would meet the truth. And Marpasse's expectations came back limply to roost like birds that had been drenched in a thunder shower. She had struck a spark into Denise's soul, and the spark blazed up into a beacon that Marpasse could not smother.

Aymery came riding down past the great pool where troopers were watering their horses, the beasts trampling and splashing in the oozy shallows, and sucking lustily despite the mud. Marpasse soon marked him down, and watched his face as they came within his ken. Marpasse saw

Aymery go red as a boy, and being comforted by the man's colour, she stole a glance at Denise. Denise's face had been shining like the face of one inspired. Marpasse saw it cloud suddenly as though a shadow had fallen across it.

So they met, with the women under the yew tree fifty paces away watching them, and the splashing of the horses and the voices of the men merging into the great murmur that seemed to fill the woods. For the moment Aymery had nothing to say. Marpasse could have pricked him with the point of her knife to make him leap out of that slough of silence. Denise stood in the long grass, a whorl of golden flowers brushing her grey gown, her face white and troubled in the sunlight. Marpasse might have had a pair of dumb and irresponsive puppets on her hands. There was nothing left for her but to pull the strings.

"I am the brown woman who mended a wound, lording," she began.

Aymery remembered her well enough. His face resembled a grey sky through which the sun was trying to shine and could not. He had his heart in his mouth but Denise did not help him. She stood there, as though her thoughts soared into some cold and brilliant corner of heaven. Yet only the surface had the sheen of ice. The deeps beneath were full of flux and tumult.

Marpasse, being a plain and impetuous woman, could have nudged both of them, and prompted both, at one and the same moment. Matters were not moving as she had forecasted, and these two people looked afraid of one another.

"A kiss on the mouth, lording, and your arms round her," that was what she would have said.

Her words were:—

"Earl Simon may have told you the news."

By the sharp look that Aymery gave Denise, Marpasse guessed that he knew the truth.

"To Lewes?" he asked her, with the uneasy air of a man urging himself to do something that seemed strangely difficult.

"Oh, we women, lording, can be of use."

He repeated the words, looking at Denise.

"To Lewes?"

Marpasse grimaced.

"God knows, we shall be walking on hot bricks," she said; "but then, this blue gown, and this face of mine, are better than passwords."

Aymery's eyes were still upon Denise, as though waiting for one word or look from her. He could not see that she was as passionately mute as he was, and that a spasm of self-consciousness held her in thrall.

Marpasse broke in, feeling the silence like thorns in her flesh.

"I can do without her, lording. Listen to me, Golden-head. They shall put me within a mile of Lewes town, and wait in the woods for any news that I can gather. You need not play the moth to the candle."

Marpasse saw Aymery's eyes flash something at her that made her less uneasy. The judgment lay with Denise. They looked at her and waited.

Denise looked at neither. She hid everything, nor was there a ripple of emotion about her mouth.

"I shall go with you, Marpasse," she said.

The big woman shrugged her shoulders.

"Bah, I can as well take one of the others with me. They would play the part better, and look less dangerous."

Denise kept her eyes from Aymery, as though her pride had set itself a pilgrimage, and would not see anything that might hinder it.

"Say what you please, I shall go with you, as I promised."

Marpasse nodded her head, and seemed to consider the situation. Biting her lips, she looked from Aymery to Denise. Neither of them helped her, and Marpasse could have stamped her foot at the man, and told him what to do. "Fool, take her away from me, and hold her fast!" She shrugged her broad shoulders, and laughed a little mockingly.

"We are all talking so much," she said, "that we shall get nowhere to-night unless we tie up our tongues. You, lording, can find us a couple of mules or asses."

Marpasse's sarcasm sank into sand, for Denise turned and walked back towards the rest of the women who were making a meal under the yew tree. Some of them were using their needles, and sewing the white crosses on to the surcoats of the men.

"I will say good-bye to them."

Perhaps there was a set purpose in this act of hers, for Denise would have Aymery see the comrades with whom she had travelled.

Aymery was turning his horse when Marpasse caught his bridle.

"Lording," she said, "keep the fog out of your eyes. We, and the rest yonder, followed the host to do what we could when men were knocked out of the saddle. I have changed my cloth, if not the colour of it. She has done that for me."

She looked up almost fiercely into Aymery's eyes.

"Speak to her on the way, lording. Women are not won by looking, charge home, and let the trumpets blow, unless," and she let go the bridle, "unless my lord has changed."

The man's eyes answered her that.

"Marpasse, have you forgotten that night?"

"No, not I, nor you, lording."

"It seemed death then, but now — —"

Marpasse's eyes flashed up at him.

"Man, man, what makes the hills blaze, a wet fog, or the sunset?"

Dusk was beginning to fall when they set off into the woods, Denise upon a grey palfrey that a priest had lent them, Marpasse perched on a mule, Aymery and his men in full battle harness, their spears trailing under the trees. They had a guide with them, a swineherd who knew every path and ride even by night, and though the sun was touching the horizon, they had before them the long twilight of a clear evening in May.

Aymery sent the guide on ahead with the men-at-arms, and Marpasse, knowing what she knew, manœuvred her mule so as to leave Aymery with Denise. But the priest's palfrey seemed to have conceived a great affection for Marpasse's mule. Denise had hardly a word to say. She kept close beside Marpasse and appeared blind to the glimmerings of that good woman's impatience.

Marpasse could bear it out no longer. She struck her mule several resounding smacks with her open hand, and the beast went away at a lazy canter, leaving Denise and the man on the black horse together.

"May God untie their tongues," Marpasse said to herself; "it is a curse to have too quick a conscience. I shall be hoisted on my own fire unless the man can bring her to reason."

So Marpasse rode on behind the men-at-arms, leaving the two to work out their own salvation.

The woods were steeped in a green twilight, and a great stillness reigned everywhere, save for the song of the birds. Here and there a great tree stood tongued as with fire. The foliage grew black against the golden glow in the west, while long slants of light still stole in secretly along the solemn aisles.

The birds were at their vespers, and a cold dew was falling, drawing out the fresh perfume of the woods at night.

Aymery and Denise were riding side by side, the woman pale, sad-eyed, yet resolute, the man sunk in that deep silence that follows some ineffectual and passionate outburst of the heart. They seemed afraid of one another, nor could they meet each other's eyes. Denise's white face might have stood for the moon. And though the birds sang, their voices gave the dusk a sadder and a stranger mystery.

Aymery spoke at last, passing a hand over his horse's mane.

"Our Lady keep you," he said, "I will not quarrel with your desire."

Denise's lips were dry, and she felt as though the old wound had broken over her heart.

"If I have suffered," she said simply, "I have learnt what life is."

"Self-martyrdom?"

His voice woke echoes that she strove to smother.

"It is God's whim in me, perhaps, that I should prove myself. Marpasse and I will go together."

Night had come and the glare of many fires lit the southern sky when they reached the edge of the woodland and saw the great downs black, and vague and ominous. The men were waiting under the woodshaw, and Marpasse stood rubbing the nose of her mule. She could hear voices, slow, suppressed, stricken into short, pregnant sentences like the disjointed fragments of a song struck from untuned lutes.

Denise had left her palfrey under a tree. She came out from the shadows, and taking Marpasse in her arms, kissed her.

"We go together, you and I," she said. "No, no, say nothing to me, it is my heart's desire."

Marpasse held her, and was mute. She looked towards a shadowy figure on a shadowy horse, and Denise understood the look.

"I have told him, he will not hinder me in this."

"Heart of mine, stay here in the woods. I can go alone, my carcase is of no account."

Denise would not be put away.

"Marpasse," she said, "this is our Lord's true passion working in me. Nor shall the cup from which He drank be snatched from me to-night."

Marpasse was silent, feeling a greatness near her that awed her rebellious impulses. She kissed Denise, and was very humble, thinking that she herself had brought this thing to pass.

"Come then," she said, "it may be that God goes with us to-night."

Aymery, standing with one arm over his horse's neck, watched them disappear into the darkness, the swineherd going with them to show them the road to the town. The whole northern sky still burnt with a faint glow of gold, and in the south a hundred fires flickered amid the black folds of the downs. And Aymery watched these distant fires, thinking with grim impatience of the King's host that lay yonder like a great dragon ready to tear and slay.

CHAPTER XXXVIII

The King and Richard the Roman were lodged that night at the Priory of St. Pancras, Prince Edward with De Warenne in the castle of Lewes. Nor would it have been easy to choose between St. Pancras Priory and Lewes Town in the matter of furious and indiscriminate drinking. Some said that the King's host mustered sixty thousand men. One thing was certain, that a very great number of them were drunk that night, and that the lords and captains were no better than the men.

"The King will hunt swine to-morrow."

Such was the night's apothegm, and men flung it with variations and with a liberal garnishing of oaths into each other's faces. The metaphor was acceptable to those who were in their cups, and much repetition piled assurance upon assurance. The great army of the King had its head full of drunken insolence. Its mouth uttered one huge oath. It would only have to show itself on the morrow, and De Montfort's dirty burghers would take to their heels and run.

Bonfires had been lit everywhere, and round them were crowds of grotesque faces that bawled, and gulped, and fed. There was no lack of food and drink, sheep and oxen were roasted whole; men gorged themselves like dogs about the carcases. Cressets flared upon the castle towers, and Prince Edward had set twenty trumpeters to blow fanfares before the gate. The Priory bells were jangling like fuddled men quarrelling with one another. There was no discipline anywhere, no sign of a high purpose, no forethought for the morrow. "The King will hunt swine!" Men bellowed it to one another, and the superstition contented them.

When Denise and Marpasse came near the west gate of the town, they saw a huge fire burning there, the flames lighting the black battlements above. A great crowd had gathered about the fire, and the noise might have equalled the noise at Barnet Fair. Men were running about half naked like hairy-legged satyrs mad with wine. The platform of the town gate was crowded with a roaring, squealing mob that amused itself by emptying nature upon the equally repulsive mob below. Mounted upon a tub, a man with one eye, dressed like a Franciscan, spouted indecent skits on the clergy, pretending the while to be zealously in earnest. Elsewhere a crowd of excited and contorted figures made a ring round two women who, stripped to the waist, were wrestling, their faces smeared with the blood of a dead ox. Drunken rascals were scrambling about on all fours, and pretending to be dogs. If any mad whim came into a man's head, he acted on it, and did not stop to think.

Marpasse had taken Denise by the wrist, and they had melted back into the darkness, holding their breath over the chance of being plunged into that simmering human stew. Marpasse was no innocent, but her face went hard and ugly with the sincerity of her disgust.

"Drunken swine! We will keep away from your sty, I warrant you."

She spoke in a harsh whisper, her pupils contracting as she stared at the gate and the bonfire that was half hidden by live things that swarmed like beetles. Denise shuddered inwardly, and was silent. She thought of the cool, dark woods over yonder, and of the grim and quiet men who waited for the dawn.

Marpasse waved an arm towards the town.

"You see," she seemed to say.

"They are like wild beasts."

"What did you think to find, my dear; blessed banners and crosses, and priests galore? Or perhaps so many Sir Tristans keeping watch under the stars, and thinking of noble and great ladies. No, no, the King and Earl Simon handle their hot coals differently. Come away, we shall do no good yonder."

They retreated along the road, and hearing loud squeals of laughter near them, drew aside, and hid themselves in a ditch. Marpasse could feel Denise shivering. When the laughter had gone by them towards the town, Marpasse stood up and looked about her in the darkness.

"We were walking into the cattle market," she said in an ironical whisper. "The Priory lies yonder, most likely the King is lodged there. Pick your feet up out of this mud."

They scrambled out of the ditch, and leaving the road, went on cautiously hand in hand. Marpasse's eyes seemed like the eyes of a cat. Sometimes they stopped to listen, standing close together as though for comfort. The darkness, rendered more weird and baffling by the glare of the watch fires, seemed to threaten them with all manner of evil shapes.

An overbearing desire to talk mastered Denise. The sound of her own voice tended to smother the whisperings of panic. Marpasse let her run on till the mass of the Priory began to blacken the clear sky.

"Ssh," she said, "we shall need our ears now, more than our tongues. If we are stopped by any of these gentry, leave the talking to me."

Aymery's face flashed up into Denise's consciousness. Her hand contracted convulsively upon Marpasse's wrist.

"If Earl Simon could have fallen on them to-night," she whispered.

"To-morrow will do, or I am no prophet," answered Marpasse.

The Priory of St. Pancras was shut in by its great precinct wall, but Marpasse and Denise found it only too easy to make their way within. There was a guard at the Priory gate, but the men were drinking and dicing, letting the night look after itself. People did what they pleased, and St. Pancras had no heavenly say in the matter. The men of the sword had pushed the good saint into a corner, his monks, too, were exceeding meek and docile, holding to the Christian doctrine that one must suffer in the spirit of patience. Yet their patience was largely a matter of discretion and of necessity, for put power in a priest's hands and he is a tyrant among tyrants.

Booths had been set up inside the precinct wall, and there were clowns who kept the crowd a-laughing, and minstrels who sang songs fit for the lowest ear. Women in bright-coloured clothes went to and fro between the bonfires, fierce, hawk-faced women who knew how to take care of their own concerns. Marpasse and Denise kept in the shadow, though there were things to stumble over in the darkness, as Marpasse found when she trod on something that kicked out at her and cursed. They wandered into the cloisters, and through the dark passage-ways and slypes; all doors were open, and no one hindered them, for no one seemed to boast any authority that night. Sometimes they stood in dark corners, and listened to what was said by those who passed. St. Pancras might have stood with his fingers in his ears, for the humour was very broad, and the language primitive. "The King will hunt swine to-morrow." The same snatch served here as in Lewes town, and Marpasse understood the significance thereof. The King meant to attack De Montfort on the morrow, and was letting his men debauch themselves into reckless good humour.

The great church was full of tawny light, all the doors stood open, and Marpasse and Denise gliding from buttress to buttress, looked in through the door of the north transept. Torches had been stuck about the walls, the smoke pouring up, and filling the dim distance of the vaulting with drifting vapour. The church was full of men and women in cloths and silks of the brightest colours, men and women who danced and drank, and sprawled about the flagged floors. Nor were the men from the common crowd of the King's army; they were the lords, the knights, and the esquires, wild captains of free-lances who held a debauch before to-morrow's battle. The high altar was like a rostrum in old Rome, seized upon by a drunken crowd, and covered with creatures that laughed and howled, and clung to one another. Some of the women had put on the men's helmets, others wore garlands of half-withered flowers. A party of young nobles had broken open the sacristy, and dressed themselves in precious embroidered vestments. The scene was a scramble of colour, a scene of perpetual movement, of flux and reflux, of strong sensual life throbbing in and out of half-darkened sanctuaries.

Marpasse had seen enough, and Denise too much. They were moving away, when Marpasse started aside and drew Denise into the shadow of a buttress. A blur of movement disentangled itself from the darkness, and took shape in a knot of figures that approached the transept door. The party halted, and the two women saw a man wearing a cloak of sables, and a surcoat of some golden stuff, come forward alone and stand looking into the church.

The glare from the torches fell upon the face of the man who wore the sable cloak. It was a handsome face, yet weak and troubled, the face of a man without great self-restraint, a man who would attempt to be violent when he should be patient, and who would betray his weakness when he needed strength. There was something tragic about the figure standing there alone, and looking in upon the wild night before the dawn of the morrow. It might have been the figure of a magician gazing upon the fierce and elemental things that he had brought into being, and who had lost the power of holding them under his spell.

Marpasse saw the man cross himself, and turn away with an air that suggested foreshadowings of disaster. It was a figure full of infinite significance, in that it had striven continually to strut upon the world's stage, and yet had never succeeded in being more than a puppet.

Marpasse had whispered in Denise's ear.

"The King!"

And then:—

"The poor fool! He is not a shepherd like Earl Simon. Even his sheep dogs are out of hand."

As he had come out of the darkness, so he disappeared, silently, almost furtively, with no blare of trumpets and no tossing of torches. Men who were wise saw in him a thing that was sometimes a saint, sometimes a mean, contriving Jew, often a firebrand, more often still a beauty-loving fool. Brave enough in battle, and a clean liver, yet the grim, animal energy of his father might have served him better than his own flickering and inconstant brilliancy. Henry could delight in the colour of a painted window, and he had the heart of a sentimental woman. In one thing alone he may have been of use, for his follies taught the stronger son to be warned by the mistakes of a weak father. Henry made war against the spirit of liberty stirring in the heart of a great people. Edward the Strong was wiser in knowing the nature of his own strength.

Marpasse nudged Denise, and pulled her hood forward over her face.

"We have seen enough," she said; "they are to hunt swine to-morrow! Good, very good, let them beware of the boar's tusks."

They made their way back towards the gate, and St. Pancras, kind saint, blessed them, for they escaped unscathed out of the place. And coming out to the cool darkness that covered the downs, they sat down side by side to wait for the dawn.

CHAPTER XXXIX

Marpasse was up as soon as the first grey light began to spread above the hills, and it was possible for them to see their way. Denise had passed the night, lying with her head in Marpasse's lap, and sleeping soundly despite her promise to remain awake. Marpasse had smiled, and let her sleep, trusting to her own ears and eyes to warn her of the approach of any peril.

They were on the move while the land was still half in shadow, for Marpasse was as eager as any man to let Earl Simon know the truth about the King. Standing and looking back on Lewes as the dawn increased, Marpasse could gauge how cheaply the King and his captains held their enemy. There were Gascons too with Henry, and the Gascons should have known what manner of man they had to deal with in Earl Simon. Yet the green slopes of the downs, gleaming with dew as the golden light of the dawn began to play on them, were utterly deserted. The King's host lay snoring after its debauch, without a single troop of horse to patrol the hills. Only on the hill that was afterwards called Mount Harry could Marpasse distinguish what appeared to be a solitary sentinel. And he, too, was lying like a grey stone on the hillside, asleep at his post while the sun made the east splendid.

Marpasse clapped her hands.

"The fools!" she said; "come, there is no time to lose. We ought to bear more yonder towards the west. They will be on the watch for us. I know of one man who will have been awake all night."

She looked at Denise and saw her redden.

"Give him one kiss, heart of mine," she said, "for a man fights the better with his woman's kiss upon his mouth."

"Then, it will be the last, Marpasse," she retorted.

"Bah, have you had him killed already!"

"It will be the last whatever happens," said Denise sadly. "Do you think that I would let him make so poor a bargain."

Marpasse would have taken her to task for showing such hypersensitive self-consciousness, had not a horseman appeared above the crest of a low hill, and come galloping down into the freshness of the May morning. Marpasse looked at him as he came up, and the man's face shone in the sunlight. He was out of the saddle, and standing by Denise, as though it was not easy for him to keep his hands from touching her.

Marpasse laughed, and looked brown and joyous.

"You see, lording," she said, "I have brought her back fresh as a white may bough."

None the less the may bough had a rich colour. Marpasse turned her back on them, and looked intently towards Lewes.

"Lording," she said, "I give you while I count fifty. There is no time to lose, for the King means to fight to-day."

Whether she wished it or not, Denise found her hands in Aymery's. He stood and looked into her eyes, and neither of them said a word.

"Ten," quoth Marpasse.

Aymery's face came nearer to Denise's.

"My desire," he said, "if I live through it, I would have your heart for mine."

Denise had gone red at first, but she was as white now as her shift.

"Lord," she said, "I cannot."

"Bah! Twenty!" called Marpasse.

Aymery's eyes were like the pleading eyes of a dog. He remembered what Marpasse had said to him. Yet despite her vigorous counsel the great love in him made him reverent.

"Why *cannot*?" he asked her simply.

She looked up at him and her eyes swam with tears.

"Because of—of the pride in me, because of all that has happened."

"Fool, kiss her! Thirty!" murmured Marpasse.

Aymery still held Denise's hands. Yet he was looking beyond her towards the town hazy with the golden mist of the morning.

"It was I who brought it on you," he said.

He felt Denise shudder, and the impulse mastered him, he drew her to him, and kissed her upon the mouth. She did not resist, but her mouth was cold, and her eyes troubled. Gaillard's shadow seemed to come between them.

"Forty," called Marpasse, "and a buxom age for a woman."

Aymery let go of Denise's hands. He stood with bowed head, looking into her face.

"Whatever God wills to-day," he said, "remember the words that I have spoken."

"Fifty," trilled Marpasse. "I will see to it, lording. Up on your horse, my gallant. They are all in a drunken sleep yonder at Lewes, and there is not a man of them on the watch."

She turned, and glanced sharply from Aymery to Denise. And the wet, passionate trouble in Denise's eyes betrayed to Marpasse how things were tending. It was best to leave the tenderness to ripen of itself that day, for none but a woman understands a woman's heart.

Aymery was in the saddle. His man's face had grown tense and keen, the face of the strenuous fighter who puts softer things aside. And Marpasse loved him for that hawk's look of his, and the way he spread his pinions to the wind.

"Simon is marching through the Newick woods," he said; "if he can but come in time, he can seize and take the ground that pleases him."

He looked down at Denise, and Marpasse understood the look.

"Ride, lording," she said, "leave us to follow."

Aymery drew his sword, and kissed the blade.

"Denise!" and wheeling his horse he went away at a gallop.

De Montfort had the news soon after dawn that May morning as his host came streaming through the woods of Newick. Sending forward a company of knights and men-at-arms under young De Clare and William de Monchesny, Simon followed on with the main body, climbing the narrow coombe that led to the chalk ridge running westwards from Lewes town. The vanguard had found Marpasse's solitary sentinel still asleep on the hillside, and they woke him roughly, and laughed at his gaping and astonished face. Meanwhile the main host gained the ridge, and pouring on steadily in the morning sunshine, did not halt their banners till they could see the bell tower of the Priory of St. Pancras.

Simon, who had been carried in a litter through the Newick woods because of a wrenched tendon in the leg, mounted his horse, and rode out in front of the ranks. Standing in the stirrups he spoke a few brave words to hearten his men, pointed to the white cross he wore, and commended himself and the host to God.

"God, and the Cross," the shout came back to him.

Some knelt, others prostrated themselves, with arms outspread, and kissed the earth. The King would have to fight an army of zealots that morning.

De Montfort soon had his battle in order. He divided his host into three main bodies, each holding one of the promontories or spurs into which the chalk ridge broke on the side towards Lewes. On the northern spur that stretched towards the castle stood the Londoners under Nicholas de Segrave. Young Gilbert de Clare had the centre, and with him were John Fitz-John and William de Monchesny and the pick of the Barons' host. On the southern spur were De Montfort's two sons, Guy and Henry, and with them Humphrey de Bohun and John de Burgh. Simon himself remained with the reserve, and he had called about him some of the men whom he could trust to the last blow, men whom he could weld together, and hurl like rock into the fight, to beat back a charge or to tear a passage. Aymery and Waleran de Monceaux were with Earl Simon, knee to knee, and speaking hardly at all. To deceive the King, De Montfort's litter was packed with certain London merchants who had plotted against the cause, and set with the Earl's standard on the higher ground towards the west. There also was stationed the baggage. Young William le Blund had command of the guard.

The Barons' men, resting in their places after a nine miles' march, and quietly making a meal, were able to watch at their leisure and to their own comfort the scurry and alarm in the town and Priory below. The King's host ran to arms amid infinite confusion. Trumpets blew, bells rang, banners went tossing hither and thither like bright clothes blown abroad by the wind. Something suspiciously like a panic had seized some of the less disciplined troops camped about the Priory. Knights and captains who had scrambled into their battle harness, had to ride in among their men and beat courage into them with the flat of the sword. Prince Edward, who had the flower of knighthood with him in the castle, was the first to take the field. They came pouring out from the town and the castle, a gorgeous cataract of heavily-armed men, surcoats ablaze, shields flashing gules and or, azure, argent, and vert; pennons jigging, banners aslant from gilded banner staffs.

Their van curled like a brilliant billow carrying the masts of many ships, and flecked with steel for foam. The great, grotesque war helmets were like the masks of strange creatures called up by a magician's wand. Their trumpets rang out cheerily, sending a thrill through the hearts of Simon's men. The Londoners, who faced this mass of lords and knights, and burly free-lances, began to talk too much, and to give each other orders.

Denise and Marpasse were with the baggage behind De Montfort's standard. They had climbed into a waggon, and could see a great part of the field stretched out before them. Dark columns were pouring up from the Priory, and Marpasse, who was watching them, caught Denise by the arm.

"Look yonder, they have hoisted the Red Dragon."

The whole of Simon's host had seen it also, for a long sullen roar rose like that of a wave breaking upon shingle.

"What does the red banner mean?"

"Mean!" and Marpasse bit her lips in her excitement; "death to all, no prisoners, and no quarter if the King wins. That is the song of the Red Dragon."

Denise said nothing. Marpasse glanced at her with a sudden, sidelong stare.

"You will not grudge him that one kiss," she said, "for to-night we may go a-searching for dead friends by torchlight."

The two dragons of war were trailing their coils nearer to one another. The King's red banner came tossing up the slope, he himself riding before it, holding his shield aloft with the lions of gold thereon.

"Simon, *je vous défie!*"

That was his cry that morning, a cry that his men took up, and screamed at the silent masses that watched and waited on the slopes above. The royal host was flushed now and confident, trusting in their numbers and in the great lords whose banners blew everywhere.

Edward the Prince was the firebrand that morning. He was pricking his horse to and fro like a mad boy, and his lips were bloody under his great helmet. For he had the Londoners before him, those Londoners who had thrown offal and foul words at his mother. The son had taken a vow to wipe out those words with blood.

Trumpets rang out on the King's right. Edward threw his spear into the air, caught it, and stood up in the stirrups.

"Death to the dogs! At the gallop, sirs, come."

He was away, a splendid and furious figure, with many thousand horses trampling at his heels. The iron ranks roared, and rocked and thundered. Those who watched saw a tossing sea of horses' heads, a whirl of hoofs tearing the grass, a mist of slanted spears, a confusion of grotesque heads bending behind painted shields. The mass plunged in on the Londoners like a rock that falls with a deep sob into the sea. There was no submerging of that mass of steel, and flesh, and leather. It went in and through as a fire leaps through dry corn, terrible in its red ruin, unquenchable and splendid.

Marpasse, on her waggon, caught her breath, and held it. Simon's left wing was wavering. Its spears went down in long swathes, and did not rise again. Black puffs of panic started out from the rear of the shaken mass, and spread like smoke over the green hillside.

"The Londoners have had enough! The fools always suffered from too much tongue. Dirty dogs, run, run, the devil is at your heels."

She had hold of Denise's arm, and Denise drew her breath in with a short, sharp sound, for Marpasse's nails had made blood marks under the skin. But Marpasse never so much as noticed that she had hurt Denise. Her heart was a man's heart as she watched the Earl's left wing streaming away in rout with the mailed knights and men-at-arms scudding through it, and spearing the burghers as they ran. Away down the slope of Offham Hill, and across the level towards Hamsey and Barcombe went the tide of slaughter. The flying Londoners trailed a fatal lure for Edward the Prince that morning. The paradox proved true in the main, that by running away they won Earl Simon the battle, for Edward hunted them for a league and a half, wiping out the insults they had thrown at his mother. And while he trampled the Londoners into the grass, and drove many of them into the river, Earl Simon won the battle of Lewes, and taught Prince Edward a lesson in the self-restraint of war.

The reckless assurance that possessed the King's army betrayed itself in an incident that followed the routing of Simon's left wing. A crowd of women had followed on the heels of Edward's lords and gentlemen, their lovers of the night before. The women had come out prepared to enjoy the battle as a spectacle, and perhaps to gain their share of the plunder. Some of them were mounted on mules and palfreys, others went on foot. And no sooner had the Londoners been driven off the field than these bona-robas came laughing and shouting up the hill, waving their kerchiefs and making a great to do. Most of them followed in the track of Prince Edward's victorious banners, though a few spread themselves abroad to plunder the dead.

Marpasse and Denise had a distant view of all that happened after the flight of the Londoners down Offham Hill. They saw the massive centres of the two hosts come to grips, and stand like two bulls with locked horns, neither able to budge the other. Then Earl Simon's genius gleamed out. Reinforcing his right wing with the reserve, he fell upon the left of the royal army under Richard, King of the Romans, crushed and scattered it in rout. Turning, he fell furiously with his flushed troops on the exposed flank of the King's centre, broke through their ranks, and gave Gloucester's men their opportunity.

From that wild mêlée the royal centre streamed away like ragged clouds driven by the wind. The green hillsides were covered with savage and furious figures, charging, and counter-charging with a riot of colour and glittering harness that sank slowly towards Lewes town. Henry, who had had his horse killed under him, and was wounded, was dragged away in the thick of a knot of desperate men, and carried off at a gallop to the Priory of St. Pancras. The battle was over as a struggle between two great masses of men. It dwindled into a series of scattered episodes, and of wild scuffles that rose suddenly like small dust storms, and then dispersed. A few of the sturdier spirits fought it out before they surrendered, happier in their valour than the King of the Romans who took refuge in a windmill and was besieged by a mocking and exultant mob till he delivered up his sword to Sir John de Befs. The fighting flowed in scattered trickles down to Lewes town, the west gate was taken by assault, though the King's men held out in the castle and in the Priory of St. Pancras.

Now those about De Montfort's standard were so taken up with watching the rout of the King's army that they were caught open-mouthed when one of the last episodes burst on them like a thunderclap. There was a shout, the scream of a trumpet, a quivering of the earth under the thundering hoofs of galloping cavalry. Prince Edward was riding back from the slaughter of the Londoners, assuming the battle won, having spent precious hours in hunting down mere lads amid the windings of the Ouse. He and his men burst in among the waggons and the baggage, hot and bloody, their horses covered with sweat. And since Simon's standard and litter were there, they thought they had him in their hands.

Young William le Blund was cut down under De Montfort's banner, and his men slain and scattered. The servants and camp-followers fluttered and flew like frightened chickens in a farmyard. De Montfort's litter was overturned, and the London merchants dragged out by the heels, and put to the sword despite their babblings and their protestations. It was shouted abroad that Simon was hiding somewhere amid the baggage, and the camp was turned into chaos, men tearing the loads out of the waggons, thrusting their swords into trusses of fodder, yelping like dogs about a fox's hole. The women who had followed them shared in the scramble. And since that traitor Simon was not to be found, the whole rout took to plundering the baggage, not troubling to discover that the battle had been lost down by Lewes town.

Marpasse had dragged Denise out of the empty waggon, and set to at once to pull bales out of a cart.

"Play the game."

She had to scream at Denise because of the uproar.

"Play the game. Swear, curse, be one of them."

Denise fell to, and helped Marpasse. The big woman had whipped out her knife, and slit the sacking of the bale she had dragged down over the tail board. The bale contained nothing more than rolls of white cloth.

Marpasse spat on it, and swore, for other men and women were crowding up.

"White bibs for the fools, curse them! May Simon's corpse be a bloodier colour."

She seized Denise by the wrist, and dragged her off as though to hunt for richer spoil. But in the thick of the scramble she ran against the chest of a white horse that came out from behind one of the waggons. Marpasse saved herself by holding to Denise.

The rider on the white horse broke into a shout of laughter.

"Great, fat sheep, where are you running?"

And Marpasse stood open-mouthed, for it was Isoult, Isoult in a man's hauberk, and red surcoat, her black hair bundled up under a steel cap.

"Black cat!"

Isoult reached down, caught Marpasse by the cloak, drew her in, and kissed her.

"You big brown devil, how I love the smell of you. And sister Denise, too, with all the fun of the fair."

She tossed her head and laughed, and shouted to a knight on horseback who was watching his men scrambling over a coffer full of plate.

"Lording, come you here. I have found your red head for you. Though you will not be wanting her now, unless you would like a touch of my knife."

The knight turned in the saddle; he had taken off his great helmet, both Denise and Marpasse knew him at the first glance.

"Gaillard!"

Marpasse took Denise by the hand, and kept very close to Isoult's white horse.

CHAPTER XL

Aymery had searched the hillsides that day for a blue surcoat shining with golden suns, but since Gaillard had charged among Prince Edward's spears, he was miles away on the heels of the Londoners while the men of the White Cross were driving the King back in rout upon Lewes town.

But Simon had not forgotten to look for the return of the Prince. He had gathered the pick of his knights and men-at-arms together, and when they brought him news of the plundering of his camp, he smiled and bided his time. Steady and motionless, a mass of steel half hidden by a rise in the ground, De Montfort's cavalry waited in the evening light for the coming of the Prince.

And a riotous and disordered troop it was that marched back towards Lewes after plundering the Barons' camp. Edward and his lords seemed to have accepted their victory as assured, and never doubted but that the White Cross had been trodden into the dust. The scene that stretched before them, flooded by the evening sunlight, was deceptive in the extreme. De Warenne's banner still flew from the castle, and that of the King from the bell tower of St. Pancras. There were scattered bodies of armed men moving over the slopes and about the town, and the dead strewing the field made no confession of victory or defeat.

It was then that the most tragic thing of the day happened, for the mob of fighting men under the Prince, marching as they pleased, had some hundreds of women mingled with them, unfortunates who had thought of nothing but making a joyous night of it after the great victory, and the plunder that they had won. De Montfort's mass of knights and men-at-arms, rising suddenly like a grey sea out of the twilight, came on at a gallop, fresh and lusty after a long rest. Isoult was one of those gay queans, riding with Gaillard's arm about her, chattering and laughing to keep her man amused. Following these two, half as comrades, half as prisoners, came Denise and Marpasse, mounted upon cart-horses, that had been taken from the Barons' camp. Luckily for them they were in the rear of Prince Edward's host or they would have been trampled down at the first charge, as were many of the women.

Marpasse and Denise were riding close together, watching Gaillard as sheep might watch a dangerous dog, and waiting their chance to break away in the gathering darkness. Although he had an arm about Isoult's body, Gaillard's eyes wandered round towards Denise, stealing half-furtive glances at her, as though he were already tired of Isoult, and suffered his passions to embrace a contrast. Marpasse saw how it was with Gaillard, and hated him for Denise's sake, and because she could tell what manner of man he was, insolent, lustful, ever ready to throw aside things that had sated him. He was like a great lean spider with his long legs and his sinewy arms, and Marpasse could have stabbed him for the way he held Isoult.

They were crowded together, and Marpasse and Denise saw nothing of the storm that was tearing down upon the Prince's following. A strange silence fell suddenly on that mass of humanity, broken here and there by a loud and querulous cry. A moment ago there had been nothing but singing, shouting, and coarse jests.

A shudder seemed to pass through the whole mob. It wavered, stood still, swayed to and fro. Marpasse heard women shrieking. Then a roar of voices rose, the furious voices of men caught at a disadvantage with death rushing upon them like a flood. Utter confusion spread, trumpets screaming like frightened beasts, spears swaying this way and that. Then the shock came. The bodies of men were thrown in the air like stones torn from a sea wall by a furious wave.

Marpasse saw Gaillard rise in his stirrups, draw his sword, and turn a bleak, wolf-like profile towards them. He caught his battle helmet from the saddle bow, dipped his head into it, and came up a grotesque monster with a face like a gaping frog. Marpasse had a vision of sloped spears pouring down on them through the golden haze of the evening. Then chaos seemed to come again, and the world crumbled with the rushing of many waters and the rending of solid rock.

Marpasse had a glimpse of Denise clinging to her horse that had reared in terror. Gaillard had left Isoult, and was trying to clear a path with his sword, making his horse swerve to and fro in the press. Then Marpasse had no sense left in her, but the sense of falling, of being thrown hither and thither, of being trampled on and hurt. A horse crashed to the ground close to her and lay still, and with the blind instinct of the moment, Marpasse flung herself down and huddled close under the beast's body as an Arab shelters behind a camel when a dust storm sweeps the desert. Yet with swiftness and tumult and fierce anguish the storm passed, and was gone. Marpasse found herself peering up over the horse's body, and looking at a splendid sky against which dark figures struggled together as on the edge of an abyss.

Marpasse scrambled up, wondering how she had come out of the storm so easily, and stood and stared stupidly about her, dazed for the moment by the violence of it all. A tempest of horsemen was rolling away over the hillside like a grey cloud curling over a mountain. Broken bodies lay everywhere, some still squirming like worms that have been trodden under foot; others motionless, contorted, and grotesque, like bodies thrown at random from a high tower. And where life and noise and movement had been but a few minutes before, a slow silence seemed to ooze in and to stagnate under the melancholy of the coming night.

Marpasse's wits came back to her, and she looked round for any sign of those who had been with her a few moments ago. Gaillard had gone, Denise also, like people swept off a rock by an ocean wave.

Looking about her, Marpasse saw a white horse lying dead upon the hillside, and something that moved half under and half beside it, with the whimpering cry of a child. Marpasse stumbled forward, for one foot had been bruised, and found Death sitting upon the carcase of the white horse. Isoult lay there with the beast's body upon her legs, and her back broken. She could stretch out her hands to Marpasse, with a shuddering spasm of cursing that was piteous and futile.

"Curse Simon, and his bulls, curse Gaillard, the great coward! I am done for, and this white hog, this devil's bitch lies on my legs like a rock. Hold off, great fool. Do I want to be pulled about when my back's broken, and my ribs are pricking my liver."

Marpasse tried to drag her clear of the horse, but Isoult's screams and curses sobered her. She saw that Isoult was near her end, crushed like a wild cat in the steel jaws of a trap. The girl, too, had the spiteful valour of a cat, and pushed Marpasse's hands away when she tried to fondle her.

"None of your spittle," she said, biting her lips with the anguish in her; "it is jolly, I tell you, to be trampled into the dirt! Just the sort of end I was made for. Who cares? Oh, yes, I shall go straight to hell."

She chattered on at random, laughing, sneering, and biting her lips. Marpasse sat by her, her heart full of inarticulate and half-angry pity.

"What are you sitting there for, great fool? There is that red-headed Denise of yours; you left me for her; I know, Gaillard told me the story. Oh yes, you had what you wanted, Messire Gaillard, you held me in your arms, devil; you saw me trampled on, and rode after the red head. God curse you, my Gaillard, you bundle of burning straw in a body of clay. Tell me, Marpasse, are not we women accursed fools?"

She began to curse Gaillard bitterly under her breath. Marpasse saw a change come over her, for she seemed to grow thinner and greyer in the dusk. A great sob gathered in Marpasse's throat. She fell a-weeping, and hung dearly over Isoult.

"There, child, what does it avail? Lie in my arms now, and fall asleep."

Isoult ceased her cursing suddenly, and shuddered a little as she felt Marpasse's tears falling upon her face. Her black eyes became dark, and very wistful.

"What are you weeping for, great fool?"

Marpasse hung over her, and smoothed her hair.

"You were a little slip of a thing when we first were friends," she said, "and you often slept in my bosom. We had rough days and rough weather together. All the roads were rough for us, and so is the last track."

Isoult lay very still, though her cold hands crept up, and rested in the warmth between Marpasse's breasts. She grew very grey and feeble, and blood came into her mouth. Isoult spat it out, and looked up at Marpasse.

"What a fool of a world," she said hoarsely; "but if I could work a miracle, I would just mend you, and set you on your feet. And if God and His saints are harder hearted, let them keep their pride, I would rather sup with the devil."

Isoult gave a great sigh.

"How could I help it all," she said; "I was branded when I was born, and I was no man's child. No one ever taught me prayers, or fed me on white bread. And when I was kicked, I learnt to scratch back."

Marpasse lay down beside her, and in a little while the end came. Nor did Isoult die easily, but with pain and revolt, and blood choking her throat. Marpasse put her arms about her, and held her till she died. And with the passing of Isoult's spirit, something seemed to break in the heart of Marpasse.

The dusk deepened, and the living woman was sitting there with her head between her hands, and staring at the dead woman's face, when a gaunt man in the dress of a priest came by, and seeing them, turned aside. He had a wooden cross in his hand, an axe thrust into his girdle, and a buckler at his back. If Grimbald had served the White Cross with his axe that day down amid the windings of the Ouse, he had put the iron aside now, and taken to compassion.

He spoke to Marpasse, but she did not hear him. Grimbald touched her on the shoulder.

"Peace, sister," he said.

Marpasse jumped up and looked Grimbald over in the dusk. Her glance lighted on his cross.

"What is the use of that," she said; "bah, take it away, my brother!"

Grimbald nodded his head. Marpasse spread her arms, and then pointed to Isoult.

"See, there, what has God to say to such a thing? When we are born in a ditch, and kept in a ditch, and kicked into a ditch at the end, what has the Cross to do with it?"

Grimbald knelt down quite solemnly, and looked at Isoult.

"What a child! Who said that she had sinned, sister?"

Marpasse's mouth was full of scoffing.

"We have stones thrown at us. We are too black for the good folk to soil their hands in washing us."

Grimbald turned his face to her, and his eyes shone.

"The Lord said 'let those who are without sin cast the first stone.' What do you make of those words, sister?"

"That the devil must put his tongue in his cheek when the good people go to church," said Marpasse.

Grimbald got up, and went and stood in front of Marpasse. They looked each other in the eyes like two sturdy souls sure of hearing the truth.

"Do you see her in eternal flames, sister?" asked the man.

"On my oath, I do not. The child had good in her, when people did not thrust thorns into her face."

Grimbald nodded his head solemnly.

"I would have the flaying of all hypocrites," he said, "as for such lives, I would mend them in heaven."

"You will put up a prayer, Father. I have money."

Grimbald almost glowered at her.

"Will my tongue do any better for the stuff! Help me to pull the child away. We can find her a clean grave somewhere. As for my prayers, God knows the ways of the world."

Marpasse had an impetuous heart. She took Grimbald by the girdle.

"I could kiss that mouth of yours, Father," she said, "because it talks out straight, and is the mouth of a man."

The river Ouse took toll that evening from the King's host, drawing many a rider into its deeps, while the bogs and the morasses opened their slimy mouths for food. The Prince had saved a portion of his following from the rout upon the hillside, and breaking away he found the west gate of Lewes held against him, and was compelled to gallop round the town to join the King at the Priory of St. Pancras. The greater number of the royalist leaders had fled, riding for the castle of Pevensey, whence they could cross into France. The King's brothers, William de Valence and Guy de Lusignan, were galloping for their lives, and with them a crowd of adventurers and free-lances who knew that they would be hanged on the forest trees if the country folk could lay their hands on them. Hugh Bigot and Earl de Warenne were with the fugitives. The King of the Romans and his son, the Scotch nobles, many English lords, and a crowd of lesser men had been taken by Earl Simon.

Meanwhile Denise had been saved by the terror of her horse from being trampled and crushed like Black Isoult. The beast had broken through, and fled at a gallop, with Denise lying out like a child along his neck. There were other horses galloping about her, some with riders, many with empty saddles, and one common instinct seemed to shepherd the beasts together, so that Denise found herself swept along in the thick of the herd.

Lying upon her nag's neck, with her cheek laid against the coarse coat, and her hair blowing in the wind, Denise became conscious at last of a black horse galloping beside hers, stride for stride. At first she saw only the beast's head with its red nostrils, and ill-tempered ears laid back, and the whites of its eyes showing. Then a man's figure drew into view, and she had a glimpse of a blue surcoat with a blur of gold thereon, and a great iron helmet that gaped like a frog. Denise was no longer a piece of wreckage carried along in the thick of the flood. The black horse seemed to know his master's mind, and began to guide Denise's nag as one beast will guide and rule another.

The man, who had been sitting stiffly in the saddle, bent forward and caught the trailing halter of Denise's horse.

"Hold fast, Sanctissima," he said, "we shall soon be out of the mill race."

Denise knew that it was Gaillard, but fate carried her at the gallop, and she was too conscious of the wind in her ears and the way the ground rushed under her.

"If I can save you a broken neck," he went on, shouting the words through the black cleft in the great helmet, "I shall deserve your forgiveness. The fools yonder are rushing like a drove of pigs for the river. They will drown one another. We will take our own road."

Denise felt like one falling and falling in a dream. There was no end to it, and she had not enough breath in her to feel the finer, spiritual fear. It was impossible to so much as think in the rush and welter of all those flying, thundering shapes. Her body was taken up with holding to the body of her horse.

They drew clear of the main torrent at last, and went cantering in the dusk over the rolling grassland. Gaillard was sitting straight in the saddle, and watching a gush of flame that had leapt up over Lewes town. The King's men who still held the castle, had thrown springalds of fire down upon the houses, setting the thatch ablaze so that the houses should not cover Simon's men who were crowding to the assault. The glare of the burning town seemed an echo from the red sunset above the western hills. A distant uproar rose into the twilight, though the summits of the downs were solemn and still. Denise felt her horse slacken under her now that they had turned aside from the rush of the pursuit.

The power to think and to feel came back to her. She escaped from the chaos of things to a consciousness of self, and of that other self beside her. The blind life-instinct that had carried her over the hills into the twilight, gave place to a quick, spiritual dread of the man at her side. She had not seen Gaillard desert Isoult, and leave the girl to be trampled under foot. But her own being had a passionate loathing for the man, a loathing so great that it tempted her to throw herself from her horse. Her broken and unconscious body would be nothing to Gaillard, and he would leave her as a drunkard would leave a broken and empty jar.

Gaillard, alert and masterful, reined in suddenly as though to listen. He had caught some sound following them out of the dusk, but the trampling of their own horses had smothered it, and robbed it of significance. Gaillard kept his hold of the halter of Denise's horse, and towered over her as he turned in the saddle to look back.

The ridge of a hill ran bleak and sharp against a stretch of yellow sky. And outlined against this streak of gold came the figure of a man riding a black horse. He was not two hundred paces away, and Gaillard saw him shake his sword.

Denise also saw that solitary rider black against the sunset, and the heart leapt in her, and beat more quickly.

Gaillard kicked in the spurs, dragging Denise's rough nag after him.

"Hold fast," he said, "if that fellow is after us, he will not rob a Gascon of his supper."

They were galloping again, rushing on into a vague and dolorous dusk. The wind swept Denise's hair, and once a shout followed after them, but Gaillard kept her horse at the gallop, and Denise was at the mercy of the two strong beasts, and of that yet stronger beast, man. A streak of dull silver parted the darkness in front of them. Before Denise had understood the nature of the thing before them, water was splashed over her, and their horses were swimming the river.

Gaillard had not spoken a word. When they were out of the muddy shallows and on the firm ground beyond, he reined in, turned the horses, and looked back over the river. An indistinct figure loomed out of the dusk with a scamper of hoofs, and the heavy breathing of a hard-ridden horse.

Gaillard had drawn his sword. He lifted his helmet, and putting it on the point of his sword, stood in the stirrups, holding sword and helmet high above his head. Denise was near enough to see his face in the dusk. It was half fierce, and half amused, yet wholly confident, the face of a strong man and a libertine whose strength made him take a bully's joy in cheating weaker men of their women.

"Hallo, there!"

The pursuer had drawn in on the farther bank, with his horse's hoofs sucking the spongy grass.

"Keep over there, my friend, if you value a sound skull. I am not to be meddled with when I ride with a gay lady."

There was a splashing of hoofs in the shallows, and a voice came over the river.

"Denise!" it said, "is it Denise, yonder?"

Gaillard looked down at her, and opened his mouth scoffingly when she answered the man's call.

"Hallo, Golden-head, you would have a lover in your lap, eh! We will see to it to-night, my desire. I promise you it shall not be the fool yonder."

The water had broken into fresh ripples that came lapping among the sedges. Aymery's horse was swimming the river.

Gaillard dropped his great helmet on to his shoulders, and holding the halter in the same big hand as held his sword, turned the horses, and rode off so close to Denise that his knee touched hers.

"Grace before meat," he said, laughing under his helmet, "your man is probably clumsy enough. I know how to deal with such a windmill."

He dragged Denise's horse to a canter, and turning in the saddle, saw Aymery floundering up through the crackling shadows.

"Some people are in a great hurry to get to heaven," said Gaillard; "it is a pity, Sanctissima, that you have such a head of hair, and such a body. They are things that make a man cut other men's throats."

CHAPTER XLI

The plunge through the cold Ouse freshened Aymery's horse, and Gaillard, who rode only to put some miles between him and Simon's host at Lewes, heard the rhythm of the hoofs behind him drawing ever nearer. The knowledge that he was chased by one man did not bustle the Gascon in the least, for Gaillard knew his own strength, and had never taken a thrashing. The day's battle had beggared him, and his brother adventurers, for the lords who had hired them would soon be scattered over the sea. Moreover Gaillard remembered De Montfort in Gascony, and that Earl Simon had dealt very roughly with hired gentlemen of the sword who meddled where they had no cause. Yet Gaillard did not snap his jaws at the chance that had beggared him. He felt in fettle, and ready for a scrimmage, arrogantly confident in himself, and with sufficient animal spite in the mood to put him in an excellent temper. He would thrash the fool who followed them, have his way with Denise, and make Pevensey on the morrow, and sail with some of the King's lords who were seized with a desire to visit France.

Had Gaillard had a glimpse of the face of the man who followed him, he might have taken the escapade more grimly, and talked less of "Sussex boors who could better fix a spiggot in a barrel than handle a sword." The Gascon could not keep the froth from the surface. Loquacity was a habit of his when he had anything strenuous in hand. He gabbled away to Denise as they cantered on in the dusk, keeping a sharp eye however on the ground before him, very wide awake in spite of his loquacity.

"Come, now, Sanctissima," he said, "tell me when you are tired of your horse, and we will stop and talk to the gentleman behind us. A gallop at night makes one sleep more soundly. We shall find a bed somewhere, and no one shall wake you early if you would play the sluggard."

Denise, listening to the rhythm of hoofs behind them in the dusk, hated Gaillard for his flamboyant spirit and his arrogance. She held her breath for Aymery's sake. If Gaillard should kill him! If she should see him beaten, and crushed! She cast frightened brown eyes over Gaillard's figure, and hated him the more because he seemed so big and lusty.

"Hallo, we are coming up fast behind there! The gentleman is very hot, and in a great hurry, Sanctissima! Do you see a wood over yonder. We can make a bed under the trees when we have had our talk with Messire Meadhorn. Beer, Sanctissima, makes these boors hot in the head and quarrelsome."

Denise felt the canter slacken, for Gaillard was drawing in. A swift and inarticulate horror, a vivid sense of what was to follow, seized on her. These two men would be at each other's throats. And in the dusk and the silence of that night in May she might see lust conquer and strangle love.

The dull plodding of hoofs behind them beat a measure in her brain. She would have cried out to Aymery, and could not. And on that hard, brown face under the helmet she imagined a callous and self-assured smile.

They neared the trees, masses of fresh foliage hanging motionless under the quiet sky. It would be peaceful, and odorous, and silent in among those trees. Yet their black plumes had a sinister sadness for Denise. They were so calm, and black, and motionless, with never the sound of a night wind in them.

Gaillard reined in abruptly, threw a sharp glance over his shoulder, and then pushed Denise roughly from her horse.

"Try to run, my minion, and I will ride over you," he said, "no fool of a mesne lord shall stand in the way of it."

He still had her horse by the halter, and Denise saw him jerk it, so that the beast tossed its head. And the brutal thing that Gaillard did sickened her to the heart, so that she stood still with wide eyes and quivering mouth. For Gaillard had slashed the horse's throat, and Denise saw the poor beast rear, break free, and then sink on its knees with a smothered sound that was all too human.

Denise forgot even the maimed horse with the coming of Aymery out of the dusk. Gaillard had circled round so that he stood between Denise and the trees. He had begun to sing some southern song, throwing his sword from hand to hand, his voice reverberating in his helmet.

Denise stood and watched and waited as though her whole soul had withdrawn into her eyes. Aymery was quite close to her, yet she neither moved nor spoke to him. Perhaps she was dazed by the imminent dread of what would follow.

Gaillard broke off his song, drew his shield forward, and crowed like a cock.

"Good evening, my little gentleman," he said; "there you are, white cross and all. I will put a red mark on that cross of yours. Ladies are always pleased by a red rose."

Aymery said nothing, but glanced aside at Denise. Then Gaillard came cantering up, tossing his sword, and crowing in his helmet.

"Up with your shield, my friend, I have a lady to love, and the night is ready."

Denise watched them, half in a stupor. The men were sword to sword, shield to shield, and horse to horse. Confusedly, like one half asleep, she heard Gaillard prattling as they began the tussle, a grim and half playful babble, like the chatter of a waterfall when men are struggling in the pool beneath.

Soon, however, Gaillard grew very silent, save for a sudden and spasmodic oath. To Denise there seemed nothing in the world but two strong men lashing at each other from the backs of two ever moving and circling horses. Then in the thick of the clangour, and the heavy breathing, she heard Gaillard give a sharp, fierce cry, the cry of a strong man cut beneath his harness. A horse swerved, stumbled, and rolled over. Whose, Denise could not tell for the moment, in the whirl of the tussle, and the darkness.

It was Gaillard's horse, but he was free of the beast, up, and no longer the complacent sworder, but a man fighting with the valour of a beast that fights to live. He blundered against the other's horse, grappled a leg, and twisted Aymery out of the saddle. They were on foot now, still close to her, dodging, striking, circling round and round. Denise could hear the sound of their breathing above the rattle of blows, and the dull rustling of feet.

Then she saw a man stumble, jerk forward, and recover though cut across the shoulders with a sword. A head was bare, the great helmet had fallen, and a white face showed in its stead. Denise knew Gaillard by his greater height. His shield was up, sure as a pent-house at the foot of a wall, and Denise would have crushed that shield had the power of a Greek goddess been hers that moment.

Gaillard had blood on his face, she saw the dark smirch thereof above the eyes and down one cheek. A broken shield was thrown aside, Aymery's, and fell like a dead crow with flapping wings into the grass. Gaillard sprang on him. There was a meeting of swords, a moment's locking of the blades, a swift up-thrust by the one that first broke free. Again Denise heard that great cry of Gaillard's with more of the roar of the wild beast in it than before.

He rolled from side to side as though drunk, and then throwing aside his shield, made a blind and blundering charge with an upheave of the sword. Aymery sprang to the right with a twist of the body, using that swing of the body for the sweep of the counter-blow. Gaillard sprawled, spun round, caught Aymery's ankle, and dragged him to earth. For a while there was a confused struggle in the grass. Denise heard a man groaning, and straining like a giant trying to lift a rock that is crushing him into the ground. Then there was the sharp sound of steel wrenching its way through steel. The end had come, and one of the men lay still.

Why the horror of the thing should take possession of her as it did Denise did not consider. She saw the wood, dark, cool, and still, before her, and fled into it, seeing nothing but hearing ever Gaillard's cry. And though she fell often, stumbling against the great trees in the darkness, she ran like one without reason, not noticing whether anyone followed, and that the silence of the place closed on her like water over a stone.

CHAPTER XLII

From a chance word that Marpasse let fall while they were burying Isoult, Grimbald discovered all that she knew concerning Aymery and Denise, and he made her tell the story. Marpasse had been breaking up the ground with a sword, and Grimbald using a shield for a shovel, scooped a shallow trough for the body wrapped in its scarlet surcoat. That labour together over the grave, and the way Grimbald made her talk of herself and Denise, brought Marpasse and the parish priest to a sudden sense of comradeship.

With Isoult laid to rest they trudged off together to Lewes town, but could gain no sure news of Aymery there, though Grimbald found a Sussex man, Geoffrey de St. Leger, who swore that the Knight of the Hawk's Claw had ridden in that last charge against Prince Edward's company. Grimbald and Marpasse had already searched the ground in the dusk without coming upon Denise's grey gown. A truce had been called, and torches were moving to and fro over the battlefield like corpse candles in the darkness.

The parish priest and the bona-roba watched the night out under a hedge, and Marpasse fell asleep while Grimbald watched. They were up before dawn, however, and breaking bread as they went, they searched the scarred track along which Simon's knights had ridden in pursuit of the flying royalists. Grimbald bent over many a body in the twilight, and though there were women lying dead and stiff upon the grass, Denise was not among them, nor did they find Aymery among the slain.

The dawn was just breaking when they came to the river; grey fog hung there; and it was very still. The dead were here also, horse and man, and Grimbald saw that the richer bodies had been plundered, even stripped naked and left upon the grass. Their search had lessened the chances, save what the grey river might be hiding under its shroud. But Grimbald chose to be an optimist that morning, and swore, as though he had seen the thing in crystal, that neither Aymery nor Denise was under the quiet water. He chose the simplest explanation, and put it forward so confidently that Marpasse believed also, and fell in with his plan. Aymery had found Denise, and taken her away with him out of reach of the storm.

"As sure as I live," he said, "we shall find them at Goldspur. It is not the first time that I have prophesied the truth."

And Marpasse accepted Grimbald as a prophet, and he looked the part with his gaunt face and fiery eyes.

They were walking towards the bridge when a splashing sound came up the river, and a black boat glided out of the mist, driven along by a man who wielded a long pole. A second man was drawing in a rope, and there was something at the end thereof, for the rope was taut and straight, with drops of water falling from it. The first man shipped his pole, and went to help his comrade with the rope, nor had either of them noticed Grimbald and Marpasse.

A thing that glistened rose to the surface. The men reached over, and between them, dragged the body of a man in gilded harness into the boat. They grunted cheerfully over the catch, and disappeared below the gunwale. The boat lay in mid-stream, and there was the plash of the grapnel as one of the men heaved it out again into the river.

Grimbald held up a hand to Marpasse, slipped down the bank, and dropped quietly into the water. A few long strokes carried him under the boat's stern. And the great brown head that appeared suddenly over the gunwale so scared the two spoilers of the dead that they gaped at Grimbald, and lost the chance of knocking him back into the river. The bottom of the boat was littered with plunder from the bodies along the bank; and one of the men was cutting the rings from the hands of the knight they had fished up with the grapnel. Grimbald scrambled in, axe in hand. But he looked so huge, and fierce, and fateful in the grey of the morning that the men jumped for it, and swam like water rats, leaving the parish priest lord of the spoil.

Grimbald poled the boat to the bank, lifted the dead man out, and laid him on the grass. He knelt and said a prayer for him, while Marpasse stood on guard with the axe, watching the two thieves who had crawled out on the near bank and were skulking behind a bush. Grimbald ended his prayer, and stood up and shook himself like a great dog.

"Providence is at work here," he said; "my prophecy will come true."

They climbed into the boat and ferried across, watched by the men who were waiting to recover their spoil. But Grimbald cheated them of their desire, for he stove out the planks with the end of the pole, and pushed the boat out to sink in the deeper water.

"Let it return to the dead," he said. "Those rogues shall catch no more fish to-day."

Grimbald and Marpasse set out on their five-league trudge to Goldspur, both of them being stout walkers, and eager to come to the end of the tale.

These two warm, rough natures were quickly in sympathy, for Grimbald discovered the "woman" in Marpasse, and being nothing of the Pharisee he had no exquisite dread of soiling his robes. Marpasse talked to him on the way as she had never talked to a man before. Grimbald was so strong and so honest that the woman's eyes gleamed out at him approvingly. Isoult's death had stirred her deeply, following as it had on her comradeship with Denise. Marpasse put her life in its crude and simple colours before Grimbald's eyes, not justifying herself, but talking as though it helped her to talk to a priest who understood.

"It is just like climbing a ladder," she said, "to get inside a castle. The good people above throw stones, and potsherds, and boiling oil. And if you get to the top—they try to pitch you down again. If I had my way I would have a door in the side of the world, and the poor drabs should be let in quietly, and put out to work to earn their bread."

"Sometimes it is very dull—being good," said Grimbald with a twinkle.

"It is often very dreary being sinful, Father. Give me a chance to choose, and I would have a fire-side, and a bed, and a broom to use, and a man to cuff me—at times—if he kissed me an hour afterwards. A smack on the cheek does a woman a world of good."

"And a kiss on the mouth?" asked Grimbald.

"Oh, that makes the puddings turn out well. And I have a taste for puddings."

Grimbald's prophetic instinct fulfilled itself that morning, for they were not a mile from Goldspur village, and following a track that ran over a stretch of heathland between the woods, when they saw a man ride out from a woodland way. He was not a furlong from them, so near that they could see the red stains on the white cross sewn to his surcoat, and the way the reins were slack upon the horse's neck. In fact, the horse seemed to carry the man, and not the man to guide the horse. It was Aymery himself, grey-faced, battered, forlorn as a ship struggling home after a storm.

Grimbald's long legs left Marpasse far behind. Aymery smiled at him as a sick man smiles at the face of a friend. He had grown gaunt and haggard in a night, and the unshaven stubble on his chin showed black against his pallor.

"Victory at Lewes."

Grimbald took his bridle.

"And a wound—somewhere," he said.

"Wounds—plenty of them. I am tired, Grimbald—tired as a dog."

Aymery left his horse to the priest, for it was as much as he could do to steady himself in the saddle by holding to the pommel with both hands. Marpasse came to meet them, and Aymery looked at her stupidly, as though his brain were clouded.

A faint gleam passed across his face as he recognised Marpasse.

"I have killed him," he said; "yes—it was on the edge of the woods—over yonder."

He relapsed again into a half stupor, staring at Marpasse with eyes that seemed heavy with sleep.

"Denise?" she asked him.

He echoed her, slowly. Marpasse nodded.

"Denise was with Gaillard—I killed him. She had disappeared when we had ended it," and he looked at Marpasse as though it was she who was wise in the matter, an appealing look like the appeal of a dumb child.

Grimbald gave Marpasse a most unpriestly wink.

"Bed and bread," he said in a whisper, "and good wine to wash it down. The oil is low in the lamp. Keep it burning."

Marpasse understood, and was all cheerfulness.

"Never was I better pleased by the thought of a corpse," she said; "as for Denise, she was born to run away—as I always tell her. She knows the woodways hereabouts, Father, eh? To be sure. Madame will not be long on the road."

Aymery was at the end of himself, and lay along his horse's neck, his arms hanging down on either side. Grimbald looked fierce, being combative where death, sickness, and the Devil were concerned.

"Hum—white as a clean dish clout!"

Marpasse touched Aymery's cheek.

"Asleep," she said.

"Speak out; no metaphors."

"I speak what I mean—and your long words can go to the eel pond, Father. He is asleep. What could be better? Gaillard, Messire Gaillard, you met your match! And Denise—the fool—ran away!"

She went close, kissed Aymery's neck, and then turned on Grimbald with a defiant glare of the eyes.

"Mayn't I kiss a brave man?" she asked.

Grimbald threw up his head and laughed.

"Who said you 'nay'?" he retorted; "you women are in such a hurry."

"Then I shall kiss you, Father!"

"Will you!" quoth he grimly.

Goldspur manor house was still a mute gathering of charred posts, though some of the lodges and the barn had been rebuilt. Aymery was taken that day to the priest's house that stood on the edge of a glimmering birch wood, whose boles rose like silver pillars above the brown wattle fence about the church. Grimbald carried him in in his arms, and laid him on his own bed. There was no *focaria* or servant, and Marpasse was soon as busy as any hearth-ward. She found the aumbry where Grimbald kept his oil and wine, gathered sticks from the wood lodge, lit a fire, and hung the iron pot on the hook. Grimbald was stripping Aymery of his harness, unfastening the gorget and greaves, peeling the heavy hauberk off him with much trouble, and unlacing the gambeson beneath. Marpasse came in with the wine and the water-pot, for Grimbald had his bed in the little room at the end of the great hall. She began to covet and handle some of the parish priest's vestments that hung on pegs along the wall. Marpasse's brown hands made a white alb scream into strips for bandages. Grimbald glanced round at her with philosophic consent.

"I shall never get such another," he said.

"Shall I put up an oath for you, Father?"

"Quiet, fool! His mother gave it me—five years ago."

"It has washed well," said Marpasse.

And the alb was used to bind up Aymery's wounds.

Much loss of blood from a few deep flesh cuts, that was the main mischief, and Grimbald and Marpasse soon had him under the coverlet. He was half asleep all the while they were handling him, heavy and stupid with long hours in the saddle, the death tussle with Gaillard, and lack of food. There was no epic heroism in the episode. Aymery was put to bed like a small boy, and the washing that Marpasse had given him had made the illusion more complete. Beyond making him drink some wine they did not trouble him, but left him to have his sleep out, and wake—if God willed it—hungry.

Marpasse's thoughts turned to Denise, but she and Grimbald were sufficiently carnal to rejoice in a good round meal of bread and mead and bacon. They sat at the table with the door of the house wide open, so that they had a glimpse of the green and mysterious world beyond. Grimbald had little to say, and Marpasse was very hungry, and so little overawed by a seat at a priest's table that her hunger walked boldly, and would not be abashed. And Grimbald was amused by it, and commended the healthiness of the instinct, the more so because it proved its value in the person of a very comely woman with a sunburnt face, clear eyes, and a mass of tawny hair.

They began at last to talk of Denise, and Marpasse made Grimbald take her to the door, and point her out the way to the beech wood where Denise had had her cell. Grimbald could show her the wood itself, a green cloud adrift across the blue of the May sky. Marpasse saw to her shoes, dropped half a loaf into her bag, and made it plain to Grimbald whither she was going.

"Birds fly back to the same haunts in the spring," she said; "nor do I see, Father, why you alone should be a prophet."

Grimbald looked at her as a wise man of five and forty looks at a mischievous yet lovable girl.

"Go—and prove it," he said; "I shall get down to the village and send the people out to search the woods. Not a word to them—mind you—of all that has happened in the past."

Marpasse showed the curve of a strong brown chin.

"Am I so much a fool?" she asked.

Grimbald appeared to consider the question. He did not give his verdict till Marpasse had reached the gate.

"Death alone saves us from being fools," he said, and his eyes had a seriousness as he watched her go.

Marpasse went down the hill, leaving the village on her left, and crossing the valley, climbed the slope to the great beech wood. The trunks were black and smooth under a splendour of green that shone in the sunlight. The earth still seemed virginal, for the flowers that had been touched by the bees were lost in the rich, rank lustiness of early summer. The valleys rippled with gold, and the may trees were still in bloom, and full of infinite fragrance.

Marpasse made her way through the wood, and came at last to the place where the beech boles stood like great pillars about an open court. There was a blur of colour against the green, the pink blush of an early rose that had run in riot over the wattle fence, and flowered like a rose tree in a garden of Shiraz. The dark brown thatch of the cell showed ragged holes where birds had burrowed in and built their nests. The grass stood knee deep in the glade, grass that seemed asleep in the warm sunlight, dreamed over by moon-faced daisies bewitched by the song of the bees.

Marpasse had taken cover behind the trunk of a beech tree. She had seen a track in the long grass where someone had passed but a short while ago. And Marpasse's eyes beamed in her brown face. Her prophecy had also been fulfilled, for there, under the shade of the rose tree she saw Denise amid the grass, her knees drawn up, and her chin resting in the palms of her two hands.

Marpasse watched her awhile, indulging her own philosophy much like a nurse commenting upon a child.

"Heart of mine, but somebody should be here in my place. What a sad, white face, to be sure, and what eyes—as though the whole world were on its death bed! We will change all that, my dear. You shall be the colour of the rose bush before the day is out."

She slipped from behind the tree, and crossed the grass, singing a song that she had often sung upon the road. And she saw Denise's face start up into the sunlight out of its mood of mists and sadness. A tendril of the rose tree caught Denise's hair as Marpasse pushed open the rotting gate.

Marpasse laughed, happy, yet with a lovable shyness in her eyes.

"See what it is to be desired," said she, "even the rose tree must catch at that hair of yours. Heart of mine—how you tremble!"

She took Denise and held her, kissing her mouth.

"So you ran away—for the last time, hey—when St. George had finished slaying the dragon! That was a mad thing to do, my dear. You should have stopped to succour him, should he have been wounded."

Denise's brown eyes searched Marpasse's face, looking beyond the other's playfulness.

"Gaillard?" she asked.

"Dead, heart of mine; the best thing that ever he did was to die. Those brown eyes of yours need not look so frightened, St. George has been put to bed to sleep till he is hungry."

Marpasse sat down under the rose tree, and drew Denise into her lap.

"Try to smile a little, my dear," she said, "for summer is coming in, and the cuckoo is singing."

Denise did not rest long in Marpasse's lap, nor would she touch any of the bread that Marpasse had brought with her. She drew aside in the grass, turned her face away, and sat staring into the shadowy spaces under the trees. Marpasse watched her, and let the mood take its course. She could be patient with Denise as yet, knowing that suffering and sorrow leave the heart sore and easily hurt.

Denise spoke at last in a low voice, still keeping her face hidden from Marpasse.

"Where is he?" she asked.

"Down yonder—in the priest's house."

"Wounded?"

"He killed Gaillard, heart of mine, and Gaillard was a good man at his weapons."

Her vagueness did not work as a lure. Denise did not swoop to it; so Marpasse told the truth.

"There is nothing to fear. Messire Aymery was not born to die a bachelor."

"Does he know that I am here?"

"How should he, heart of mine, when I left him asleep—tired out, and came up here at a venture."

Denise fell again into a long silence. There was something in the poise of her head—and in the way she sat motionless in the long grass that betrayed troubled thoughts and deep self-questioning. Denise had the mirror of her life before her, and found it full of shadows, and of reflections that she could not smother.

"Marpasse."

"Heart of mine."

"He must never see me again; no—I could not bear it."

"God help us now! Why, it is the month of May—and the sun is shining——"

"It is the truth, Marpasse. How can I—I——? Look; it all happened here! How can I put that out of my heart?"

Marpasse stretched out a hand and touched her.

"Come, come, look at the sun, not at the shadows."

"It is not in me—to forget everything."

"Even that the man loves you?"

Denise turned on her suddenly with eyes full of a fierce light.

"Yes, and should I take his love, I—who cannot go to him as a woman should! It is not in my heart, Marpasse, whatever you may say. God help me, but I love him better than that!"

Her passion spent itself, and she lay down in the grass, covering her face, and trying to hide a rush of tears. Marpasse bent over her, moved by great pity, and yet impatient with Denise for pulling so simple a thread into a tangle. But Denise would not listen to Marpasse. She was even angry with her own tears.

"No, no—let me be; I am a fool; it will soon pass."

Marpasse grimaced.

"Why will you walk on thorns?" she said; "some people can never satisfy their consciences!"

Denise still hid her face in the long grass.

"It is for Aymery's sake."

"Bah!" quoth Marpasse; "you will give him a stone, will you—when he is hungry."

She got up from under the rose tree, and went towards the gate.

"I have left you the bread," she said, "and it is better to eat bread and be contented than to look for rents in one's own soul. Messire Aymery shall not know that you are here, if you will promise me one thing."

Denise raised herself upon her elbow.

"Stay here till to-morrow. I will put it all before Father Grimbald. He is a man with a head and a heart. For the rest, my dear, put that bread into your body and sleep ten hours by the sun."

CHAPTER XLIII

Aymery was still in a deep sleep when Marpasse returned to the priest's house an hour before sunset, and found Grimbald baking cakes on the hearth. Marpasse might have laughed at his housewifeliness had she not been in a very earnest temper about Denise. So she drew a stool up and sat down as though to make sure that Grimbald did not burn the cakes which he had made while she was away.

"I have found her," she said, and Grimbald had only to listen, for Marpasse's generous impatience had ample inspiration.

"Never tell me women are not obstinate, Father, for I swear to you that Denise was born to make misery for herself. A Jew hunting for a farthing in the mud is not more careful than Denise to hunt out something to grieve over. I should like to cut the conscience out of her, and bury it."

Grimbald held up a hand, and rising from the stool, went to the doorway of the inner room, and looked in to see that Aymery was asleep. He closed the door softly, and came back to the hot cakes and Marpasse.

"You are a great battle-horse, my child," he said bluntly. "Denise's flanks are not for the same spur."

Marpasse took the rebuke with the best of tempers.

"Dear Lord, but the pity of it. All this to-do, and blood-spilling, and no marriage bed at the end of it. There is no law of the Church against it, Father, surely? The monks clapped vows on her, and pulled them off again with their own hands."

Grimbald bent forward, and methodically turned the cakes.

His strong face shone like burnished copper in the firelight; a gaunt, good face, honest and very shrewd. Marpasse watched him, and the thought flashed on her from somewhere that it would be an excellent thing to have the baking of such a man's bread. And with a quaint impulsiveness she put her hand up over her mouth, symbolising the smothering of so scandalous a conceit.

Having turned all the cakes, Grimbald gave his judgment.

"I have no love for the convent women," he said, "and there—I am out of fashion."

Marpasse saw the worldly side of the picture, and smoothed away a smile.

"Then you would make them man and wife, Father if the chance offered?"

"Against all the monkish law in the kingdom," he said stoutly; "we put no vows on her when she had her cell up yonder. And some of the folk here would have been burnt for her if she had asked it. Only that lewd dog of a Gascon— —Well, we broke their teeth at Lewes."

Marpasse stared solemnly into the fire as though looking for pictures amid the blaze of the burning wood.

"If Denise could only forget a year," she said.

Grimbald nodded wisely.

"God wastes nothing," he answered; "those who never suffer, never learn."

Aymery slept the whole night, and woke soon after dawn with a rush of memories like clouds over a March sky. He found Grimbald sitting by his bed. Grimbald was dozing, but his eyes opened suddenly and looked straight at Aymery like the eyes of an altar saint in the dimness of the room.

The first word that Aymery uttered was the name of Denise.

Grimbald's gaunt face remained thoughtful and placid.

"Marpasse has found her," he said.

Aymery's eyes asked more than Grimbald had the heart to tell.

"She is safe," was all that he would say, and acting as though there were no secret to be concealed, he went out to lay the fire on the hearth of the great room.

Now Marpasse showed a most managing temper that May morning, and went about as though she had some grave work on hand. She herself took food in to Aymery, remained awhile with the door shut, and came out looking very set about the mouth.

"I have told him a lie," she said to Grimbald in a whisper, "his eyes asked for it. Go in and barber him, Father; a lover looks best with a clean chin."

Grimbald stared her in the face.

"What have you told him?"

"That we kept her away last night—for the sake of his wounds."

Grimbald's lips came together for a "but." Marpasse whispered on.

"Get your razor and barber him, Father, and keep a clean edge on the lie. His eyes asked for it—I tell you, and I had not the heart to dash in the truth. I have the yoke on my own shoulders. Two lies sometimes make the truth."

She took Grimbald's holly staff from the corner, and put on her hood.

"I am going to fetch her," she said; "no—I shall not scold. I have my plan. You may sit in the wood-shed out of sight, Father Grimbald, when I bring her back with me. If she sees you it will spoil the whole brew."

She turned on the threshold, and Grimbald saw suddenly that her eyes were wet.

"Pray for them both, good Father," she said to him, "my heart's in the thing whatever rough words my mouth may say."

And Grimbald promised, and let her go. Yet when she had gone, and he was left alone in the great room with its black beams and smoking hearth, he saw through his prayers the brave, brown face of Marpasse.

Yet Marpasse's warm-hearted, yet coarser, nature could not vibrate to the subtler emotions that stirred in Denise. The two were like crude sunshine and moonlight; Marpasse healthy and vital in herself, yet lacking mystery and the glimmer of visionary things. Denise had often been more a spirit than a body, though the woman in her had been awakened, and the rich warm scent of the earth had ascended into her nostrils. Suffering had made her very human, and yet the soul in her still beat its wings, even though those wings should carry it away from the world's desire nearer to the cold stars in a lonely sky. To Marpasse, Denise's self-condemnation might seem a kind of futile and pitiable sanctity, but then Marpasse had more blood and bone in her, and less of that spirit that is crucified by its own purity.

Denise had passed the whole night in the long grass under the rose tree, looking at the stars and the vague, black shapes of the great beeches. The cell had a horror for her, and she would not enter it, as though her other self lay dead within. That other memory was more vivid than the memories of those nights when Aymery had lain there wounded little more than a year ago.

Give herself to the man she felt she could not, for she was too sensitive, too much a sad soul in a beautiful body not to feel the veil of aloofness that covered her face, that veil that was invisible and impalpable to Marpasse. Her own innocence made her more conscious of that other life—that other innocent soul that had been born in her, and which had taken from the mother that which she would have given to Aymery whom she loved. Only a pure woman could feel what Denise felt in her heart of hearts. The divine girdle had been torn from her. Love might be blind to it, but Denise's soul could not be blind.

And yet a sense of great loneliness rushed upon her that night, weighing her down into the long grass, and making her heart heavy. The petals of the rose fell dew drenched into her lap. The night was still and fragrant, and no wind made the trees mutter like the hoarse whisperings of an oracle in some ancient forest. The heart of Denise was heavy within her. The sad deeps of life seemed between her and the world, a dark voiceless gulf that no living soul could cross.

So the day came, and with it Marpasse, holly staff in hand, alert, and on her guard. But she was disarmed that morning by Denise herself. The first glimpse of that tragic and troubled face drove the rougher words out of Marpasse's mouth. She took Denise in her arms, and kissed her, seeing in those brown eyes such deeps of sincerity and sadness, that Marpasse humbled herself, feeling herself near to something greater than a woman's whim.

Marpasse guessed what Denise had to say. The renunciation lay in the brown eyes like a dim mist of tears.

"I am going away, Marpasse," she said. "I have thought of it all the night."

Marpasse hid her impulses, and was patient and very gentle.

"Heart of mine, where will you go?"

"To Earl Simon."

Marpasse opened her eyes.

"I shall go to him, and put everything before him. He has a great heart, Marpasse, and his lady has the soul of Mary—Our Mother. Nor shall I go in vain."

She spoke very simply, like one resigned, but Marpasse felt the wild heart of a woman who loved palpitating beneath her courage. It was the purpose of one whose knees shook under her, and who strove to keep herself from looking back. A touch, and love would break out, with a great passionate cry. Marpasse saw it all, and took her inspiration.

"So be it, heart of mine," she said, looking sad enough; "and yet—before you go—there is Father Grimbald yonder. The good man strained a sinew last night, or he would have been here with me this morning. He would not forgive your going without seeing him."

Denise breathed out the answer that Marpasse was expecting.

"But I cannot go! He—is there."

Marpasse, brazen-faced, told the lie of her life.

"Messire Aymery? He is so little the worse that he was in the saddle at daybreak, and searching the woods to the west, and half the village with him."

Denise looked into Marpasse's eyes.

"That is the truth?"

"Heart of mine, why should I tell you a lie!"

Denise seemed to hesitate. She shrank from the sight of any familiar face that morning, and yet her heart reproached her because of Grimbald. The thought was often with her that she might have trusted him more deeply.

Marpasse, dreading to seem too eager, put in a frank plea.

"Why shun a good friend?" she said; "he would be grieved. The man is no Ursula, God forbid!"

Denise surrendered.

"I will come," she said; "but I will see no one but Grimbald."

"Leave it to me, sister; we can keep to the woods."

Marpasse played her part so well that no flicker of suspicion passed over Denise's face as they made their way across the valley to the priest's house under the silver birches. Only here and there had they to leave the woodlands to cross a meadow or a piece of the wild common where the villagers pastured their cattle. Denise walked with her hood drawn forward, looking about her wistfully at the hills and valleys that were so familiar, and had been so dear. She felt like a stranger in the Goldspur woods that morning, a bird of passage that passed and left no loneliness in the heart of the land she left. Marpasse talked much upon the way, entering into Denise's plans as though she were resigned to them, the most loving of hypocrites who lied for the sake of love. She even warned Denise to take care of her long-suffering body. "Two nights without sleep," she said, "is enough for any woman. Live your life in such a hurry and you will be as thin as a post in three months, with wrinkles all over your face. The pity of it! Like a piece of fine silk left out in the wind and rain."

So they came to Grimbald's house amid the silver stems of the birches, Marpasse alert and on the watch lest some piece of clumsiness should make her plot miscarry. Denise was shy and wild as an untamed falcon, her brown eyes half afraid of the birch wood, as though Aymery might come riding out with half Goldspur village at his heels. Marpasse saw the look in Denise's eyes. One clap of the hands and the bird would be skimming on frightened wings.

"Courage, sister," she said, "there is not a soul to be seen. I will keep guard and watch while you are talking with Grimbald. No, the good man will not try to over-persuade you. If I whistle, then you will know that there is danger in the distance."

They entered the porch, Marpasse first, Denise following.

"The good man is abed resting that sprained ankle of his. I will see whether he is ready."

Marpasse crossed the outer room, peeped in, held up a hand to Aymery, and turned and called Denise. There was an iron catch on the door that hooked into a staple, so that the door could be fastened on the outer side. Moreover the door opened outwards into the larger room, and Marpasse stood with her hand on the catch.

"She is coming, Father," she said, keeping her eyes upon Denise.

The grey figure brushed past Marpasse, and crossed the threshold in all innocence. No sooner was Denise within, than Marpasse clapped to the door, fastened it, and ran like a mad woman out of the house.

In the wood-shed at the end of the rough garden she found Grimbald sitting patiently on the chopping block behind a screen of faggots.

"I have shut her in with him," she said; "now love must win—or never."

CHAPTER XLIV

The morning sunlight poured through the window and struck upon Denise as she stood leaning against the door that Marpasse had closed on her. The first impulse had been one of anger, the anger of one caught in an ambuscade. For it was not Grimbald that she saw, but Aymery, propped against a pillow, with a face like wax, his eyes shining at her, eyes full of that truth which she had sought to shun.

"Denise!"

He held out his hands to her, rising in the bed so that the sunlight fell upon his head and shoulders. And Denise, leaning against the door, found her anger sinking into a kind of stupor. Her face was as white as Aymery's, and she shrank like a bird when the hand of the fowler comes into the trap.

Aymery's eager face was still luminous, as though the soul shone through the flesh. Denise's hood was drawn, yet beneath it he caught the gleam of her splendid hair. She did not move or utter a word, but stood there helplessly, hearing her own heart beating like a thing that struggles to be free.

There was a sudden sense of a shadow stealing across the room. The man's face had clouded. A troubled, questioning look came into the eyes, the look of a dog trying to understand. His hands sank slowly to the bed, and were no longer stretched out to her, but lay open, palms upward, the hands of a man waiting for alms from heaven.

For the moment Denise saw nothing but those hands. The rush of blind anger against Marpasse went out before a spasm of compassion. The silence of the room seemed the silence of a great church where the Holy Blood is uplifted. Then a mystery of infinite, dim things swept over her like a cloud of incense. She shivered, and held her breath.

"Denise."

She struggled to find words.

"I thought that it was Grimbald here. Marpasse deceived me."

How poor and miserly the words seemed, and the sense of their ineffectual coldness drove her to glance at Aymery's face. He was lying back in the shadow, his eyes watching her with that same puzzled, questioning, and wistful look. She saw them fill suddenly with understanding, and the generous gleam that followed, humbled her heart.

"I did not know——" he began.

"Marpasse told me——"

She bit her lips, and was silent.

"Denise—it was no trick of mine, God knows that!"

She leant against the door, hiding her face.

"I lost you—after Gaillard and I had ended it. They brought me here, and told me that they had found you, but that they would not bring you to me—because of my wounds. That—is everything. Call Marpasse. She shall open the door and let you go."

Denise glanced at him, half furtively, and that one glance seemed to make the metal of her purpose melt and flow into a stream of living fire. She turned with an inarticulate cry, and threw back her hood, letting the sunlight fall upon her face.

"Lord, how can I, I who remember all the past!"

"Denise!"

He was up, leaning towards her, stretching out his hands.

"God! What is all that—to me! Can you not understand?"

She swayed, closing her eyes, her hands feeling the air as though she were blind.

"My heart—oh—my heart!"

"Denise!"

"May the sin of it be forgiven."

She was on her knees beside the bed, her arms flung out over it, her face hidden in the coverlet.

"Lord—save me——!"

Aymery's arms went round her, and she clung to him with sudden passion, as though life were there, and love, and hope.

"Hold me—keep me—let me not go! Oh, but the shame of it—the selfishness! Closer, closer to you! I am afraid—I am afraid!"

She was trembling like one lifted from the torture of the rack. Her hands clung to him, the hands of a frightened child, and of an impassioned woman. Aymery turned her in his arms, so that her hair fell down across the bed, and her face was under his.

"Rest here, my heart. Who—on God's earth—shall take you from me?"

Their eyes met and held in one long look.

"Lord, lord—ah—do not pity me," she said, "not in the way that hurts a woman's heart."

Aymery kissed her upon the mouth.

"God forgive me," he said, "if ever I have made you think that."

Meanwhile Marpasse had returned, leaving Grimbald in the wood-shed, and creeping softly across the room she stood listening at the closed door. Such a true friend was Marpasse that the two within might have forgiven her her eaves-dropping. It was no inquisitive spirit that waited there silent, and open-mouthed, listening with wet eyes to words that were sacred. Marpasse soon knew the truth, and she crept away on tip-toe.

But Marpasse was no sooner out of the house than a delirious mood seized her, and she ran like a girl, her wet eyes ablaze, her face exultant. There was no need for Grimbald to ask her how things sped.

"Love is lord of all," she sang; "and I have the weight of a lie off my shoulders! Good saints, good saints—I wish I could give you a lapful of silver!"

She laughed up to Grimbald in her delight, caught him by the shoulders, and kissed him full upon the mouth.

"*Mea culpa*, Father; I am a mad fool, but my heart was in the venture, and when I am glad—like a dog—I must show it."

The sunlight pierced the faggot wall of the shed, and burnt like golden tongues on the sombre cloth of the man's cassock. Something in Grimbald's eyes sobered Marpasse abruptly. It was not anger, not an amused and fatherly tolerance, but a look in which the deep strong heart of the man betrayed itself. Marpasse caught her breath, and went fiercely red under her brown skin. Then, a sudden virginal softness seemed to steal over her face. She hung her head, but not foolishly. For the moment neither she nor Grimbald spoke.

Marpasse gave a short, curious laugh, picked up a rotten stick, and began to snap it into small pieces between her hands.

"May they be very happy," she said; "the love of a strong man is life to a woman, Father—and the children that may come of it."

She looked up quickly at Grimbald, and her bold eyes had grown like the eyes of a girl.

"I might have made a good mother—but there——!" and she threw the pieces of broken wood aside, and spread her hands "children have not come my way—nor the man who will master me," and she was silent, staring at the ground.

Grimbald's face shone like a rock with the sunlight on it.

"To some of us such things are not given," he said; "my children are down yonder—and yet——! I chose what I chose—when I was a lad."

Marpasse seemed to be struggling to say something that would not shape itself into words.

"It is so lonely—sometimes," and her eyes looked into the past; "dear heart, I have often spat at the thought of myself! It is always 'the might have been,' with some of us. The world often leers at a woman, Father, when it offers her a penny. I was just as tall as the harvest wheat when they pushed me out on the road. But I am not bad to the core, Father, though few people would think it the truth."

She heard Grimbald draw his breath.

"The core of the world is a generous heart," he said; "look at me, Marpasse. Many things might happen, but for what I am."

He took Marpasse's hands, held them a moment, and then dropped them reverently, looking at her to see that she understood. And these two brave souls gazed in each other's eyes, knowing that they could come no nearer, and that their lives might cross but never travel the same road.

Yet Marpasse went out from the wood-shed into the sunlight with a smile upon her face, the smile of a woman who has re-discovered mystery in herself. A look of the eyes, a few words, a touch of the hands—that was all! Marpasse pressed her face between her two hands, and stood staring and staring away towards the distant woods. The scoffing voice was silent in her, the mouth strangely soft, the eyes the eyes of a young girl.

And Denise, who kissed her that night, as a woman who is loved kisses the woman who loves her, saw no shadow of sadness on the brave, brown face of Marpasse.